Conten

C000174731

1-99

Vile things

EXTREME DEVIATIONS OF HORROR

EDITOR: CHERYL MULLENAX

COMET PRESS
NEW YORK

VILE THINGS:
EXTREME DEVIATIONS OF HORROR

A COMET PRESS BOOK

All rights reserved. Printed in the United States of America. No part of this book may be reproduced or transmitted in any form or by any electronic or mechanical means, including photocopying, recording or by any information storage and retrieval system, without the written permission of the publisher, except in the case of brief quotations embodied in critical articles and reviews.

The stories in this anthology are works of fiction. People, places, events, and situations are the products of the author's imagination or are used fictitiously. Any resemblance to an actual persons, living or dead, events, or locales is purely coincidental.

Vile Things: Extreme Deviations of Horror copyright © Comet Press, 2009
"The Fisherman" copyright © Brian Rosenberger, 2008
"Fungoid" copyright © Randy Chandler, 2009
"Tenant's Rights" copyright © Sean Logan, 2009
"Again" copyright © TZ Publications, 1981
"Maggots" copyright © Tim Curran, 2008
"Going Green" copyright © Stefan Pearson, 2007
"Coquettrice" copyright © Angel Leigh McCoy, 2009
"The Fear in the Waiting" copyright © C.J. Henderson, 2000
"The Worm" copyright © John Bruni, 2008
"Sepsis" copyright © Graham Masterton, 2003
"What You Wish For" copyright © Garry Bushell, 2009
"The Devil Lives in Jersey" copyright © Z.F. Kilgore, 2009
"Rat King" copyright © Jeffrey Thomas, 2009
"The Caterpillar" copyright © Charles Moore, 2008
"'Poor Brother Ed' or The Man Who Visited" copyright © Ralph Greco, Jr., 2004

"Again" first appeared in *Rod Serling's The Twilight Zone Magazine*, November 1981
"The Fear in the Waiting" first appeared in *Crypt of Cthulhu*, Fall 2000
"Sepsis" was first published by Cemetery Dance, 2003
"Rat King" first appeared in *Dark Regions* magazine #3, 1998

Cover art by Phil Fensterer, Creative Schism, www.creativeschism.com

ISBN: 978-0-9820979-1-5

First Comet Press Trade Paperback Edition June 2009

As always, my thanks and love to Andre for all of your help and support.

The Fisherman

Brian Rosenberger

IN THE TOWN of Winterhaven, fishing was a way of life. The first word out of an infant's mouth was more likely to be bass instead of mama. Most children learned how to bait a hook before they were taught to tie their shoes. Men didn't discuss who would win the Superbowl or the World Series; they didn't care. The bottom line was who would capture the Bass Master Classic and walk off with the coveted Angler of the Year award. In a town where TV fishing host Bill Dance was regarded as a Saint and the local reverend spoke more of Jonah than Jesus in his sermons, Silas McGee was a fisherman among fishermen. And that's what caused Lester Wilkes to break more fishing poles than any five men in angler history.

Lester was a damn good fisherman. He could coax fish to bite when everyone else was already microwaving their fishsticks at home. He could seduce them with little more than spit and a paper clip. He was good.

Silas was a legend. He looked the part. He had more wrinkles than a fat lady had stretch marks and walked like the fat lady was riding piggyback. His face was so pale from walking hunched over one wondered if Silas ever saw the sky. The beard didn't help. It reached to his navel and was the color of a well-used toilet bowl. Ancient as he was, he could be seen everyday with his brown bag of medicinals (as he liked to call the 40 ouncer), his rods and his can of bait, fishing to his heart's content. When the day was done, he left with the bottle empty and his stringer full.

Lester had an unhealthy distrust and dislike for Silas. Distrust because Lester distrusted anything older than he was, even though he was almost 27. Lester still partied as hard as he did in high school. Dislike because Silas was a better fisherman. Not that Lester would ever admit to it. And there was another reason too.

As a little minnow, Lester had caught Silas with his dirty overalls around his ankles, masturbating with a fish. Lester was about 13 and was no stranger to masturbation. He milked the walleye himself. But to see this old hillbilly with a fish on his dick saying, "Bite it, bite it." with his eyes rolled back in his head was something else all together. When Silas realized he was being watched he turned to Lester and said, "Maybe you'd like to give your mouth a try, boy?" Lester lit out of there faster than a fart at a baked bean buffet.

As an adult, Lester had avoided Silas. Lester complained that Silas always smelled like he had just stepped in dog shit and had taken the extra effort to ensure both shoes got equal amounts. Hygiene was not a priority. Not that it was a high priority with Lester either. If some lady was kind enough, dumb enough, or drunk enough to spread her legs on Lester's face, he wouldn't wash for days, instead letting the smell sit on his mustache so he could savor his conquest long after the battle was over.

Lester usually saw Silas' mug in the *Winterhaven Gazette*, in the Catch of the Week feature. That damn goon face every week. He thought the paper should carry an advisory. *Warning—Extreme Ugliness may result in a loss of appetite.* Even if someone was reported missing or got caught desecrating one of the local graveyards, or someone found a ten-inch mushroom, Silas and his lunatic grin always took center stage.

There's no way in hell that increased sales, Lester swore.

Lester remembered last summer, when he had nailed a fifteen-pound large mouth. Damned if he wasn't excited. He figured on being a lock for the Catch of the Week. No telling what kind of pussy he'd get being a celebrity. All smiles, he brought the fish to be weighed and the first thing the photographer said was "That's the biggest fish I've seen all week except for the one Silas brought in this morning. Now that was a whopper!"

Lester shook his head, muttered something about carp fucker and smacked the photographer in the head with the bass. It was enough to make a man take up quilting.

Their paths had last crossed two weeks ago. Lester had taken the boat out, hoping to try a few holes in preparation for the upcoming walleye tournament. He had hoped to try a different kind of hole the night before without any luck. He took Mary Ellen out to eat. Slopped the hog but no pork was pulled.

He had been hung over as hell. The lake was anything but calm, causing Lester to heave his morning breakfast of Doritos, cold pizza, and PBR into the water. Who should be there, but Silas with his $5.99 orange lifejacket and that rusted piece of shit he called a boat.

Lester steered well clear of the old man and started casting. To pass the time, he thought about all the pussy he didn't get last night. That started him thinking about all the beaver he hadn't tongued, fingered and banged over the years, which was a lot. Getting depressed, he imagined Silas was a modern day Noah but instead of gathering animals, he collected turds. Big turds, small turds, corn-filled, stinky feces of all imaginable geometric shapes. He imagined Silas's boat full of shit and still seeking more poop. Even when the boat began sinking, his quest for dung continued. With each turd, the boat sank a little more. Finally Silas noticed and panicked. There's too much shit.

Lester imagined himself sliding his boat up against Silas's, yanking his pants down and taking the crap of a lifetime, a gorilla shit, we're talking poop measured in pounds, right on to the steamy mound that was Silas's boat, sending that fish-sodomizing bastard into whatever watery hell would have him.

Splashing woke Lester from his daydream. Maybe Silas's damn boat had sprung a leak. No such luck. Silas had caught another fish, about his seventh in the last hour. He put it on the stringer, took another hit from his bag, scratched his crotch, and re-baited the hook.

Lester, using a big fat night crawler imported from Texas, had caught nothing except for moss and the sniffles.

Super pissed, Lester yelled out, "Whatcha using for bait, Silas?"

Silas lowered the bag, sneered, and replied, "Taint none of your damn business, boy."

With that, the fisherman reeled in his line, gunned the Mercury outboard and sputtered off across the lake, muttering as he went. After landing the remains of a tennis shoe, Lester returned to town to see if he could find out where the damned fish were biting. He was greeted with the best news of the day.

Apparently, Jerome Hickey had finally gotten tired of his fat wife and his equally obese kids and left them. No one had seen or heard from Jerome in the past ten days.

Lester thought Jerome was about as useful as a bleeding hemorrhoid. He was the type of guy who would smell his fingers after wiping his ass. Lester had knocked his front teeth out a few years ago in a heated argument over which color of Roostertail, white or yellow, was more effective for trout. Lester had screwed Jerome's wife Martha too. Sweat meat.

Meat was the word for Martha, all 240 pounds of her. For a cow, she sure did have a tight pussy. She had a little Hitler Mustache on her snatch. Lester always gave her a *Sieg Heil* salute when she dropped her drawers. And could she suck peter? With such force, it would make your asshole cringe. Lester planned to go over and comfort her when he had time.

Jerome had been one of the odds on favorite to win the walleye tournament and the five hundred dollars that went along with it. With him out of the picture, Lester was thinking of ways to spend the prize money. Maybe treat Martha to a meal at Big Don's Barbecue—We pork it and you fork it.

Days passed. There was still no sign of Jerome. With the tournament a few days away, Lester was talking to P.J., his best friend and beer-drinking buddy. The first time they had met in grade school, P.J. was charging people a dollar to smell his finger. There was quite a line. P.J. said he had fingered Rosie Lee Marshall, every male fifth grader's jerk off fantasy, at last night's school carnival and had yet to wash his hand. Lester was skeptical but stink was still stink. Opportunities like this didn't arrive every day. Sure enough, there was a distinctive odor. A few months later in detention hall, P.J. revealed that he had stuck his finger in a can of tuna before arriving at school. He had cleared almost thirty bucks.

They were at P.J.'s combo junkyard and used car lot, plenty drunk, and talking about the usual, fishing, fucking, and fighting, when Lester mentioned his meeting on the lake with Silas.

"Don't surprise me none. He's a sneaky bastard," said P.J.

"I don't know what he was casting but it was working."

"Yeah, for a man who looks as if he's older than Methuselah he sure as hell has brought in some biggun's. Surprised he ain't had a stroke yet, bringing some of them in," replied Lester.

"That Silas, he's a living breakfast. Flakes, fruits, and nuts all in one bowl," snickered P.J.

At that both men broke out laughing. Wiping tears from his eyes, P.J. said, "Yeah I sure as hell wish I knew what the old geezer was using for bait."

"So do I," agreed Lester, his face as contorted as a question mark.

Later that evening, after being rejected by Martha, the blond clerk at the gas station, two teenagers walking home (damn dykes), and after downing a few more beers and flexing the five knuckle shuffle while watching a rerun of *Baywatch*, Lester had an idea.

Under the camouflage of night, Lester drove his pick-up to Silas' shack in the woods. Not taking any chances, he parked out of sight and staggered the rest of the way, stopping to answer nature's call once as he went.

Silas wasn't poor, but you couldn't tell that by his living conditions. His home was a log cabin that looked more like a log pile. In his yard were the remains of five cars. It was like a demolition derby and all the cars had come there to die. An outhouse stood near the shack. Judging from the grunts coming from within, the king was on his throne, thought Lester. With that bit of information, drunk on courage and cheap beer, he headed for the shack. The door already opened, he entered.

Inside he saw a couch that had seen better days, the remains of a chair that had seen much better days and a broken television with an axe firmly embedded in the screen that would never see the light of day again. Trophies of fish decorated the walls. Bass, catfish, walleye, bluegill, the place looked like a mounted aquarium. It smelled of beer, fish, and urine. It was like a garbage can with windows and the windows were closed. Damn, it stank.

He moved into the kitchen. More fish decorated the walls. On the stove were some fresh bluegill, fried in cracker crumbs and another type of meat. His stomach growling, Lester sampled it. The fish was delicious and the meat mouth watering. Kind of like squirrel but less gamey. Was that a fucking hair? It was. More than one. Didn't affect the taste, Lester thought as he swallowed.

Lester opened the refrigerator and found it empty, except for what looked like potato salad gone mutant, a jar of pickles and some baloney. He wondered what Silas did with all of his catch. Surely, it had to be here somewhere. He moved towards the window and tripped. He looked down and saw a handle. The entrance to the cellar.

Descending the narrow staircase, Lester looked around and saw poles, reels, and tackle boxes galore. On a small worktable, among the knives, saws, and hammers were lures by the hundreds, poppers, jigs, spoons, spinners, crankbaits, and buzzbaits. Odd the lures looked as if they had not been used in quite some time. Rust covered the once glistening hooks. Pondering this, Lester saw an ice-box in the corner of the cellar.

"So that's where the old man keeps his catch. He wouldn't mind if I borrowed some, would he. No sir," Lester said.

Lester opened the freezer. Among the packs of frozen fish and other meats was what remained of Jerome Hickey. His left arm was filleted to the bone. His right hand was missing three fingers.

Bile rising, Lester turned to puke. He looked into the worm eaten, maggot infested face of Wally "Whiskers" Malone who had disappeared months earlier. Scanning the room he saw bones and parts and pieces that caused him to gag. Hanging in a corner looked to be a skinned deer. But deer didn't wear *Hanes* underwear. Screaming "Jesus on a crutch", Lester rushed upstairs and into Silas' murderous glare.

Instead of liquor or a fishing pole, Silas was holding an axe.

"So ya done gone and discovered my secret, did ya. Too bad, ya won't live to tell anyone. Usually, I like to use eight-pound *Trilene* monofilament to choke 'em. Sneak up all quiet like and *snap*. Just like crappie on a jig. But for a sneaky, gopher-cheeked peep thief like you, Betsy will do. Betsy meet dead boy."

With the grace of a fly fisherman trying to catch a stubborn trout, Silas lifted the axe, lunged forward and fell down, gasping for breath.

Clutching his chest, Silas looked up into Lester's saucer wide eyes and whispered, "Shit. And I'm outta toilet paper too." Lester seized the opportunity. He kicked the fallen fisherman in the head once, twice, three times because it felt good.

Lester, regaining his composure, left as fast as his drunk-ass feet could carry him, staggering like a three-legged Daddy Longlegs back to his truck.

Lester reported his findings to the Sheriff Schlagsteiner who wrote him up on a public intoxication charge and put his ass in jail. The following morning, a hung over Lester explained what had happened. Skeptical at first, the sheriff agreed to check things out. An investigation was conducted. The coroner concluded that Silas really could've used a bath and that he died of heart failure. Four corpses, sixteen skeletons, including one horse skeleton, and an assortment of fingernails were found on Silas' property.

In wake of the grisly findings, Winterhaven's tourist population flourished. P.J. sold authentic fishhooks from the insane killer's very own tackle box made of human bone. At least, he said they were authentic. Needless to say, he made a killing.

Widow Martha and her fatherless children became media darlings. In fact, Kirstie Alley was rumored to play Martha in *Lifetime* movie of the week. The walleye tournament was postponed and Silas made the front page for one last time. For once, Lester stole the spotlight. Everybody loved a hero. Although his sex life didn't improve much, Lester did receive a free Roland Martin signature series rod and reel courtesy of the local bait and tackle store, a free membership to B.A.S.S., ten spin-n-glow triple teasers and a set of *Baywatch* Season one DVDs.

Lester graced the cover of the *Winterhaven Gazette* several more times that year for winning four fishing tournaments and for breaking one county fishing record. A lot of people commented on the pictures, saying he looked fat. Lester shrugged it off, saying the camera always added at least fifteen pounds. He didn't care. He was famous. In fact, his breaking the state record for striped bass even eclipsed the disappearance of little Amanda Southern and little Ricky Jameson for the headline in that week's paper.

Fungoid

Randy Chandler

IT WAS A FILTHY JOB but Frank was in no position to turn it down. When your life is in the toilet, you do what you can to stay afloat and keep your hand off the handle. Some days you have to fight the unforgiving urge to flush it all away and send the whole wretched mess spiraling down the tubes, yourself with it.

But this was not one of those days. So Frank pulled on the black rubber knee-boots, stomped his feet a couple of times to imprint his humanity, and stared grimly into the sludge-filled swimming pool.

Even after the electric pump had siphoned the stagnant brown water out of the pool and ejaculated it into the patch of woods on the other side of the backyard's chain-link fence, the sludge-encrusted pool still reeked of floodwater and bottom-rot.

Frank stretched the elastic band of the blue surgical mask behind his head and positioned the mask over his nose and mouth. It wouldn't keep all the bacteria or moist spores out of his airway, but at least it would cut down on the stench. The instructions printed on the box warned that facial hair would prevent a proper face-seal. No way was he going to shave his close-cropped battleship-gray beard for a three-day job. He would take his chances with whatever-the-fuck-kind of bugs that might be hiding in that shit-brown sludge, waiting to set up housekeeping in his body's susceptible cells.

"Come on in, boys," he said to microscopic culprits. "Make yourselves at home, if you can pay the freight. But I warn you, this old abode is way past fixer-upper, and I reserve the right to evict your ass without notice."

Christ. Talking to microbes now. "I could use a drink," he said—to himself, not to the lurking nasties.

But he knew he couldn't take that first one. Not if he wanted to get this job done and get paid three days from now. One drink would lead to the next, and by the third one, he would slide into Take-This-Job-And-Shove-It mode, load his wheelbarrow and shovel into the back of his rattletrap GMC pickup and boogie on down the road. But he wouldn't get far on an empty tank, and he didn't have enough scratch to buy a six-pack or a pint of vodka anyway, so fuck it, get in there and get it done, bro. Stop whining and hop to.

He glanced up at the deserted two-story brick house and wondered how it would've been to live here before the floods and before the Airport Authority decided to buy up all the residential properties in the area and add new runways where all the now-empty houses stood forlornly waiting for the bulldozers and wrecking ball. Janet had always wanted a house with a pool in the backyard, and for a while they'd both believed it would happen, but then he got laid off from his Lockheed job, started the really heavy boozing, and she left him for a computer-programmer with a golfer's tan, a big bank account and a bigger cock. The "bigger cock" thing had come out during one of Frank and Janet's last fights, and by that time the gloves were off and every bare-knuckle verbal hit was a body-shot meant to do lasting emotional damage. The jab to his manhood hadn't been as devastating as the blow to his earning power, or lack thereof. "Fuck him and his big bank account," Frank had said as he clenched his fists and tried his best not to smash her pretty little upturned nose. Janet had been ready for that one and countered with: "Oh, I will, Frank. I surely will."

He looked away from the empty house as he realized that not even a mansion with a top-of-the-line pool could have saved his doomed marriage. He put on heavy-duty work gloves, picked up the shovel and started spading the sludge off the shallow-end steps, dumping each shovelful of the foul brown gunk into his rusty wheelbarrow parked on the deck's edge just above the top step.

Frank tried not to think about the futility of the work at hand. His job was to clean up the pool and the gone-to-seed yard so the appraisers wouldn't knock thousands of dollars off the fair-market value when the agents of the Airport Authority made their offer on the property. It wasn't enough that the area residents were forced to give up their homes; the take-over artists would scam the poor saps at every turn and pay them as little as possible.

Frank thought this clean-up gig was a little like nursing a sick death-row con back to good health so the state could execute him. Tradition held that you couldn't have your executioner dispatch a guy who wasn't healthy enough to ride Old Sparky or take the Last Spike in the vein. Wouldn't be civilized. A man needed a healthy glow to go to his appointment with the Grim Reaper.

Frank's job was getting this muck-choked pool into ship-shape condition, spotless and sparkling enough for a bevy of bathing beauties to swim in it, so the powers-that-be could fill it up with dirt, pave it over and fly jetliners off it. Made perfect sense in this gone-to-shit world, didn't it? Runways to hell were also paved with good intentions. And with back-breaking work for joes like Frank.

He put his back into the digging and soon the first barrowful was ready for transport to the back fence. The sludge wasn't too heavy with most of the water drained out of it, so he hoisted the wheelbarrow onto the top of the fence and dumped the sludge on the other side, then rolled the barrow back to the edge of the pool and started shoveling up the next load, keeping a wary eye out for snakes hiding in the muck.

Soon he and the wheelbarrow were down in the shallow end of the pool. His rubber boots squished sludge. He shoveled and shoveled. His mask was damp with sweat, as was his old Grateful Dead T-shirt with the skeleton in the stovepipe hat sticking a bony fingertip in the groves of a vinyl disc to play a phantom dirge for the dead.

"Big job," said a gravelly voice.

Frank looked up at a white-haired elderly man leaning on a silver-handled cane.

"Yeah," Frank said, pausing to lean on his shovel. He pulled off the mask and let it hang under his chin. "Tell me about it."

"They have machines that can suck that stuff out in an hour's time."

Irritated, Frank said, "Yeah well, I ain't in the sucking business, Pop. I do things the old-fashion way."

The old man grinned. He was toothless. He licked his gums and said, "They declared all the real estate hereabouts a floodplain after that last airport expansion and then went ahead like fools and cleared all that land back yonder and built them apartment buildings. Then every time Sullivan Creek overflowed, all these here backyards was swamped with that foul goddamn floodwater. That's the damn government for ya. Always finding a way to fuck up a wet dream and stick it to you dry."

Frank nodded sagely. "You live around here?"

"I do. I'm the last holdout. Everyone else's vacated."

"Holding out for more money, huh?"

"Nope. I ain't selling. I'm going down with the house."

"Good for you," said Frank. "Give 'em hell." Crazy old fart.

Frank pulled off his gloves and lit an American Spirit. It seemed as good a time as any for a low-budget smoke break. "Must be kinda spooky, living all alone in a deserted neighborhood."

The old man grunted and said, "Reckon the only spook hereabouts is me."

Yeah, the old guy was a nutjob, sure enough. "I hear ya."

"It ain't ghosts you should worry about."

Frank blew a little cloud of smoke up at the October overcast. "Meaning?"

"Meaning you should get out of that crud you're standing in, go away from here and don't come back."

"Why would I do that? That'd be the same as throwing away seven hundred bucks."

"It's only money, son. Can't buy salvation."

"If you're revving up for a sermon, save your breath. I'm not looking to get saved."

The old man shook his head disgustedly. "And I ain't preaching one. I'm just saying you should get out of that muck before it's too late to save yourself."

"From what?"

He nodded at the swimming pool. "From that fungus and everwhat else is in there. Them floodwaters run through an old graveyard before they get here. Means we was flooded with *grave water*. But it's the fungus that'll get ya. That stuff you're shoveling, that crap's et up with it. You're digging your own grave."

"So? I'm not putting down roots here. Ain't like it's gonna grow on me."

The old man shrugged. "Your funeral," he said, then turned and walked up the driveway. He paused at the gate, raised his cane in gentlemanly farewell and toddled toward the street.

"Crazy old coot," Frank muttered. He ducked his cigarette butt in the damp sludge, pulled the mask over his mouth and nose, and then went back to work.

Shoveling shit.

Cynically, Frank thought it was fitting that his life had come down to this. He'd been shoveling shit of one kind or another for most of his life, so there was a certain karmic symmetry in his standing in a swimming pool of this brownish goop, working to dig his way out. It was perfect, really. The shit-shoveler finds his true niche. Frank wasn't feeling sorry for himself; he was finally accepting his true lot in life. His low place in the uncaring cosmos.

He whistled a sappy tune through the surgical mask as he worked.

You coulda been a contenda, said the voice, ala Brando.

Frank knew the voice well. The voice of failure, the one that mocked him and kicked him when he was down. This time he was ready for it. He said, "Coulda-woulda-shoulda. What's the diff. Contender, dead-ender—it all comes down to shoveling this goddamn shit."

And what *was* this shit, anyway? What was its precise genesis? Heavy rains drive the creek water over its banks, the water washes over the land, collecting animal-vegetable-mineral detritus, including animal droppings (and probably human droppings from winos and crack addicts), road grit, dead leaves, moss, twigs, small rocks, litter—you name it— and then the cold roiling stew washes over the cemetery, bringing up groundwater with chemical juices and miniscule flecks of waxy flesh from rotting corpses, the grateful dead . . .

Frank shuddered.

He found his rhythm in the digging. The wet metronomic plops of the sludge hitting the belly of the barrow formed his mushy background music, all rhythm and no melody. Busting his move in the burbs. One . . . two . . . three . . . four . . . Toss the shit and dig some more.

The gray overcast darkened, leaching color from the autumn day. The air chilled. Frank sweated. He wanted another smoke but he kept digging because there weren't many Spirits left in the pack and he had to ration them to make them last.

Just before he broke for a meager lunch of potted meat and Saltines, the hairs on the back of his neck prickled and he was sure somebody was watching him. He stilled his shovel and scanned the surroundings, expecting to see the old coot bent over his cane, but he saw no one. Just a squirrel twitching its bushy tail on the thick limb of an oak. And a crow taking flight from the woods on the backside of the backyard fence.

He shrugged off the feeling of being watched, wishing he had a beer to quench his deep thirst and to keep off the jim-jams, those creeping willies that crawled his skin and twisted his imagination into crazy knots whenever he went too long without a drink.

By mid-afternoon he'd cleared the shallow end of the pool. The bottom and sides still wore ugly brown stains but he would hose those off after all the sludge was gone. Then he would scrub the whole shebang with caustic cleanser, knock out the yardwork, go collect his pay and get drunk as a lord.

He heard something plop in one of the isolated little pools of water nestled in the sludge in the deep end, and he spun around to see a frog rippling the brown water.

"Froggy went a-courtin', he did go, uh-hah . . ." Frank crooned. Then he scooped up the frog with the shovel's blade and tossed it out of the pool and watched it hop across the weedy lawn. "The Great Frog God just gave you new life, warty little dude."

He worked until twilight, which came earlier than he'd expected. Then he remembered that Daylight Savings Time had ended last weekend and the world was back on "real" time now. He dropped the shovel in the wheelbarrow, trudged up the pool's steps, sat down to pull off the rubber boots, and then got up and walked toward the dark house. He stopped at his truck to grab his sleeping bag, his gym bag and his sewer snake.

He fished the house keys out of his jeans pocket. The owner had given him the keys so Frank could snake the shower's clogged drain in the downstairs bathroom. He didn't have the energy to do it tonight, but he saw no reason why he shouldn't crash for the night in the empty house rather than waste gas driving back to his depressing rented room in College Park. The utilities were still on for the appraisers, so he'd have lights and hot water for a shower. No soap, but crashers couldn't be picky.

He let himself in through the back door, went through the kitchen and found the tiny bathroom at the foot of the stairs. He stripped naked, ran the shower until the water was warm enough and then slipped under the stinging jets. He cranked the "H" knob and let the hot water knock fatigue from his muscles. He stayed in the shower until the water started to cool. He pulled an old beach towel out of his gym bag and dried off, then put on a clean set of sweats.

He laid out his dirty sweat-wet work clothes on the carpet since there was no good place to hang them to dry, and then unrolled the sleeping bag under the dining-room window and stretched out on it with a paperback he'd remembered to bring along: Kerouac's *On The Road*, recently scored from a used-book store. Sad Jack was long dead, having destroyed his liver and pickled his once-brilliant brain with booze, but the youthful exuberance of his early Beat days lived on in the yellowed pages.

Frank found his dog-eared place and started reading. He would've liked nothing better than to hit the road and take his carefree adventures where he found them, but he knew that was just so much wishful thinking. If he hit the road, the road would hit back—with gleeful vengeance. His ancient truck wouldn't survive a cross-country trip and he probably wouldn't either. Frank's carefree days and *his* youthful exuberance were way behind him.

Ahead of him was another day of shoveling sludge.

A howling dog woke him. Sounded like the mutt was right outside the bare window. Frank rose to his knees and looked out but didn't see the howler in the hazy glow of streetlights. Other hounds howled in the distance, answering the feral call. Frank banged his fist against the pane, hoping to scare off the unseen mutt. It must've worked; the closer howling ceased.

He flopped back onto the sleeping bag and scratched a sudden itch on his right wrist. The scratching only set off more itching, and soon he was scratching his forearm, upper arm and shoulder.

What the hell? Had he gotten into some poison oak or ivy?

He got up and turned on the light. An angry red rash had risen in the flesh around his wrist. He pushed up his shirtsleeve to see that the raised pimply skin ran all the way up his arm. He pulled off the sweatshirt, went to the bathroom to examine his torso in the mirror.

"Jesus . . ." he said when he saw the extent of the rash's rapid spread. Its rosy fingers already reached from his right deltoid to his chest. ". . . Christ!"

The old man's gravelly warning came back to him. *It's that fungus that'll get ya. That crap you're shoveling is et up with it.*

In the brightness of the bathroom's light Frank could see that the rash, though crimsoned, had a blackish tint. A closer look showed that each little red pimple wore a greenish-black cap. He did his best to resist the maddening urge to scratch the infested skin.

He kicked off his sweatpants and jumped back in the shower. He stayed in the jetting spray until the hot water petered out again. The shower only intensified the itching. Finally, Frank gave in and feverishly scratched his arm, shoulder and chest. The relief was short-lived, instantly followed by worse itching—this time accompanied by the stings of a thousand tiny needles in the flesh. He raked his nails everywhere the rash was. He fell into a dreamlike state of tortured bliss, scratching on autopilot. Scratching . . . scratching . . . scratching . . .

The dog howled again. The beast was in the bathroom with Frank. How the hell . . .?

Then Frank caught his reflection in the mirror and realized he was the one howling.

Losing my fucking mind.

His fingernails were ragged—a long way from his last half-assed manicure—and had drawn smears of blood from the rash. He washed off the blood at the sink, then slipped into his sweatshirt, put on his shoes and rushed outside.

The old man with the cane was in one of the neighboring houses, and Frank intended to find the geezer and make him make him spill, no bullshit now, make him tell what he knew about the fungus or whatever the fuck it was that was consuming Frank's flesh and driving him mad with itching and making him howl like a moon-drunk mutt with a bad case of mange.

Lunatic itch, said the voice. Not the Voice of Failure this time. Nor one of those inevitable voices given to haunting alkies in desperate need of a drink.

A new voice, smarmy and insinuating. A voice too shrewd to sound judgmental, speaking in tones of phony intimacy. Like the cool voice of a cruel god.

Ignore it. Move on.

He walked up the driveway and stood in the middle of the street. All the houses were dark, the streetlamps shrouded in thick fog. It hit Frank hard that he was in the middle of an abandoned neighborhood at the edge of the world. He shivered, chilled to the bone by the profound aloneness he felt. He itched but refrained from scratching. He chose a direction and started walking.

Down the middle of the deserted street.

Closer to the rim of the world and whatever lay beyond.

There.

Down there on the right. A light in a window. Found the son of a bitch.

Frank ran.

Ran toward the light in the window of the two-story brick house with an old hearse parked in the drive. What the fuck, a hearse? Sure as hell. Seventies-vintage death wagon darkly shining in the streetlight.

As he ran, Frank made disturbing connections. If the old man was a retired undertaker, he might actually know what he was talking about, might know about a flesh-infecting fungus and about disease-bearing fluids washed from the graveyard and into the pool where Frank had spent most of the day. But anybody could buy an old hearse, so the old guy might be nothing but a senile fart with a head full of fungoid delusions.

Your funeral, said the dreamlike voice.

"Fuck you," said Frank, running past the hearse and up the steps to the front door. He banged his fist on it. He stabbed a finger at the doorbell button. "Hey! Old man! Open up!"

The itch had him by the balls now. His groin prickled with fierce itching. He stuck his hands in his pockets to keep from scratching. He kicked the door. "C'mon, open up. I gotta talk to you."

He can't help you.

"Shut up," Frank told the voice. And then he knew.

Oh, Jesus . . .

He *knew.* The fungus was talking to him.

The old man answered the door in a shabby silk robe. He raised his cane as if to strike the crazed man on his doorstep.

"Please," said Frank, "you gotta help me. This shit's eating me up."

"Toldja. But *no,* you wouldn't hear it. Too late now." The old man grinned. His toothless gums resembled a raw wound.

"Who the fuck *are* you?" Frank slipped his right hand out of his pocket and balled his fist. The urge to hit the irascible bastard was almost as great as his desire to scratch his own rash-riddled skin.

"I ain't nobody. Go away."

Rather than hit the man, Frank gave his hands free rein to scratch at the spreading itch. He scratched his belly, his groin, his thighs, then went back to scratching his arms and the backs of his hands.

"See there?" The old man pointed with the cane's crooked handle at Frank's right hand. The silver handle was an ornate ram's head with jeweled eyes.

The rash on the back of Frank's hand had cracked open, and yellow liquid oozed out, followed by a greenish foul-smelling discharge. Followed by blood.

Frank swayed on his feet. He grabbed the door's edge to steady himself. "Oh God . . ."

"Flesh-eating fungus," said the old man. "Feasting on your ass already, ain't it. Same kinda shit killed off half the frogs in Australia couple years back. Ain't no cure neither."

"Please . . ." Frank's vision dimmed, then blurred.

You're delicious, Frank.

"It's talking to me," said Frank, desperately thinking this might convince the man to somehow help him.

"That's it eating your brain. Fungus don't talk, you idjit. Now go away 'fore I call the law. You're dripping them contaminating fluids on my doorstep."

Frank saw red.

Rash-red. His sudden impulse to do violence was like an itch that had to be scratched. He snatched the cane out of the gnarled hand and cracked the old coot's skull with the silver ram's head. The wizened scarecrow went down like a lumpy sack of rotting potatoes, knobby knees, elbows and head ka-thumping, deadweight on the door stoop.

Frank whacked him again for good measure, cracked him dead-center on the back of his cranium.

That's it. Hit him again.

Frank obeyed the talking fungus. He struck again and again. Until he'd crushed the old man's head like a mush-melon and the cane's silver handle was blood-plated. Then he grabbed the dead man by the ankles and dragged him inside and shut the door.

Good job, said the fungus.

"Fuck you," said Frank. "You're not real."

The fungus laughed. It was a wet laugh, a dirty *basso profundo* bubbling up from subterranean depths.

Frank looked at his oozing hands. "Okay, maybe you're real. But you're not . . . not natural. You're . . ."

Supernatural? Again with the dirty laugh.

"What the fuck *are* you? Who ever heard of a talking fungus?"

Once upon a time you believed in a talking burning bush.

"God," said Frank, the stench of the fluids erupting from his fungus-infected flesh making him sick to his stomach.

The fungus began to whisper conspiratorially. It told Frank exactly what to do.

Frank obeyed. He found the keys to the hearse hanging on a hook by the front door. He dragged the old man out to the hearse, opened the rear door and dumped the body in the back. Only thing missing was a casket, but what the hell? They weren't going to a funeral. The fungus had whispered: *Feed him to me.* Frank obeyed because he knew something bad would happen if he tried to disobey the Fungus God. Something worse than bad. *Bad* was already happening.

He climbed behind the steering wheel, cranked up and drove back to the jobsite. He backed up to the swimming pool, dragged the old man out of the death wagon and dropped the corpse into the deep-end sludge. It hit with a sickening splat.

"There ya go," he said. "*Bon appétit!*"

He couldn't see what was happening in the dark pool but he heard a god-awful slurping-sucking sound that made him turn away and stumble toward the house.

The fungus spoke in a language Frank had never heard before, though it sounded vaguely French, with a smattering of silky Japanese. The voice was inside his head but it was also resounding from the pool.

He pressed his palms to his ears to shut out the nerve-racking voice and immediately realized his mistake when the gooey stuff leaking from his ulcerated hands seeped into his ear canals. "Gah!"

The Voice of Failure slipped a few words in edgewise: *Gonna let that fungus get the best of you, you miserable fuck? Be a man. If you still can.*

"I *am* a man, goddammit," he said, stumble-bumming through the back door.

All at once his groin was on fire with needling pain. A deep slicing ache brought him to his knees. He whimpered. This was worse than the time he'd passed a kidney stone. Way worse. "Ah God, it's inside me." So much for being a man. How could you be a man when a flesh-eating fungus was devouring your waterworks from the inside-out?

Snake your drain, said a voice. Frank didn't know whose voice it was, nor did he much care. He took the command as the way to his salvation. The only way.

He shed his sweatpants and crawled over to the sewer snake he'd left by his gym bag. He uncoiled the metal auger, dragged it to the corner and sat with his legs spread wide. He held the pointed end of the metal snake in one hand and his flaccid penis in the other. Green liquid oozed out of the tip of his cock. Good. He figured the goop was plenty thick to provide lubrication for plumbing his prick.

Snake your drain.

"Shut up, I am." With his thumb and forefinger he spread his prick's slit as wide as it would go, then he slowly brought the sharp point of the snake to the opening and inserted it with trembling, pus-dripping hands. Then he shoved it up his burning chute.

He screamed as the snake punched through his urethra and ripped a ragged path all the way to the bladder. With a delirious heave, he yanked the snake out. Blood and slime-streaked urine poured out of him, and he passed out screaming.

A kick in the face woke him. Frank looked up at the old geezer with the rotten mush-melon head looking down at him with one dangling eyeball. The dead guy's flesh was furred with greenish-brown fungus, shot-through with black. Parts of his brain showed through the jagged chinks in his skull. Swatches of his blood-spiked white hair were hung with strings of slimy brown sludge like dark tinsel on a dead tree. His toothless mouth, slack jaw, and sagging posture added to the illusion of a melon-headed scarecrow that had slipped down from its makeshift wooden cross and shambled out of a cornfield and into Frank's fevered nightmare.

The scarecrow kicked him again, but Frank hardly felt it. The incandescent pain in his groin blocked out all lesser sensations.

Get up.

"Fuck you," Frank roared, hands clasped over his ruined plumbing. "I'm dying."

The dead geezer worked crooked fingers into a crevice in his broken head, seized a handful of fungal muck and slapped it on Frank's groin. Its narcotic effect immediately took away the pain. And stopped the bleeding. Miraculous shit!

You're not dying. Get up. It's time to go.

"Go? Where?" The absence of pain was blissful. Frank leaned into the corner, breathing easier now and savoring the relief that washed over him.

South. Away from the coming cold.

Frank tumbled to the scheme. The old man's walking corpse was the temporary vessel for the Fungus God's essence, and Frank was the designated driver, wheelman of the hearse that would take the foul entity to warmer climes, where it could flourish in fungal delight. It needed Frank severely injured and dependent on its pain-relieving narcotic. That was how it intended to control Frank, the predictable addict.

Don't do it, dumb-ass, said the nagging voice of his disgruntled ex-wife. *Be a man for once. Stand up to this disgusting shit. Stop it!*

"Janet? What the hell are you . . .?" But then he knew what she was doing in his head. The particular part of his out-of-whack off-the-tracks mind that was still his own was using Janet's intractable voice to get through to him. To *warn* him: *Stop it.*

"Fuck you, fungus," he said. "My mind is mine."

The scarecrow kicked him again, smashing Frank's nose. Then once more, pulping his lower lip.

"All right! All right, I'll do it, goddammit," Frank shouted with a fat-lipped lisp. "You win."

That's it, whispered Janet, *play along and then cream the sonofabitch when he ain't looking. Just the way I taught you. You still got a little juice left in you, Franklin. Just enough to do something right for once in your miserable goddamn life.*

"Shut up, bitch," Frank muttered. "I got this." He slipped carefully into his sweatpants. He didn't want to do anything to undercut the blessed numbness in his urinary tract. His rash no longer oozed and the itching had abated, thanks to the healing properties of the slimy balm the Fungus God had slapped onto his crotch and belly.

He wished he could have one last double-shot of vodka with a beer chaser. See the sunrise one last time. But . . . fuck it. Janet was right. He had one last chance to do something right. Fucked if he was going to blow it. And anyway, there was no point in living when your dick was split open from the inside. He put his crushed pack of smokes and Zippo in his pocket.

He followed the limping dead scarecrow out to the hearse. "Need gas," Frank said as he grabbed the plastic gas can with a faded red rag tied to its handle from the bed of his truck. He uncapped the hearse's tank and fed it half the can's contents, then he soaked the rag in gasoline and stuck it into the mouth of the tank, turning the death wagon into a giant Molotov cocktail.

"Get in the back," he told the dead geezer/Fungus God, "so nobody can see your ugly fucking head."

That filthy fungal voice hissed angrily in Frank's head, warning him to show proper reverence and awe.

"Yeah, yeah, I hear ya. Not to worry. We're going south right now." Frank flicked his Zippo open, lit his last cigarette and then held the flame to the gas-soaked rag hanging like a red tongue out of the vehicle's tank. He slid behind the wheel and keyed the ignition. The hearse's motor sputtered, coughed, and then rumbled to life. He slapped it into reverse and gunned the engine.

The death wagon lurched backward, rolled over the edge, undercarriage shrieking, and bumped and bounced down the steps and banged into the shallow end of the pool. Something snapped in Frank's back. He gritted his teeth and waited for the explosion.

The voice of the fungus screamed incoherent curses inside Frank's head.

The hearse rolled in reverse until the mound of sludge in the deep end stopped it.

"C'mon," Frank said around the Spirit clamped in his teeth, "blow!"

Then he saw the burning rag flame out on the shallow-end steps.

"Sonofabitch," he said, realizing his Molotov hearse was a dud.

What a fuck-up, said Janet.

When he heard the geezer bumping around in the back of the vehicle and then the creak of the rear door swinging open, Frank figured it was time to get the hell out of there.

But he couldn't move his legs. Couldn't move anything below the waist. The loud snap when the hearse bounced down the steps had been the sound of his lower spine cracking.

He would have to crawl out on his forearms. *Shit!*

He threw open the door, leaned left and fell out onto the sludgy floor of the pool. He heard the shuffle of the dead guy's bare feet behind him. Pain flared in his groin, renewing the hot-poker sensation in his devastated urinary tract.

Smoke from the bent cigarette still clenched in his teeth burned his eyes. He looked back at the open mouth of the gas tank on his left, and crawled toward it. *One shot*, he told himself. *Make it good.*

He sucked on the butt until its ember glowed bright red, then rolled onto his back, took aim and tossed it at the target. The remains of his last American Spirit struck just below the tank's mouth and fell harmlessly in a shower of tiny sparks.

"Fuck!"

He saw the walking dead man coming at him with arms outstretched, zombie-style. The voice of the Fungus God gibbered madly, but there was no mistaking its rage.

Give it up, Frank, said his ex. *You're fucked. And I'm outta here. See ya. Wouldn't wanna be ya.*

Since when did Janet speak in sports clichés? he wondered.

Easy answer: Since your maximum fuck-up landed you in this giant toilet bowl in the middle of a deserted suburb, trapped with a pissed-off talking fungus that fancies itself a god. Capische?

Frank screamed in frustration. Old Melon Head reached down for him. Frank grabbed both of the fungus-furred wrists and fended the monster off as best he could. But the geezer fell upon him and gave Frank a big, slimy kiss on the lips.

When he opened his mouth to spit and bellow his disgust, the thing vomited a gushing torrent of stinking slime into Frank's nose and mouth and down his throat.

Gagging, Frank flung the geezer aside and tried to catch his breath through the foul, viscous fluid blocking his airway. The putrid stuff wheezed obscenely in his throat.

That was when Frank knew he really was going to die here in this giant toilet. His remains might go on as something else, but Frank would be no more.

Defeated by fungus.

Then he remembered the Zippo in his sweats' pocket.

He dug it out as Melon Head was getting up to come at him again, no doubt to heave another barrage of fungoid stew at him. He flicked open the Zippo's metal lid, thumbed the roller and struck the flint. A slender flame danced in Frank's fist.

He rose up off his belly with a snake-like motion and lobbed the lighter at the mouth of the old gas tank. The flaming Zippo disappeared through the opening.

From the belly of the tank came a whooshing sound and then a blinding light—

Frank was grinning when the explosion flushed him out of the world.

Riding updrafts and thermals on dihedral-angled wings, the turkey vulture soars, then glides closer to the earth and begins to circle the manmade pool below. With its acute sense of smell it scents food, descends gracelessly and alights beside the dead thing in the bottom of the waterless pool.

Designated "peace eagle" by the Cherokee Nation because it does not kill, the turkey buzzard dips its bald red head into the broken skull of the dead thing that isn't as badly charred as its carrion companion. The vulture pecks brain tissue from the fuzzy fungus growing inside the shattered skull and eats with great appetite.

Two cold hands suddenly seize the bird's stubby neck. The buzzard flutters its wings and dances on air but cannot escape its captor's grasp. The dead thing vomits a thin stream of gummy liquid into the bird's mouth and eyes, then it releases its hold and the buzzard takes to the air.

Ruffled by the unexpected encounter, the buzzard nevertheless rises into the autumn air and catches a southwesterly current.

Tenant's Rights

Sean Logan

NOTHING MADE ALBERT MORE ANGRY than Lance's hair. It was messy, but that wasn't the bad part. The bad part was that it was messy *on purpose!* The guy spent an hour in the mirror every day to get his hair that messy. When he woke up in the morning, that hair just wasn't messy enough. It took a strained and concentrated effort to make every odd clump stick out in a different direction, poking up from his scalp like it was trying to get the hell out of there.

That was the bad part, but that wasn't the worst part. The worst part was that all the girls liked him. They didn't even seem to care that his hair was a disorganized disaster. Once, when Albert was on surveillance—looking through Observation Hole Excelsior on the south end of the attic, which spied down on Lance's bed—he actually heard Sally-Ann, Lance's most recent conquest, say she "loved" his hair and asked who "styled" it.

It didn't make any sense. Why did Lance get all the girls when Albert was the one with perfect hair? It was thick and dark, neatly trimmed, and he had a flawless part. He took great pride in that part. It took years to cultivate. And now it was as straight as the barrel of a Remington 12-gauge, a sharp white line cutting precisely through the dark forest on his head.

And yet it was mussy-maned Lance that got the girls. Infuriating. Simply unjust. It took a tremendous display of willpower for Albert to keep from vomiting when he heard Lance's girlfriend slobbering over his sloppy locks like some hair worshiping nymphomaniac. But thank God he hadn't, because he would have given away his entire surveillance operation, and today his efforts had uncovered an invaluable nugget of information.

He was looking down through Observation Hole Delta-Bravo over the kitchen phone, listening to the tapped line with his earpiece as Lance talked to his girlfriend, leaning back on a kitchen chair, holding the receiver with one hand, adjusting his crotch through his $300 jeans with the other.

"Do you really mean it?" Sally-Ann squealed.

"That's right, baby," Lance crooned. "Pack your bags. You're moving in. End of this month."

"What about your roommate?"

"He's not my roommate, he's my tenant."

"What about your tenant?"

"Well, he's gotta go. I don't trust that freak—I think the guy's half crazy and I don't want him around you. I'm gonna miss the eight hundy his old man sends every month, but it's all about you now, baby."

"We're gonna have to tell Grammy and Gramp-Gramps."

"Fine. Dinner here this weekend. We'll break the good news."

"They might not like me moving in with you, us not being married. You're gonna have to make a good impression."

"How can I not? I'll just make sure the freak keeps his pimply face in his room. Other than that, we're golden."

So I'm out and that skinny little nympho's in, huh? Albert thought, wanting to cough something up and spit it down the observation hole right in pretty boy's hair. *Keep my pimply face in my room, huh? I don't think so, Mr. I'm-too-cool-'cause-I'm-tall-and-got-a-square-jaw-and-a-cool-guy-patch-of-hair-under-my-lip-and-I-wear-a-different-outfit-every-day-and-drive-a-convertible-sports-car. I don't think so! I'll keep my pimply face anywhere I choose.*

He looked around at the attic, all his hard work, the stealthways, observation points, secret hatches, video equipment. If he left here, he'd have to start his work all over again from another location. And he'd be leaving this area vulnerable. He may not be able to protect this entire nation from overseas threats, but by God, this 1,500 square foot region was secure. He knew with a soldier's heart and a general's wisdom that there were no terrorists or foreign invaders on these grounds. And he wasn't going to let Lance change that.

We'll just have to see how good an impression you make at that little dinner of yours, Lance. We'll just have to see if things don't go quite as planned.

"Well, look at Mr. Handsome—aren't you just too sexy for words," Lance said, winking at himself in the mirror. It really was amazing. He saw that face every day and was just a little surprised every time. Could that really be his face? Was it even possible to have a face that attractive? No prosthetics, no special effects, that is what it actually looked like! It was like standing across from a movie star. No, better than a movie star—a soap star, or an entertainment TV reporter. And he never got complacent about it, because year after year it always got just a little better. He was getting older, pushing up on thirty, but he was only looking more distinguished. Less boyish and more ruggedly handsome. More manly. His body continuing to fill out.

He smiled his signature smile, flashing those big white beauties. He tried a few other smiles to see which was the most charming. There was a coy sideways number that had some possibilities. Probably keep that one on the back burner for awhile, see how it develops. Stick with the tried and true for now.

He pointed his index fingers and raised his thumbs, shooting his reflection. "Pow, pow! I got you, good-lookin'."

Maybe he was too good looking for Sally-Ann? Maybe this was a mistake, letting her move in? Maybe he was selling himself short? She was about the best looking girl in this shit town, so what could he do? He could always move to the city, sell the house, find someone his caliber.

Relax, Champ, he told himself. *When you feel like moving on, those big-city broads will still be there. Go ahead and give a townie a shot for now.*

Sounds like a plan. And see that? Not only was he ridiculously handsome, he was also humble. But it was time to turn his mind to other matters. There was official business that needed his attention. He sat at his desk and took out a sheet of paper. This had to sound official, like it came from a lawyer. So he put himself in a lawyerly frame of mind and wrote:

June 13th
Dear Mr. Albert Flapp:

It is with the deepest and most utmost regret that I must expunge our co-habitationary relationship. Situational changes have necessitated the need for you to relinquish residence in this domicile. Please cease and desist your tenancy no later than June 30th. At such time, any monies due to yourself (e.g., cleaning deposit, et. all) will be rended.

Sincerely yours,
Lance Masterson

Lance was sweating and had a sharp, piercing headache when he was done writing, but the letter was perfect. With that taken care of, he spritzed his face and touched up his hair for awhile. He checked out the new smile one more time—not too bad, might be something there—and headed upstairs to Albert's room. He knocked and the door flung open, the little freak jumping back into a karate stance, dressed head to toe in camouflage. When he saw it was Lance, he straightened up to his full five foot four and shook it out.

"Sorry, Lance. Can't be too careful."

"Yeah, that's right," Lance said, "I could have been a gang of ninjas. Look, Albert, I need you to take this and read it."

He gave Albert his notice. The freak opened the letter and stared, his bushy bottle-brush eyebrows scrunched together—for a twenty-year-old that couldn't grow a mustache, he sure did have some dynamite eyebrows. He strained over the letter, concentrating like he was trying to light it on fire with his mind.

"It says you have to leave by the end of the month," Lance said patiently.

"*That's* what this says? Okay, I was expect . . . I mean, this really comes as a shock."

"Yeah, sorry for the short notice. But I'm sure a smooth operator like yourself won't have any trouble hooking himself up with a swinging bachelor pad." Saying that made Lance feel kind of dirty, but little creeps like Albert usually responded to flattery. "I've got my girlfriend, Sally-Ann, moving in. You know how it is, my man."

Albert stroked his small recessed chin and raised one of his eyebrows dramatically. It looked like a caterpillar trying to crawl up his forehead. "That's too bad," he said. "I really thought we had a good thing going on here." He raised his index finger like a professor about to make a key point. "Say, Lance. Hypothetically, if Sally-Ann couldn't move in for some reason—say, I don't know, she joined the Marines and got deployed to Uzbekistan or maybe she was mauled to death by a giant Kodiak bear—would I still need to move out?"

"You know, pal, there's nothing I'd like more than to have you stay, you really have been a breath of fresh air around here, but with Sally-Ann coming on board it's just going to be too crowded." Maybe he was laying it on a bit too thick. The freak was buying the flattery, but Lance was starting to feel nauseous. "Oh yeah, I also wanted to tell you that I'm planning a dinner party for Sally-Ann and her grandparents tomorrow evening."

"Great, what time should I be there?"

Lance felt his stomach lurch. He tried to smooth the repulsed look off his face. "I'm afraid it will just be the four of us."

Albert counted on his fingers. "No, I get five. Or, what, can one of the grandparents not make it? Does grandpa have a goiter? That's all right. The four of us will have a good time."

"I mean it will just be Sally-Ann, the grandparents and myself."

"I don't get it."

"I mean I was hoping you'd keep to your room that night so we can have some privacy."

"What kind of an invitation is this?"

Lance thought his head might explode if he didn't end this conversation. "It's not an invitation. I don't want you to come downstairs. I want you to stay in your room and not come out until everyone has left. Do you understand?"

Albert's upper lip, covered in a soft pubescent dusting of fur, quivered just a bit. "I understand."

"And don't forget, I need you out by the end of the month," Lance said as Albert shut the door.

Jesus, Lance thought, *thank God that freak will be gone soon.* Now his shoulders were knotted with tension. This stress wasn't good for his complexion. He should head down to the gym and hit the free weights. His deltoids needed some attention. And his pecs hadn't exactly been setting the world on fire lately.

Maybe when he was done he should get an exfoliating massage. Maybe a mani-pedi.

Albert prepared for his next mission with renewed zeal. He was wavering there for a moment. Lance had been apologetic and so full of kind, appreciative words that Albert nearly thought he should move out after all. Then Lance played that cruel trick of inviting him to the dinner but telling him he couldn't leave his room. Well, he may keep to his room, but his presence would most certainly be felt at that dinner.

Albert removed his camo jacket and pulled on his long black trench coat. He had sewn pockets and secret pouches inside for his weapons, spy equipment and ninja gear. What he needed was a better utility belt. He had a grappling hook attached to a launcher on the buckle, but it only threw the line about five feet before it thudded to the floor. And when he did manage to get the hook over a ledge and tried to climb up, it pulled his pants up to his chest, crushing his testicles. But he wouldn't need any of that for this mission.

Albert climbed onto the shelf in his closet and lifted the hatch to the attic. He scanned his immediate surroundings for terrorists and spiders. Clear. He hoisted himself up and crawled along the stealthway to the lockbox hidden under the insulation in Sector Alpha. He removed a small baggie and a vial of liquid, slid them into a secret pouch in the left arm of his trench coat and returned to his room.

He dumped the contents of the baggie into a silver alchemist's mixing bowl (they said it was a dog's water dish at the pawn shop, but that seemed unlikely). It was a fine brown flaky powder, like silt and dried skin. He looked closely and thought he could detect a slight movement, which made sense, because down there at a microscopic level were millions of tiny insects. Itching power, the professional kind. Those little bugs crawled under the skin and caused unbearable itching. Albert had to have it mailed in from Mexico—it was illegal in the United States. And when Lance showed up at dinner tomorrow, itching like a mangy dog, not able to stop scratching throughout the meal, there was no way

Sally-Ann's grandparents would want her living in this unsanitary, vermin-ridden hovel with that disease-carrying hobo.

And just to make sure it was effective, Albert implemented the next phase of his plan. He poured the clear liquid from the vial into the silver bowl, creating an even more powerful concoction. He was like an evil scientist—but an evil scientist for good! But he supposed if he was for good, then he really wasn't an *evil* scientist at all. He was a good scientist. But he supposed most scientists were pretty good already, so that wasn't really a distinctive title. It didn't matter, he could think of a proper title later. What mattered now was gently stirring in the growth agent.

Albert got the vial from his friend Doug from ninja class. Doug's older brother was studying chemistry at the community college but dropped out to start a meth lab in his trailer in the woods. One of his side projects was trying to mutate a bovine growth hormone. He was hoping to make something he could use on his marijuana plants to make the buds swell to gigantic proportions. It didn't work on the "reefer," but it did work on a fly that landed in the solution. Doug said the next day that fly started growing, and before long it was the size of a softball. It fluttered lazily around the trailer, barely able to lift its own bulk, buzzing like it was breaking wind. They had to swat it with a tennis racket, and Doug said it was like popping a fuzzy black balloon filled with chunky red and yellow yogurt.

And now that Albert had the mutated growth hormone, he'd do to this itching powder what had been done to that fly—and Lance was in for a long, uncomfortable dinner party tomorrow.

Once the concoction was thoroughly blended, Albert blow-dried it until it was light and flaky and put it into the baggie. He returned to the attic and crept to Sector Omega over Lance's room, opened Ceiling Hatch Enduring Freedom and lowered the rope ladder. He climbed down and pulled back the silk sheets on Lance's king-sized bed, then changed his mind. If Lance started itching too early, he'd have time to cancel the dinner. So instead Albert went to Lance's underpants drawer, which was filled with fancy little bikini briefs. He sprinkled the powder into the crotch of each pair. Lance was the kind of guy who changed his underpants every single day, so tomorrow when he put on a new pair he'd start getting an itch right where he'd least want it.

Albert returned to his room and undressed for bed. He checked out his physique in the mirror. Not bad. He was skinny—he barely weighed a hundred pounds—but he was pretty cut. When he flexed his arm, it was very clear where the bicep was. There was a distinct line indicating where the muscle started. No one could mistake it.

He got into bed and thought that if this mission went well, if his planning and stealthwork resulted in him being able to stay in the house, then maybe he should consider being a mercenary. The Marines wouldn't take him, but being a mercenary was freelance. No one would know if he was asthmatic, anemic, and had a pilonidal cyst on his coccyx. He liked the idea of being a sniper, but he didn't know how much he'd like running around the jungles of South America. He assumed he probably couldn't get any mercenary jobs here in the house. But maybe he could get an assignment in the neighborhood. Maybe he should get a subscription to *Soldier of Fortune*.

Lance woke up late the next morning. He took a long, hot shower and tried out his new shampoo. *Mangos—nice!* When he got out, he carefully shaved his face, chest, shoulders and upper arms. He applied a layer of lotion—*Lancôme Aqua Fusion, very refreshing, fragrant but not unmasculine.* He slid on some festive red bikini briefs, a pair of vintage jeans and a crisp white long-sleeve shirt. He was also excited to try out the new French cologne he found—*J. Cousteau, the smell of adventure!* A squirt on the neck and another down the pants, just in case Sally-Ann was staying over. Now it was time to get to work on that hair.

An hour and twelve minutes later he'd achieved perfection. He checked himself out in the full-length next to his bed. Perfect. He took another look on the second full-length on the inside bathroom door. Different lighting. He took a third pass on the full-length on his closet door. Still perfect. Grammy would be creaming her Depends.

It was already after noon, and he told Sally-Ann to bring the fossils over at three. He figured that's about when old people ate dinner. So he started vacuuming, and as he did, he started getting a tingling sensation in his crotch. It felt like his foot when he sits on it too long. When this happened to his foot, he'd stomp on it until the circulation came back, so he squeezed his Johnson, pulled on it, punched it a few times, but the tingling didn't stop. Maybe his briefs had shrunk in the wash and were cutting off the blood to Stretch Armstrong.

He tossed out the red pair and slipped on some tiger-stripes. This was a party, right? He went back to vacuuming. The tingling didn't stop, and now it was starting to itch. He went to the bathroom to look. It was red, but that could be from scratching it.

It was getting late and he had to go pick up the food. He drove to the restaurant with one hand on the wheel and the other stuffed down his pants, raking at his sack. The whole area felt like it was on fire. A horrible itchy fire. It had to be that new cologne he'd sprayed down there. If he ever found out who that J.

Cousteau was, he'd track his French ass down and stab him in the nuts with a fork.

Lance picked up the food—a cream of asparagus soup, mashed potatoes, a creamed white fish and tapioca pudding for desert. He wanted to get soft food because he didn't know if the dinosaurs still had their teeth or not. As the zit face at the counter got his order together, Lance had to stuff both hands down his pants, scraping at his crotch like a rototiller. Zit face wasn't too thrilled to take Lance's money when he handed it to him.

Back at the house, Lance threw the food in the oven and ran to the bathroom to see what sort of cooling salve he could slop on his knob. He pulled down his pants, and the whole area was hot and bright red. It had spread a few inches down his thigh and up his lower belly, and there seemed to be some blisters or welts rising on his skin. He really needed to make an emergency appointment with one of his dermatologists, but it was almost three. He smothered the area in calamine lotion until it looked like it had been formed from clay, then turned the blow-dryer on it until it was hard, dry and cracking.

The doorbell rang. Lance zipped up his pants and rushed out into the living room. He gave his package one last good squeeze and opened the door. Sally-Ann was smiling, looking good in a tight white dress. "Hey, baby! This is Grammy and Gramp-Gramps!" she said, presenting a pair of stubby prune-like creatures who only came up to her shoulders.

Gramp-Gramps was wearing an oversized brown suit with an orange tie as wide as his head. The lower half of his face was mostly covered with a whopper of a pushbroom mustache, and he wore a toupee so bad Lance honestly thought for a moment that it was some sort of fur hat. It was matted flat and wide, so it stuck out on the sides of his head. And the dull salt and pepper color was in stark contrast to the wispy silver that grew naturally around the sides of his scalp.

"So you must be Gramp-Gramps," Lance said, displaying a warm smile and extending his hand.

"Gramp-Gramps?" the old man harrumphed behind his mustache. "What are you, a child, for Chrissake? My name's Eugene. Call me Mr. Makeweather."

"Of course, Mr. Makeweather," Lance said, lowering his hand and dying to shove it down his pants, the skin of his crotch crawling and tickling.

He turned to Grammy, dressed up in an old lacy blue dress, a shawl wrapped around her shoulders even though it was eighty degrees out. Her wig was even worse than Gramp-Gramps' toupee. It had big looping curls and looked like something a medieval prosecutor might wear. Her pasty, make-up caked face looked tiny and shriveled under all those dull gray curlicues.

Lance grabbed her cold plasticy hand. "So this must be Sally-Ann's sister," he said, charmingly.

"What?!" she yelled, turning to Gramp-Gramps. "What did he say?!"

"Oh, good God, son, are you insane?" Gramp-Gramps said. "This is Sally-Ann's grandmother. Her *grandmother*! For crying out loud."

"I'm, uh, sorry," Lance said, taken aback. He looked over at Sally-Ann for help, but she was trying to signal to him, pointing down below his waist. He looked down and saw a big pink handprint on his crotch from when he'd squeezed before opening the door. "Uh, come in everyone, please, and, uh, excuse me for a moment."

He race-walked to his bedroom, yanked off his pants and scratched like he was trying to dig himself out of a premature grave. He washed his hands, put on a new pair of jeans and returned to the living room.

"So, can I get anyone a glass of wine," Lance said. "I've got a nice Bordeaux and a very nice Viognier from the Rhône valley."

"I have no idea what the hell you're talking about," Gramp-Gramps said, slumped on the couch, his feet dangling half a foot from the floor. "Get me a Scotch. Single malt."

Shit, he didn't have any Scotch. What liquor did he have? Jaegermeister, tequila, melon liqueur. "How about some Southern Comfort? That's sort of like Scotch."

"Fine," the old man said, waving him off.

"I'll have some white wine if you've got some," Sally-Ann said brightly. She was either putting on a good act or she hadn't realized that five minutes into this little get together it was already a disaster.

"What can I get you, Mrs. Makeweather?" Lance said.

"What?!" she said, looking around at Sally-Ann and Gramp-Gramps. "What did he say?!"

"You really have to speak up with her," Sally-Ann said.

Lance leaned in closer, raising his voice. "What can I get you to drink, Mrs. Makeweather?!"

"What?!" She looked at Sally-Ann. "I can't hear what he's saying."

"You really do have to speak loudly, Lance. She doesn't hear so good anymore."

"Mrs. Makeweather . . ."

Sally-Ann made a lifting motion, mouthing the word "louder."

Lance leaned in right next to the old lady's ear and yelled as loud as he could, "WHAT WOULD YOU LIKE TO DRINK?!"

She covered her ears in pain.

"Holy Christ!" the old man yelled. "What's the matter with you? Are you trying to make her *completely* deaf?"

"Why don't you just bring her a glass of white wine," Sally-Ann said, putting a consoling arm around the old lady.

Lance slinked off to the kitchen and shoved his hands down his pants. He shouldn't have gotten that manicure yesterday—he couldn't scratch hard enough. He snatched a fork off the counter, shoved it down his pants and dragged it hard across his skin. It hurt like hell, but it felt so damn good he didn't want to stop. But he did. He didn't want to whip out his junk with everyone in the other room, but it felt like the rash was spreading down his thighs, around to his hips and up his belly. And it itched worse than before, which he didn't think was possible. It felt like bugs were crawling under his skin.

He poured the drinks and returned to the living room. He gave Gramp-Gramps his glass. The old man took a sip and his wrinkled face got even more contorted. "What the hell did you just give me? Is this cough syrup?"

"Be nice, Gramp-Gramps," Sally-Ann said, taking her glass of wine.

Lance started to hand the other glass to Grammy when he felt the horrible, sickly sensation of an insect running down his inner thigh, making him jerk, kicking Sally-Ann in the shin and throwing the wine in Grammy's face.

Suddenly, everyone was on their feet, Sally-Ann hopping on one foot, Grammy stunned, blinking the wine out of her eyes, Lance diving in, dabbing at her face with his shirtsleeve, smearing the thick make-up, Gramp-Gramps shoving him out of the way, looking like he wanted to fight.

"Good Christ in heaven, what's gotten into you?!" Gramp-Gramps yelled.

"I'm so sorry, I, uh, had a muscle spasm. Are you all right, Sally-Ann?"

"I'm fine," she said, grimacing.

"Should I get a towel?" Lance said.

"Of course you should get a towel, you imbecile." Gramp-Gramps might have been snarling, but it was impossible to tell behind his massive mustache.

Lance ran to the bathroom, kicked off his shoes and jumped out of his jeans. He looked for the bug that had run down his leg but didn't see it. Then he felt a tickle on the back of his right knee. He reached back and felt a lump. He picked at it and the lump darted up the back of his leg—*under the skin!*

Lance shrieked.

"What the hell are you doing to yourself in there?" the old man called from the other room.

"I'll be out in a minute," Lance called back, feeling a light tingling in his head and a gurgling queasiness in his stomach. He felt around for the lump but it seemed to have disappeared. He pulled up his pants. He didn't even want to think about where the lump had gone.

Jesus, there's some sort of bug under my skin, he thought, but pushed the idea out of his head before he passed out. *Let's just get through this quickly. Shove some food down their crotchety old throats, get their wrinkled asses the hell out of here and get to the hospital.*

Lance brought Grammy a towel. She dried off, knocking her wig askew and leaving half her face on the fabric.

"So what do you guys say we have some dinner?" Lance said.

"I think that sounds like a fine idea," Sally-Ann said, staring Gramp-Gramps in the eye and nodding insistently.

The old man grumbled, leading a dazed Grammy into the adjacent dinning room.

Everything between Lance's waist and his knees was achieving a supernatural degree of itchiness. It was hard to think of anything other than the creepy-crawly heebie-jeebieness in his pants. He walked behind the others with his knees together, thighs scraping, both hands in his pockets scratching at anything he could reach like a cat wrapped in a pillowcase.

Once everyone was seated around the dining room table, Lance excused himself and ran to the kitchen. He took his chances and dropped his pants. His thighs and waist and groin were a throbbing, glowing red and lumpy. He raked the area over fast and hard with the fork, leaving bloody corn rows. The tines hit a set of lumps on his lower belly, and *sweetjesuslordinheavengodalmightly* the lumps ran up his stomach, three of them, Lance stabbing at his stomach and chest, chasing them up toward his shoulders where they seemed to disappear.

Lance stood there, breathing heavy, the fork stuck in his upper chest through the shirt, the end of the fork bobbing with each breath. *Where the hell did they go?* he asked himself, then replied, *I don't want to know. There was nothing there and it didn't go anywhere.*

He yanked the fork out of his skin and filled four bowls with soup. He loaded them onto a serving tray and brought them out to the dining room, praying one of those cursed subcutaneous bugs didn't start running around inside him, making him toss scalding soup onto his elderly guests.

He made it. Everyone got their soup and started slurping.

"Honey," Sally-Ann said. "Are you all right?" She pointed at his chest. Half a dozen bloody splotches were soaking through his white shirt where he'd stabbed himself with the fork.

"Yeah, I'm fine," he said, almost whimpering. "I guess I should change this."

Lance stood, and as he did, he felt a hideous scrambling of bugs around his lower back.

"Oh, oh, oh!" he yelped, thrusting his hips out three times in quick succession, smacking his pelvis hard against the table, scooting it across the dining room floor, Grammy chasing after her soup with her spoon as it slid across the table.

"Baby, are you sure you're all right?"

"Oh, you bet, honey, I'm . . ."

Suddenly, there was an explosion of crawling and squirming and scurrying under his skin. He felt the bugs scrambling through him, up his back, down his legs, his arms, across his chest. He ripped open his shirt and saw dozens of lumps, hundreds, the size of wide, flat jelly beans crisscrossing beneath his flesh. He grabbed one on his stomach, isolating it with his thumb and index finger, just able to make out a crab-like shape, like a boney spider. It vibrated and wiggled under his grasp.

Lance panicked, grabbed Gramp-Gramps by both shoulders, put his face right up against the old man's and screamed, "AAAARRRGGGGHHHHH!!!!" He tried to ask the old man to help him, to do something, but all that came out was a deafening shriek that made the old man's eyes bulge and his mouth hang so low it was visible beneath the curtain of his mustache.

The old man wasn't helping, so Lance flew to the other side of the table and shoved his face right up against Sally-Ann's.

"AAAAAARRRRRGGGGGHHHHH!!!!!"

She started screaming too, the two of them wailing in stereo.

"AAAAAAARRRRRRGGGGGGGGHHHHHHHHH!!!!!!"

"You two keep it down over there, I'm trying to enjoy my soup," Grammy said without raising her head from the bowl of creamed asparagus.

"Zip it, you bald cunt!" Lance screeched. "I'm being eaten alive over here!"

"All right," Gramp-Gramps said, throwing down his spoon and stomping his feet as he stood, "I think I've had just about enough of this young man's disgraceful behavior. Come along, Sally-Ann."

Sally-Ann dragged Grammy away from her soup, and the three of them headed for the door.

"Wait, you can't leave," Lance said, dizzy and frozen in place, watching the frantic activity transpiring beneath his outer layer.

"We can and we will," Gramp-Gramps declared.

Sally-Ann narrowed her eyes at him. "You really shouldn't have yelled at poor Grammy."

They left and Lance was alone. He didn't know what to do. He grabbed a steak knife from the dinning room table, zeroed in on the slowest moving lump on his forearm. He stabbed and missed, the knife sticking in a half inch, sending a sharp jolt of pain up his arm. He yanked the knife out and aimed more carefully. He jabbed, got it, and the hideous subdermal insect started vibrating violently on the tip of the blade like it was being electrocuted, sending a teeth-rattling shiver through every bone in his body.

He ran through the house screaming—through the living room, into the kitchen, the dining room again, back into the living room, the knife dangling from his arm. He plucked it out and all the little creatures seemed to gather at the site of hole, crawling over each other, making the skin swell, creating such an overwhelming agitation that he barely felt the knife as he laid it across his skin, pressed down and dragged it hard over his forearm, splitting the skin. He had to get those tiny monsters out. He pushed down on the wriggling mound and three of them slid out of the open wound. They were as big around as quarters and looked like thick bone-white spiders, trailing blood as they scurried across his forearm and down to his fingers. He flicked them off onto the floor.

They were followed by about two dozen others.

Lance felt his head going light, spots popping off in the corners of his vision.

And then a funny thing happened. Lance was standing in the center of the living room, facing the south wall and the stairway that lead up to Albert's room. But this section of the room slipped down toward his feet as the ceiling slid forward in front of him, and the floor came up from behind, smacking him on the back of his head.

The world righted itself and he realized that he was lying on his back, watching the room grow dark around him.

Albert attached the CO_2 cartridge to the grappling hook launcher on his wrist. It stuck out awkwardly, but it should throw that line like nobody's business. And the wrist mount wouldn't give him a wedgie like the belt attachment.

He put a handful of diversionary smoke bombs and a few throwing stars in the secret interior pockets of his trench coat. He wanted to bring his two-handed broad sword, but it was too heavy and made his coat pull off one shoulder.

He saw Sally-Ann and her grandparents leave, so now that he was adequately equipped, it was time to talk to Lance about letting him stay here. He may be excited about the idea—after all, Lance had called him "a breath of fresh air"—or he may be upset about the lengths Albert had to go to in order to make it happen—he did seem to be in excruciating discomfort. It was impossible to tell, but in either case he was prepared.

Albert cracked the door and peeked out. Clear. In a crouch, he crept downstairs to the living room, where Lance lay unconscious, bleeding from his arm.

Albert nudged his leg with the toe of his clawed ninja grappling boot.

Lance opened his eyes and started choking. He sat up and coughed out a mouthful of wriggling white insects. Then Albert noticed the bulges on his face, other insects moving under the skin across his cheeks, several making his upper lip bulge. One was under his left eye. It crawled out from under his lower eyelid and across his eyeball.

He passed out again.

Albert had to shake him by the shoulder to rouse him this time. When his eyes opened, Albert said, "Hey, Lance? This may not be the best time, but now that Sally-Ann's not moving in, do you think I can stay?"

"Albert? Oh my God, you've got to get me to the hospital."

"Right. Sure. But what do you think about me staying?"

Lance coughed up another bug, which scurried across the laminate floor and under the couch. "Now's not the time for that. You've got to get me to the hospital."

"Oh, of course. But I was thinking that now that we've gotten rid your girlfriend, there's no reason I should . . ."

"What do you mean 'we got rid of?'"

"Well I guess you could say that *I* got rid of her since you didn't know about my plan up front, but you did play a crucial part and deserve a lot of the credit."

Lance pushed himself up to a sitting position and started to stand. "What plan?"

"The itching powder I put in your underpants to scare off your girlfriend. It obviously worked, so should I just assume I can stay then?"

"You did this to me?" Lance said, looking irrationally angry, his eyes wide, lip curled up in a sneer. He bent down and grabbed a steak knife from the floor next to where he'd been lying. "I'm gonna kill you. I'm gonna kill you dead right where you stand, you sick fucking freak."

This is why Albert came prepared. "You can't kill me," he said, waving one hand slowly across his face as he reached into his coat pocket with the other, "because I'm not even here."

Albert threw a handful of the diversionary smoke bombs on the floor in front of him. They were the professional kind that magicians use, but all these produced was a faint pop and a tiny wisp of smoke, like he'd lit a few sticks of incense.

"You're dead," Lance said, lunging at him. Albert needed to get to his room to get his two-handed broad sword, but Lance had gotten between him and the stairs.

This is where all of Albert's hard work paid off. He ran to the side of the stairs, underneath the banister. He pulled back his sleeve, revealing the grappling hook launcher on his wrist. He pressed the release button. The CO_2 cartridge hissed out cold air, freezing the hairs on Albert's forearm, but it didn't throw the line.

Lance moved toward him, stopping after each step to itch frantically at a different part of his body.

Albert pulled the full line out of the launcher. He threw it up toward the banister, but it was too short. He threw it again, this time jumping as high as he could.

The hook caught on the banister!

And Albert came down with a jerk, the line on his wrist nearly yanking his arm out of the socket, leaving him dangling a foot and half from the floor like a piñata.

Albert tried to pull himself up and climb to the second floor, but he didn't have the upper body strength to raise himself more than a couple of inches. He tried to move but could only flail his arm and legs helplessly, suspended in midair.

Lance raised his knife.

This is it, Albert thought, *all of my good deeds and hard work keeping this country safe, and this is what it comes down to.*

Lance moved in, ready to stab, then stopped. He doubled over. "Ah, Jesus! Holy mother of Satan!"

He ripped open his pants to reveal a misshapen lump of flesh that Albert barely recognized as part of the human anatomy. There was a penis, but it was grotesque, bulging and changing shape, the white crab-like insects spilling from the end like some evil ejaculate. There seemed to be an incredible amount of roiling activity concentrated in the groin area, making it expand and swell like the tinfoil trays of popcorn you heat over the stove until they burst open.

Looking down at this, a strange calm seemed to fall over Lance. He turned serenely away from Albert, walked over to the coffee table, knelt down, placed his penis on top of it, raised the knife over his head and brought it slashing down, chopping the penis clean off, insects spilling from the dismembered organ and the stump from which it had been removed. Lance flopped back, the bugs continuing to pour from the hole in his groin.

It took Albert nearly half an hour to unstrap the wristband, sending him crumpling to the floor, his hand so numb it felt like an inanimate piece of rubber. He went over to Lance and tried to shake him awake—he'd never said explicitly whether or not Albert could stay in the house—but he was cold and lifeless, and in all probability dead.

So that meant the house belonged to Albert now. It was never his intention to kill Lance, but now that he was dead, it really was the best possible outcome. He took a look around. That sleek modern couch, that widescreen TV, that bloody coffee table, it was all his now. And he could probably keep the checks his father sent each month, which meant he could really beef up the surveillance equipment around here.

Albert walked through the dining room, checking out his nice oak table. He went through the kitchen to admire his appliances and take an inventory of all his food.

He went to the bedroom. It sure will be nice sleeping on those silk sheets tonight. He also had a new wardrobe. He didn't think Lance had any camo or ninja gear, but Albert wouldn't mind wearing some of those fancy underpants. He pulled open the drawer to get a look—

—and found it filled with a sea of bone-white insects, which engulfed his arm, traveling up over his shoulder, down his chest and up his neck, covering his face, filling his mouth, his nostrils, crawling under his eyelids, wiggling into his ears.

As Albert began to black out, he pulled his throwing stars from his coat pocket. But didn't really know where to throw them.

"Boy, I never can figure why a fella would want to go and castrate himself," Hoyt Butterfield said as they put the shriveled corpse onto the gurney.

"Well, I sure can agree with you there, Mr. B," Lloyd said, placing the penis on the cadaver's chest. "But I think castration is when the testicles are removed, and this here fella seems to have held onto his set."

"I imagine you're right on that score. But it sure is a shame."

"That it is, Mr. B. Say, the officer says we got another fella back in the bedroom. You think we should go load him up too?"

"I suppose we should."

They went to the back bedroom and found the other corpse, just as dried out and shriveled as the first.

"Well, would you look at that," Hoyt said.

"What's that, Mr. B.?"

"Even in death, that poor kid has just about the nicest head of hair I ever seen."

"Oh, doesn't he though."

"And would you just look at that part. It's just as straight as an arrow. What I wouldn't give to have a part like that."

"Like you said, Mr. B., it's a real shame."

Again

Ramsey Campbell

BEFORE LONG BRYANT TIRED of the Wirral Way. He'd exhausted the Liverpool parks, only to find that nature was too relentless for him. No doubt the trail would mean more to a botanist, but to Bryant it looked exactly like what it was: an overgrown railway divested of its line. Sometimes it led beneath bridges hollow as whistles, and then it seemed to trap him between the banks for miles. When it rose to ground level it was only to show him fields too lush for comfort, hedges, trees, green so unrelieved that its shades blurred into a single oppressive mass.

He wasn't sure what eventually made the miniature valley intolerable. Children went hooting like derailed trains across his path. Huge dogs came snuffling out of the undergrowth to leap on him and smear his face, but the worst annoyances were the flies, brought out all at once by the late June day, the first hot day of the year. They blotched his vision like eyestrain, their incessant buzzing seemed to muffle all his senses. When he heard lorries somewhere above him, he scrambled up the first break he could find in the brambles, without waiting for the next official exit from the trail.

By the time he realised that the path led nowhere in particular, he had already crossed three fields. It seemed best to go on, even though the sound he'd taken for lorries proved, now that he was in the open, to be distant tractors. He didn't think he could find his way back even if he wanted to. Surely he would reach a road eventually.

Once he'd trudged around several more fields he wasn't so sure. He felt sticky, hemmed in by buzzing and green—a fly in a flytrap. There was nothing else beneath the unrelenting cloudless sky except a bungalow, three fields and a copse away to his left. Perhaps he could get a drink there while asking the way to the road.

The bungalow was difficult to reach. Once he had to retrace his journey around three sides of a field, when he'd approached close enough to see that the garden that had surrounded the house looked at least as overgrown as the railway had been.

Nevertheless someone was standing in front of the bungalow, knee-deep in grass—a woman with white shoulders, standing quite still. He hurried around the maze of fences and hedges, looking for his way to her. He'd come quite close before he saw how old and pale she was. She was supporting herself with one hand on a disused bird-table, and for a moment he thought the shoulders of her ankle-length caftan were white with droppings, as the table was. He shook his head vigorously, to clear it of the heat, and saw at once that it was long white hair that trailed raggedly over her shoulders, for it stirred a little as she beckoned to him.

At least, he assumed she was beckoning. When he reached her, after he'd lifted the gate clear of the weedy path, she was still flapping her hands, but now to brush away flies, which seemed even fonder of her than they had been of him. Her eyes looked glazed and empty; for a moment he was tempted to sneak away. Then they gazed at him, and they were so pleading that he had to go to her, to see what was wrong.

She must have been pretty when she was younger. Now her long arms and heart-shaped face were bony, the skin withered tight on them, but she might still be attractive if her complexion weren't so grey. Perhaps the heat was affecting her—she was clutching the bird-table as though she would fall if she relaxed her grip—but then why didn't she go into the house? Then he realised that must be why she needed him, for she was pointing shakily with her free hand at the bungalow. Her nails were very long. "Can you get in?" she said.

Her voice was disconcerting: little more than a breath, hardly there at all. No doubt that was also the fault of the heat. "I'll try," he said, and she made for the house at once, past a tangle of roses and a rockery so overgrown it looked like a distant mountain in a jungle.

She had to stop breathlessly before she reached the bungalow. He carried on, since she was pointing feebly at the open kitchen window. As he passed her he found she was doused in perfume, so heavily that even in the open it was cloying. Surely she was in her seventies? He felt shocked, though he knew that was narrow-minded. Perhaps it was the perfume that attracted the flies to her.

The kitchen window was too high for him to reach unaided. Presumably she felt it was safe to leave open while she was away from the house. He went round the far side of the bungalow to the open garage, where a dusty car was baking amid the stink of hot metal and oil. There he found a toolbox, which he dragged round to the window.

When he stood the rectangular box on end and levered himself up, he wasn't sure he could squeeze through. He unhooked the transom and managed to wriggle his shoulders through the opening. He thrust himself forward, the unhooked bar bumping along his spine, until his hips wedged in the frame. He was stuck in midair, above a greyish kitchen that smelled stale, dangling like the string of plastic onions on the far wall. He was unable to drag himself forward or back.

All at once her hands grabbed his thighs, thrusting up towards his buttocks. She must have clambered on the toolbox. No doubt she was anxious to get him into the house, but her sudden desperate strength made him uneasy, not least because he felt almost assaulted. Nevertheless she'd given him the chance to squirm his hips, and he was through. He lowered himself awkwardly, head first, clinging to the edge of the sink while he swung his feet down before letting himself drop.

He made for the door at once. Though the kitchen was almost bare, it smelled worse than stale. In the sink a couple of plates protruded from water the color of lard, where several dead flies were floating. Flies crawled over smeary milk bottles on the windowsill or bumbled at the window, as eager to find the way out as he was. He thought he'd found it, but the door was mortise-locked, with a broken key that was jammed in the hole.

He tried to turn the key, until he was sure it was no use. Not only was its stem snapped close to the lock, the key was wedged in the mechanism. He hurried out of the kitchen to the front door, which was in the wall at right angles to the jammed door. The front door was mortise-locked as well.

As he returned to the kitchen window he bumped into the refrigerator. It mustn't have been quite shut, for it swung wide open—not that it mattered, since the fridge was empty save for a torpid fly. She must have gone out to buy provisions—presumably her shopping was somewhere in the undergrowth. "Can you tell me where the key is?" he said patiently.

She was clinging to the outer sill, and seemed to be trying to save her breath. From the movements of her lips he gathered she was saying "Look around."

There was nothing in the kitchen cupboards except a few cans of baked beans and meat, their labels peeling. He went back to the front hall, which was cramped, hot, almost airless. Even here he wasn't free of the buzzing of flies, though he couldn't see them. Opposite the front door was a cupboard hiding mops and brushes senile with dust. He opened the fourth door off the hall into the living-room.

The long room smelled as if it hadn't been opened for months, and looked like a parody of middle-class taste. Silver-plated cannon challenged each other across the length of the pebbledashed mantelpiece, on either side of which were portraits of the royal family. Here was a cabinet full of dolls of all nations, here was a bookcase of *Reader's Digest* Condensed Books. A personalised bullfight poster was pinned to one wall, a ten-gallon hat to another. With so much in it, it seemed odd that the room felt disused.

He began to search, trying to ignore the noise of flies—it was somewhere further into the house, and sounded disconcertingly like someone groaning. The key wasn't on the obese purple suite or down the sides of the cushions; it wasn't on the small table piled with copies of *Contact*, which for a moment, giggling, he took to be a sexual contact magazine. The key wasn't under the bright green rug, nor on any of the shelves. The dolls gazed unhelpfully at him.

He was holding his breath, both because the unpleasant smell he'd associated with the kitchen seemed even stronger in here and because every one of his movements stirred up dust. The entire room was pale with it; no wonder the dolls' eyelashes were so thick. She must no longer have the energy to clean the house. Now he had finished searching, and it looked as if he would have to venture deeper into the house, where the flies seemed to be so abundant. He was at the far door when he glanced back. Was that the key beneath the pile of magazines?

He had only begun to tug the metal object free when he saw it was a pen, but the magazines were already toppling. As they spilled over the floor, some of them opened at photographs: people tied up tortuously, a plump woman wearing a suspender belt and flourishing a whip.

He suppressed his outrage before it could take hold of him. So much for first impressions! After all, the old lady must have been young once. Really, that thought was rather patronising too—and then he saw it was more than that. One issue of the magazine was no more than a few months old.

He was shrugging to himself, trying to pretend that it didn't matter to him, when a movement made him glance up at the window. The old lady was staring in at him. He leapt away from the table as if she'd caught him stealing, and hurried to the window, displaying his empty hands. Perhaps she hadn't had time to see him at the magazines—it must have taken her a while to struggle through the undergrowth around the house—for she only pointed at the far door and said "Look in there."

Just now he felt uneasy about visiting the bedrooms, however absurd that was. Perhaps he could open the window outside which she was standing, and lift her up—but the window was locked, and no doubt the key was with the one he was searching for. Suppose he didn't find them? Suppose he couldn't get out of the kitchen window? Then she would have to pass the tools up to him, and he would open the house that way. He made himself go to the far door while he was feeling confident. At least he would be away from her gaze, wouldn't have to wonder what she was thinking about him.

Unlike the rest he had seen of the bungalow, the hall beyond the door was dark. He could see the glimmer of three doors and several framed photographs lined up along the walls. The sound of flies was louder, though they didn't seem to be in the hall itself. Now that he was closer they sounded even more like someone groaning feebly, and the rotten smell was stronger too. He held his breath and hoped that he would have to search only the nearest room.

When he shoved its door open, he was relieved to find it was the bathroom —but the state of it was less of a relief. Bath and washbowl were bleached with dust; spiders had caught flies between the taps. Did she wash herself in the kitchen? But then how long had the stagnant water been there? He was searching among the jars of ointments and lotions on the window ledge, all of which were swollen with a fur of talcum powder; he shuddered when it squeaked beneath his fingers. There was no sign of a key.

He hurried out, but halted in the doorway. Opening the door had lightened the hall, so that he could see the photographs. They were wedding photographs, all seven of them. Though the bridegrooms were different—here an airman with a thin moustache, there a portly man who could have been a tycoon or a chef— the bride was the same in every one. It was the woman who owned the house, growing older as the photographs progressed, until in the most recent, where she was holding onto a man with a large nose and a fierce beard, she looked almost as old as she was now.

Bryant found himself smirking uneasily, as if at a joke he didn't quite see but which he felt he should. He glanced quickly at the two remaining doors. One was heavily bolted on the outside—the one beyond which he could hear the intermittent sound like groaning. He chose the other door at once.

It led to the old lady's bedroom. He felt acutely embarrassed even before he saw the brief transparent nightdress on the double bed. Nevertheless he had to brave the room, for the dressing-table was a tangle of bracelets and necklaces, the perfect place to lose keys; the mirror doubled the confusion. Yet as soon as he saw the photographs that were leaning against the mirror, some instinct made him look elsewhere first.

There wasn't much to delay him. He peered under the bed, lifting both sides of the counterpane to be sure. It wasn't until he saw how grey his fingers had become that he realised the bed was thick with dust. Despite the indentation in the middle of the bed, he could only assume that she slept in the bolted room.

He hurried to the dressing-table and began to sort through the jewellery, but as soon as he saw the photographs his fingers grew shaky and awkward. It wasn't simply that the photographs were so sexually explicit—it was that in all of them she was very little younger, if at all, than she was now. Apparently she and her bearded husband both liked to be tied up, and that was only the mildest of their practices. Where was her husband now? Had his predecessors found her too much for them? Bryant had finished searching through the jewellery by now, but he couldn't look away from the photographs, though he found them appalling. He was still staring morbidly when she peered in at him, through the window that was reflected in the mirror.

This time he was sure she knew what he was looking at. More, he was sure he'd been meant to find the photographs. That must be why she'd hurried round the outside of the house to watch. Was she regaining her strength? Certainly she must have had to struggle through a good deal of undergrowth to reach the window in time.

He made for the door without looking at her, and prayed that the key would be in the one remaining room, so that he could get out of the house. He strode across the hallway and tugged at the rusty bolt, trying to open the door before his fears grew worse. His struggle with the bolt set off the sound like groaning within the room, but that was no reason for him to expect a torture chamber. Nevertheless, when the bolt slammed all at once out of the socket and the door swung inward, he staggered back into the hall.

The room didn't contain much: just a bed and the worst of the smell. It was the only room where the curtains were drawn, so that he had to strain his eyes to see that someone was lying on the bed, covered from head to foot with a blanket. A spoon protruded from an open can of meat beside the bed. Apart from a chair and a fitted wardrobe, there was nothing else to see—except that, as far Bryant could make out in the dusty dimness, the shape on the bed was moving feebly.

All at once he was no longer sure that the groaning had been the sound of flies. Even so, if the old lady had been watching him he might never have been able to step forward. But she couldn't see him, and he had to know. Though he couldn't help tiptoeing, he forced himself to go to the head of the bed.

He wasn't sure if he could lift the blanket, until he looked in the can of meat. At least it seemed to explain the smell, for the can must have been opened months ago. Rather than think about that—indeed, to give himself no time to think—he snatched the blanket away from the head of the figure at once.

Perhaps the groaning had been the sound of flies after all, for they came swarming out, off the body of the bearded man. He had clearly been dead for at least as long as the meat had been opened. Bryant thought sickly that if the sheet had really been moving, it must have been the flies. But there was something worse than that: the scratches on the shoulders of the corpse, the teeth-marks on its neck—for although there was no way of being sure, he had an appalled suspicion that the marks were quite new.

He was stumbling away from the bed—he felt he was drowning in the air that was thick with dust and flies—when the sound recommenced. For a moment he had the thought, so grotesque he was afraid he might both laugh wildly and be sick, that flies were swarming in the corpse's beard. But the sound was groaning after all, for the bearded head was lolling feebly back and forth on the pillow, the tongue was twitching about the greyish lips, the blind eyes were rolling. As the lower half of the body began to jerk weakly but rhythmically, the long-nailed hands tried to reach for whoever was in the room.

Somehow Bryant was outside the door and shoving the bolt home with both hands. His teeth were grinding from the effort to keep his mouth closed, for he didn't know if he was going to vomit or scream. He reeled along the hall, so dizzy he was almost incapable, into the living-room. He was terrified of seeing her at the window, on her way to cut off his escape. He felt so weak he wasn't sure of reaching the kitchen window before she did.

Although he couldn't focus on the living-room, as if it wasn't really there, it seemed to take him minutes to cross. He'd stumbled at last into the front hall when he realised that he needed something on which to stand to reach the transom. He seized the small table, hurling the last of the contact magazines to the floor, and staggered toward the kitchen with it, almost wedging it in the doorway. As he struggled with it, he was almost paralysed by the fear that she would be waiting at the kitchen window.

She wasn't there. She must still be on her way around the outside of the house. As he dropped the table beneath the window, Bryant saw the broken key in the mortise lock. Had someone else—perhaps the bearded man—broken it while trying to escape? It didn't matter, he mustn't start thinking of escapes that had failed. But it looked as if he would have to, for he could see at once that he couldn't reach the transom.

He tried once, desperately, to be sure. The table was too low, the narrow sill was too high. Though he could wedge one foot on the sill, the angle was wrong for him to squeeze his shoulders through the window. He would certainly be stuck when she came to find him. Perhaps if he dragged a chair through from the living-room—but he had only just stepped down, almost falling to his knees, when he heard her opening the front door with the key she had had all the time.

His fury at being trapped was so intense that it nearly blotted out his panic. She had only wanted to trick him into the house. By God, he'd fight her for the key if he had to, especially now that she was relocking the front door. All at once he was stumbling wildly toward the hall, for he was terrified that she would unbolt the bedroom and let out the thing in the bed. But when he threw open the kitchen door, what confronted him was far worse.

She stood in the living-room doorway, waiting for him. Her caftan lay crumpled on the hall floor. She was naked, and at last he could see how grey and shrivelled she was—just like the bearded man. She was no longer troubling to brush off the flies, a couple of which were crawling in and out of her mouth. At last, too late, he realised that her perfume had not been attracting the flies at all. It had been meant to conceal the smell that was attracting them—the smell of death.

She flung the key behind her, a new move in her game. He would have died rather than try to retrieve it, for then he would have had to touch her. He backed into the kitchen, looking frantically for something he could use to smash the window. Perhaps he was incapable of seeing it, for his mind seemed paralysed by the sight of her. Now she was moving as fast as he was, coming after him with her long arms outstretched, her grey breasts flapping. She was licking her lips as best she could, relishing his terror. Of course, that was why she'd made him go through the entire house. He knew that her energy came from her hunger for him.

It was a fly—the only one in the kitchen that hadn't alighted on her—that drew his gaze to the empty bottles on the windowsill. He'd known all the time they were there, but panic was dulling his mind. He grabbed the nearest bottle, though his sweat and the slime of milk made it almost too slippery to hold. At least it felt reassuringly solid, if anything could be reassuring now. He swung it with all his force at the centre of the window. But it was the bottle which broke.

He could hear himself screaming—he didn't know if it was with rage or terror—as he rushed toward her, brandishing the remains of the bottle to keep her away until he reached the door. Her smile, distorted but gleeful, had robbed him of the last traces of restraint, and there was only the instinct to survive. But her smile widened as she saw the jagged glass—indeed, her smile looked quite capable of collapsing her face. She lurched straight into his path, her arms wide.

He closed his eyes and stabbed. Though her skin was tougher than he'd expected, he felt it puncture drily, again and again. She was thrusting herself onto the glass, panting and squealing like a pig. He was slashing desperately now, for the smell was growing worse.

All at once she fell, rattling on the linoleum. For a moment he was terrified that she would seize his legs and drag him down on her. He fled, kicking out blindly, before he dared open his eyes. The key—where was the key? He hadn't seen where she had thrown it. He was almost weeping as he dodged about the living-room, for he could hear her moving feebly in the kitchen. But there was the key, almost concealed down the side of a chair.

As he reached the front door he had a last terrible thought. Suppose this key broke too? Suppose that was part of her game? He forced himself to insert it carefully, though his fingers were shaking so badly he could hardly keep hold of it at all. It wouldn't turn. It would—he had been trying to turn it the wrong way. One easy turn, and the door swung open. He was so insanely grateful that he almost neglected to lock it behind him.

He flung the key as far as he could and stood in the overgrown garden, retching for breath. He'd forgotten that there were such things as trees, flowers, fields, the open sky. Yet just now the scent of flowers was sickening, and he couldn't bear the sound of flies. He had to get away from the bungalow and then from the countryside—but there wasn't a road in sight, and the only path he knew led back toward the Wirral Way. He wasn't concerned about returning to the nature trail, but the route back would lead him past the kitchen window. It took him a long time to move, and then it was because he was more afraid to linger near the house.

When he reached the window, he tried to run while tiptoeing. If only he dared turn his face away! He was almost past before he heard a scrabbling beyond the window. The remains of her hands appeared on the sill, and then her head lolled into view. Her eyes gleamed brightly as the shards of glass that protruded from her face. She gazed up at him, smiling raggedly and pleading. As he backed away, floundering through the undergrowth, he saw that she was mouthing jerkily. "Again," she said.

Maggots

Tim Curran

THE FEW BLAZING STICKS in the shallow pit did little to dispel the frigid winds that howled through the winter dead forest. The trees were snow-heaped sculptures, the landscape blasted white with drift. Francois Jarny sat there, shivering, teeth chattering, hugging his greatcoat to him for all the good it did. His knapsack was empty and had been empty for days, still he pawed through it with frostbitten fingers, hoping for a stray crumb of biscuit that he might have missed.

But there was nothing.

Jarny had been hungry for weeks it seemed, at least since the Grand Armee had retreated from Smolensk, harassed by Cossacks and filthy peasants the entire way. Smolensk was a plague city, thousands smitten with typhus fever. So many dead that the locals were throwing corpses out into the streets.

That long? Jarny wondered. *Has it been that long since I ate some decent food?*

Studying his gnawed leather belt, he knew it was true. There had been a few crumbs of stale bread since, a thin soup of rotting turnip tops at a farmhouse, and, ah yes, the fine meal of roasted dog in Dorogobouche. A starving, slat-thin hound, they had savored its juices and meat, gnawing bones and sucking out the marrow, making a soup from the poor thing's thin blood.

To taste of the meat. To eat of it.

Around him, huddled by the small flickering fires, Jarny could hear men moaning and crying out, many dying from infected battlefield wounds, many more from fever and starvation. Each day there were fewer that moved on. Less soldiers. Less stragglers. Frozen corpses were iced to trees, standing upright.

Footsteps crunched through the snow. "Friend Jarny . . . what a terrible sight you are," said a voice.

It was Henri Boulille, his greatcoat hanging open, his blue tunic beneath streaked with dirt and dried blood. He grinned with yellow teeth. Jarny ignored him, knowing who and what he was.

Boulille squatted by the fire, warming his fingers as the snow fell in frigid sheets. "Why is it, friend Jarny, that you shiver with cold and hunger when there is food to be had? When there is meat that will fill you and keep you strong."

Jarny stared at him with narrow eyes. "I do not care for your meat."

Boulille laughed. "Oh . . . tsk, tsk, Jarny . . . you wish to die in the Russian winter? You wish to never see the warm green hills of France again? How terrible. How very terrible." He looked around. There were two other soldiers at the fire. One had fallen over, freezing to death. The other was delirious, speaking at length with his mother.

Boulille brought his foul, seamed face in closer. "What is it you think I eat, Francois? Do you think I chew upon corpses in the snow? That I gnaw upon their leathery flesh? Oh, but how mistaken you are! How terribly mistaken!"

But Jarny did not think he was mistaken. For he had heard the stories of Boulille and the others. He had seen them dragging frozen corpses from the drifts. And as he squeezed his eyes shut and pretended not to hear, he had heard the sound of knives and bayonets working the carcasses of men. There was a word for what Boulille and the others were, but Jarny would not let himself think it.

Boulille continued to speak, but Jarny would not listen. He could smell death upon his breath.

But to taste of the meat. To eat of it.

He was so hungry, so terribly hungry.

It had only been six weeks now, six weeks since Napoleon's Grand Armee had marched into Moscow, fresh from their valiant victory at Borodino. 100,000 men. They marched into the city unopposed only to find that the Russians had fled. The city was burning. Even miles out on the steppe, the sky had been blotted out by a black haze of smoke. The Russians had deliberately set their beloved city afire, then evacuated en masse. Those that remained were either insane or infected with typhus and dysentery, rat-bite fever. There was no food in the city. The water was contaminated. Two-thirds of Moscow was blazing, the air congested with smoke and ash.

But even there, in the hollowed, smoldering corpse of the city, Boulille had proven himself an apt survivor. The troops were starving and Napoleon himself ordered immediate withdrawal. On the way out, Boulille had gathered the emaciated around him and led them into the ruins of a medical school. The only meat in the city was in specimen jars there in the dissection rooms. Boulille, no stranger to eating men by that point, had organized a feast. The men ate what they found pickled in jars. Organs, limbs, diseased masses of tissue. They fished meat from vats. They feasted, glutting themselves on white, bloated carrion.

Within days, most were dead from formaldehyde poisoning.

But not Boulille. He was fit. He was strong. A ghoul with chattering yellow teeth sharpened on bones, his eyes black lusterless shoe buttons betraying a void of seething madness in his brain.

And now, here he was, making obscene offers of meat to Jarny. He, full and fat and rosy-cheeked, while Jarny, half his age, was a stick-thin, trembling thing with mad eyes and hollow cheeks, the skin bitten off his lips, his leather belt well-chewed, ribs thrusting out beneath his lice-infested tunic which hung on him like a winding sheet.

He was so terribly hungry.

But one taste . . . one taste and you will never be a man again. You will be a thing of graves and gallows.

But to taste of the meat. To eat of it.

How it came to be, Jarny could not say. But his next awareness was stumbling through the snow on broomstick limbs, Boulille supporting him, holding him up like a father with a favored child. They moved among the dead and dying. Men crying out. Men boiling with typhus fever, steam rising from them in a mist of pestilence. Corpses jutting from the snow, dead-white faces sparkling with frost. The meat stripped from throats and gouged from bellies.

"Come, friend Jarny," Boulille said, grinning at the death around him here in this fine kitchen of hell with abundant foodstuffs laid out upon the cutting boards of ice. "Walk with me. Soon you will know strength . . . and wisdom."

Jarny had some delusional half-memory of being deposited in the snow before a blazing fire. His eyesight was blurred from starvation. He could barely move his limbs or think a coherent thought. Men around him. Soldiers he knew. Brave men. Cowards. Officers. Enlisted rabble. Yes, circled around him, all grinning like desert-picked skulls, faces streaked with grime, eyes huge and black and empty, grease glistening on chins, gore hanging from mouths.

"Eat, friend Jarny, good friend Francois Jarny," they said. "Fill yourself."

Jarny, dangling somewhere between dream and waking, nightmare and harsh reality, remembered Dorogobouche. The Grand Armee, tattered from malnutrition, disease, and exposure, fought a rear-guard action out of the city as the Russians reclaimed it. The streets were clogged with the mangled carcasses of horses and human corpses frozen in stiff white heaps, both of which had been flayed before death by ravaging gangs of cannibals that haunted the bones of the city. Everywhere, smoke and flames from shelled buildings, burning powder wagons. Naked peasants huddled around fires, yellow-faced and pockmarked from typhus fever and rat-bite, dancing madly until they dropped and were ground underfoot by their fellows. And through it all, the hunters of men skulked in cellars and ruins, waiting to rush out and claim the wounded. To roast them on crude spits. And it was no fable, for Jarny had seen it. Seen their firepits. Seen their smooth white faces and glistening hungry eyes peering from pockets of shadow.

Boulille had fed quite well in Dorogobouche.

But even then, starving, Jarny would not even think it.

But to taste of the meat. To eat of it.

Yes, through foul mists of fever, he remembered, remembered as the fresh corpse of a soldier was laid in the snow before him, charred and crisping from the flames. And it was the bayonet in *his* hands that split the pig open until the redolent, hungry smell of fine, juicy meat roasted on a spit rose up before him, enveloping him in a hot, salty cloud of appetite.

After that . . . they all feasted. Knives and bayonets hacking. Slabs of steaming, dripping meat shoved into greedy mouths. Faces glistening with grease and yellow fat grinning up at the moon. Lunatics luminous with profane delight. Bellies filled. Fingers licked. Entrails divided. Bones gnawed of scraps and sucked of marrow. Then nothing left in the snow but that blackened, rent carcass, broken and scattered in all directions.

Jarny had never felt so strong or so deathless.

Months later, Paris.

Warm, sultry.

Jarny, more dead than alive, searching for food. For the dead.

There were few cemeteries in Paris by that point, most having been banned because of the foul odors and seeping rot that began to contaminate the air and streets and cellars of nearby neighborhoods. By the late 18th century, the miasmic stench of putrefaction could be smelled across the city where it hung in a pestilential haze and was thought to be the cause of one epidemic after another. The cemeteries were closed. The largest of which, the *Cimetière des Innocents* had been shut down in 1786.

The *Cimetière des Innocents* had once been the central burial ground for Paris. Located next to *Les Halles,* the central Parisian market, on the corner of *rue Saint-Denis and rue Berger,* the dead had been heaped here since the Gallo-Roman days. In 1786, when it was closed down with all the other smaller graveyards, the dead were taken to the newly opened catacombs at *Denfert-Rochereau,* far south of the city. Jarny knew this well, for his father had been one of the laborers. Night after eerie night, a grim procession transferred the draped remains from the Paris cemeteries to the catacombs.

All that remained now were *St. Parnasse, le Cimetière du nord Montmartre,* and the *Cimetière de l'est,* known as the *Père Lachaise* cemetery. And this is where Jarny went. To his favorite hunting grounds at the junction of *rue des Rondeaux* and *avenue du Père-Lachaise.* Standing at the cemetery gates, heart palpitating with strange desire, driven by depraved forces that had long since driven him mad with absolute horror, he listened for watchmen. His teeth were chattering. But it was not from the chill evening air, but hunger.

Quiet, you must be quiet, he told himself.

Yes, what was to be done was secret. How clever he had been this night as every night. All of Paris in an incensed uproar because some skulking ghoul was violating the tombs of their dead, yet he, Francois Jarny, had slipped out of the sleeping barracks with a shovel in his hand, right past the guards with their drawn bayonets and breech-loaders. Now he stood before the cemetery gates, panting and delusional, a cold and sour-smelling sweat beading his face. He stood there with his hands wrapped around the uprights of the fence, trying to fight what was inside him, what slithered and shifted in his belly making an insatiable hunger roll through him in queasy waves.

Some worn shred of humanity in him would not allow it. Not again. This time he would not give into it. This time he would be master of his own flesh. He would not weaken, he would not lose control.

"I'll kill myself if I have to," he said under his breath. "I'll do whatever it takes . . . do you hear me? You won't make me do this, you won't . . . make me do it . . ."

And that's when the pain came. It brought him to his knees, squeezing tears from his eyes and making his mind spin until he could do nothing but moan and thrash on the concrete. The pain was like razors sliding through his belly, needles bursting his stomach, nails and tacks filling his entrails until he begged for it to stop. Dear God, anything, anything just make it stop, *just please make it stop—*

And then it did.

Jarny lay there, dripping wet with perspiration, the agony slowly subsiding until he could breathe again and his heart stopped hammering. He was being taught a lesson and knew it. Just a lesson. He had to learn not to ignore the hunger, not to fight against it.

He coughed out a black, oily mass of phlegm and then felt better.

Using the uprights, he pulled himself to his feet and pressed his moist, feverish face to the fence. The wrought-iron was cool. Like death.

Picking up his shovel, he scaled the wall and dropped down on the other side, panting. Not exertion. Not really. Something else. *Père-Lachaise:* a winding maze of crypts seemingly piled one atop another like some morbid excrescence of graveyard stone. The hunger bloomed inside him like funeral orchids. It wanted, it needed, it desired. Jarny moved along through the battalions of leaning headstones and moon-washed sepulchers. The cemetery was a study in silence, a marble forest that held its breath. Tree limbs creaked overhead, rats scratched in the darkness.

As always, he deluded himself. It was the only thing that kept him comparatively sane.

He tried to convince himself that if he wandered in circles long enough, maybe he would get confused and not be able to find the grave. It was a nice ruse, but it did not work: for the hunger knew where the grave was. It could smell the black soil and oak box, what rested within. It had the scent and like a bloodhound straining at its leash, it led him there. A small, conservative tombstone the color of a blanched skull. Jarny looked up through the intertwined tree branches at the sullen eye of the moon, but there was no solace there.

Something hitched in his belly.

Spikes were driven through his stomach wall.

"Yes, yes," he said. "Quit being so greedy."

He touched the stone and silently read the name there: ELIZABETH DUPREE. She had drowned in the Seine. Fifteen years old, she had been in the ground nearly a week. The hunger increased in his belly. Yes, she would be seasoned properly.

Forgive me, he thought. *Forgive me.*

He took the shovel and cut away the sod. That was easy enough; it hadn't the time yet to properly take root. He rolled it away and began to dig. At first, he dug into the soil almost languidly as if he planned on never finding what was buried below. But the pains kept rising and falling and he began to dig through the wormy black earth in earnest, taking it down foot by foot and squaring off his excavation as he went. Three feet, four, five.

The hunger rolling though him made him practically giddy now.

He kept digging, his pile of dirt getting larger as the moon slipped across the sky. And then . . . the shovel struck wood. Breathing hard, drenched with sweat and black with earth, he began pawing the soil away from the polished box. When it was clean and gleaming with dirty moonlight, he raised the shovel over his head and let out a wounded, agonized cry, breaking the catches one by one.

Jarny hoped, God how he hoped, someone would hear him, that the noise he purposely made and his cry of loathing would bring someone. The gate swinging wide, men with rifles rushing through the grass. Finding him, seeing him for what he was.

Yes, yes, yes, seeing the thing I am and killing me, shooting until their guns are empty and—

The pain again. Not a full-fledged attack, not an out and out violation, but more like a groping of filthy, unwanted hands, an obscene kiss in the dark. Shaking, tears running down his cheeks, he gripped the lid of the box and threw it open.

The stench.

Oh, the high foul stink of it.

It came rolling out of the casket in a mephitic cloud, green and wet and sickening. Jarny fell back against the side of the grave while his stomach lurched and roiled. Thick and noisome and utterly offensive, it was also . . . *delicious.*

He lay there, shaking his head, in complete denial of the perversions to follow. Bile climbed his throat, spitting hot and acidic onto his tongue. He couldn't do this. Dear Lord, he couldn't do this *again.*

But the hunger was a living thing inside him, huge and silver-toothed and unwieldy. It was so irresistible that it blotted out who and what he was, made him into a host, a vessel with hooked fingers and teeth and insatiable desires.

The corpse of Elizabeth DuPree was not a pretty thing after nearly a week in the damp, rank earth. Her white lace burial gown was mottled and water-stained from seepage and a dark mildew had grown up her neck and over her cheeks like a beard. Her folded hands were likewise meshed with morbid fungi. Her face was sunken, lips shriveled away from the teeth so that it looked as if she were grinning.

Please don't make me do this, don't make me touch . . . that . . .

But then as always, Jarny's will was no longer his own.

Things like defiance and self-control and resolution no longer existed. They had been crushed beneath the stark and vile immensity of the hunger and the need of what lived inside him. He was just a vehicle, a machine with no conscious volition of its own. And that's what made him jump into the casket, on top of the corpse, feeling its feel and smelling its smell, disgusted beyond earthly bounds. He pressed his face to that of the dead girl until her putrescence filled him and the hunger went mad inside him. His tongue came out and licked her blackened lips, tasting the powders and chemicals the undertaker had used on her, and something beneath all that, something repellent and nauseous.

He dragged the body up into the moonlight, dumping it on the damp grass.

And what was inside him said, *Fill us . . . we're starving . . .*

There was no more waiting.

Jarny sank his teeth into the gelid flesh of her throat, yanking out damp flaps of fetid meat, chewing and tasting, driven insane by the textures and revolting flavor on his tongue. He tore her gown away, gnawing at the greening meat of her thighs and belly, tearing at her cold breasts and nibbling at her mottled buttox. He licked and sucked and tore. He used his teeth and his hands, shredding and devouring and spitting out gobs of black juice that ran from his mouth. The taste was disgusting, the feel of that rotting meat sliding down his throat made him feverish and disoriented. And when he was filled, satisfied with his charnel meal of pulp and bone and graying meat, he screamed and mutilated what was left, tearing the corpse asunder and rolling in the scraps until its feel was his feel and its stink was his own vile perfume.

And then it was done.

Jarny slowly came back to himself, ribbons of decomposing tissue hanging from his mouth, his uniform splashed down with drainage and oozing black ichor. The sickly-sweet stench of putrefied meat clung to him in a ghastly bouquet. His first impulse was to scream and his second was to vomit. To throw out his guts and everything that was in them: that warm and slushy mass resting in his belly. But he didn't dare. For *they* would not allow it. They would never have that, never have him denying him their feast of grave-meat.

Show us, they said. *Show us.*

So Jarny stood up, unbuttoning his filthy tunic, revealing the yawning hollow in his side that was eaten away and infested by a squirming mass of white maggots. No ordinary graveworms, these were impossibly fat and pale and sluglike, a coiling and slinking mass even then lengthening and thickening and bursting with eggs from the feast he had given them.

It was enough.

They were happy.

Whimpering, Jarny retreated from the plundered grave as the worms inside him grew fat and lazy and torpid. As they went to sleep, he ran from the cemetery, a hot wind of dementia blowing through his head.

By the time they marched into Vilna, Napoleon's Grand Armee had been reduced from 100,000 to barely 7,000. Weakened to a deplorable state by fevers and plagues and starvation, the bitter cold did the rest and this in a matter of weeks. Jarny, now having supped upon the meat of men, was not like the others. Strong, vital, full-blooded, he fought the Russians and peasants at Boulille's side. While the others fell dead at his feet from exposure or cowered in the trees, Jarny fought like an animal, taking sheer savage joy from the men he killed. When he emptied his rifle, he drew his saber and charged into the Russian ranks, slashing and hacking, delighting in the screams of the enemy and laughing with merciless sardonic humor at their pleas for mercy.

His saber fell a forest of men, leaving a writhing carpet of carcasses underfoot. Limbs were scattered, heads rolling free, bowels spilled steaming to the snow. There was purity and glacial joy in the killing that he had never experienced before. There was nothing finer than the brutal act of the saber, laying open one's enemies and staining the snow red. And there was no sweeter joy than having their blood sprayed over you in reeking gouts, splashing over your face so that you could taste the life you had taken, knowing it, feeling it, filling yourself with its hot wine.

This is how it was for Jarny.

He saw his enemies as cattle to be slaughtered, to be brought under heel and blade, swine to be carved and smoked over a hot fire. And while the others died in numbers, laid low by fever and famine, his belly was full. And who could know of the secret joy Jarny felt bursting into the miserable huts of peasant farmers with others of like appetites? The screaming, the cutting, the rich heady aroma of spilled blood? The slabs of juicy meat roasted on spits, entrails cooked on sticks over hot fires? He lived for the kill, the feeding, and his prey was abundant.

Then, just outside Vilna, a Russian reprisal. Musket balls whizzing through the air and shells bursting, men screaming as they were cut down in the snow. The air was wet with a fine mist of blood. Everywhere, bodies and parts of them scattered about in a gruesome hodgepodge. Jarny was hit by shrapnel as he jumped over the shattered anatomies of his fellow soldiers in a vain attempt at escape. The shrapnel nearly tore his right leg off, it sheared open his belly and filled his gut with burning fragments of metal. Unwilling to die, he crawled through the snow dragging his viscera behind him in freezing loops. He left a trail of blood and slime.

After that, his mind fell into a fog.

He and dozens of others were dragged into Vilna, seeking food, shelter, and medical aid. But there was none to be had. Vilna had been ransacked by peasant riots and fighting. The typhus plague had swept the city and corpses were heaped in untidy, loose-limbed stacks right out in the streets. The population was starving, diseased, and filthy. They crowded into stinking little huts infested with cockroaches.

Jarny was dumped with the rest of the sick and wounded in the field hospital at St. Bazile. It was an awful place even by the standards of the day. Crowded, steaming, and stinking, jumping with lice, men were packed in wards shoulder-to-shoulder, sometimes right on top of one another on floors that were a seething pool of human waste infected with disease germs. Typhus raged, as did influenza and dysentery. The wounded and ill literally drowned in their own vomit, blood, bile, and excrement. The corridors were stacked with thousands of corpses. So many that a crude maze-like path had to be opened through them. Rats fed on the dead and dying. Broken windows and ruptured walls were stuffed with torsos and limbs in a grisly rampart to keep the polluted air from infecting the living.

Jarny was thrown in a tight, close room with hundreds of others that were delirious from hunger and fevers. The floor was covered with rotting straw fouled with urine, bile, and feces. There were bodies everywhere, many rotted right to mush. He was tossed atop the wormy, spongy mass of a bloated corpse. A corpse infested by . . . *maggots.* And no ordinary maggots were they, he soon learned. But a race of graveworms with a perverse communal intelligence, a single overriding need to infest and feed. Jarny landed on the body of their previous host, in fact, who was too rank and polluted by that time to be of any further use to them.

So they entered Jarny.

They came in through his eyes and nostrils and mouth, up his ass and through the numerous holes in his hide where sharpened staffs of bone jutted forth. They filled him, infesting and breeding.

You won't die, they told him. *We won't let you.*

And that's how it began. He did not die: they would not allow it. They repaired him, rebuilt him, and soon he was well again . . . as well as a man can be that is little more than a host for hundreds and hundreds of worms.

Out in the streets of Vilna, as the plague overflowed every house, every barn, every makeshift morgue and spilled out into the streets until it was possible to cross them by walking over bodies, it was a horror as well. Constantly harassed by Cossacks and insane peasants, Napoleon pushed on as the Russians poured in to fight, leaving the sick and dying behind to their gruesome fate. By the end of December there were 25,000 people in Vilna, nearly all of them stricken with typhus fever. By June, only 7,000 would still be alive.

Jarny was one of them.

But by that point, colonized as he was, he could no longer call himself human. What the worms had given him was secret and what he would have to do for them was no less secret.

And it was always the same: *Feed us.*

It was in the streets and all over the Paris papers the next morning: the awful slinking ghoul had struck yet again. This time it had violated the grave of a young girl. The body had been carefully unearthed then savagely mutilated, torn to fragments in a deranged frenzy. Parts of her were scattered over the walks and dangling in the trees.

He learned of it as did all and hearing it, remembered that once he had been a man named Francois Jarny. A human being.

* * * *

When he woke in the barracks several days later after another hideous night of mania, sweating and shaking, the worms had been busy. They had spun a cocoon of new pink flesh over the gaping hollow in his side. It was their gift to him so he did not have to look on their wriggling, industrious masses.

Yes, a gift and it filled him with a loathing that was absolute.

He vomited bile into the basin, then, wiping his mouth, he fell against the tub, shaking and whimpering. He could still smell the grave ooze on his hands, his breath.

After the tears had finally dried up and that stark insanity stopped scratching inside his skull, Jarny stood up and allowed himself to look at that patch of pink skin just below his ribs. It was very shiny, almost waxy-looking. And warm. Very warm, almost hot. Like a child intrigued by a scab, he pressed his fingers against the patch of skin. The new flesh was squishy, flaccid. When he applied pressure to it, his fingertips sank into it like it was not human skin but the flesh of a soft, rotting peach.

He pulled his hand away, fingers stained with a dirty brown liquid. The smell was horrid like the drainage of gassy corpses. More of that liquid ran in tiny streaks from the holes his fingers had punched into his side.

There was revulsion, of course, a deep-set physical revulsion that had become an almost common thing with Jarny, a natural rhythm like happiness and sorrow. He subsisted on a daily diet of it. Knowing that he was host to them. That they owned him. That they would make him violate more graves, feed upon the rot within, stuff himself with it like a glutton at a buffet. He was infested by graveworms and there really was no way out.

They were small and he was large.

They were weak and he was strong.

But he was one and they were a multitude, forever starving. Forever demanding.

They felt what he felt. Tasted what he tasted. Knew what he knew. And, oh yes, they could see what he saw. They could look through his eyes and make him experience things as they experienced them. And to Jarny, there was no greater horror in this world beyond the feasting itself. To look out through his eyes, *as* them, feeling their lust and depravity and knowing their cold, cutting, metallic hunger. To become a corpse-worm appraising a shank of greening meat and not feel repugnance or simple disgust, but a joy and pleasure that was almost sexual. A noxious hunger, an overwhelming chemical desire to crawl over the offered putrid mass, to bore into it, chew and suck upon the grave bounty, and, yes, meet others of your kind in those moist, tainted depths, to mate, to spawn, to lay your eggs in hot pearly masses within.

That was horror . . . to do such things and *love* it.

He couldn't even kill himself, because they would not allow it. They would repair whatever damage he incurred and make him walk again, a mindless and demented cadaver, a shell that existed only to find and feed upon the carrion they desired. Not that he hadn't tried. Again and again. But they always patched him up and would until he was so polluted by their larva and waste that he was of no further use to them . . . except as food.

He could feel them wriggling about in his side repairing the damage he had done. They did not punish him. The feel of them slinking and slithering inside him was punishment enough.

Already, they were hungry and he would have to feed them. Such was the penalty of resurrection and morbid symbiosis.

Jarny thought it was months now, but maybe it was years. It was hard to remember. Yes, he had a fine new sheath of pink skin at his side . . . but what of the rest of him? He was bony and pale, tiny red lumps of infection broken out all over his body. They were soft to the touch, filled with discolored pus. He was rotting from the inside out and the maggots kept him alive, kept him going even as he drowned in their own diseased filth and poisoned wastes. For he was their home. A home that needed constant maintenance. But they were ambitious, diligent, they would not let him fall to disrepair.

Not just yet.

The *La Gazette* reported that the ghoul had been active again. This time at the cemetery of *St. Parnasse*. Watchmen of the *Gendarmerie Royale* had fired at the creature, but it escaped over a wall. They claimed it had the face of a wolf or perhaps a hyena.

Jarny laughed at that.

Laughed and remembered Henri Boulille . . . and hated.

He stood before the mirror, looking at the cadaverous thing he was. Hollow-socketed, sallow, gums pulling back from yellow teeth sharpened on corpses and gray bones. The worms moved within him, digging and tunneling and forever burrowing. He could see their plump shapes moving just beneath his skin. Down his arms and over his chest, like peas pressed beneath the flesh of his face and in constant, busy motion, writhing through his honeycombed tissue.

Yes, he looked at himself in the mirror.

But what looked back was a monster.

The horrible destruction of the Grand Armee in Russia was final testament to the vulnerability of Napoleon's forces. As the tattered, ragged remains retreated through Poland the Russians continued to harass them, circling ahead of the scattered army of the living dead and practicing a scorched earth policy. They burned villages and farms, slaughtered animals and heaped wells and ponds with the carcasses of men and cattle. Food was scarce. Water contaminated. Peasants began to join the remnants of the Grand Armee, forming a wandering parade line of refugees that stumbled along, at a distance, behind the broken, zig-zagging march of soldiers seeking France. And as they moved, they spread ty-phus and influenza in their wake.

In many of the fractured, smoldering villages they came to, the peasants burned their dead in great pyres, already infected by forward units of the Grand Armee. They huddled around fires, burning dung to keep pestilential vapors at bay. It did them little good.

Jarny often walked alone.

The other men knew what he was by then, an associate of Boulille, the corpse-eater. They shunned his company. Often he could hear them speaking: *Regarder là, il est Jarny, l'ami de Boulille. Il mange les cadavres des hommes, remplit son ventre de charogne.* Yes, they were right. He was a friend of Boulille's, and he did eat the corpses of men and stuff himself with carrion. How right they were.

Covered in lice and sores, his greatcoat a soiled threadbare thing, his tunic crusty with urine and excrement, bloodstains and the grease and fat of his noc-turnal feedings, he was a hunched-over goblin with hollow cheeks. Face dirty, teeth chattering, cataleptic eyes staring, forever staring, the mind behind them diseased and dirtied by what it had seen, what it had done, and what it yet would do.

Jarny was mad, infested. Jarny was a ghoul.

As he wondered alone, far from the others one day, he came upon a filthy little hamlet. A woman in rags was stirring a pot over a fire. Her eyes were like wet glass set in a yellow pocked face, her decaying teeth jutting from sallow gums. She was insane and Jarny knew it. She motioned him over and he drank from her foul well. Afterwards, she offered him a tin cup of soup. It was quite good, though the meat was seasoned unpleasantly sweet. And too familiar to the taste.

She giggled as he ate, scratching through the snow like an animal to the dirt and roots beneath. Finally, in perfect French, she said, *"Ah! Je vous avais attendu, ami Jarny! Un autre dit vous viendriez! Ici . . . mon mari et enfants sont morts de la peste, ainsi j'ai fait un potage heary fin à partir de leur chair et os!"*

But it wasn't the roots she was scratching for, but to show him the well-boiled bones of her family. Her husband and children, from whom she had made a special hearty soup anticipating his arrival. Yes, Boulille had been there.

Telling the mad woman to expect another of similar appetites.

The column, as it were, marched on and bitter winter gave way to slopping, wet spring. With the warmth and wetness, the typhus fever raged and dropped dozens of men each day. The dysentery worsened as did the influenza. Diseased men leaned against one another just to make it another mile, a few more feet. The pestilence was blowing through Eastern Europe on a hot wind of plague. The lice were unbearable, breeding in the warmth and damp. The ragged clothing of the soldiers actually moved they were so infested. Jarny was teeming with them. As he tried to sleep at night by his pitiful fire, they nipped and bit, making him tremble and sweat there on the moist ground.

One night, a soldier named Betrand jumped up in a mad frenzy, stripping his clothes off and throwing them into the fire. They burned with a popping sound, the noise of hundreds of lice being incinerated. Hopping about in the mud, naked, he was delirious, slapping and scratching at his emaciated, lice-bitten body, calling out, *"Grêle vers la France! Grêle à Napoleon!"*

Another man raised his musket and shot him dead so the others might sleep. His body did not lay long before soldiers and peasants slipped out of the shadows and dragged it away to be quartered by bayonets and roasted. This is what they had become. No longer were they the Grand Armee. Now they were beggars and criminals and scavengers, skulking things less then men. Filthy with their own waste, human rats that spread disease, parasites that fed upon one another.

Tormented by thirst and hunger, the stragglers marched ever forward through the rains that turned the fields and roads to rutted mud holes. Pools of standing water were putrid with the corpses of men and animals. Only the mad sipped from them. It was to these ponds of carrion that Jarny was driven by what burrowed inside him. At night, while the others were scattered away from him, he would seek out especially deep pools of rank water that were seething and steaming with dozens of waterlogged corpses and carcasses, greening and flyblown as they broke the oily surface in putrescent tangles and staffs of white bone. He would dive amongst them, peeling mucid flesh from fungi-slicked skeletons, gnawing on jellied hides and innards boiling soft with rot. These were the ponds he swam in, bathed in, and filled himself with.

And this, ultimately, was the hideous creature called Francois Jarny that returned to France.

After days of stuffing himself with whatever was convenient—gassy rats and flyblown dogs found in alleys—the maggots led Jarny on a wild chase down in the sewers where they smelled something delicious, something ghoulishly tantalizing. Beneath the metal grating, it was a place of stagnant waters and sucking black mud, sewage and rats and rotting things.

Amongst all that misting decay and nauseous stench, they had scented something they wanted.

They pushed Jarny on and on. He slopped through the smelling muck of those winding, echoing tunnels, scattering vermin, his arms specked with insect bites and curious rashes. Long after midnight, in a clogged leaf-covered backwash where leeches clung fatly to his legs, they found what they wanted.

The corpse of a little boy.

Jarny had seen his sketched face in the papers. Everyone had. He disappeared and no one could find a trace of him. But they could not smell like the maggots could. Once he went soft and pulpy and fragrant, the worms could scent him easily. Jarny dragged the boy's gas-bloated, swelling body out of the foul water and laid it on the concrete embankment. By moonlight, the child was an atrocity. He had bloated so badly that the buttons of his little shirt had popped free.

He looks wonderful, the maggots said.

Jarny frightened off the rats that had been nibbling at him and did what he must do.

In the wan light of the leprous moon peering through a sewer grating, he licked the boy's bluing face, revolted and insane, touching him and squeezing his distended bulk like a butcher with a fine cut of beef. The maggots went wild within him, biting and pulsing and digging into the loam of his intestines. And Jarny was pushed, as always, into higher realms of depravity. He tore open the boy's belly with his teeth, swooning as a nauseating sickly-sweet cloud of corpse-gas blew into his face. Then he was biting and tearing, screaming into the night as he sank his teeth into pulpous flesh. He buried his face in the putrescent mush of the boy's abdomen, yanking out soft entrails with his teeth, sucking down rivers of carrion-slime, tearing and biting and ripping until his jaws were sore and his face oozing with corpse-jelly.

Panting and gagging in the rank, sluicing water, Jarny cackled like a lunatic. And the maggots said, *Show us...let us see.*

Shuddering and convulsing, gore dropping from his mouth in clots, he stood and let them look through his eyes and their delight was almost hallucinogenic: carnal and hot-blooded. The boy was nothing but a mangled gray-green heap of mildewed meat, marrow-sucked bones, and shattered, gnawed wreckage.

Now finish, Jarny, they said. *The sweet-meats, don't forget the sweet-meats.*

With a loose brick, he broke open the skull, gnawing and licking at the jellied gray matter within, spitting out beetles and worms that dared defile this rarest of cutlets. At first, he was gently passionate with the sweet-meats, but soon the ravenous ghouls within pushed him to new heights of frenzied gluttony. He yanked the buttery-soft meat out in rancid handfuls, shoving it greedily in his mouth, chomping and feeling it crush to a sweet, juicing paste beneath his teeth. He smeared it over his face and danced madly in the dappled moonlight. In the end, breathless and horrified, he licked the skull clean as a soup bowl.

And then, satisfied, the maggots went to sleep.

Jarny scrambled up out of the sewers and vented his horror in a whooping, hysterical scream.

He lay awake that night.

Barely breathing.

A vile-smelling juice ran from his pores like sweat. He stank of corpses and graves and decomposition. Inside, he was infested. As the worms slept off their hideous repast, Jarny lay shivering and polluted with their wastes and drainage.

It couldn't go on much longer.

The next day he was summoned before Captain LeClerq. He was a stern, gray-haired man that had absolutely no tolerance for anyone. But he had a soft spot for Jarny. They had both survived Napoleon's invasion of Russia and had crossed the Neiman together—the Russians laying waste to what remained of the Grand Armee as they crossed the freezing river, hundreds cut down, hundreds more drowning, but the majority rafting across on corpses. They had both received the *Légion d'Honneur* for their valiant actions.

"Sergeant Jarny," LeClerq said, not looking up from his daily reports. "You have, no doubt, heard of this ghoul haunting our cemeteries and of the vile things he or it has been doing."

"Yes, sir." Jarny waited, at full attention, the maggots looping in his stomach.

"All Paris is angered. There are cries from the highest offices."

Yes, Jarny was certain of that. He could just imagine the vociferous outcries of condemnation coming from the plush salons of the aristocratic and the social climbing upper bourgeoisie. Were they truly offended? Truly outraged? Probably not. Decadent to the core, these people lived lives of leisure while the masses starved in the streets. They frequented their salons and cafes of the *Champs-Elysées,* talking at length of poetry, art, and politics. Many subjects they were equally ignorant of. But when something like this happened . . . they feigned outrage . . . but secretly *delighted* in it. Anything to escape the self-imposed dull sameness of their regal prisons.

The vegetable sellers, ragpickers, rat-catchers, and common tradesmen of the *Les Halles* and the *rue de Venise* were probably the ones truly incensed. And the prostitutes who sold themselves nightly for fifty *centimes* or a head of cabbage to eat. Yes, incensed probably, but not surprised. Not in this city.

"I suppose they are angered," Jarny said.

LeClerq removed his spectacles. "Come now, Jarny. Let us speak openly."

Jarny sighed. "That is . . . sir . . . I wonder if these people are truly angered or secretly relish the gruesome details."

"Ah! You speak of the culturally elite? The privileged? The aesthetics? It is well you have no political ambitions, Jarny. But I prefer, as do you, to think that I serve the all not the few. It is important to remember this."

"Yes, sir."

"But this business at hand . . . it is a most . . ." He paused, studying Jarny through his wire-rimmed spectacles. "Are you well, Jarny?"

"Yes, sir. I but slept poorly last night."

LeClerq merely nodded . . . though for one trembling instant, Jarny was certain that the man suspected him, was about to stand up and cry out for Jarny to confess his evil sins, to admit to what he was. But he did not.

"Monsieur Betreaux was here, Jarny," LeClerq said with a certain gravity behind his words. "Betreaux is the Police *Commissaire* for this quarter as you probably know. What he told me was most disturbing. You will not read of it in the newspapers or scandal sheets. His men at *St. Parnasse* Cemetery . . . they claim the man they fired at was a soldier."

Jarny felt woozy, his head spun and his eyesight seemed to blur. "But . . . but," he stammered, "such a thing . . . it is impossible . . ."

"Yes, Jarny. So thought I. Until I was given this." LeClerq dropped a small brass disc on the desk. "Do you recognize it?"

Jarny tried to lick his lips, but it would have taken rivers. He swallowed, tried to stay on his feet as his world careened madly around him and the maggots gnawed hungrily at the lining of his stomach. Of course he recognized what that disc was: a button. A button from a military infantry tunic. Why, his tunics had the very same buttons . . .

"Watch your men closely, Jarny. I told Betreaux I would personally make an inspection of every tunic in the barracks." But LeClerq waved that away. "But I will not. I find the idea distasteful. Besides, it would create a certain amount of suspicion, yes? So you and my other sergeants shall do it. Check your platoon, Jarny. Check their tunics."

Look at me, you fool! Can't you see guilt, the horror, the madness in these eyes?

"Yes, sir. I shall."

Jarny saluted and turned to the door, amazed that he was able to stay on his feet, amazed that he did not fall to his knees and cry out his obscene crimes. If only he had but the strength.

"And Jarny?"

"Sir?"

LeClerq studied him with typical flat indifference. "Watch your men closely."

"Yes sir."

"This fiend must be found and destroyed."

His eyes welling with tears, Jarny said, "I couldn't agree more, Captain . . ."

A popular pastime in those grim days was to visit the Paris morgue. Passers-by and the morbidly curious would enter that forbidding stone building, immediately making for the display room. Here, behind a large viewing glass, arranged on slabs, were the unclaimed corpses laid out like meat in a butcher's window. Engulfed in a sweet stench of decay and less definable odors, the curious could study, at their leisure, the bloated white bodies fished out of the Seine, the crushed remains of workmen, suicides with the burn of the rope cut into their throats, and street women found hacked in dim alleys, their eyes glazed in horror. All were laid out naked in grisly splendor, there being no secrets in death. Tacked to the wall behind were personal articles: trousers, coats, petticoats, hats, scarves. It was thought that if a particular slab of moldering meat was no longer recognizable, perhaps an article of clothing or a favored watch might be.

It was not, of course, a pleasant place.

But pleasant or not, people stopped by in droves. For unlike many other Parisian exhibitions, this one was free to the public. At any given time of the day one might glimpse workmen with their satchels of tools standing about, gnawing on fresh loaves of bread from nearby vendors. They stood shoulder-to-shoulder with high-born melancholic ladies in their silken gowns and lacey parasols, self-styled intellectuals and street poets chiming graveyard verse, upscale businessmen with top hats and walking sticks, dozens of giggling girls fresh from the mills and shops who moved around in rosy-cheeked swarms. They all came: lower classes, bourgeoisie, intellectuals, aristocrats. They looked upon dead faces that were swollen blue from the river and eaten to the bone by fish; faces waterlogged to the point that they were coming apart like boiled chicken; faces that were sliced, jabbed with holes, chewed by rats and dogs, burnt and mutilated by forces unknown; faces that were like so much molten wax, heated by the sun and infested with larvae, until their soft pulping flesh literally slid from the skulls beneath; faces that were the shriveled dusty yellow of mummies or lacked eyes or smiled the autopsy grin of the death rictus; and, now and again, the face of some young woman who'd thrown herself into the Seine only to find exquisiteness in death: lustrous sweeping hair, flawless marble skin, high skullish cheekbones, lips pulled into a soft gray pout. Life encapsulated and death personified in the ravishing beauty of the charnel. The undertakers often made death masks of these poor girls. One of which—known as *L'inconnue de la Seine*—was copied and sold in great numbers, decorating sitting rooms and parlors across the country.

By day the morgue was a thriving place, by night just as still and quiet as the flyspecked faces in the display case.

And it was here, in the dead of night, that a man named Francois Jarny came, driven by what starved within. It was not his first visit to the *maison des morts,* as it was known. He knew there were troublesome attendants in the cellar where the most select cuts were to be found. But the maggots were smart. They made Jarny hide in a broom-closet until first one attendant slipped off for his lunch and another napped in an empty office.

The buffet was open.

The maggots, of course, had Jarny bring an iron prybar with him. After a bit of straining and grunting, he popped the door to the cellar and went down the sweating steps. The postmortem room was of no interest to them . . . though there were certain lingering odors that were positively succulent.

In the cold room, Jarny opened the drawers set in the wall. The fare was adequate. The crunchy flesh of a burn victim. The rheumy eyeball of a suicide. The soft fingers of a drowning victim. The sweet belly fat of a strangled infant. Snacks, mainly. Appetizers. Enough to drive the maggots into contortions of rapture, but hardly enough to sate them. They kept at Jarny, piercing and biting, tearing his internals raw. Filling his bowels with shards of glass.

Feed us, they said. *We need real meat. Find it.*

In one of the last drawers, he found what they wanted. A murder victim plucked swollen and gas-blown from the cloying soil of a cellar floor. A woman. She was wrapped tightly in a stained, gray sheet like a Christmas present. Jarny hefted the package from its chamber and shook it. What was inside sloshed about lusciously as if the present were filled with a thick mint jelly. He opened it slowly, teasing and almost seductive. The maggots appreciated a fine presentation. Much of the woman splashed out in a repellent surge of watery meat and sludgy tissue. The stench was pure joyous putrefaction: gamy and yellow and marvelously brined in its own heady juices. Perfectly repulsive and perfectly appetizing.

Taste her, they said, *sip her.*

Jarny, a wet distorted scream breaking in his throat, dipped his fingers into the gelatinous mass of her remains like she were fondue. He licked them clean, nibbling at the green mossy bulge of her throat, yanking her blackened tongue from her mouth and licking it like it was still alive . . . then chewing upon it. As the hunger rose up inside him and his mind was thrown into a blank gray haze, he began ravenously tearing and snapping at the goodies.

And, the maggots said: *Behind you!*

The sleeping attendant had stole back in, stealthy thing he was. He stood there with a look of absolute, revolted horror on his face. "You!" he shouted. "You! What . . . what in God's name are you doing?"

Jarny grinned at him, corpse-slime running from his mouth, a flap of stringy tissue hanging from his jaws. *"Je mange la chair des cadavers!"* he told him.

His fingers curled into malicious claws, he jumped up with a demented, gibbering shriek. But the attendant was a stout, powerful man. He snatched up the forgotten prybar and put it to use. As Jarny raged and howled, the prybar rose and fell, swung by a man whose soul was sickened by what he saw. It shattered Jarny's left arm, cleaved open his head, smashed-in his ribs. He hit the floor and the attendant, worked up into a maniacal hatred, continued to swing his weapon. Finally, panting and dizzy, he looked down at the ghoul. He was still alive, eyes wide and glassy and aware, but he was broken, bleeding, his neck snapped and his body splayed limply. Blood was running freely from all orifices.

As the bar came up for the death-blow, Jarny smiled with red-stained teeth, saying, "Thank God, Thank God . . ."

Francois Jarny no longer moved.

Jarny was not dead.

He only waited while the worms attempted to put him back together again. But his wounds were massive, grievous, it would take many days and they could not bear the idea of starving all that time.

At midnight the next evening, a new attendant came on shift. He saw to all the trifling tasks his job entailed. When he was finished, and quite alone, he peeked in the drawers at the cold cuts, looking for anything that might be of use. When he reached Jarny's and looked upon that white grinning face, he gasped.

Jarny saw him through filmed eyes. That long cadaveric face fanning out with deep-set lines, the narrow discolored teeth, those dead gray eyes. He knew this man, God yes, how he knew this man. He could almost smell the powder and battlefield stench, feel the cold and nits biting him.

"Oh, ho, ho," said Boulille, "friend Jarny, good friend Francois Jarny. So you are the ghoul of the cemeteries, eh? Tsk, tsk, my old friend. What a state you are in."

Jarny did not speak, but inside his head he spoke to the maggots: *Look at him! He's fat and healthy and cunning! I'm ruined, but he is perfect . . . for a host.*

Yes, they said with great breathless fervor. *Yes . . .*

Happily, Jarny waited. He did not wait long. Alone, ever obscene and deranged, Boulille thought he would sample a scrap of meat from his old compatriot of the Napoleonic Wars. As he sank in the knife, Jarny sprang up with the last drop of vitality available, seizing Boulille by throat. Oh, but how Boulille fought! He jumped away, dragging Jarny right from his berth. He fought, he tore, but Jarny would not release him. They fell to the floor in a heap, Jarny on top. And then, black toxins running from Jarny's flesh and dripping from his nostrils and ears, a heaving muscular convulsion swept through him and he voided what was inside. He vomited a foamy peristaltic river of slime and worms, hundreds and thousands of worms that kept pouring out in moist tangles with each convulsion. They were fat and white and glistening. They covered Boulille's screaming face and thrashing body.

But not for long.

They entered him. Through his mouth and nose and ears, through tiny cuts and abrasions. They wriggled up his ass and worked their way down the head of his penis. Wherever there was an opening, they swarmed. And many of them just tunneled straight in, melting into his flesh until he was no longer Henri Boulille, craven cannibal, but merely a host for something ancient, evil, and undying.

Jarny hit the floor, quite dead.

Boulille collapsed beside him.

By the next evening, following a cursory examination, Boulille was placed in an unused drawer. The maggots gave him the semblance of death for it suited their purposes. And now, he could begin his new life amongst the sepulchers and mortuaries and graveyard damps.

Boulille did not lose consciousness.

He laid there, praying for the darkness, for release. But it was far too late for that. Infested by the graveworms, globby masses of eggs laid in the hot charnel earth of his flesh, he was forever theirs now. When they hatched, the new generation got right down to work, setting things to right.

The next night, Boulille sat up and walked. He left the morgue in search of a fresh grave. But not *too* fresh of one as he would soon discover.

And this, then, was the final vengeance of Francois Jarny.

Going Green

Stefan Pearson

THE NIGHT AFTER THE FUNERAL was muggy and moonless, purple black clouds hanging in the night sky like ripe Merlot. Simon West stole from the house, spade and Maglite in hand. He'd insisted that the fully biodegradable metal-free coffin was buried in no more than a few feet of earth; "If we bury her any deeper her nutrients won't reach the topsoil." Germaine had resisted of course, but caved eventually—she knew he knew best. Truth was he just didn't fancy digging and refilling a six foot hole.

Luckily the ground was loose and hadn't begun to settle. Simon glanced back to the converted farm house—all was still and his no night-lights policy for the kids' bedrooms meant that the only glimmer came from the winking burglar alarm mounted high on the wall. The pale blades of the wind turbine turned sluggishly on the roof. It was a sultry night and before long his shirt clung to his back, a lock of lank hair plastering itself across his forehead.

After what felt like an age the spade finally thunked off wood. A muffled groan escaped from the half-buried coffin. On hands and knees, Simon clawed the remaining dirt aside and prised away the lid, bringing his small torch to bear. The ex-mother-in-law growled, groaned and gnashed her false teeth at him, teeth that worked themselves loose and slid across her face on a thick strand of paste-like saliva. He stifled a disgusted shiver.

Dragging Margaret across the lawn was a pain, her twig-like limbs squirming from his grip. The only way he could get a proper purchase was to wedge his fingers into her bones. If he held her skin she just slid from his grasp.

Back in the lab he tossed the old woman onto the table and strapped her down. He'd have preferred to administer his serum before she was buried, but knew from bitter experience that he had a window of hours at best in which to inject the life restoring elixir. It just didn't seem to work if the body was any older. His recently deceased mother-in-law groaned and gnashed gummily.

"I wouldn't moan just yet Margaret," he quipped, splashing his face in the sink and pulling a beer from the mini-fridge. She fixed him with milky yellowed eyes and hissed, working her toothless jaw. "I'd reserve my moaning until I'd been on this for a week." He strolled over to the recently wall-mounted water-wheel, cracked open his can, and patted the heavy wooden frame. Margaret growled. Rebuilding the waterwheel in the basement had been a stroke of genius. The extortionate bloody thing had failed magnificently in the property's stream, barely moving in the turgid current. Turned out some bastard farmer had diverted the flow further up the valley. The house was struggling to generate enough power and the solar panels and wind turbine were disappointingly feeble, even if they looked the part. Free electricity didn't come cheap.

Margaret was ominously silent as he fastened her into the treadmill, but then he had ripped her larynx out before securing her to the waterwheel. Her open throat hissed, popped and gurgled, but it was infinitely better than that incessant moaning. He'd had enough of that when she was alive. He stood in front of her and contemplated his handy-work. She lumbered towards him. The wheel began to turn, its complex gears whirring into life. Simon tapped the side of the generator. A definite current! The needle bobbed, Margaret channelling her stumbling anger into readily stored free kilowatts.

"Paying your way at last you old bitch," he grinned, finishing his can and tossing it to the floor. Simon flicked off the light and locked the cellar behind him.

In the best scientific tradition, Simon West had stumbled across a serum that effected the reanimation of necrotic tissue pretty much by accident. He'd been working on a cure for baldness at the time, a pet project since his hairline had begun creeping inexorably across his skull. Simon's serum contained a particularly virile bacterium that he'd isolated from the stomach of a dead cat. The agent underwent radical physical changes immediately after the host's death, taking on an almost regenerative role, a last ditch attempt to adapt to its unliving environment. West had introduced the bacterium into an artificial blood plasma serum. The idea was you pasted the stuff on your head and it brought dead hair follicles back to life. In hindsight he was glad he hadn't road tested it on himself, although it could be argued testing it on the deceased Mr Frisky had been ill conceived. Particularly as the once dead cat had hopped off the slab and dragged a coil of its guts across the room, mewling at his feet. The thing rubbed a bloodied cheek against his trouser leg. A hanging eyeball stuck to his cords. Simon had stuffed the ex-pet into a heavy sack and stashed it in the corner of the cellar, scrubbed his trousers and contemplated his discovery.

"You haven't seen Mr Frisky have you Dad?" Peter asked.

"No, sorry son. When did you last see him?"

"A few days ago. Mum and Sammy haven't seen him either."

"He's probably off prowling around the woods. He was a house cat. Probably got a lot of catty catching up to do—eating voles, fighting, peeing in the garden. I'm sure he'll be back soon."

"Mr Frisky wouldn't eat a vole!" his youngest protested, running from the kitchen.

"And the little bastard won't be peeing in my leeks anymore either," Simon muttered.

He finished his breakfast and took a stroll around the farm. It was another dull, languid day, grey clouds ambling across the sky directionless and obtuse. The solar panels had given next to fuck all juice and there was barely a breath of wind either. He glanced up at the wind turbine to see a crow sitting nonchalantly on one of its immobile blades. He'd have thrown a stone if he didn't know that, sod's law, he'd probably hit the blade and break it.

It seemed like the *ennui* had spread to his writing too. This late in the morning he should really be in the cellar and cracking on with his self help opus, *Green not mean*, which he was sure was going to be a big hit. He billed it as the ultimate guide to living an ethically and ecologically sound life without compromising on those essential creature comforts, and felt like he'd really caught the *zeitgeist*. People wanted to be green, of course, but they wanted wi-fi, plasma screens and air-conditioned cars too. And he reasoned they could have both with the right economic management. He called his system Ecolonomics. A sound bite he felt sure the reviewers would latch on to. But he just wasn't getting anywhere. Even more annoying, it seemed that Margaret wouldn't turn the treadmill unless he was in the room with her. In fact, it seemed like the old witch wanted to attack him. Fair enough, he wasn't exactly her biggest fan, but it was a drag sitting there in the cellar listening to her gurgle while he tried to find his creative mojo again. He'd hooked up the Mac's speakers and played Haydn to drown her out, but it never entirely masked it. Still, at least it meant the house was generating some power. In fact, the farm's electricity was coming almost exclusively from Margaret's frenzied stumbling so the more time he spent in there the better.

Back in the house, he took his keys from his trousers and unlocked the cellar. Once he was sure the door was locked behind him he flicked on the light. Margaret's creme egg eyes fixed on him, her arms stretched out, and the gurgling began. Seconds later the wheel was in motion.

"Hi honey, I'm home," he quipped. He turned on the CD player and sat in front of the screen, the little vertical cursor winking needily. He watched it for a while, then spun slowly in his chair. Margaret pulled on her restraints. He stared at her for a moment, sighed, picked up the catapult, selected a stone from the tub of gravel on his desk and fired it at her. The corpse gave a start as the projectile thwacked off its forehead, a forehead (and face) that was already peppered with tiny black welts and contusions.

"That's black again," he said. Margaret wheezed. He selected another stone. The second lodged in the ruin of her throat, a thick gloop of blood dribbling down her neck. "That's red number 3!" he intoned in what he thought was a northern accent. "That's the dead granny on a treadmill. None darts player next." He fired again. The third stone burst one of her eyes and milky white fluid slid torpidly across her cheek. "It's a bull's-eye! And Bully's special prize is! Another magic tree!" He hung the air freshener around her neck, clapping his hands. He felt like Jimmy Savile. The corpse suddenly lunged for him taking him unawares. He stumbled back, losing his footing and grabbing for the waterwheel. The cadaver's claws were on him in a flash, tearing at his clothes, Margaret's toothless jaw gumming at him. He staggered quickly away cursing and wiping dead spittle from his shirt. She'd torn the damn thing and there were livid red scratch marks on his arm. He rinsed his wound under the tap, cursing and rubbing on some Savlon. He sniffed tentatively at his sleeve. It stunk. In fact she was pretty high in general, even if she did look like some un-dead Mr-T wannabe. She wore a heavy necklace of air fresheners, and stick-ups were stuck liberally to her. He gave her a blast of Oust for good measure.

Simon wasn't sure what had woken him: a noise, a full bladder, a bad dream? He slid his legs out of the bed and nudged into his slippers. The house was dark, a faint grey rectangle marking out the bedroom window. He tugged on his dressing gown. His throat was dry as shale and his head pounded, like the onset of fever. Maybe he was coming down with something? He had been pushing himself a bit hard lately. A glass of fresh orange and a Paracetomol would sort him out. He was halfway to the kitchen when he noticed that the door to the cellar was hanging loosely open. A feeble light illuminated the wall and top of the stone steps—had he left his desk light on down there? The least of his worries. His heart plummeted. "Fuck!" How the hell had Margaret managed to escape her bonds and unlock the door from inside? He scanned quickly around the hallway, kitchen, living room—a standby light winking red. He'd have to pull the kids up about that tomorrow—and the dining room. Nothing. Back in the hall his eyes snagged on the leathery cylinder of his golf bag. He felt around for his trusty 7 iron. Scared as he was, facing the undead Margaret was infinitely preferable to explaining to his family why their dead gran was wandering about the house.

Simon edged towards the open door, teasing it a little wider and placing his foot on the first step. The house was black, cold and silent as the tomb. He was almost half way down the stairs when there was a horrific, blood-curdling hiss from below. A black shape streaked past him brushing wetly between his legs. Quick as a flash, he stepped smartly on the black coil slithering up the steps in Mr Frisky's wake feeling a sudden jerk. The dead cat gurgled hideously. Stooping quickly he grabbed the beast's sticky innards and dragged it back towards him. The cat struggled, digging its rotten claws into the floor boards. He had to loop the stuff around his fist to stop the thing writhing free, a macabre tug of war. It came in range and he grabbed the cat by the neck, smacking it smartly on the back of the head. The club embedded itself in its skull with a sickening, but satisfyingly wet, crunch. "That's two you little bastard," he hissed, "don't think you're getting another seven." He twisted Mr Frisky hard in his hands, breaking its spine. Even if the little fucker was resurrected again, it wouldn't be going anywhere.

He closed the door behind him and hurried down the remaining steps. That was when he saw the empty collar hanging limply from the waterwheel's motionless frame. His heart beat hard against his dressing gown. He gripped the club, tossed the cat to the ground and steeled himself for the attack, eyes darting around the cluttered cellar space for his adversary. A groan from behind the table. He crept slowly forward, club raised above his head, and leapt around the corner, stopping himself short before he dashed his son's brains out.

"Peter!" he hissed, dropping the club and taking the boy's head in his hands. Peter was barely conscious and had a large bloody scratch on his chest. An empty sack—the one Mr Frisky had been in—lay by his side and Simon's cellar keys were on the floor at the boy's feet. He wiped granny dribble from his son's hair and face and stuffed the keys into his pyjama pocket at exactly the same time as Margaret's taloned claws wrapped around his throat. He fell forward, gurgling, barely managing to swerve aside before he crushed the boy. The ex-mother-in-law was on him in an instant, her rotten mouth straining for this throat. Simon twisted desperately trying to dislodge the thing but couldn't get a good grip. A ragged sliver of flesh fell from her rotting throat and an Airwick stick-up came away in his grasping hands. He managed to get a slippered foot under her midriff and propelled her backwards as hard as he could. She hit the ground with a nasty crunch, but was quickly on her feet again. A lump of shiny white plastic protruded from the torn flesh of her hip. The corpse lumbered forward and Simon grabbed for the 7 iron, bringing it smartly down on top of her head. Margaret tottered for a moment, sighed one last time, and crumpled to the ground. Stepping over the corpse, he placed a foot on her back and tugged the golf club free. He hit her again just to be sure.

Peter was regaining conscious. Simon wrapped the boy quickly in his dressing gown and dressed his wound in the sink. He found a jar of chloroform, tipped some onto a rag and held it over Peter's nose. The boy passed out again. Simon carried him gently up stairs and put him back to bed.

Simon sat in front of the Mac, head in his hands, desperately trying to stay awake. Not only was he utterly exhausted, but his head still pounded and he had an awful case of the shakes. In the bathroom mirror this morning his eyes had looked horrible, pallid and bloodshot. But no wonder. When he should have been asleep he was up all night dismembering Margaret and Mr Frisky. He'd heaped the bits into his wheelbarrow and trudged through the garden to the pig pen at the back of the house, where Pinky and Perky had made short work of them.

A scream from upstairs. The fucking kids. When were they back at school? The summer holidays seemed longer every year. He turned the music up a little more, hoping Haydn's Symphony number 11 in E Flat Major would sooth his pounding head and drown the little bastards out. It didn't. They were still at it ten minutes later. If he'd known Peter was going to be this hyperactive the morning after his nocturnal escapades, he'd have used more chloroform. The boy had complained of nightmares, naturally, and Simon had told Germaine that he'd found Peter sleepwalking—"He must have scratched himself on the banister." Germaine had molly coddled him for a bit, naturally, but when Sally had started teasing, Simon took his breakfast to the cellar and left them to it. His fruit and cereal still sat on his desk. He just didn't seem to have the stomach for it. He pushed the bowl aside and stalked upstairs.

"Peter! Leave your sister alone," he hollered through the living room's open door. The boy had his big sister pinned to the floor. She screamed and thrashed but he wouldn't relent. Simon smiled. He and his younger brother had been exactly the same at that age.

He drifted through to the kitchen looking for Germaine. He was making for the fridge when he tripped over his wife's prostrate body and hit the tiles with a thud that almost winded him.

"Fuck!" He scrambled backwards, slipping on the blood-slick floor. Germaine lay in a mangled heap, a huge chunk torn from the soft flesh of her innards, her torso a Rorschachian nightmare of organs, flesh and glistening ribs. Simon was about to throw up when she groaned. Definitely groaned. Particularly disconcerting as her lungs, in plain view, hadn't moved. His dead wife sat up, glared at Simon with white, pupiless eyes and began to drag herself towards him, growling and drooling.

"Fuck!" Simon jerked himself to his feet and scanned the kitchen for a weapon. He snatched the nearest thing to hand. Germaine was on her feet, lumbering purposefully towards him. He hit her as hard as he could with a Fissler saucepan and she fell to the ground hard. She was struggling to her feet again but Simon managed to make for the hall, grab another golf club, and dash back to the kitchen. Germaine launched herself at him in a frenzied attack, scattering salad bowls and mugs. Simon pushed her back as hard as he could and took an almighty swing. The club connected smartly with the side of her head. A clod of hair, skull, blood and cranial tissue arced across the room splattering the Smeg fridge. His wife went down, groaned and lay still. Simon let the club drop. He was hyperventilating, breathing fast and concentrating hard on not fainting or pissing himself when he felt tiny teeth sinking into his right buttock.

"AAAhhhhg!" He spun round, staggering back. Peter hissed, glaring with those now all-too-familiar sour milk eyes, and gurgled. The boy's face and t-shirt were thick with gore. Peter's jaw snapped as he launched himself at his father. Simon's first swing missed—the shock was beginning to sink in and he could barely control his shaking limbs. The dead boy managed to bite his kneecap this time. In desperation, Simon brought the other knee up sharply and sent his son three feet into the air and sailing across the hallway. Simon had steeled himself by the time his un-dead son had regained his feet. The boy staggered forwards and collided with the doorframe, head lolling backwards, eyes fixed skyward, a stalk of ragged spine protruding from the side of a broken neck. Simon stepped quickly forwards and finished it. Exhausted, he slumped to the floor and the tears began to flow, great sobs wracking his body, so much so that he barely heard the groaning form the living room.

"Sam! No!" he dragged himself to his feet one last time, picked up the gore-caked golf club and made for the living room. His daughter lay on the floor where Peter had left her. She fixed him with dead eyes, belched out a blood-curdling moan and began to drag herself towards him. As she did, her legs and lower torso were left behind, joined to her upper body by an ever expanding loop of intestine. Simon vomited, clutching at the door frame. If he fainted now it was over. Sam hissed and pulled herself forwards with slow and hideous resolve. With the vestiges of sanity and strength, Simon brought the club down hard on his daughter's head.

Simon sat in front of the Mac, head in his hands. The little vertical cursor winked needily. He groaned. He was making slow process and doubted *Green not mean* would ever see the light of day. He was hungry too. He dipped into the Tupperware box on his desk and took a bloody bite. It was good. Something fell onto the pristine white keyboard. He picked it up. One of his ears, grey and rotten. A maggot landed on the Z key and squirmed away. Simon groaned and began to type.

Coquettrice
Angel Leigh McCoy

THE COCKATRICE clucked its tongue and sniffed the steam rising off the eviscerated corpse. It narrowed its eyes. Gently, it pushed its hands through the coils of intestine and the lumpy organs to savor the dissipating heat.

A sound at the end of the alley alerted the cockatrice to the intruder. It lifted its head and peered through the darkness with black-amber eyes. Those eyes tracked the man as he faced a wall and opened his clothing to piss upon the brick. The cockatrice stood slowly, unfolding its long, lean body. It swayed there seductively. Its bare skin reflected what little luminescence lingered in the twilight of the man's life.

Even intoxicated, the man sensed something. In mid-stream, member in hand, he turned sharply toward the cockatrice. He looked confused, shocked even, and the cockatrice smiled. In a heartbeat, his last, the cockatrice struck.

There was no warning, that morning, in the subtle shift of nebulae across the sky. I entered the bus, as usual, riding the same line to the same stop. The same dull faces shared my commute. The same inane conversations grumbled at the periphery of my consciousness.

And then, "Hi," she said. "Mind if I sit here?" It was such a simple opening to such a complex story. At the time, I didn't hear the weight in her request. Remembering back, I don't see how I could have missed it. Her smile alone, so sweet, should have made me wary.

I looked her over: high breasts, flat stomach, jeans tight enough to camel-toe in her fleshy crotch, long legs, pretty face and that smile.

Momentarily, "Sure," I replied and moved my books off the seat, holding them in my lap with the spines facing her so she could see the titles.

She looked.

"Oh. You're a doctor?" They all asked that once they'd seen the clues and always with that same feminine squeak of interest in their voices.

I gave my customary chuckle and response, "Soon. I start my internship this fall." Offer the hand. Smile. "Name's William. What's yours?" Tip the head with interest and look straight into the eyes. My choreography worked every time.

"Tiffani." She turned toward me and slid her hand into mine. I noticed how soft it was, how frail and light. The kind of hand a man loves to have stroking him.

I got her phone number and called her after my last class. I asked her out. She agreed. Readily. Dinner and a walk along the river led us back to my place.

I rubbed my fingertips in lazy circles at the base of her spine, naked with her upon the stain of our union. Her hand languidly coaxed me up from the languor into which I had drifted.

"What are you doing?" I asked dreamily.

"Playing."

"Playing? Are you having fun?"

"Oh, yes."

"Good. Me too."

"Good."

I realized that this was a woman I could love.

The German shepherd growled and bared its teeth, so the cockatrice twisted its head off. Afterward, the monster looked up at the house, holding the decapitation by an ear. Blood and other fluids drained from the dog's neck onto the lawn. Stepping over the twitching body, the cockatrice rounded the corner of the house and peered through a window. It purred deep in its throat at what it saw. It cut through the screen with one, sharp claw and crawled inside. Television noise came from another room. The cockatrice quietly shut the nursery door. It walked to the crib and held up the dog's head for approval, bobbing it above the railing like a puppet with a ribbon tongue and blank, button eyes. The child giggled. For several minutes, the cockatrice amused itself, making the baby laugh. Predatory peek-a-boo pleased it for awhile, but not forever. The sour-sweet aroma of infant-meat made its mouth water.

An idyllic summer, spent in the arms of my sunny-tressed Tiffani, turned into a cruel autumn. The leaves gathered age-spots; they cringed, dried up and died. Tiffani and I moved in together. I started my internship and began my decline.

Indian summer they called it, but that only brought images of hatchets and scalpings—blond hair clutched in my fist. She wasn't home when I returned. It wasn't the first time. Tiffani said she got bored while I was on duty. She went out with *friends*.

At first, I believed her. I waited with a book, pretending to read between glances at the clock, the door, the window. My mind buzzed with questions that grew more and more urgent, more and more bitter with each passing minute. Finally, the key turned in the lock, and I was up and at the bedroom doorway in a second. I watched her sneak into the darkened apartment and saw her surprise as she caught my eyes upon her.

"Hi, William," she said with that smile.

"Where have you been?" I accused.

"Out."

"Out where? Who were you with?"

"Shopping, silly." Tiffani set her packages aside and slithered up to me. She pressed her cold hands against my cheeks. Her lips grazed mine, and her tongue flickered to taste me.

My gut sensed another man, but I wanted desperately to believe her. I kissed her deeply, searching for hope. That night, we made love like never before. I had something to prove: my manhood, my love, my ownership. I proudly chained her to me with three solid orgasms. Foolish as I was, I thought that would be enough, enough to keep her satisfied and tied to my bed.

The pretenses helped for awhile. Tiffani and I discussed the weather. We made love. We did our weekly shopping. We curled up on the couch to watch movies. We kissed hello and good-bye. We ate, and we slept, but time and again, I came home to an empty apartment. I found bus tickets to odd parts of town. I smelled cigarettes on her clothes and in her hair, and I overheard quickly-ended phone conversations, "No. Don't worry. He doesn't suspect a thing. I have to go."

On a Sunday, a strange woman came to the door saying her name was Debora and claiming to be a friend of Tiffani's. I let her in. Tiffani was dressing in the bedroom.

"So," Debora said with a conspiratorial wink, "you're the cock?"

"What?"

Debora looked past my shoulder, her face suddenly pinched with guilty secrets. I looked too.

Tiffani stood there. I caught the tail-end of her head shaking, her eyes hard with warning, then she showered me with one of her pearlescent smiles.

I left them to their lame excuses and isolated myself in the bedroom. The cock. The Cock. That's what they called him. My beautiful Tiffani was screwing the Cock. The crudeness of it turned my stomach.

Over the next couple weeks, I noticed dark clouds gathering under my eyes. I lost my appetite for food. My clothes irritated me, and finally, my libido left me. Tiffani swore it didn't matter, but I could feel the chains weakening.

My suspicions haunted me. The hallways of the hospital echoed with her name. Thoughts of her breezy, frail hands stalked me as I inserted catheters. Images of her thighs, spread wide, plagued me as I drove needles through the walls of veins. I saw her mouth open and willing as I threaded tubes down throats. The specters of her sexuality, however, had lost their eroticism. They bedded in betrayal.

October was coming to an end, burying the corpse of autumn in the grave of winter. Anyone who ever said winter didn't start until December had never lived in Minneapolis. The season cheated there. It snuck in early. It double-dealt doubt and dread throughout the city long before its victims admitted that it had arrived.

I remember the date: October 29. Tiffani wasn't home when I got off work. I pretended to read until midnight. From midnight to two, I paced. By two-thirty, I was cursing her and the Cock, raging and swearing. By four, I was in bed. She came home, and I pretended to be asleep.

With dawn came a new understanding of what I had to do. I climbed carefully out of bed. I showered, shaved and brushed my teeth. I dressed in my usual work clothes. I left the apartment at the usual time and walked to the usual bus stop. I got on the usual bus.

I got off again at the very next stop and sneaked back to spy.

Despite everything, despite her lies, and despite her slip-ups, a part of me still wanted to believe her. That hope-filled morsel stirred up enough doubt that I *had* to find out for sure. I couldn't just leave her. I'd wonder for the rest of my life whether I'd been wrong. Maybe she really had been telling the truth. Maybe 'the Cock' *was* just her pet name for me, as unflattering as it was. Maybe. Maybe. Maybe. Too many maybes.

For two long hours I stood on the street, in the cold, waiting for Tiffani to leave the apartment. Following her was a lot easier than I'd expected. She didn't take a bus or a taxi. Her destination was a three-story brownstone only five blocks from where we lived. The front door of the building opened with a squeak as I followed her inside. It startled me. Guilt stirred in my brain-stem, but I was beyond listening to my feeble conscience.

Tiffani's footsteps echoed in the staircase that spiraled squarely overhead. I could just make out the edge of her coat as she ascended. She was on the second floor, turning to climb to the third. Her slim hand wrapped delicately over the railing, gliding along as she went.

I tracked her with my eyes to the third floor. She knocked. I could tell the sound came from the rear of the building, but I couldn't tell which apartment. Cautiously, I climbed halfway to the second story, peering upward, and heard a door open on the third. I froze.

"Hi," Tiffani said. Simple, straightforward: that was her way.

I strained my ears, but heard no response aside from the eventual closing of the door and the slide of a deadbolt. I don't know how long I stood there on the landing between the first and second floor. My heart raced, and my head pounded. I considered leaving, forgetting the whole thing, but I couldn't. My need to know rooted me. I stared at the wall's chipped plaster and flaking paint. I imagined Tiffani upstairs in some other man's arms. Before I could change my mind, I climbed the rest of the stairs.

The light fixture on the third floor cast a jaundiced glow. Two apartments sheltered at the back of the building, numbers 11 and 12. One was fronted by a flowered mat. I discounted that one and turned to inspect the other. A Halloween decoration hung on the door, but not the usual cutesy witch or jangling skeleton. An oil painting, approximately five by seven inches, it flaunted the kind of imagination I would never possess and triggered a sort of morbid fascination that escalated as I studied it. A taxidermied snake framed the painting. The creature's markings were a subtle pattern of brown and black diamonds. Its skin flaked in places and its tail tucked neatly into its mouth at the top.

Upon the canvas, the artist had rendered the profile of a rooster, just the head. Its feathers were a bruised black-and-blue, iridescent. Its comb was swollen and ruddy; its visible eye was dark and dirty amber with a circular iris. As I examined it, I realized that the rooster's beak purposely resembled a penis, erect with a natural, downward curve. Its wattle hung below like wrinkled, scarlet testicles. The image disgusted me. Whoever this guy was, he was sick.

This guy was the Cock. The connection fired in my brain like a flare and left behind the acrid taste of fury. Of course.

I glared at the painting.

The rooster stared back at me, unblinking.

Tiffani's laughter whispered out to me—yes, she was in there. I raised my fist to knock, but hesitated. The hackles at the back of my neck tickled and gave me a violent shiver. I tried to rub the feeling away.

The rooster stared at me.

Suddenly, I lost the courage to go on. I realized abruptly that if I knocked it would end my relationship with Tiffani, whether she was guilty or not. Defeated, I turned to leave.

A man stood at the top of the stairs behind me. I hadn't heard him approach. He wore all black: trenchcoat, shirt and twilled-cotton trousers. His head was ragged and scruffy, despite the clean lines of his body and the penetrating sharpness of his ice-blue eyes. I waved my hand negligently at the painting and muttered some pseudo-excuse for loitering in the hall, then tried to hurry past him. He stopped me with a hand on my arm. I bristled.

"Beware the Basilisk," he uttered, his voice full of apocalyptic melodrama. He nodded toward number 12.

"What?" I was flustered. The man stood several inches taller than me and was built for a boxing ring. Something about him regressed me into a child caught in a misdemeanor.

The man scrutinized my guilt. He said nothing more, but withdrew a flyer from his pocket and thrust it into my hand.

I watched him walk to number 11, unlock the door, wipe his feet on the flowered mat and disappear inside. I shoved the brochure into my coat pocket and hurried back down the stairs. In the foyer, I paused only long enough to read the name on mailbox number 12: 'P.J. Price'. I repeated it to myself, several times, and then I rushed out the front door. The cold air hit my cheeks like water on embers.

Through the peephole at apartment number 11, Father Matthew watched the young intern flee. Previously, he had only seen William in pictures taken by a local priest to document the coven and the people connected to it. Immediately, Father Matthew had recognized William's innocence. How could he have missed the brush-strokes of embarrassment upon William's cheeks and the pain in his eyes?

Humming a simple hymn, Matthew crossed his meagerly-furnished apartment and hung his coat in the closet. He made tea and plain toast for dinner, gave a short prayer of thanks for the meal, then ate in silence. When finished, he pushed aside his plate and settled in to study. First, he picked up the file on the intern, William Jason Leake. It included the young man's birth certificate, baptism certificate, I.Q. test scores, grade school report, high school transcript, university transcript, credit report, residential history, medical records, gun license, psychological evaluation, and finally, the report on William's habits and internship. Matthew had already memorized nearly everything in it, but he knew the value of thoroughness. Browsing through the pages, Matthew wished he could do more to help William, but he had more to worry about than a young man who was going to walk away with only a broken heart.

The priest knew William was in no danger. The historical profile indicated that Tiffani Cerastes had probably chosen William as her cover. She lived with him to preserve an illusion of normalcy. His mundanity helped her disassociate herself from her crimes. Matthew figured Tiffani would dump William shortly before the ritual and move in with the Cock to raise the newborn cockatrice.

Matthew looked over at his rooster. It stirred, scratching its feet in the sandy floor of its cage. Matthew tossed it a piece of left-over crust from his toast and watched as the animal eyed the offering. The rooster didn't wait long before snatching up the bread. It ate with a ruffle of red-orange feathers. Matthew turned back to the table. He closed William's file and set it aside. Then, he picked up his Bible and opened it to "Psalms."

The light coming in the window turned from golden twilight to cold streetlight, and Matthew read aloud the words that most comforted him, "Thou shalt not be afraid for the terror by night; nor for the arrow that flieth by day; nor for the pestilence that walketh in darkness; nor for the destruction that wasteth at noonday. A thousand shall fall at thy side . . ." So many had died at Matthew's side. So many had given their lives in the Holy War that all mortal wars emulated. He knew that someday he too would die in the Lord's service.

". . . And ten thousand at thy right hand." Matthew had killed in the name of the Lord. He had lost count, long ago, of the minions he had sent to Hell. Sometimes innocents got in the way, and that may have been a shame, but it was also a necessary price to pay.

". . . But it shall not come nigh thee."

Taking a deep breath, Matthew closed the Good Book and said a short, silent prayer, finishing aloud with, "Lord, give me strength and wisdom to overcome Basilisk and his cockatrice. Amen."

In the candlelit room, the orgiastic pile of bodies writhed. The cockatrice had one in its mouth and one in its sex. It moaned its pleasure and lifted its eyes to gaze up the body of its future husband. When in its true form, as it was then, the change in its eyes gave everything a fire-shimmer, as if it were looking through an amber lens. It preferred this demon's form to the soft, weak femininity it hid in most of the time, but it had too many enemies to show its unvarnished visage to the mortal world.

The cockatrice sucked and licked as its lover ejaculated into its throat. So succulent, he was. His musky-sweet seed tantalized the cockatrice's bloodlust. The taste thrilled the monster, but it wasn't beast enough to kill this one. No, this one had a purpose. The cockatrice growled as its own orgasm rippled through its body.

Back at home, I tossed my coat aside and paced, waiting. I barely noticed the shadows shifting across my apartment as night's darkness menaced the day away. All I could see was that genital-faced rooster and my Tiffani. In my mind, it pecked at her, and she laughed. She laughed again and again. Eventually, she was laughing at me, and then he joined her, crowing at the gullible boyfriend. I cursed them both, and I cursed my own stupidity. I was ready for her when she finally came in the door. By then, I had settled onto the couch like a crucified saint, ankles crossed and arms spread along its back. That's how I felt, me and my martyrdom.

I hadn't bothered to turn on any lights and I took some satisfaction in her startlement when I spoke to her out of the darkness, "Get enough?"

"Jesus, William. You scared me." She turned on the lights and must have seen the accusation in my face, or perhaps in my eyes. She did a double-take, then began to explain without having to be asked, "Debora and I went shopping."

"Where's your bags?"

"I beg your pardon?"

"Your bags. You went shopping, but you didn't buy anything?" I liked the taste of self-righteousness.

"Oh. I must have left them at Debora's place. We stopped there afterward for coffee."

"Does Debora live in a three-story brownstone?"

Tiffani muttered something unintelligible and walked into the bedroom. I arose and followed. She had thrown her coat on the bed and was sitting beside it, removing a boot. I leaned against the doorjamb.

"Excuse me?" I said, cool as a snake. "I didn't hear what you said."

"I said yes, she does." Tiffani paused, then asked, "How do you know that?"

I ignored her question. I had to ask, despite or maybe because of the cliché, "Was he good?"

"What? Who?"

"The guy in number 12. The Cock." My mouth opened obscenely around the last word.

"You followed me?"

I responded with a crooked, drunken grin, even though I hadn't had a drop of alcohol. It fit.

"How dare you follow me!"

I used my doctor voice, the one she hated, logical and cold. "How dare you screw around on me."

"I'm not."

"No? Then who's P.J.? Who's the Cock?" I was beginning to like the vindictive, violent feeling that word had in my mouth.

"P.J.?"

"Yeah. P.J. Price. You know. The one you're screwing?"

"P.J.? Oh. You mean Paul. He's just a friend. I'm not sleeping with him!"

I should have expected it. How could I argue with that? I hadn't *seen* her in bed with the guy. I'd only seen her go inside and heard her laugh. She had blown my case right out of the water. She knew it too. She came over to reinforce her words with kisses and caresses. It was my word against hers, and all I had was jealousy and conjecture in my corner.

My confidence was abandoning me, but I made one last feeble attempt to rally my side. "Then why did you lie and tell me you went shopping with Debora?"

"Because," she pouted, "you're so jealous. I didn't think you'd understand if I said I'd spent the afternoon hanging out with a male friend. I'm sorry, honey."

A man knows when a woman has him by the balls.

The morning sun cast a flaccid light down upon Father Matthew. He stood on the street across from William and Tiffani's apartment building, rocking on his heels. He buried his hands in his pockets and tried to ignore the cold's saturation into his bones. He watched. Heaven only knew what he expected to see or what great influence he hoped to have by being there, but some divine hint of instinct had sent him.

Eventually, the young intern emerged from the building. Matthew noted William looked tired and tense. Innocent, the priest thought. Innocent enough that he sensed the truth about his lover only on a subconscious level.

Their eyes met. Matthew stood firm, knowing that William had seen him. He gave the young man his most intense stare. 'Listen to your gut, boy,' the look sent. 'Run. Run away as fast and as far as you can. Go. Go. Go.' A city bus drove slowly past. Matthew watched as William ran to catch it.

The hospital buzzed, coughed, gurgled, cried, and blip-blip-blipped. I hated it. I intended to go into private practice where I could diagnose my patients, then refer them to a hospital or specialist for treatment. I liked solving puzzles, but hated doing the hands-on dirty-work. I had learned two important lessons as an intern: one, that the textbooks did a thoroughly cosmetic cover-up on the truth of human anatomy—bodies were actually disgusting, filthy things that oozed, stank, and housed parasites—and two, that people were unbelievably stupid. They all thought they were invulnerable, that they could stick anything they wanted in any orifice, play with dynamite, or leap tall buildings in a single bound, and walk away intact. They were usually wrong.

My dinner break came at seven p.m., and I took it promptly. Getting through the line at the cafeteria chewed up fifteen minutes; eating took another fifteen. To pass the rest of the time, I found a quiet phone cubicle and called home. It rang through, and I muttered to Tiffani to pick up. She didn't. I hung up and redialed only to reach more emptiness. The hollow rings sounded like sonar pings searching for something solid off which to bounce, but they found only a growing void. I began to feel sick.

Father Matthew saw her through his peephole. Tiffani Cerastes knocked on the door across the hall. Her delicate fingers brushed over the beak of the painted rooster. Matthew admired her beauty, as any man would. He had taken a vow of celibacy and dedicated his life to a higher purpose, but that didn't mean he couldn't feel the stirring in his loins at the sight of an attractive woman, especially a cockatrice. He briefly touched himself through his pants, drawing strength from the physical energy that fired at the sensation.

The door opened at number 12. Paul Jefferson Price stood there dressed only in a pair of blue jeans. His upper torso rippled with muscles—smooth, full and strong. The young man was handsome, of course. Basilisk would have it no other way. Matthew waited until Tiffany had entered, and the door had shut behind her, then he went back to the kitchen table.

The clock struck eight, with soft, reminder chimes. Matthew picked up his notebook, opened it to a new page and began to write in his economical, masculine script:

8 p.m. Tiffani Cerastes arrives at no. 12 and enters. Price inside. I no longer have any doubt that Cerastes is the Mother for the unholy birthing. She now wears Basilisk's mark upon her left hand. I saw it only moments ago while she waited for the Cock to let her inside the coven room. She will guide the ritual and tend to the Cock. Once the egg has hatched, assuming I fail in my attempt to stop the entire process, she will mother the infant cockatrice to maturity.

The ward remains on the door, making it impossible to enter, even when the apartment is empty. They're careful. So much is at stake. Tonight, Basilisk will manifest, and once he is in this world I can banish him back to Hell. I pray for the innocent and ask that the Lord . . .

A knock on the door drew Matthew from his journal. He closed it, stood and crossed the room. Peering through the peephole, he spied a little devil with baby horns, rosy cheeks, and a pointed tail that bounced on its own. He unlocked and opened the door.

"Trick or treat!" the children cried in relative unison, holding up their bags.

Matthew smiled and reached for his plastic pumpkin of candy.

I called the apartment every fifteen minutes after that first time. My agitation grew with each unanswered ring. Finally, I made the hospital let me go home.

My stomach had knotted up a half an hour earlier. I knew what I had to do.

The 8:30 bus arrived five minutes late. I pushed through the waiting commuters to get to it, my pardons growing more urgent and less polite as the bus's doors slowly closed without me.

"Wait!" I called, stepping up and pounding on the glass. The driver reopened the doors. I climbed in, paid my fare, found a seat near the middle and stared out the bus window. My hands clenched into fists over and over on my thighs, until I felt eyes upon me. I looked over to see a woman watching me. I caught her gaze, and she turned away. Irritated, I shifted my posture toward the window and stuffed my hands in my pockets. My fingers brushed the flyer. I thought of the strange man who had given it to me, and remembered seeing him outside my apartment that morning. I pulled it out and looked at it.

"Judas walks among us," it said, superimposed over a dull reproduction of 'The Last Supper,' and I almost threw it away right then and there. I had little interest in sanctimonious propaganda. I opened it, however, curious about the man himself.

Even as upset as I was, the interior text made me laugh, albeit wryly. It talked about demons and their servants. In particular, it mentioned Basilisk, the Snake King, who impregnated roosters that then laid eggs out their bowels. From these eggs, the cockatrice hatched. According to the flyer, the cockatrice were monsters that served Basilisk and could change form to become beautiful women. They "seduced innocent men into sin." The brochure went on to explain how they killed for fun, ate human flesh and had uncanny powers, including the ability to mesmerize their victims. I tossed the flyer on the floor of the bus.

When I got home, the apartment was dark.

"Tiff?" I called, on the one small hope that she had fallen asleep. No answer. No *fucking* answer. She wasn't there. I knew what *was* there though: my gun.

Father Matthew's evening dragged. He busied himself with scripture and prayer. He double-blessed his primary weapon: the rooster whose crow could return Basilisk to Hell. He also prepared his other weapon. The revolver felt good in his hand as he cleaned and then reloaded it.

Matthew had finished his last journal entry a few minutes earlier at 9 p.m. In it, he had documented the arrival of the other coven members, four of them, two men and two women. Finally, he had gathered up all his files and placed them, with the journal, in the Little Black Box. The clergy would look for that if anything happened to him. He locked the box and duct-taped it to the inner frame of the couch. As he replaced the piece of furniture, his scalp crawled and itched. He scratched it, turning slowly to stare at the locked door. The unholy rituals had begun across the hall. The rooster felt it too. It fretted, ruffling its feathers uneasily.

The priest sat at the table and prayed over his rosary, "Though I walk through the valley of the shadow of death . . ." A sharp pain lit up his calf. Matthew cringed and drew his leg up protectively. He raised his pant-leg and examined the source of the pain. Two puncture wounds sat side-by-side on his calf, already swelling and bleeding. Looking down to the floor, Matthew spotted his attacker.

The snake wasn't large, only about two feet long and meaty. It looked like braided leather, its markings a series of diamonds all fit neatly together. The beast lifted its ovoid head and swayed. It delivered its second strike to the priest's other ankle, sinking fangs deep into Matthew's flesh.

Matthew threw himself to the floor, toppling the chair toward the snake in an attempt to escape another bite.

The viper struck again.

Matthew grabbed the chair with both hands. He beat the creature. Chair-legs splintered and the sound of cracking wood filled the apartment. With desperate satisfaction, he saw portions of the snake's body split and smear, flatten and bleed. He hit it again and again. His arms and back ached with the effort, but Matthew didn't stop until the snake ceased moving. The animal died as it had arrived: silently.

Matthew dragged himself toward the counter. He reached up to pull himself to his feet and his gaze landed on the rooster. It lay wrong, one foot twitching. Matthew's legs denied him and he slumped back to the floor. He easily imagined, if not actually felt, the venom coursing through his blood-stream.

"Help!" he shouted, trying to reach anyone. "Help!" He called again and again. Eventually, he whimpered his pleas, "Oh . . . Lord . . . oh please, God . . ." A heavy, black shroud enfolded Matthew. His eyes froze in place, unblinking, and his throat constricted on the prayer, unheard. He had failed.

I climbed the stairs to the third floor of the brownstone. The gun felt heavy in my coat pocket; its solid presence bumped against my thigh with each step. I had lost all feeling and all reason. Draped in a veil of sanguine rage, I stood at the door to number 12. Someone had removed the rooster painting.

Without hesitation, I reached for the doorknob and turned it. I swung the door wide and stepped across the threshold. A giant bed stood in the middle of the room, draped with red and black, sheeted with satin. Candles cast a carnal glow. Two faces looked over at me. His, so handsome, so smug, had a smile. Hers, so beautiful, so familiar, showed surprise. They were naked. He rolled over and sat up. I saw his erection.

"William?" she murmured, moving to the edge of the bed. "What are you . . .?"

I pulled my gun.

"William!"

I didn't think. I just pulled the trigger. The explosion rebounded off my nerves and hit the wall. My finger twitched again. The second bullet threw the Cock back onto the pillows. He was bleeding. His blood drained slowly, creating a scarlet river that meandered down his heaving chest to pool in the basin of his stomach. He hissed, deflated and died.

Someone closed the door behind me, and I felt two people, one on either side, take my arms, take my gun, and take my freedom. I didn't struggle. It was too late for that.

"What do we do now?" The others whispered among themselves. "The Cock is dead. We're doomed."

I began to shake.

Tiffani stood. She smiled that smile and tilted her head just so, "William. Will you never cease to surprise me?" She crossed toward me, her breasts swaying with each step. Dribbles of splattered blood, P.J.'s blood, ran down her hip. Her eyes looked strange. The whites slowly darkened to black crystal sparked with amber. Her pupils became discs of obsidian. As she approached, she changed. Like some walking special-effect, she transformed before my eyes into a snake woman with talons and rippling muscles where feminine curves had once made her so shapely. Her skin took on a snake-like texture, and her body swallowed her hair leaving her completely bald. The bones in her face elongated and her mouth widened into a slash with the hint of a cleft lip. When her tongue flickered out, it had a forked tip. I stared, trying to see through the hallucination to the Tiffani I knew, but she eluded me. Hot urine ran down my legs and soaked into my shoes.

Tiffani announced, "We have a new Cock. Basilisk has sent us a sign." She touched her slim, cool fingers to my cheek. Her gaze mesmerized me. I relaxed.

Time and reality slipped away. They stripped me, the five of them. The two men held me in place while the three women bathed me thoroughly. Tiffani's friend Debora was there, but I had never seen the others. They bent me over an armchair. The enema made me uncomfortable. I cried. I begged.

I shat soup into an iron bucket.

Tiffani soothed me with tender caresses, as she always had. She assured me everything would be all right. She told me that Basilisk had chosen me. She stroked my penis with her frail, soft hand.

They tied my wrists to my ankles and placed me on the bed with my ass in the air. I turned my head to avoid looking at P.J. Price's gaping eyes and mouth. My cheek lay upon soft satin. Tiffani rubbed me with sharp-scented oils, massaging away my tension and fears. This *was* my Tiffani, after all. She wouldn't let anyone hurt me. She loved me. I closed my eyes. Her hands spread the oils over my skin and into my pores. She lubricated my anus with it, inside and out.

At some point, the chanting began. Deep and throaty, the lullaby made me sleepier. It wrapped me with a blanket of security. I even forgot that the underside of my naked body was exposed to the room. I wanted to forget everything.

"Soon, darling," Tiffani hissed into my ear. "It will all be over soon, and then we can go home." She blindfolded me, and I welcomed the darkness. No one could look at Basilisk and survive, she explained.

Their voices rose. I smelled burning hair and sulfur. I tracked their softly padding steps as they danced around the room. I was losing sensation in my hands and feet. I made fists and curled my toes to pass the time. Cool air fanned across my buttocks. The chanting grew louder, ecstatic and more insistent. The air itself crackled with energy, and the hair on the back of my neck stood on end. Someone touched me, and I instinctually tried to look behind myself. The blindfold denied me.

They were hands—large, masculine hands. They rubbed harshly over the fleshy hemispheres of my ass, kneading and spreading them. Something insinuated itself inside me. It was thin, limp and alive like a snake. Panic enveloped me, and my heart thundered. I cried out for Tiffani, for mercy and for God. I squirmed, but those hot hands held me firmly in place. The tentacle wiggled inside me, delving deeper and deeper. It swelled, filling me and spreading me wide. I screamed, I'm sure of it.

I thought my intestines would rupture from the sheer girth of it. It pulsed with a seductive new rhythm, with an alien heartbeat that tried to derail my own. The pain was excruciating.

Suddenly, the hands viced down on my hips. Basilisk raped me with a hard, heavy beat. He grunted with each thrust, then abruptly, the expanding tentacle erupted. It released its load of molten semen into my body. I heard Basilisk's unearthly groan as the demon came inside me, and I felt hopeful relief thread through my soul. Soon, the pain would end. The tentacle slithered out of me and went away. Basilisk loosened his hold on my hips, and I swear I felt him caress me, tenderly, just like my Tiffani had done. My screams subsided into sobs. I think I lost consciousness.

When I awoke, my anus hurt. Sticky with drying semen and blood, it burned. I couldn't move. My testicles descended from their clutch of fear and horror, to hang between the A-frame of my thighs. My knees ached. The sheet was hot beneath my cheek, wet with my own spit and rank with the perfume of anointing oils. The skin of my face tightened with dried brine and my throat felt as if I'd swallowed a handful of thistles.

They gathered around me; their master had retreated to his unholy realm. I felt their kisses, their caresses and their licking tongues as they cleaned me and adored me. They plugged me up, to keep the precious seed from escaping. Tiffani untied me, pulled away the blindfold and smiled into my eyes. She loved me.

The next couple days passed in a blur. The others took P.J. away and put new sheets on the bed. Tiffani stayed with me. We slept, ate and held each other, always naked. Tiffani insisted on doing everything for me. She fed me, spooning an herbal pudding into my mouth, and held the cup as I drank honeyed tea. She washed me and combed my hair. I began to feel like a king.

The egg formed slowly, soft and tender at first. The pressure coalesced into one place, like beads of mercury all rolling together to form one big, shimmery pool. Tiffani explained it all to me. I was going to be a father.

On the morning of the third day, the egg was a solid presence in my body. The thought of excreting it frightened me, but Tiffani assured me that everything would be fine. She was right. The egg came that evening. I squatted upon the bed, tears streaming down my cheeks, my groans and screams echoing in my head. It stretched me. It tore me. I thought for sure I would die, but finally, it was out. The egg was large, the size of a man's fist, enough to hold a supernaturally tiny infant. The shell gleamed with black and blue opalescence. The others cleaned it off while I lay gasping on the bed.

Later, Tiffani and I curled around it, keeping it warm between our bodies. I petted its dappled surface with awe-struck fingers. My baby grew inside it. For two weeks, Tiffani and I took turns leaving the bed to stretch, wash and use the bathroom. Most of the time, we cuddled, stroked each other, and made love with our baby lying beside us. The bed became our love nest.

On November 13 at 7:53 a.m., the egg cracked. Tiffani and I cried together as our child stretched a perfect, little arm out of her shell. We helped her emerge and cleaned away the thick, clear fluid in which she had incubated. She was beautiful and healthy. I loved her immediately. We had already chosen her name, Coquette. In French, Coquette meant 'flirtatious'. Lying there with my new family, I held Coquette's hand carefully in mine and kissed the delicate, baby fingers with their tiny talons and cool skin. She looked up at me, beguilingly, with her mother's black-amber eyes. I vowed to give her the world.

The Fear in the Waiting

C.J. Henderson

REPORT OF MEDICAL OFFICER MAJOR ERNEST T. WHITTAKER
OPENING STATEMENT:

I do not quite know where to begin. As any who read this report and whom also know me or my work will attest, this is not a usual state of affairs. But, of course, as the select few who will read these pages already know, there is nothing usual about what I have been asked to analyze here.

When I was first assigned the examination of this report's subject, various facts were withheld from me. I am not yet certain as to whether or not I should look on this as a disservice or not. Surely, if I had been told everything that was known of the madness into which I was being sent before I had entered, I would have been better prepared for all I was to be told. However, would I have been less receptive, more curious, cautious enough to wear perhaps a more skeptical layer of armor? And even if I had done any of these, could they have helped?

I can not answer. Nor, maybe, should I even attempt to. My orders were quite simple. With the death of Dr. Herbert West, I was to discover all I could from one of the only survivors of the disaster known as Project Starchaser, his assistant, Dr. Daniel Cain—not to whine on inordinately about how such orders affected me. Dozens of people are dead. Scores more are missing. Damages total-ling in the hundreds of millions have been estimated, with the more pragmatic of the ledger keepers predicting that the final total will be over a billion dollars. A billion dollars. Even in the heavy inflation of the late forties, still the thought of a billion dollars worth of damage, all of it incurred in a matter of minutes . . .

I stopped where I did and began once more because I was losing my train of thought as well as my perspective. A dangerous admission, I suppose, when the psychiatrist begins to rant and ramble. I reveal this, not to make the case for sloppy emotionalism, or to suggest that my need to assess my own stake in this matter outweighs your own need for precise, uncluttered information, but as a means of supplying you a subtler type of intelligence that you yourselves might assess without my putting any kind of favorable "spin" on things.

I will admit to you now that this is the fourth draft of this report which I have begun. When I found myself rambling in earlier versions—hands shaking, mind wandering—I destroyed the copies and began anew, fearing that you might find me in need of more help than my own patient. But, I have decided after a long night of soul-searching that to get my thoughts down and then to revise them until they are pure and safe and reflective only of terror voiced from other throats would be a disservice to you, my superiors, and to our country as a whole.

It is my decision in the final analysis that you need to feel what I have felt, the horror, the disbelief, the agony and pain, and ultimately, the hysterical fear that has left me trembling and doubting and no longer in any way certain that the world is what I once thought it to be. Cold ink on bright white paper will not suffice. To understand what you have charged me to explain, then you must touch the mantle of chaos as I have, as I did when I walked into the cell of Dr. Daniel Cain and stared into his eyes and learned the terrible truth that, for at least one man in this cosmos, there is no God.

BACKGROUND:

July 8th, 1947, First Lieutenant Walter G. Haut, the Public Information Officer out of the Roswell Army Air Base released what has already become known as "The Roswell Statement." This is the document in which he announced to the world that the military had recovered the remains of a flying saucer.

This report was almost instantly dismissed in favor of a new release which claimed the supposed "UFO" was actually an experimental weather tracking satellite.

At the same time, two captured war criminals, Doctors Herbert West and Daniel Cain, Americans who had been working with the Nazis in the death camps, were sent to New Mexico, specifically, to U.S. Army Restricted Area 51, to spearhead a hastily put together covert project known only as Operation Starchaser.

West and Cain, unbelievable as it might sound, were supposedly experts in, and at this point I quote from General Order #25-A-892, "the highly experimental field of reanimation—that being the resurrection of dead tissues to a once more living state."

So simply said, so casual a statement—isn't it? Such deceptively calm words. I would imagine the scientists working on the Manhattan Project spoke in such pleasant euphemisms. Pleased to meet you, Dr. West. You're the creator of the reanimation process everyone is talking about, aren't you? Didn't I read something about you in the latest journal? No, I remember, I heard it from your colleague, Dr. Cain. Something about the ashes of concentration camp victims being molded into a living, humanoid monster, and about the resurrected body of our Holy Lord chewing on your chin. And what's all that about you transferring the essence of your consciousness from your mind to that of a young woman so that you might secretly become your assistant's lover, then his son . . .

Again, I stop.

But, do not mistake this for some simple pause to reflect, a moment's rest so that I might compose a sentence in my head. The above was not simply some clever bandy to help convey my disgust for this assignment. Actually, I am at present trying to keep from screaming. My hands are shaking so badly, they are so covered with the slime of my own perspiration that I can barely make contact with my typewriter without my fingers slipping across the keys. My brain is afire with the sins Cain has outlined for me, a hundred disgusting, abominable tales that have left me morose and fearful.

Suffice it to say that my patient claims to be close to sixty years in age, despite the fact he appears to be only in his late twenties. He claims to have died and been resurrected by West. He claims to have killed West more than once to try and halt his horrible experiments, only to have failed time and again. In short, Cain claims many things, each of them more repugnant than the next, and Heaven help me, I believe every word he said to me to be true. With what I have seen, how can I not?

I met Cain in a darkened room. I was told that due to his condition the patient himself had requested that no one be able to see him. He was fed only by intravenous drip, the tube extending from its bottle to his arm through the heavy curtains drawn around his bed.

Cain did not leave his bed throughout our conversation. I saw nothing unnatural in this at the time. Such a number of people had been injured in the New Mexico tragedy that I merely assumed him to have suffered some crippling wound, like so many of the others I saw in the same ward. I would later discover that I was correct. Hideously, monstrously correct.

Enough.

I have hinted at Cain's past, and that shall suffice us for now. This report was to concentrate on Cain and West's activities at Project Starchaser only. From here on in, it would probably be best if I were to allow Dr. Cain to speak for himself.

THE INTERVIEW:
"I think you should leave, Dr. Whittaker. For your own good, I think you should leave this room now."

These were the first words spoken to me by Dr. Cain. He did not sound tired or sedated. Nor either did he sound deranged or lacking of the proper facilities to respond to the questions I needed to ask. Still, he insisted, "You don't understand. I think something is going to . . . I mean, there is a danger . . . something is . . ."

And then, the most peculiar thing occurred. Cain suddenly broke off his attempt to get me to flee his chambers and began talking to himself. It was a mad buzzing noise of hisses and snaps. I could make out few of the words clearly, my patient's none-too-internal debate muffled by the curtain around his bed. Finally however, he spoke to me once more.

"You think I'm crazy, don't you? It's all right. I am crazy, you know. Crazy to have allowed all that has happen to me to occur, crazy not to have killed West decades ago. But, but . . . of course, I did, didn't I? I killed him. And then I killed him. And I think I may have killed him again somewhere in there. I'm not certain anymore, you know."

The man rambled for some time after that, telling me in great and horrid detail the abominable tales I have but hinted at in the preceding pages. After several hours I attempted to get my assignment under way by abruptly changing the subject. Without warning, when my patient paused for a breath, I said, "Tell me about what happened at Project Starchaser."

"What do you want to know?"

"Tell me what you saw, what you did, what you were brought there to do. Tell me what went wrong."

There was a long pause at this point. Cain made small gurgling noises for a while, interrupted with disturbing, dry whistles. I must admit, despite my many years of medical service it was a noise I had never quite before heard. Finally, however, he managed to begin to answer my question.

"West."

"What about Dr. West?"

"You asked what went wrong. It was West. He is what was wrong. What went wrong. What *is* wrong. What is wrong with the world, with the human mind, with existence itself!"

"Why do you say this, Dr. Cain? What makes you feel this way?"

"What makes me *feel* this way? Are you an idiot? Have you heard nothing I've said? What more does the monster have to do?"

"Yes, I understand that you believe Dr. West responsible for a great many horrors over the years you've been with him. But, even if I accept everything you say as true—all of it without any critical reflection—still, I need to report to my superiors exactly what occurred in New Mexico. There are considerations of national security."

No response was made to that statement, merely the same dry whistling noise slithering outward from between the weighty curtains surrounding the darkened bed. I despaired for a moment. Normally I would want to work with a patient such as Dr. Cain for months before tackling the root center of his problem. But, I had not the luxury of time. My assignment was to get answers as quickly as possible—through whatever methods possible.

God help me, I did as I was ordered.

"There were reports of a flying saucer recovered by the Army Air Corp. The rumor is that this was what lie at the heart of Operation Starchaser. Can you tell me about that?"

"There was no saucer."

I expected more, but again, the air was filled with only the rasping whistle. I was about to question this further, when Cain suddenly snapped fiercely.

"Am I an engineer? A physicist? Is West? We're doctors, you fool. *Reanimators!* We were not taken to New Mexico to examine a space ship. Think, you idiot. What would they take us there for? What possible reason could your masters have to bundle us off to their desert prison?"

"My assumption had been that you were taken there to examine, and possibly revive whatever bodies might have been recovered from the wreckage."

"Oh, we went to revive a body all right, but there was no wreckage. Well, not from any unidentifiable flying objects."

And then, at that point, my patient began to chortle. It was a thin, drooling sound, as if the notes were being strained through a thick gauze heavy with blood. After fifteen years of working in various mental wards, the laughter of the hopeless and the frightened is nothing new to me. I have waited by patiently while murderers and rapists have laughed themselves into stupors without so much as blinking. But this, this was different.

Cain's gaiety was an inhuman thing, the noises of howling dogs and shrieking crows mixed with the various sounds one hears around wood-cutting machinery. It was shrill and piercing, yet somehow mournful. At the same time my brain held both contempt and yet pity for the creature which could produce such a noise. Finally, however, Cain broke off his wild cackling. The dry whistling returned, a grating irritant so unnerving I almost wished for the laughter instead. Then suddenly, the terrible noise ceased and Cain's voice began speaking to me once more.

"I'm sorry, Dr. Whittaker. I'm sure you're only here to help. You're doing your duty, but still, you think it somewhere within your powers as a healer to rescue me. I suppose you deserve a decent chance at both. I will tell you about Project Starchaser."

I waited in silence. Something puzzled me about Cain's voice. The trembling in it, the hatred, had somehow become subdued. But, they had been replaced by a snide authority, a type of mocking piety I found most troubling. It was a tone I am quite familiar with, the range of vocal pitch used by the worst psychopaths when they are attempting to beguile.

It did not make sense to me, though. Unless Cain were harboring multiple personalities . . .

Enough. There is little to be gained by reviewing my inability to perceive what was happening then. All shall be revealed to you as it was to me.

Continuing, I should add that by that time my eyes had become quite used to the darkness in the room. From the thin lines of light leaking in around the door, I could make out a tiny bit of the bed before me. I tried greatly to see through the curtains, begging providence for even an outline, a bit of shadowy reflection on which I might build some sort of picture of the man to whom I was speaking.

But, even as my eyes adjusted to the near pitch dark gloom, I found the barrier to be complete and unyielding. Embarrassed by my insensitive curiosity, I directed my attention to my recording equipment as much as I could. From then on my patient gave me a great deal to record.

"Yes," he said, "New Mexico released news of a cosmic mishap, then sent out another story insisting that it was a weather balloon that had crashed. Tell me, doctor, could you believe me if I told you that *both* stories were true?"

Cain chuckled again, then explained himself.

"You see, Dr. Whittaker, there actually was a weather balloon, some new, larger type of experiment, capable of reaching much greater heights. It had been sent up with mannequins inside it to record some sort of reactions—not much beyond that was ever made clear to myself . . . or West." My patient chuckled briefly, then continued. "But there was a weather balloon, a massive affair of rubber and wire and aluminum, and that was what the beast crashed into."

"The beast?"

"Yes, the thing from space. Oh, it was an incredible sight. Of course, we were not the first to see such a being. Similar creatures were first reported back in the thirties." When I but stared blankly, Cain continued.

"You must remember the news stories, the Miskatonic Expedition to the Antarctic continent. Pabodie, Lake, Atwood—their wild radio reports—none of them returned? The expedition that followed found their land point and their encampment, but the mountain ranges and caverns they claimed to discover had collapsed upon themselves, wiping out all traces of the tool-using prehistoric civilization they reported finding."

When I showed no memory of the event, Cain confided, "The officer in charge of Starchaser said that some small evidence of the underground cities they reported had indeed been uncovered over the past two decades, but excavations at the bottom of the world are slow things. Still, why dig for corpses when they deliver themselves to you so neatly, eh?"

"But, Dr. Cain," I said, more than slightly confused and somewhat convinced that his stories was mere lies, "what are you trying to tell me? Cities under the Antarctic, monsters flying in the stratosphere . . . what does all of this have to do with Project Starchaser?"

And then, the dry whistling returned, and in the ensuing silence, somehow my brain filled with a dread combination of leaps, a horrible epiphany of wild connections that allowed me access to Cain's incredible tale.

Decades in the past an expedition discovers traces of an ancient city beneath the southern polar region. An intricate, advanced metropolis created before humanity had found fire or the wheel. Now, a monster similar to those discovered then is found in the upper atmosphere. It crashes into a weather balloon and falls to Earth. Its otherworldly appearance, combined with the wreckage of the balloon, is mistaken for a flying saucer. But, I thought, that would mean . . .

"Yes," agreed Cain with an eerie precision, almost as if he could hear my thoughts, "creatures that can transverse the ether of the galaxy the way fish do the ocean. Magnificent things they were . . . ten feet tall, dark grey, infinitely dense. The one we were taken to within the brightly lit confines of Hanger 18 was an extraordinary specimen. Nine foot membranous wings, flexible and yet impervious to torch or saw, and its magnificent, five-pointed head . . . the wonders within it . . ."

Cain stopped talking for a moment at that point. Or at least, he ceased talking to me. Despite several attempts by myself to coax a response from him, my patient engaged in an internal dialogue, yammering under his breath to himself for nearly a minute. Then, the dry whistling returned, slicing keenly through my nerves, followed again by my patient speaking to me once more.

He begged my apology, again in the suspiciously mocking tone I had noted earlier. I bade him continue without mentioning anything. Chuckling as he spoke, he told me,

"Anyway, the beast. That magnificent specimen, fantastically, it was a thing almost completely preserved. Our guess was that the creature, capable of transversing the flowpaths of space itself, had managed to glide most of the way to the planet's surface and thus avoided being severely damaged."

"But, it *was* dead, correct?"

"Oh, yes," agreed Cain. "As some fabrics can turn or blunt a bullet and yet still be slit through by a knife blade, so was this wondrous beast slain. An almost humorous irony, its skin, capable of turning meteors, had been pierced by one of the recording struts of the weather balloon. The more the great Old One struggled, the more entangled it became, the more it drove the broken strut into its vitals."

The sudden cheerful edge Cain's voice had taken on disturbed me greatly, although I could offer myself no reason for the uneasy feeling. In fact, I suddenly became aware that everything about the interview was beginning to disturb me. I felt that the darkness was closing in on me. I felt myself growing suspicious of the strange noises that interrupted Cain's monologue, and the bizarre—what could I call them—arguments, perhaps, that my patient lapsed into from time to time.

I even found part of my brain listening to Cain's tone and the rhythm of his speech, positive that his voice had changed significantly since the beginning of the interview. Reminding my paranoia that differing emotions can cause fluctuations in the pitch and meter of human voices, I snarled at the runaway edginess slithering through my body, trying to get myself back under control.

And yet, as Cain described the procedures he and West used to examine the great star creature, I could not shake the violent conviction rooting itself throughout the soil of my consciousness that something was dreadfully, terribly wrong. I cursed my unexplainable lack of nerve. There was nothing so unusual, so bizarre to require me to respond in such a fashion, I told myself. Yes, certainly the subject matter being discussed grew more fantastical by the minute, but since when was a psychiatrist supposed to be disturbed by the rantings of one of their patients?

In many ways I was simply furious with myself. So I was sitting in the dark. So Cain's voice had taken on an almost sinister tone. So he wove tales of nightmare and horror. So what? I could not believe the reaction the situation was inducing within me. But, no matter what I could believe, the reaction was real and growing.

I felt an unease I had not known since I had found myself sitting in the back of an Army medical vehicle on the German front only a few short years ago. I was supposedly safe, safe enough. And yet, you always found yourself thinking, all it might take was an errant shell, an off-course bomber, a land mine . . . maybe this was the day, any minute, something could go wrong—just one misstep, one tiny error . . .

My hands were slick with a cold, yet sticky sweat that I seemed incapable of wiping away no matter how hard I tried. My bones ached, my muscles knotted, my nerves were inflamed. Insanely, I closed my eyes against the darkness, grinding my teeth together to keep them from chattering.

At that point it took the rigid summoning of all my will power to keep myself from fleeing the room. And why—why, I did not know. I begged myself for an answer, but none revealed itself. Why was Cain's voice so frightening to me? What could possibly be so terrifying about a man so withdrawn from the world that he insisted on living in darkness, surrounded by a double layer of windowless walls? What it was, I did not know. I could only think that something in the air of the room had chilled me so utterly that I no longer felt I could control my actions.

My arms began shaking uncontrollably at that point, my fingers trembling. As I wrapped them around myself, hugging myself, pressing my chin to my chest, doubling over, forcing my feet flat against the floor, I could feel tears forcing themselves through my tight clamped eyes, could taste the bile and mucus clustering in my throat.

"Are you listening to me, doctor?"

Terror and confusion blasted through my mind as I sought to answer Cain's smirking question. When later I played back the tape, I realized my patient had talked for almost fifteen minutes without my hearing a word. He had gone through the complete checklist of his examination of the creature, as well as the application of West's potions to the deceased alien.

Knowing from Cain's condescending tone that he knew the truth about my inattention, still I pretended otherwise at that moment, asking him to continue. With a damning snicker, he went on with his story.

"Actually, there isn't much more to tell, Dr. Whittaker. At that point it was only a matter of moments until the creature began to stir. It was, of course, West's greatest moment of triumph. No matter what happened from that moment forward, he had proved himself, had carved for himself a place in the annals of medicine for all time. For, he had not merely reanimated simple human tissue this time. No, finally he had proved that his formulas were not just tied to the basic molecules of human life, but to the firmament of *all* life— to the very building blocks of the universe *itself!*"

Cain fell into another sudden bout of strangled whispers. This one was quite prolonged, accompanied by sounds which could mean nothing else save that my patient was slapping himself. In the thin silver coming from under the door, I watched his intravenous bottle shaking on its hanger, but I did nothing. I did not call out, I did not go to him. I simply waited for the unknown inevitability which I knew with sickening certainty was racing toward me.

"It sat up on the table, staring at us, at everyone in the room, the five points of its star shaped head taking in the entire chamber. I thrilled to see its various membranes, the delicate gills and pores of it, testing themselves, instantly deciding what kind of atmosphere it was in, involuntary reactions reasserting their independence. The creature stood up on the table, its wings half-folded, staring about itself. For a brief moment, it was like a utopian vision, the wise and advanced stranger staring down on its lesser brothers, grateful for its life, ready to share the bounties of the universe with us." There came a cold laugh from behind the curtains, after which my patient added,

"And then, reality came crashing down upon us all."

At that point if I had possessed the strength—*any* strength, *any* of my own will—I would have fled the room. I no longer cared about this report, about my patient or my country or anything but escaping the vile and odious sound of the belittling voice oozing toward me from behind the curtains. Helpless I had been, though, and helpless I remained.

"Amazingly, from within a fold of its own skin, the creature removed a marvelously intricate device. It was delicate in both size and design, fashioned from some alloy that shone with a blue-green radiance. Despite its appearance, however, the instrument's function was decidedly not delicate. Before any of us could sense the device's purpose, the creature aimed it at the largest knot of men within the hanger and released a shimmering ray utilizing some principle of energy unknown to this world."

"What happened?" I choked.

"Men died," said my patient simply. "By the dozens, possibly by the hundreds. Their clothing and skin exploded into flame, blood boiling, erupting through their flesh, hair afire, nails and teeth melting, bones burning, eyes sizzling, popping—fluid bursting from their bodies, steaming away to mist as it arced away from each ruined host."

"And yet," I somehow found the strength to say—to accuse, really, "You survived."

"Of course I survived, Dr. Whittaker," came the voice from beyond the curtain once more. "I always survive."

I knew the truth then. Actually, I'd known it far earlier. I'd simply refused to believe it until that moment. As I forced myself to my feet, a hand grabbed at the curtains.

"The beast took maybe only a half dozen rounds from the bewildered, frightened troops surrounding it. Peanuts hurled at an elephant. It shrugged off their attack and murdered them all. I had shoved Cain out of the line of fire, knowing that the alien would first slaughter those who seemed an immediate threat."

"How?" I demanded, knowing the answer. "*How* did you know?"

A second hand grabbed at the curtains beyond.

"Because I had transferred my mind into the alien's brain, of course. Do you think I would let such an opportunity pass me by? Do you think me such a fool?"

Another hand grabbed the edge of the curtain, and then another, and finally, the walls of cloth began to part.

"I felt my body being cut down, but it did not matter. Housing myself within the mind of the great Old One—to be given a chance to raid its storehouse of otherworldly secrets—was ample reward for something so trivial as a sack of oh-so-easily replaced flesh and blood and bone."

I staggered up out of my chair. In doing so I inadvertently kicked over my recording machine. Thus, I have no audible record of what happened from that point on, but it does not matter, for I will never forget any aspect of what happened next. Hearing the curtains sliding apart, metal rings grating against metal piping, I felt my fingers gliding along the wall near the door.

Part of me was searching for the exit knob, but another, braver, far more insane part of me was fumbling for the light switch. Cursedly, curiosity won out. I heard the multiple thud of bare feet striking the floor. My fingers found the light switch. The room was flooded with brilliance. I was blinded for a moment, and then I was damned.

"Now, Dr. Whittaker," came the mocking voice once more, "be a good boy and take off your clothes."

I stared numbly, my fingers moving to do West's bidding. My mouth hung open, saliva dripping. My eyes bulged, unblinking. Before me stood Cain, exactly as he looked in the photographs I had been shown previous to entering his room. And, there next to him, *growing out of his side*, was a newly born Herbert West.

Suddenly, all made sense. The insistence on extreme privacy, the continuous intravenous drips, the strange noises and bizarre arguments. And, other things as well.

"You entered my mind as well, didn't you?"

"Of course, doctor. I really didn't have the time to wait for you to reach all those conclusions by yourself. In fact, I'm there right now, exerting enough pressure to ensure your cooperation. Now, you will give me your clothing and then you will climb into the bed here and there you will remain until someone finds you. What you do after that, Dr. Whittaker, frankly, I don't care. The entirety of the world is within my reach now. Nothing you do or say is going to change that . . . is it, Daniel?"

The pitifully drooped and defeated head of West's assistant shook itself sadly from side to side. And then, West jerked his new body savagely, ripping away the already drying umbilical membrane that had been connecting them together. There was a horrid ripping, a splash of congealing fluids, and a gurgling laughter which promised horrors I could only guess at.

Shamefully, I confess I fainted at that point, my brain overloaded to the point of insanity. But, even in abject defeat, I could not escape the monster's grasp. Much as I wanted to simply surrender to unconsciousness and crumple to the floor, since that did not fit West's plans, I did not fall.

At the madman's mental direction, my body continued to undress itself even as I sat back in a hysterical dither, silently screaming within the confines of my skull. Before I knew it, West was wearing my suit and smock. With Cain in tow he left the room without another word, even as I obediently climbed into the bed they had just vacated. Without hesitation I slid into the pool of sticky purple staining the sheet. And there I stayed until found by an orderly several hours later.

Exactly as West had ordered.

From here on in, you know the rest. No trace of either West or Cain has yet to be found. Intelligence has declared that they both have disappeared without a trace, and there is nothing I can add to that report. What next will come from the fevered mind of this monster, I have no idea. And, I must admit, I believe I am glad of that fact, for already my brain can not hold the amount of foul baggage unloaded there by my brief contact with West's mind.

CONCLUSION:

I have thought on this long and hard. There is nothing more I can add. You have the tapes of the session. What happened to the great Star-Headed Old One, West did not reveal. Where either of them has gone, or what they are planning, I can not say. I can not even guess.

But, I can tell you one thing. For some time during my interview with my patient, I was somewhat hostile to Dr. Cain. I thought, if the stories he told about West were actual, if even half of them were true, then I thought Cain contemptible for not finding some way to rid the world of such a monster.

Now, however, I have felt the beast within my brain, and I know such a thing can not be done. There is no defiance possible. He is Herbert West, and we are but men. There is no resisting him. There will only be the fear in the waiting to see what it is he will do next. I am sorry to say I do not have the courage to face that moment of discovery with the rest of you.

My will is attached to these papers. I believe the place I have picked to leave them will make them easy to discover, and yet keep them safe from any splatter or ruin. I apologize to you all. I'm sorry. So sorry, I can not say.

Do not worry about me, however. You do not have the time to waste. Not as long as Herbert West remains alive. Again, I'm sorry. I'm just so sorry.

The Worm
John Bruni

THE STAIRS CREAKED, and Pete Jervis ground his teeth. A soft thump, followed by another, reverberated in his skull, and while the gentle sound shouldn't have been intrusive, to Pete it was almost as bad as a rusty chainsaw.

He forced his eyes to the papers in his hand. There were copies of several contracts on and around his desk, but most of them weren't worth the paper they were printed on. Only one showed promise, but he would have to go to great monetary risk before convincing a financer to invest. It was *step* a tough decision *step* and he really couldn't *step* have his thoughts *step* interrupted at such a vital—

"Petey?" The low tone of his mother's voice stabbed into his ears like a baby's cry in a theater, an unanswered phone ringing, and a dentist's drill, all combined into one. It took all his willpower not to yell, "What?!"

Instead he turned his gaze to her, eyebrows raised. From the look of things, she was at least five sheets to the wind, and from the way she gripped the handrail, she was ready for seven to ten more.

"I know you're busy," she said, her face scrunched up. She wasn't even looking at him. "I was wondering . . ."

"Yes?" His voice was sharp, and he didn't feel bad about it.

"Do you have anything? I'll pay for it."

He thought about the bottle of Ten High he'd hidden in a trashcan between his bookcase and a bunch of filing cabinets, where he knew she couldn't reach. He used to keep his whiskey under the bed, but he noticed some of it would occasionally go missing, and it didn't take a rocket scientist—or even a math teacher—to figure out what was happening.

"I don't have anything." Pete turned back to the contract.

"I'll give you ten bucks, just please give me something."

Pete could feel his jaw groan, and he tried to unclench his teeth. "I told you, I have nothing." He read the same sentence for a third time and hoped desperately that he could make it through the rest of the paragraph.

He did, but he didn't need ESP to sense his mother's unmoving presence at the foot of the stairs. *Maybe she's so drunk it's taking a moment for my words to sink in,* he thought.

New paragraph. Halfway through the first sentence, she said, "Could you go out and get me something. Please?"

Pete sighed through his nose. "Look, I have a lot of work in front of me. If I'm ever going to move out of this place again, I need to work, okay?"

Her nose started turning red, and she was squinting, sure signs that she was about to cry. When she inhaled, it sounded like she was snorting the dregs of a milkshake up through her nose. "I'd go myself, but I'm not well right now. I need something! Please! I'll give you money. You can keep the change. I just . . . I'm not okay right now."

There once was a time when he would have refused her request. Back then he'd been a much more optimistic man, but recent events had crushed his faith in the world. Back then he'd thought he could cure his mother, but now he knew better.

Now he knew that all he could do was get her off his back.

Pete held out his hand. "Fine. What do you want?"

She gave him a twenty. "Tequila. I need something that will put me down quick. And get the kind with the worm in it. I like the worm."

Pete grimaced. It was actually a butterfly larva, and the beverage was technically called mescal, but he couldn't understand how anyone could drink anything with an insect in it. A turd by any other name . . .

He pocketed the money. "I'll be back in a few."

As it turned out, his gas tank was nearly empty, and he only had five bucks, which was only good for about one gallon in these godforsaken times. So his mother's change would probably help out, at least until the next unemployment check showed up.

It rankled him to live with his mom at the age of thirty-seven, especially since he'd been worth several million dollars only a few years ago. Like many businessmen, Pete had been swept up in the dot-com craze, but like many less-than-shrewd businessmen, he was too busy flashing green and getting laid to notice that the bottom was about to drop out. He'd lost everything, and he spent his days writing business proposals and sending them out to any venture financer who would talk to him. It was a shame most of the contracts turned out to be stupid. The few he'd managed to get signed either went bust or he barely managed to break even.

The one that held promise was practical, but he needed to kick in fifty thousand dollars, of which he only had half. He could probably hunt and scavenge for the rest of it, pull in every favor he was owed, but if the venture failed, he'd be back to square one, and probably working at a McDonald's to make ends meet.

He pulled into the lot and parked near the door. The sign above said WILLIAMS LIQUORS, but only the latter part was lit up. The rest was dirty, gray, and cracked. A bullet hole in the window was taped over, and a dark stain by the door reeked of puke and piss. At least it was fall; the stink was worse in the summer.

Pete walked in and was greeted by the clerk. They didn't know each other's names, but they were familiar enough for the usual how's-it-going-nice-day-isn't-it-getting-lucky?-etc. He went to the tequila section. Most was of the usual non-worm variety, but on the bottom shelf he found a bottle of mescal. The worm looked different, however. Usually it was red, or on occasion white (much to the purists' dismay), but this one was flesh colored. If not for the segments, he would have thought it was a pinkie finger.

It twitched.

If he hadn't been holding the bottle with both hands, he would have dropped it, and his mom would never let him hear the end of it. When he peered in the bottle again, the worm was still, and he decided the movement had been a hallucination. Too many hours writing too many contracts.

He considered getting a different bottle, but then he realized it didn't matter. His mother was only going to swill it down; she probably wouldn't even taste the booze, much less the worm. He rubbed the bags under his eyes and went to the counter.

After dumping eight-fifty-six into his gas tank, he went home and surrendered the bottle to his mother. She didn't thank him, she just shuffled off to her room like an old Eskimo wandering into the wilderness to die.

Pete retreated to his basement bedroom, to the contracts. He considered taking a snort of his Ten High, but he knew it would lead to nothing good at this late hour.

While her son went back to work below her, Mindy Jervis settled into her couch and began flipping through TV stations. Absently, her fingers wrapped around the cap and tugged until the neck ring broke away. She placed the cold circle of glass to her lips and drank from the bottle. When she was younger, she used to pour it into a cup, but she was a much different person now.

Now she realized the futility of extra receptacles. Besides, she'd only have to wash a cup later. With a bottle, all you had to do was throw it away.

She didn't grimace as the gasoline-like fluid went down her throat; she barely felt the burn. Though many images flew past her blank eyes, she stared *through* the TV screen as if it was a Mind's Eye puzzle.

The secrets of the universe were not divulged to her.

All she had were her thoughts and memories, no matter how hard she tried to smother them with drink.

It was on this very couch that Petey had been conceived. In those days, it had been in her parents' house, but when she married Phil, she took it with her. When her mom and dad were out at a party, Mindy had invited Phil over. One thing had led to another, which had in turn led to Petey.

She was really grateful for her son's existence. After him there had been two pregnancies, and both had been stillborn. They had also ruined her body inside and out. There would be no more children for her, and even if she weren't barren, her saggy frame would repel any suitors. If they could get past her flabby breasts and floppy folds of loose flesh, they would probably not get by the ring of stretch marks around her torso. If all else failed, she was certain *no one* would get past the c-section scar. Hell, *she* couldn't get past it. She couldn't stand the sight of her own body.

Neither could Phil. He cheated on her for a while, and then he divorced her. The alimony was nice, but Mindy would trade it all in an instant for the loving touch of a man, which she had not felt for about twenty years.

The bottle was already three-quarters empty. How long had it been since Petey had given it to her? Just a couple of hours?

She tried to slow down, but her need wouldn't let her. A half an hour later—not that she was aware of the passage of time—she was down to the last inch . . . and the worm.

Mindy had drunk her share of tequila in life, and she'd never seen a worm like this one. They were usually red or white, but this one looked flesh-colored.

In fact, it looked kind of like a withered penis.

She laughed, but it sounded like a gagging noise to her own ears. *Wishful thinking*, she thought, and she sucked down the rest of the bottle's contents.

The agave worm seemed thicker in her mouth than it had appeared in the bottle. It felt as stout as her tongue when she swallowed it. For a moment, she thought it had lodged itself in her throat, and she would start choking at any moment, but then it eased down into her. All was good.

You did it the wrong way.

She started. Had Petey entered her room? She looked around to find that she was alone.

Besides, she thought, *it sounded more like Phil.* And he'd had a heart attack last year, which he hadn't survived. She shivered.

Get me out. You put me in wrong.

She felt the urge to stick a finger down her throat. There was no reason, she just wanted to do it.

No, she couldn't. The tequila would come up, and that would be a shameful waste.

As it turned out, she needn't have concerned herself with this inner struggle; her head went down, and her throat closed, clogged with rushing vomit. Though she hadn't felt sick, it came spewing out of her like water from a faucet. It stank of pure alcohol, and there were no chunks.

Except one: the worm.

And it was spasming.

Pick me up and put me in right.

Her hand moved toward it, and there was nothing she could do to stop, even if she wanted to. Once it was in her grasp, it calmed down, and when she lifted the bottom of her nightgown, it went rigid and began to hum.

She stepped so softly he didn't hear her until her hands were on his shoulders.

Pete had been pouring over the specifics of the most promising contract, trying to write in loopholes where he might escape financial culpability. His lawyer could probably come up with something, but Pete was an old hand at this, so he hoped to work a bit of fine print in on his own.

His eyelids were starting to droop. The hour was late, and he figured it was time for bed. He was naked to his boxers and very comfortable, so he knew that if he didn't get under the covers now, he'd pass out at his desk.

When her pale hands slipped over the bronze mountains of his shoulders, he thought he'd fallen off the fence between reality and dream. When she squeezed and began to massage, he looked up to see his mother's face hovering over him, her long hair nearly tickling the top of his head.

"What's up?" he asked.

"It's two in the morning," she said. "You work too hard. You should get in bed."

"Yeah, that's what I was thinking."

He stood, letting her hands fall away, and went to his bed, where he sat on the edge. Only then did he notice how red her eyes were, as if she'd been crying for hours. "You okay?"

His mom bit her lower lip. "Not really. I've been thinking about your . . . your brothers, but mostly about your dad. And how empty I feel without him."

Pete sighed. This was the last thing he needed right now. Drama before bed was never good. Still, his mother allowed him to live here, so . . . "Aw, Mom. You should go out and date, like I always tell you. You wouldn't be so lonely."

"I can't." Her voice cracked on the second word, making it almost unintelligible, but she didn't bother to try again. "I'm ugly. No one would want me."

"Oh, come on. You're fine, Mom. You'll do okay."

She looked down at herself. "Do you think I'm ugly?"

Pete didn't think she was pretty. Good-looking, maybe, but definitely not ugly. "Trust me, Mom, you'd do fine."

Tears sprouted from the corners of her eyes, and she sat next to him on his bed, pressing her hot, wet face into his shoulder. Pete put his arm around her and whispered, "Shh. It's okay. You'll be all right. Do you want me to carry you upstairs?"

She sniffed. "You couldn't lift me. I'm too fat."

"Don't be ridiculous. I can pick you up."

She laughed through a throat full of snot. "Just sit here for a moment. I just want to spend a minute with my son."

He rubbed her shoulder and clasped her tighter. "Take your time." *It's not like I'm going to miss work tomorrow, or anything.*

She kissed his cheek. "You're a good son."

He closed his eyes, hoping she wouldn't take much longer. His pillow cried out to him.

Suddenly, there was a soft pressure on his lips, and his mouth was filled with tequila fumes. His eyes popped open, and he was looking at his mother's face, which was too close to his own.

"Whoa," he said, pulling away. "I think we need to get you upstairs."

Her face scrunched up, and she began sobbing. "Oh God, I'm sorry Petey! It's just that you look so much like your father, and I wish he was here. Please forgive me!" She placed both hands on his thigh and squeezed. By pure happenstance, one of her hands clasped down on the tip of his penis, pressing it against the inside of his leg. She didn't notice, but Pete did.

Though the horror of the situation had filled his belly with roiling, ulcerous fire, his traitorous body started reacting.

He pried her hands away and crossed his legs. "It's okay. We'll just get you upstairs, right?"

Both of her hands enveloped one of his, holding it so tightly she trembled. "I'm really sorry. Please forgive me, Petey. Please!"

His captive hand was suddenly warm and sticky, as if he'd put it in a freshly baked cake. Looking down, he noticed his mom had shoved it under her nightgown. His knuckles were sinking into her flesh, and he gagged.

"Mom! Stop! You need to go to bed!"

"I want you inside me," she whispered. Her head leaned forward for another kiss.

Pete backed away. "Look, I've got to get to bed, and so do you. I'll—"

"No!"

If she started struggling, and from the way her body tensed, it looked like she was getting ready to, there was no way he was going to be able to carry her up to her room. *Maybe I should just leave her down here, and then go upstairs to sleep.*

"Here, lean back," he said.

She didn't object as he pushed on her shoulder until she was on her back on the mattress. Then, just as he grabbed a handful of his blankets to throw over her, she opened her legs wide, showing off a pad of pale flesh with a thin scrim of dark pubic hair. A river of scar tissue, not unlike the white worm found in most tequila bottles, cut through the scant foliage between her legs. She was open and sopping wet.

He threw the blanket over her and said, "Goodnight."

Much to his surprise, her eyes were already closed, and her even breath indicated that she was finally asleep. He was about to sigh, but he had to restrain himself out of fear that she'd hear and wake up.

Sickness crawled up his guts and tickled the back of his tongue. Something burned inside of him as he looked down at her slumbering form. Could this be the same mother who had raised him? The same mother who volunteered to be a den mother for his Cub Scout pack when he was a kid? The same mother who had put Band-Aids on his skinned knees when he was trying to learn how to ride a bike?

I want you inside me.

The voice in his head was his mother's, and he knew nothing would ever be the same again.

You want me as much as I want you.

Again, it was his mother, but when had she said that?

You're poking out of your shorts, Petey.

He was. It was like the air was tugging on it, aiming it at his mother, as a dowsing rod would pull toward water. Revulsion ate its way through his stomach as he pushed himself back in and to the side. Without another glance at his mother, he headed for the stairs.

Don't go! Think of the things we could do!

He ignored the voice until he threw himself down on the living room couch. Then it grew stronger.

Think of all the women you could have brought home, it said. *You couldn't because you didn't want them to know you lived with your mother. No less than seven women this year alone! Isn't that pathetic?*

It was. His erection throbbed between his thighs.

Forget about them. They may be beautiful, but I will never stab you in the back. I will never embarrass you. I will always satisfy you.

He thought about what was under her nightgown. She'd told him she'd needed a c-section to get him out, but he'd always envisioned a Frankensteinian nightmare whenever she mentioned it. It hadn't looked that bad, actually.

Come downstairs. I'm waiting.

When was the last time he'd been laid? Back when he was rich, of course. He couldn't bear to bring women home to his mother. He was thirty-seven, for Christ's sake! He should have been out on his own again! What was wrong with him?

His erection throbbed so hard it felt like the glans was going to pop off, and he was no longer thinking with his big head.

Pete stood and allowed himself to pop out of his boxers again as he went downstairs and lifted his mother's blanket.

The next day, neither mother nor son could meet each other's eyes. They pretended nothing had happened, and while both suffered from stomach flops and burning throats, neither said a word. They avoided each other, and only said hi. Their tones were terse and clipped.

Months later, Mindy Jervis—who was once barren—was pregnant, and no matter how badly she wanted an abortion, all three million of her children did not let her get one.

Sepsis

Graham Masterton

"WHAT HAVE YOU GOT THERE?" she asked him, her eyes shining.

"Nothing—it's a surprise," he said, keeping the lapels of his overcoat drawn tightly together.

"What *is* it?" she demanded. "I can't bear surprises!"

"It's something I bought specially for you, because I love you so much."

"Show me!"

She tried to circle around him and peer down the front of his coat, but he backed away from her. "Before I show you, you're going to have to make me a promise. You must promise to love this just as much as you love me."

"How can I, when I don't know what it is?"

"Because it's all of my love for you, all of it, all wrapped up in one little bundle."

"Show me!"

"Come on," he coaxed her. "If you don't promise, I'll take it back, and you'll never find out what it was."

"*Show* me!"

"Promise first!"

She took a deep breath. "All-right-whatever-you-have-in-your-coat-I-promise-to-love-it-just-as-much-as-I-love-you."

"Cross your heart and hope to die?"

"Cross my heart and hope to die."

Gently, he reached inside his coat and lifted out a tiny tortoiseshell kitten, with big green eyes. It gave a diminutive mew, and clung onto his lapel with its brambly little claws.

"Oh, it's a *darling*!" she said. "Oh, it's absolutely *perfect*!"

"What did I tell you? All of my love, all wrapped up in one little bundle. What are you going to call her?"

She took the kitten and cupped her in her hands, stroking the top of her head with her finger. "I don't know yet. But something romantic. Something really, really romantic."

She made a mewing noise, and the kitten mewed back. She did it again, and again the kitten copied her.

"There! I'll call her Echo."

"*Echo*? What's that? Sounds more like a newspaper than a cat."

"No, silly, it's Greek mythology."

"If you say so."

"Echo was a beautiful, beautiful nymph, the most beautiful nymph that ever was."

"Oh, yeah? So what happened to her?"

"Everybody loved Echo but Zeus' grumpy old wife Hera got mad at her because she kept Hera talking while Zeus had hanky-panky with another goddess. Hera cursed her so that she could never speak her own words ever again—only the last words that were spoken to her by somebody else."

He shook his head in admiration. "Do you know something, I think I love your brain as much as your body. Well, *almost* as much. Unfortunately . . . your brain doesn't have breasts."

She threw a cushion at him.

His name was David Stavanger and her name was Melanie Angela Thomas. They were both 24 years old, although David was a Capricorn and Melanie was an Aries. Their star charts said that they should always be quarreling, but nobody who knew them had ever seen two people so much in love with each other. They lived and breathed each other, sharing everything from wine to whispers, and when they were together they radiated an almost palpable aura.

Some evenings they did nothing but gaze at each other in awed silence, as if neither of them could believe that God had brought them another human being so desirable. And they *were* desirable, both of them. David was 6ft 2ins tall with cropped blond hair and a strong, straight-nosed Nordic face that he had inherited from his grandfather. He was broad-shouldered, fit, and one of the most impressive wide receivers that the Green Bay Packers had fielded for over a decade. Melanie was small and slim, with glossy brunette hair that almost reached the small of her back. She had the dreamy, heavy-lidded beauty of a girl in a Pre-Raphaelite painting, as if she passed her time wandering through fields of poppies in poppy-colored velvet. She had graduated with a first-class English degree from the University of Wisconsin in Green Bay and now she was working as a contributing editor for *MidWest* magazine.

They had met when Melanie was sent to interview pro football players about their private lives. Her first question had been, "What kind of girls appeal to you the most?" and without blinking David had answered, "You."

* * * *

David and Melanie shared a ground-floor apartment in a large white-painted house in a street in Ashwaubenon lined with sugar maples. David drove a blue Dodge pickup and Melanie had a new silver Volkswagen Beetle. The evening after David brought Echo home, Melanie was sitting on the front verandah on the swing-seat, with Echo in her lap, while David went jogging.

It was one of those evenings in late August when the moths patter against the lamps and the chilly dew begins to settle on the lawn and you can feel that somewhere in the far northwest, Mr Winter is already sharpening his cutlery.

Mr Kasabian came down from the first-floor apartment to put out the trash. He looked like Gepetto, the puppet-maker who had carved Pinocchio, with a yardbrush moustache and circular eyeglasses and a black shiny vest. When he saw Echo dancing in Melanie's lap he climbed up onto the verandah to take a closer look.

"Cute little fellow."

"Girl, actually. David brought her home yesterday."

"Reminds me of my Wilma," said Mr Kasabian, wistfully. "My Wilma used to love her cats."

"You must miss her so bad."

Mr Kasabian nodded. "It'll be three years this November 12th, but believe me it's still a shock when I wake up in the morning and I put out my hand and find that she's not there any more."

"I don't know what I'd do if I lost David."

"With the grace of God you won't have to think about that until you've both lived a long and happy life."

Mr Kasabian went back inside, and just then David appeared around the corner in his green-and-white tracksuit, his Nikes slapping on the sidewalk. "Thirty-one minutes eighteen seconds!" he gasped, triumphantly. He came up onto the verandah and gave her a kiss.

"You're so *sweaty*!" she said.

"Sorry—I'll hit the shower. Do you want to get me a beer?"

"No," she said, and clung onto his tracksuit. "Come here, I *love* you all sweaty."

He kissed her again and she licked his lips and his cheeks and then she ran her fingers into his hair and pulled him closer so that she could lick the sweat from his forehead.

"Hey—beats the shower," said David, kissing her again and again.

She tugged open his zipper and buried her face inside his tracksuit, licking his glistening chest.

"Come on inside," she said, picking up Echo and taking hold of his hand.

In the living-room, she pulled off his tracksuit top and licked his shoulders and his back and his stomach. "I love the taste of you," she said. "You taste like salt and honey, mixed."

He closed his eyes. His chest was still rising and falling from his running.

She guided him over to the couch so that he could sit down. She unlaced his Nikes and peeled off his sports socks. Kneeling in front of him she licked the soles of his feet and slithered her tongue in between his toes, like a pink seal sliding amongst the rocks. Then she untied the cord around his waistband and pulled down his pants, followed by his white boxer shorts.

While he lay back on the couch she licked him everywhere, all around his sweaty scrotum and deep into the crevice of his buttocks. She wanted every flavor of him, the riper the better. She wanted to own the taste of him, completely.

And that was how it started.

Every night after that they would tongue-bathe each other all over, and then lie in each other's arms, breathing each other's breath, their skins sticky with drying saliva. Every night he would bury his face between her thighs, licking her and drinking her, and she would suck his glans so hard that he yelped in pain. When he did that, Echo would mew, too.

One night, eleven days later, he lifted his head and his chin was bearded in scarlet. He kissed her, and she licked it off his face, and then he dipped his head down for more.

Melanie's parents took them out for dinner at MacKenzie's Steak and Seafood. They sat close to each other, their fingers twisted together, staring at each other in the candlelight.

Her father looked at her mother after a while and raised one eyebrow. He was a lean, quiet-spoken man with brushed-back silver hair and a large, hawk-like nose. Her mother looked almost exactly like Melanie, except her hair was bobbed short and highlighted blonde and her figure was fuller. She was wearing a bright turquoise dress, while Melanie was all in black.

"So . . . do you two lovebirds have any plans to get married yet?" asked Mr Thomas. "Or is that me being old-fashioned?"

"I think we're past getting married," said Melanie, still smiling at David.

"*Past* getting married? What does that mean?"

"It means that we're much, much closer than any wedding ceremony could make us."

"I'm sorry, I don't get it."

Melanie turned to her father and touched his hand. "You and mom were so lucky to find each other . . . But sometimes two people can fall in love so much that they're both the same person . . . they don't just share each other, they *are* each other."

Her father shook his head. "That's a little beyond me, I'm afraid. I was just wondering if you'd considered the financial advantages of being married." He grunted, trying to make a joke of it. "Huh—I don't exactly know what tax breaks you two can expect from being the same person."

Their meals arrived. They had all chosen steak and lobster, apart from Melanie, who had ordered a seared tuna salad. Their conversation turned to the football season, and then to the latest John Grisham novel that Melanie's father had been reading, and then to one of Melanie's friends from *MidWest* magazine, who had been diagnosed with cervical cancer at the age of 26.

"She wants her ashes spread on her vegetable patch, would you believe, so that her boyfriend will actually eat her."

"I think that's so morbid," said Melanie's mother.

"I don't. I think it's beautiful."

David poured her another glass of white wine. "How's your tuna?"

"It's gorgeous. Do you want to try some?"

"No, that's okay."

"No, go on, try some."

With that, she leaned across and kissed him, ostentatiously pushing a half-masticated wad of fish into his open mouth. David took it, and chewed it, and said, "Good. Yes, you're right."

Melanie's parents stared at them in disbelief. David turned to them unabashed. "It's really good," he confirmed, and swallowed.

The next day Melanie's mother phoned her at work.

"I'm worried about you."

"Why? I'm fine. I've never been so happy in my life."

"It's just that your relationship with David—well, it seems so *intense*."

"That's because it *is* intense."

"But the way you act together . . . I don't know how to say this, really. All this kissing and canoodling and sharing your food. Apart from anything else, it's embarrassing for other people."

"Mom, we love each other. And like I said to dad, we're not just partners, we're the same person."

"I know. But everybody needs a little space in their lives . . . a little time to be themselves. I adore your father, but I always enjoy it when he goes off for a game of golf. For a few hours, I can listen to the music I want to listen to, or arrange flowers, or talk to my friends on the phone. I can just be *me*."

"But David *is* me. The same way that I'm David."

"It worries me, that's all. I don't think it's healthy."

"Mother! You make it sound like a disease, not a relationship."

October came. David started to miss practice at Lambeau Field and Melanie began to take afternoons off work, simply so that they could lie naked on the bed together in the wintry half-darkness and lick each other and stare into each other's eyes. Their greed for each other was insatiable. When they were out walking in the cold, and Melanie's nose started to run, David licked it for her. In the privacy of their own bedroom and bathroom, there was nothing that they wouldn't kiss or suck or drink from each other.

They visited their parents and their friends less and less. When they did, they were no company at all, because they spent the whole time caressing each other, deaf and blind to everybody and everything else.

One afternoon when it was beginning to snow, the Packers' assistant head coach Jim Pulaski came around to their apartment. He was a squat man with bristly gray hair and a broad Polish-looking face, deeply lined by years of standing on the touchline. He sat on the couch in his sheepskin coat and warned David that if he missed one more practice he was off the team. "You're a star, David, no question. But the cheeseheads are more important than the stars, and every time you don't show up for practice you're letting the cheeseheads down." "Cheeseheads" was the nickname that the Packers gave their supporters.

Without taking his eyes off Melanie, David said, "Sorry, coach? What did you say?"

"Nothing," said Mr Pulaski, and after a long while he stood up, tugged on his fur-lined hat, and let himself out of the front door. As he crunched across the icy driveway out he met Mr Kasabian struggling in with his shopping bags. He took one of them and helped him up the porch steps.

"Thanks," said Mr Kasabian, his breath smoking in the cold. "I'm always afraid of falling. At my age, you fall, you break your hip, they take you to hospital, you die."

"You live upstairs?"

"That's right. Twenty-seven years this Christmas."

"You see much of David and Melanie?"

"I used to."

"Used to?"

"Not these days. These days, *pfff*, they make me feel like the Indivisible Man."

"You and everybody else."

Mr Kasabian nodded toward the green Toyota parked at the curb with *Green Bay Packers* lettered on the side. "David's in trouble?"

"You could say that. We're going to have to can him unless he gets his act together. Even when he *does* show up for practice he's got his head up his ass."

"Mister, I don't know what to tell you. I was in love with my wife for thirty-eight years but I never saw two people like this before. This isn't just smooching, this is like some kind of hypnotized hypnosis. If you ask me, this is all going to turn out very, very bad."

Mr Kasabian stood in the whirling snow and watched as the coach drove away. Then he looked back at the light in the downstairs window and shook his head.

Three days before Christmas, Echo went missing. Melanie searched for her everywhere: in the cupboards, behind the couch, under the cushions, down in the cellar. She even went outside and called for her under the crawlspace, even though Echo hated the cold. No Echo. Only the echo of her own voice in the white, wintry street. "Echo! *Echo!*"

When David came back from the store she was sitting in her rocking-chair in tears, with the drapes half-drawn.

"I can't find Echo."

"She has to be someplace," he said, picking up cushions and newspapers as if he expected to find her crouching underneath.

"I haven't seen her all day. She must be so hungry."

"Maybe she went out to do her business and one of the neighbors picked her up."

They knocked on every door on both sides of the street, all wrapped up in their coats and scarves. The world was frigid and silent.

"You haven't seen a tortoiseshell kitten, have you?"

Regretful shaking of heads.

Right at the end of the street, they were answered by an elderly woman with little black darting eyes and a face the color of liverwurst.

"If I hev, den vot?"

"You've seen her? She's only about this big and her name's Echo."

"There's a reward," David put in.

"Revord?"

"Fifty dollars to anybody who brings her back safe."

"I never sin such a kitten."

"You're sure?"

"She's of . . . great sentimental value," Melanie explained. "Great *emotional* value. She represents—well, she represents my partner and myself. Our love for each other. That's why we have to have her back."

"A hundred dollars," said David.

"Vy you say hundert dollar?"

"Because—if you've seen her—if you *have* her—"

"Vot I say? I tell you I never sin such a kitten. Vot does it matter, fifty dollar, hundert dollar? You tell me I lie?"

"Of course not. I didn't mean that at all. I just wanted to show you how much we'd appreciate it if you *did* have her. Which, of course, you don't."

The woman pointed her finger at them. "Bad luck to you to sink such a bad sing. Bad luck, bad luck, bad luck."

With that, she closed the door and they were left on the porch with snow falling silently on their shoulders.

"Well, *she* was neighborly," said David.

They searched until eleven o'clock at night, and one by one the houses in the neighborhood blinked into darkness. At last they had to admit that there was no hope of them finding Echo until morning.

"I'll make some posters," said Melanie, lying on her stomach with her night-shirt drawn to her armpits, while David steadily licked her back.

"That's a great idea . . . we could use one of those pictures that we took of her on the verandah."

"Oh, I feel so sorry for her, David . . . she's probably feeling so cold and lost."

"She'll come back," said David. "She's our love together, isn't she? That's what she is. And our love's going to last for ever."

He continued to lick around her buttocks and the backs of her thighs, while she lay on the pillow with tears steadily dripping down the side of her nose. After he had licked the soles of her feet, he came up the bed again and licked her face.

"Salt," he said.

"Sorrow," she whispered.

The next morning the sky was as dark as slate and it was snowing again. Melanie designed a poster on her PC and printed out over a hundred copies. *Lost, tortoiseshell kitten, only three months old, answers to the name of Echo. Embodies owners' undying love so substantial reward for finder.*

David went from street to street, tacking the posters onto trees and palings. The streets were almost deserted, except for a few 4x4s silently rolling through the snow, like mysterious hearses.

He came back just before twelve. Melanie said, "The head coach called. He wants you to call him back. He didn't sound very happy."

David held her close and kissed her forehead. His lips were cold and her forehead was warm. "It's not important any more, is it? The world outside."

"Aren't you going to call him?"

"Why should I? What does it matter if *he's* happy or not? So long as we are. The most important thing is to find Echo."

More days went by. The phone rang constantly but unless it was somebody calling about Echo they simply hung up without saying any more and after a while it hardly ever rang at all. The mailman went past every day but they never went to the mailbox to collect their letters.

One of Melanie's editors called around in a black beret and a long black fur coat and rang the doorbell for over quarter of an hour, but eventually she went away. David and Melanie lay in each other's arms, sometimes naked, sometimes half-dressed, while the snow continued to fall as if it were never going to stop. They ate well and drank well, but as the days went by their faces took on an unhealthy transparency, as if the loss of Echo had weakened their emotional immune systems, and infected their very souls.

Early one Thursday morning, before it grew light, David was woken up by Melanie shaking him.

"David! David! It's *freezing!*"

He sat up. She was right. The bedroom was so cold that there were starry ice-crystals on the inside of the windows where their breath had frozen in the night.

"Jesus, the boiler must have broken down."

He climbed out of bed while Melanie bundled herself even more tightly in the quilt. He took his blue toweling bathrobe from the back of the chair, shuffled into his slippers, and went shivering along the corridor to the cellar door. Their landlady Mrs Gustaffson had promised to have the boiler serviced before winter set in, but Mrs Gustaffson had a tendency to forget anything which involved spending money.

David switched on the light and went down the cellar stairs. The cellar was crowded mostly with Mrs Gustaffson's junk: a broken couch, a treadle sewing-machine, various assorted pieces of timber and tools and picture-frames and hosepipes and bits of bicycle. Dried teazles hung from the ceiling-beams, as well as oil-lamps and butcher hooks.

The huge old oil-fired boiler which stood against the far wall was silent and stone-cold. It looked like a Wurlitzer juke-box built out of rusty cast-iron. It couldn't have run out of oil—Green Bay Heating had filled the tank up only three weeks ago. More likely the burners were clogged, or else the outside temperature had dropped so far that the oil in the pipes had solidified. That would mean going out into the yard with a blowtorch to get it moving again.

David checked the valves and the stopcocks, and as he was leaning around the back of the boiler he became aware of a sweet, cloying smell. He sniffed, and sniffed again, and leaned around the side of the boiler so that he could look behind it. It was too dark for him to see anything, so he went back upstairs to the kitchen and came back with his flashlight.

He pointed the beam diagonally downward between the pipes, and saw a few black-and-gray tufts of fur. "Oh, shit," he breathed, and knelt down on the floor as close to the boiler as he could. He managed to work his right arm in between the body of the boiler and the brick wall, but his forearm was too thick and muscular and he couldn't reach far enough.

Back in the bedroom Melanie was still invisibly wrapped up in the quilt and a sickly yellow sunshine was beginning to glitter on the ice-crystals on the windows.

"Is it fixed yet?" she asked him. "It's like an igloo in here."

"I'm—ah—I've found something."

When he didn't say anything else, she drew down the quilt from her face and stared at him. There were tears in his eyes and he was opening and closing his fists.

"You've found something? What?"

"It's Echo."

"You found Echo! That's wonderful! Where is she?"

"She's dead, Mel. She must have gone behind the boiler to keep warm, and gotten trapped or something."

"Oh, no, say it isn't true. Please, David, say it isn't true."

"I'm sorry, Mel." David sat down on the edge of the bed and took hold of her hand.

"It was that woman, that woman putting a curse on us! She wished us bad luck, didn't she, and now Echo's dead, and Echo's your *love*, David, all in one bundle."

"I still love you, Mel. You know that."

"But I promised to love her as much as I love you. I promised. I swore to you."

"There's nothing we can do."

Melanie sat up. "Where is she? Did you bring her upstairs?"

"I can't get her out. I tried but the gap behind the boiler's too tight."

"Then I'll have to do it."

"Mel, you don't have to. I can ask Mr Kasabian to do it. He used to be a vet, remember."

"Mr Kasabian isn't here. He went to see his daughter in Sheboygan yesterday. No, David. Echo is mine and *I'll* do it."

He stood beside her, feeling helpless, while she knelt down beside the boiler and reached into the narrow crevice at the back. At last, with her cheek pressed right against the cold iron casing, she said, "Got her . . . I can feel her." She tugged, and tugged again, and then she drew her hand out, holding nothing but a small furry leg.

"Oh my God, she's fallen apart." She dropped the leg and quickly stood up, her hand clamped over her mouth, retching. David put his arms around her and said, "Leave it, just leave it. I'll get the handyman to do it."

Melanie took three deep breaths, and then she said, "No . . . I have to get her out. She's mine, she's the love you gave me. It has to be me."

She knelt down and slid her hand in behind the boiler again. David looked into her eyes while she struggled to extricate Echo's body. She kept swallowing with disgust, but she wouldn't give up. At last, very slowly, she managed to lift the dead kitten up from the floor, so that she could reach over the pipes with her other hand and grasp it by the scruff of its neck.

Quaking with effort and revulsion, she stood up and cradled the body in her hands. The ripe stench of rotten kitten-flesh was almost unbearable. It was impossible for them to know exactly how long Echo had been trapped, but it must have been more than two weeks, and during that time she had been cooked by the heat of the boiler during the day, and then cooled by night, and then cooked again the following day, until her fur was scorched and bedraggled and her flesh was little more than blackened slime.

Echo's head lay in the palm of Melanie's right hand, staring up at David with eyes as white and blind as the eyes of a boiled codfish, her mouth half-open so that he could see her green glistening tongue.

"We can bury her," said David. "Look—there's an old toolbox there. We can use it as a casket. We can bury her in the yard so that she can rest in peace."

Melanie shook her head. "She's *us*, David. We can't bury her. She's you and me. She's all of your love, all wrapped up in one bundle, and all of my love, too, because you and me, we're the same person, and Echo was us, too."

David gently stroked the matted fur on Echo's upturned stomach. Inside, he heard a sticky, thick, glutinous sound, which came from Echo's putrescent intestines. "You're right," he said, his voice hoarse with emotion. "But if we don't bury her, what are we going to do?"

They sat facing each other on opposite sides of the scrubbed-pine kitchen table. The kitchen was even colder than the rest of the apartment, because the wind was blowing in through the ventilator hood over the hob. They had both put their duffel-coats on, and Melanie was even wearing red woolen mittens.

"This is your love," said Melanie. In front of her, on a large blue dinner-plate, lay Echo, resting on her side. "If it becomes part of me, then it can never, ever die . . . not as long as *I'm* alive, anyhow."

"I love you," David whispered. He looked years older, and whiter, almost like his own grandfather.

With both hands, Melanie grasped the fur around Echo's throat, and pulled it hard. She had to twist it this way and that, but at last she managed to break the skin apart She inserted two fingers, then four, and wrenched open the kitten's stomach inch by inch, with a sound like tearing linen. Echo's ribcage was exposed, with her lungs pale yellow and slimy, and then her intestines, in coils so green that they were luminous.

David stared at Melanie and he was shivering. The look on Melanie's face was extraordinary, beatific, St Melanie of the Sacred Consumption. She scooped her mittened hand into Echo's abdominal cavity and lifted out her stomach and strings of bowel and connective tissue. Then she bent her head forward and crammed them into her mouth. She slowly chewed, her eyes still open, and as she chewed the kitten's viscera hung down her chin in loops, and the duodenum was still connected to the animal's body by a thin, trembling web.

Melanie swallowed, and swallowed again. Then she pulled off one of Echo's hind legs, and bit into it, tearing off the fur and the flesh with her teeth, and chewing both of them. She did the same with her other leg, even though the thigh meat was so decomposed that it was more like black molasses than flesh, and it made the fur stick around Melanie's lips like a beard.

It took her almost an hour to eat Echo's body, although she gagged when she pushed the cat's spongy lungs into her mouth, and David had to bring her a glass of water. During all of this time, neither of them spoke, but they never took their eyes off each other. This was a ritual of transubstantiation, in which love had become flesh, and flesh was being devoured so that it could become love again.

At last, hardly anything remained of Echo but her head, her bones, and a thin bedraggled tail. David reached across the kitchen table and gripped Melanie's hands.

"I don't know where we go from here," he shivered.

"But we've done it. We're really one person. We can go anyplace we like. We can do anything we want."

"I'm frightened of us."

"You don't have to be. Nothing can touch us now."

David lowered his head, still gripping her fingers very tight. "I'd better . . . I'd better call the handyman."

"Not yet. Let's go back to bed first."

"I'm cold, Melanie. I never felt so cold in my life. Even when were playing in Chicago and the temperature was minus thirteen."

"I'll warm you up."

He stood up, but as he turned around Melanie suddenly let out a terrible cackling retch. She pressed her hand over her mouth, but her shoulders hunched in an agonizing terrible spasm and she vomited all over the table—skin, fur, bones and slippery lumps of rotten flesh. David held her close, but she couldn't stop herself from regurgitating everything that she had crammed down her throat.

She sat back, white-faced, sweating, sobbing.

"I'm sorry, I'm so sorry. I tried to keep it down. I tried so hard. It doesn't mean I don't love you. Please, David, it doesn't mean I don't love you."

David kissed her hair and licked the perspiration from her forehead and sucked the sour saliva from her lips. "It doesn't matter, Mel. You're right . . . we can do anything. We're one, that's all that counts. Look."

He picked up a handful of fur and intestine from the table and pushed it into his mouth. He swallowed it, and picked up another handful, and swallowed that, too.

"You know what this tastes like? This tastes like *we're* going to taste, when we die."

They lay in each other's arms all day and all night, buried in the quilt. The temperature dropped and dropped like a stone down a well. By mid-afternoon the following day, David had started to shake uncontrollably, and as it grew dark he began to moan and sweat and thrash from side to side.

"David . . . I should call the doctor."

"Anything we want—*anything*—"

"I could call Jim Pulaski, he could help."

David suddenly sat up rigid. "We're one! *We're one*! Don't let them take the offensive! Don't let them get past the fifty-yard line! We're one!"

She woke a few minutes after midnight and he was silent and still and cold as the air around them. The sheets were freezing, too, and when she lifted the quilt she discovered that his bowels and his bladder had opened and soaked the mattress. She kissed him and stroked his hair and whispered his name again and again, but she knew that he was gone. When morning came she cleaned him all over in the way that they had always cleaned each other, with her tongue, and then she laid him on the quilt naked with his eyes wide open and his arms outspread. She thought that she had never seen any man look so perfect.

It was mid-winter, of course, one of the coldest winters since 1965, and Mr Kasabian's sense of smell wasn't the most acute. But when he returned home on Friday morning he was immediately struck not only by the chill but by the thick, sour smell in the hallway. He knocked on David and Melanie's door and called out, "Melanie? David? You there?"

There was no answer, so he knocked again. "Melanie? David? Are you okay?"

He was worried now. Both of their automobiles were still in the driveway, covered with snow, and there were no footprints on their verandah, so they must be home. He tried to force open the door with his shoulder, but it was far too solidly-built and his shoulder was far too bony.

In the end he went upstairs and called Mrs Gustaffson.

"I think something bad has happened to Melanie and David."

"Bad like what? I have to be in Manitowoc in an hour."

"I don't know, Mrs Gustaffson. But I think it's something very, very bad."

Mrs Gustaffson arrived twenty minutes later, in her old black Buick. She was a large woman with colorless eyes and wiry gray hair and a double chin that wobbled whenever she shook her head, which was often. Mrs Gustaffson didn't like to say "yes" to anything.

She let herself in. Mr Kasabian was sitting on the stairs with a maroon shawl around his shoulders.

"Why is it so cold in here?" she demanded. "And what in God's name is that *smell*?"

"That's why I call you. I knock and I knock and I shout out, but nobody don't answer."

"Well, let's see what's going on, shall we?" said Mrs Gustaffson. She took out her keys, sorted through them until she found the key to David and Melanie's apartment. When she unlocked the door, however, she found that it was wedged from the other side, and she couldn't open it more than two or three inches.

"Mr Stavanger! Ms Thomas! This is Mrs Gustaffson! Will you please open the door for me?"

There was still no reply, but a chilly draft blew out of the apartment with a hollow, sorrowful moaning, and it carried with it a stench like nothing that Mrs Gustaffson had ever smelled before. She pressed her hand over her nose and mouth and took a step back.

"Do you think they're dead?" asked Mr Kasabian. "We should call the cops, I think so."

"I agree," said Mrs Gustaffson. She opened her large black crocodile purse and took out her cellphone. Just as she flipped it open, however, they heard a bumping sound from inside the apartment, and then a clang, as if somebody had dropped a saucepan on the kitchen floor.

"They're inside," said Mrs Gustaffson. "They're hiding for some reason. Mr Stavanger! Do you hear me! Ms Thomas! Open the door! I have to talk to you!"

No response. Mrs Gustaffson knocked and rattled the doorhandle, but she couldn't open the door any wider and even if David and Melanie were inside the apartment, they obviously had no intention of answering.

Mrs Gustaffson went along the hallway to the back of the house, closely followed by Mr Kasabian. She unlocked the back door and carefully climbed down the icy steps outside. "I told you to put salt on these steps, Mr Kasabian, didn't I? Somebody could have a very nasty accident."

"I did, last week only. Then it snow again and freeze over again."

Mrs Gustaffson made her way along the back of the house. There were no lights in any of the downstairs windows, and a long icicle hung from the bathroom overflow pipe, which showed that the bathroom hadn't been used for days.

At last she reached the kitchen window. The sill was too high for her to reach, so Mr Kasabian dragged over a small wooden trough in which he usually planted herbs, so that she could climb up on it. She wiped the frosty window with her glove, and peered inside.

At first she couldn't see nothing but shadows, and the faint whiteness of the icebox door. But then something moved across the kitchen, very slowly. Something bulky, with arms that swung limply at its side, and a strangely small head. Mrs Gustaffson stared at it for one baffled moment, and then she stepped down.

"Somebody's in there," she said, and her usually strident voice was like the croak of a child who has seen something in the darkness of her bedroom that is far too frightening to put into words.

"They're dead?" asked Mrs Kasabian.

"No, not dead. I don't know what."

"We should call the cops."

"I have to see what that is."

"That's not a good idea, Mrs Gustaffson. Who knows who that is? Maybe it's a murdering murderer."

"I have to know what I saw. Come with me."

"Mrs Gustaffson, I'm an old man."

"And I'm an old woman. What difference does that make?"

She climbed back up the steps to the back door, gripping the handrail. She went back inside and Mr Kasabian followed her to David and Melanie's door. She put her shoulder against it and pushed, and it began to give a little. Mr Kasabian pushed, too. It felt as if the couch had been wedged against the door, but as they kept on pushing they managed to inch it further and further away. At last the door was open wide enough for them to step into the living-room.

"This is dead smell, no question," said Mr Kasabian. The living-room was dark and bitterly cold, and there were books and magazines and clothes strewn everywhere. There were marks on the wallpaper, too, like handprints.

"I think seriously this is time for cops."

They were halfway across the living-room when they heard another bump, and a shuffling sound.

"Oh holy Jesus what is that?" whispered Mr Kasabian.

Mrs Gustaffson said nothing, but took two or three more steps toward the kitchen door, which was slightly ajar.

Together they approached the kitchen until they were standing right outside the door. Mrs Gustaffson cocked her head to one side and said, "I can hear— what is that?—*crying*?"

But it was more like somebody struggling for breath, as if they were carrying a very heavy weight.

"Mr Stavanger?" called Mrs Gustaffson, with as much authority as she could manage. "I need to talk to you, Mr Stavanger."

She pushed the kitchen door open a little further, and then she pushed it wide. Mr Kasabian let out an involuntary mewl of dread.

There *was* a figure standing in the kitchen. It was silhouetted against the window, an extraordinary bulky creature with a small head and massive shoulders, and arms that swung uselessly down at its sides. As Mrs Gustaffson stepped into the room, it staggered as if it were almost on the point of collapse. Mr Kasabian switched on the light.

* * * *

The stripped-pine kitchen looked like an abbatoir. There were wild smears of dried blood all across the floor, bloody handprints on every work-surface, and the sink was heaped with black and clotted lumps of flesh. The smell was so acrid that Mrs Gustaffson's eyes filled with tears.

The bulky figure that swayed in front of them *was* David . . . but a David who was long dead. His skin was white, and tinged in places with green. His arms hung down and his legs buckled at the knees, so that his feet trailed on the linoleum. He had no head, but out of his neck cavity rose Melanie's head, her hair caked with dried blood, her eyes staring.

It took Mrs Gustaffson and Mr Kasabian ten long heartbeats to understand what they were looking at. Melanie had opened up David's body, from his chest to his groin, and emptied it of most of his viscera. Then she had cut off his head and widened his throat, so that she could climb inside his ribcage and force her own head through. She was actually *wearing* David's body like a heavy, decaying cloak.

She had made up David's severed head with foundation and lipstick, and decorated his hair with dried chrysanthemums. Then she had put it into a string bag along with Echo's head, and hung the two of them around her neck. She had inserted Echo's bedraggled tail into her vagina, so that it hung down between her thighs.

"Melanie," said Mr Kasabian, in total shock. "Melanie, what happened?"

Melanie tried to take a step forward, but David's body was far too heavy for her, and all she could manage was a sideways lurch.

"We're one person," she said, and there was such joy and excitement in her voice that Mrs Gustaffson had to cover her ears. "We're one person!"

What You Wish For
Garry Bushell

"OH, FUCK HIM," Jayne Titchmarsh-Harvey spat. "Fuck, fuck, fuck him." Half a day she had given up, out of her very busy schedule, to go to Uncle Conrad's funeral. That's rich Uncle Conrad, who had made his millions from property development and porn; and all the selfish old bastard had left her was *this*?

Nostrils flaring with indignation, she eyed the old-fashioned Remington typewriter with disdain.

What a shit-useless chunk of antiquated junk.

She watched the delivery guy deposit it on her coffee table and wait for a moment for the tip that never came. The words of Conrad's will, recited by his dim solicitor, played around her head. "For my talented niece, may you write your next TV hit in style . . ."

Jayne scowled. Her next TV hit would almost certainly now involve the painful murder of a rich old porn baron suffering from halitosis and erectile dysfunction; but only as an aside of course. All of Jayne's work—the entire Titchmarsh-Harvey oeuvre—was devoted to serial killers who preyed mercilessly on vulnerable women, usually hookers or lap-dancers. The killers would run rings around the male cops—sexist cavemen to a man—but they always met their match in Elizabeth 'Lizzy' Wordsworth, Jayne's steely-eyed, tough-as-any-guy-but-feminine-with-it detective inspector.

The Sunday Telegraph had been queasy about the level of sadomasochistic sex in her stories; much of Jayne's blood-thirsty TV fiction bordered on autopsy-porn with lingering close-ups of horrendous injuries and maggot-infested corpses. Her victims were always debased, butchered and utterly dehumanized.

They were raped and killed in such depraved ways that had a man written the scripts, he would rightly have been accused of misogyny. In the Sun, television critic Ally Ross observed that Titchmarsh-Harvey was "as right-on as Newt Gingrich in a peek-a-boo bra" and "a piece of work." But because Jayne's heroine was female, and all the male characters were vile, she continued to attract the moist-gusset support of admiring feminist thinkers and the vast majority of middle class broadsheet critics. The entire liberal arts establishment sang her praises. She "provoked debate" and "confounded expectations", apparently. Her ITV Southbank Show special was in the bag.

In just eighteen episodes over three successful prime time series, Lizzy Wordsworth had become part of the national culture. No high-ranking woman cop mentioned in the UK press could escape being compared to her.

This year Jayne hoped that Bafta would finally reward her efforts with a gong.

"Oh isn't it lovely?" Her mousy PA Mandy Snell was admiring the Remington. "I bet you can't wait to get these keys clack-clacking away. It'll be like being back in the newsroom for you."

Jayne shuddered. The one thing she never wanted to be reminded of was her time in the Daily Star newsroom, when she was plain Jane Watts, ashamed of her small-town Lancashire vowels, and about to have her heart broken by the news editor.

Jayne shot her PA a look she could have stored popsicles in.

"It's junk," she said. "What possible use could I have for this?"

Mandy was stung by the sharpness of her voice.

"I'm sorry," she said, her bottom lip quivering. "I just thought that it would be nice to have something permanent to remember your uncle with. Especially as he once said he planned his career on his Remington; Conrad said he felt his soul entwined with it. I read it in . . ." Her voice trailed off as Jayne's glare intensified.

"Yeah? Well let me know when your brain comes back from lunch. Have you got that new script printed out yet?"

"Not quite, still inputting it," Mandy replied, adding defensively, "I had to go into town yesterday to pick up your mourning clothes from the hire shop and . . ."

"Well you've only got until Friday. Tarquin Stanley-Clarke at Network Centre must have it before he leaves for Tuscany."

"I'll get on with it tomorrow."

"You do that."

"I'll . . ."

Jayne turned her back on her. Mandy reddened and left. Jayne wrote all of her screen-plays in long-hand. Mandy's main job, when she wasn't answering the phone, fetching papers, running errands and making coffee, was to decipher them and type them up on her PC, correcting the spelling as she went. Working here used to be fun, she reflected; but her boss had changed since the run-away success of season one. Self-important, that was the word. These days she was more full of herself than a self-catering cannibal.

Jayne poured herself a glass of Krystal champagne and sneered at the Remington. At least an antique Harris Visible would have been worth a few bob. So Conrad's soul was entwined with this piece of shit, was it? His arsehole more like. Idly, she slipped a sheet of A4 paper into the machine and typed one-fingered: 'Jayne Titchmarsh-Harvey wins the Lottery,' she wrote. Then she laughed, tore out the paper, screwed it up and threw it in the bin.

Half a bottle and a Celine Dion CD later, she placed the typewriter in a black bin liner and carried it to the kitchen for Mandy to dispose of in the morning, giggling as she went.

It wasn't until half-way through the next morning that Jayne checked the Lotto results in the Daily Mail. She nearly choked on her smoked salmon bagel. The six winning numbers were all hers. The jackpot was an estimated £2.5million. There was one winner.

Her.

"Mandy!" she shrieked.

Her PA ran in to the kitchen from the office.

"Where's that typewriter?"

"I put it out in the big bins, like you wanted."

"Fuck-wit!"

Jayne shot out of the apartment in her dressing gown and slippers, a worried Mandy trotting along behind her. By the bins, her boss cupped her hands and the PA reluctantly climbed up and into the waste to fish through the filth and find the sack containing the Remington. Jayne left her dusting herself down while she rushed the machine back to the office. Putting in a sheet of paper, she typed: 'Jayne Titchmarsh-Harvey wins Bafta . . . Jayne Titchmarsh-Harvey honoured by the Queen . . .' She paused, smiled and then added: 'Jayne Titchmarsh-Harvey meets her perfect man—six foot 2, bright, athletic, sharp-dressed toy-boy—today.' Smiling to herself, she took the sheet of paper out of the typewriter, folded it tightly and slipped it into her diary.

"Mandy," she barked. "Run me a bath!"

If she was going to meet Mr Right tonight, she was damn well going to get laid. It had been a long time.

Jayne had arranged to meet an old newspaper colleague Hillary Boisdale in a Limehouse pub—she was a frightful bore but she couldn't be seen out and about like Billy No-Mates. She should get there for six, she decided. The place was frequented by plenty of high-flying City boys.

Everything was going to plan, except that dim Mandy—she'd have to go—hadn't finished inputting the script.

"It has to be at ITV by 9 am tomorrow," Jayne told her PA sternly as she left. "So you jolly well stay late and get it all done. I don't care if you're here until midnight. If you don't finish, you're out of a job. Got it?"

Mandy bit her bottom lip to stop the tears.

The City Pride pub positively throbbed with testosterone. Eager to out-do each other, bullish market men flashed their cash and chatted up every piece of "skirt" in the joint. Several tried to hit on the two women, but only one man seemed to fit Jayne's bill. Neill was six foot two with Morrissey's haircut and what looked like David Beckham's body. He was also, it transpired, five years younger than her, buff and rich enough to be wearing a brand new La Crosse XC-55 wristwatch. As soon as he clapped eyes on Jayne, he seemed transfixed by her. And this charming man proved his worth when the power cut hit. Making his excuses to Hillary, Neill swept Jayne off her feet and drove her to Booty's riverside bar, where, for a small consideration, Dennis the owner laid on candles, champagne and lasagne cooked on a camping stove—just for them.

When Neill dropped her home at 10 pm, Jayne knew she had to have him. They embraced as soon as the front door was shut—thankfully that lazy cow Mandy had already left. The sex that followed, there on the carpet, was as wild as anything Jayne had ever experienced; her orgasm was shattering in its intensity.

She fetched him a beer from the fridge—warm because of the blasted power cut. Neill listened intently and kept her brandy glass topped up as she told him about her life, her work regime and her dreams. They talked for hours. She had never met such an attentive guy.

He asked about what she would do after the Wordsworth series. She told him about her idea for a kind of super-feminist killer; a vamp who beds scores of bad men and then tortures them and kills them. "Kind of like Dexter in a skirt," he thought, but didn't say. It would be the antidote to most serial killer stories, Jayne insisted, where women are the victims. The Guardian would love it.

"Are you in to torture?" he asked, smiling sweetly.

"A little play-bondage never hurt anyone," she replied coquettishly.

Neill scooped her up in his hands and carried her through to the bedroom where he slowly undressed and lovingly caressed her. Then he lay her gently, face down on her double bed and tied her feet and hands to the bed-posts using his belt, his tie and the cords from her dressing gowns.

The last knot was a little too tight.

"That hurts, darling," she said.

He smacked her straight round the face, roughly pulled back her head and fastened his handkerchief around her mouth to stop her talking.

Jayne was furious. She was all for a little authenticity but really, this was too much. She started to struggle. Neill hit her again and produced a scalpel from his pocket, holding it hard against her face. Jayne froze. The anal sex that followed was nowhere near as painful as what came after; as Neill went on to violate her with a series of household objects.

The wetness she felt was her own blood.

She was on the verge of passing when he began to make the first incision by the side of her right eye. Jayne snapped wide awake. How was this happening to her?

Just as suddenly she realised. The power cut! Obviously Mandy hadn't been able to finish the last scenes on the computer and print it out so she would have had to have done it on the blasted typewriter. And in the closing moments of episode one, the rich but hateful society lady was raped, beaten and then skinned alive by her latest concubine. The pitiful remains of her body would be found the next morning—or on TV in episode two—by her shocked maid, or in this case the loyal PA.

Oh Mandy, you fucking idiot.

In reality Jayne Titchmarsh-Harvey was not skinned alive and her corpse was not found until several weeks later when her neighbours complained about the smell. Mandy never came back to work. She had never finished typing out the episode either. If Jayne had bothered looking she would have found her heartfelt, hand-written resignation note on her desk, stained with her tears.

The Times was not the only paper to comment on the irony.

Jayne Titchmarsh-Harvey, who had made her name with chilling stories about serial killers, was savagely murdered herself by a killer who preyed on wealthy middle-aged widows in a manner that bore remarkable similarities to the fiend in her second Lizzy Wordsworth series.

Neill—real name Charles Beeson—was a Wordsworth obsessive; his Stepney council flat was covered in pictures of the star, and of Jayne Titchmarsh-Harvey. His City boy life-style turned out to be as phoney as his watch, which he'd bought for 25 notes in a pub in Shoreditch. There was no Lizzy Wordsworth to find him, of course; just a world-weary, scum-hating East End DI who made damn sure he hurt him before slapping on the cuffs.

Jayne's obituary noted that the Bafta-winning writer, due to be made a Dame in the Queen's Birthday Honours List, had left nearly £2.75 million in the bank.

No friends or family attended her funeral; just an odd assortment of ghouls, Wordsworth fans and weirdoes.

Shortly after, Mandy Snell contacted her closest relatives and asked if she could have the Remington as a keepsake to remember her old employer by. Mandy now lives in Dubai, when she isn't in her riverside pad in Chelsea; or with her two adorable sons cheering on her mega-rich footballer husband to another sensational victory at Stamford Bridge. It turned out to be a record-breaking season.

The Devil Lives in Jersey
Z.F. Kilgore

EX-POLICE DETECTIVE Cord Bergen merged onto the New Jersey Turnpike, away from New York City on the evening of January 20th in his blue Honda minivan, pulling behind it the small rented trailer containing all of his and his son's possessions. His wife remained in New York, refusing to leave, claiming it was because of her job, but he knew better. It was because of her boss, and she was probably already shacked up with him at this moment. Actually, he supposed, it really was because of her job. He glanced in the rearview mirror at the diminishing skyline of the city and felt a sense of relief and peace.

His sixteen-year-old son Adam sat sullen and quiet in the passenger seat staring out the window.

"Look, Adam," he said, "I know you don't want to leave New York, but it's only a couple of hours away, it's not like we're moving to California or something. It'll be good for you to have a change of scenery."

Adam rolled his eyes but continued staring out the window. "C'mon dad, I'm not stupid. You're not doing this for me. I know why we're leaving. Mom told me."

"What? What did she tell you?"

"That you were under pressure to catch that serial killer guy, and you couldn't do it. You were freaked out over it, and drinking all the time. They wanted to get rid of you anyway, and get someone who could catch him."

Bitch, he thought. Fucking bitch. Did she also tell him about her extracurricular activities and the real reason she wasn't coming with them? Probably not. Instead she had blamed it on him and his drinking.

The Manhattan Monster, as he'd been dubbed, had been terrorizing New York City women for three years. Cord had been put on the case immediately since he was the occult expert. The Monster had mutilated and killed nearly 40 women, about one a month, each on the full moon. He carved a pentagram on each victim's back. Three years and he had been no closer to catching the guy. It had driven him to drink heavily, and his wife had become fed up with it.

"Yeah okay, that's true. She shouldn't have told you that, though. But that's not the whole reason, you know that."

"Sure, I guess it's my fault, right? You think that 'getting away from the city' will help straighten me out, right? Nice, wholesome setting, and all that bullshit?"

"Well, I suppose that's part of it. But it was the house, you know. My grandmother dying and leaving it to me. Then the police chief job came up and well, I thought it would be a good opportunity."

"Why didn't you just sell the house?"

"I tried to sell it, you know that. No one would buy it though and I would have still had to pay the upkeep. It doesn't have to be permanent, just to get us both straightened out, I guess."

Adam was a good kid. Yeah, he'd fallen into a bad crowd, but nothing really too serious. The typical teen stuff; smoking pot, drinking, missing school. A lot of school. In fact he'd been held back, and would be attending the tenth grade again. Not that anyone would know, not out here. Adam was not a big kid, very slender, and he looked very young, closer to 13 or 14. His long blonde hair, blue eyes, and an almost angelic face contributed to his very youthful looks. And there was the occult stuff. The guys he'd hung out with were into the satanic music and rituals. But Cord felt he was partially to blame for that. Cord was considered one of the foremost experts on occult and satanic crimes. He had books and paraphernalia all over the house, and was usually the one called in to investigate those types of crimes in the city. So naturally Adam had been a part of that growing up. Cord didn't worry too much about it; a lot of kids went through that stage but it was just part of trying to be different. He knew Adam didn't take it all that seriously.

They drove the remainder of the two-hour drive in silence. It was just getting dark by the time he found the Route 60 exit that led to Woodbine, a small town smack in the center of the New Jersey Pine Barrens.

As they drove down the dark road lined with dark trees, Cord said, "Maybe we'll see the Jersey Devil, huh? Supposedly this is one of the areas where it's been spotted."

"Oh, yeah, sure dad. More likely we'll run into a bunch of inbred hicks who want to make us their bitches for the night."

Cord let out a laugh and said, "Yeah, you're probably right." His head turned to the faded "Welcome to Woodbine" sign off to the right and he pointed at it. "This is it. We're here . . ."

Adam gripped the dash and yelled out, "Watch out!"

Cord slammed on the brakes as something swiftly crab-crawled onto the road, stopped briefly, its eyes glowing yellow and staring briefly into the headlights, then ran off the other side.

Cord's heart thumped as he heard a faint bumping sound at the edge of the tire.

"What the fuck was that?" Adam screeched, still gripping the dashboard.

"I don't know. Are you okay?" He sat still for a moment, shaken, then pulled over slowly to the side of the road.

"Yeah, I'm fine. Did you see it? You saw that, right?"

"Yeah, but I'm not sure I really saw what I thought I did."

"I *know* what I saw. It looked like a woman crawling in the road!"

"Yeah, a woman covered in fur and running on all fours. It must have been a dog or some kind of animal."

"That wasn't like any dog I've ever seen."

"Or any woman. Except for the long hair on its head. C'mon, lets take a look. Hand me the flashlight from the glove box."

He turned on the emergency flashers, and they got out and walked back along the road. He soon found the tire marks that ended in a small puddle of blood and a bit of brownish fur.

"It's not that much blood, thank god." A line of small blood drops ended at the edge of the road and he swung the light through the trees, but didn't see anything.

Adam said, "It had to have been a dog or something. That looks like dog fur."

"Maybe," Cord murmured, but he knew what he'd seen, and so did Adam. "Go grab the camera out of the car, okay?"

"Okay." Adam jogged back to the car as Cord swung the flashlight through the trees again.

He took the camera and handed Adam the flashlight. "Just shine it right on that puddle and the fur." After snapping a few pictures, he said, "Let's just walk a little ways into the trees and see if anything's there."

"Dad, whatever it was is gone. It wasn't human. They wouldn't have crawled into the woods, would they?"

"No, but let's just look real quick." He walked into the trees and Adam sighed, then followed. But fifty or so feet into the thicket revealed nothing and they couldn't go much further, the trees were so thick. "All right, lets get out of here. I want to get a sample of that blood and fur, though."

He rummaged through the back of the van until he located his evidence kit, which he always kept handy. Using the tweezers, he stuffed the bit of fur in the vial, and swabbed the blood with gauze, adding it to another vial.

"What a way to start, huh?" he said, pulling the van back onto the road.

As they reached the center of town, Cord said, "Look, I'm just gonna stop at the police station real quick and let them know what happened, and drop off the evidence."

Adam looked around at the small, dismal, buildings lining the road. "Okay. Nice place, Dad. Looks like a real party town."

Cord chuckled, "Oh yeah, that it is."

He pulled into the parking lot of the station. "Wanna come inside?"

"No thanks, I'll wait out here." Adam stepped out of the van and pulled a cigarette out of his pocket and lit it, staring into the dark.

Inside, Cord greeted the officer he remembered as Lieutenant Johnson from his interview, who sat at his desk reading a comic book. He looked over the page, set it down quickly, then stood and held his hand out. It was a big hand. In fact, Johnson was a big man. He stood well over six feet and was, well *big*. Not quite fat, but getting there.

"Chief Bergen. Welcome to Woodbine. We're so happy you made it safely. How was the trip?"

"Fine, fine. Well, we had a little incident on the way in." He recounted the event to Johnson, who nodded and tried to look serious and interested.

"Anyway, I got a sample of the blood and hair." He pulled the vials out of his pocket and showed it to the Lieutenant, who took it from him and held it up to the light, peering into the glass at the contents.

"Yup, yup, that's animal fur. Probably coyote. We got a lot of them out here. No need to worry, sir. Surely ain't human."

"Aren't coyotes usually gray?"

"Well, yep. But they can be brown too. It could be dog fur, anyways. Got a lot of strays out here."

"I'd like to get some testing done on it anyway, just to make sure. Maybe get a few people to search the area once it's light out."

"Okay, sure, no problem, Chief. You go on and get yourself settled in. I'll put this away and get the guys out there first light tomorrow."

"All right, thanks. I'll see you in the morning as well."

"Good night, sir. And again, welcome. We're very happy to have you."

The house his grandparents had left him sat at the end of a short graveled drive, isolated and dark, surrounded by trees. It was a two story simple wood house, three bedrooms, small but neat. It had been built by his grandfather in the early 50s. All of the furniture was still there of course. On his first trip out here after his grandmother's death he had covered everything to keep off the dust.

"Well, what do you think? Lots more room than the apartment, huh?"

Adam looked quite disgusted as he walked slowly through the front room, wrinkling his nose. "It stinks."

"Yeah, well, we'll have to air it out, of course. But wait till you see your bedroom, on the top floor. It's huge."

Adam walked upstairs and to the window, staring out into the dark. He thought he saw someone out there, walking quickly past and around the corner of the house. He rushed to the window on the other wall and looked down. But what he saw what looked like a very large dog running off into the woods.

The next couple of weeks passed rather uneventfully for Cord. The crimes in the town were pretty much limited to petty theft and vandalism, committed mostly by bored teenagers. A regular Mayberry, he thought, complete with a town drunk. Bergen was happy about that and felt himself settling into life as a small town police chief. Adam had made a friend. Chris dressed in black, had black hair, and wore black eyeliner. Cord really didn't expect anything else. His son would never fit in with the clean-cut crowd.

The phone rang on his desk. "Police Chief," he answered.

"Mr. Bergen, please?"

"This is Chief Bergen."

"This is the Forensic Science Center in Trenton. You sent us a blood and hair sample for testing."

"Yes, that's right. You got results?"

"Well, no. We couldn't determine the origin of the samples, sorry. It's possible the samples were contaminated."

"Contaminated?"

"Right. We were unable to determine whether it was even human or animal. We couldn't match it with any known species, in other words."

"Odd. You're absolutely positive?"

"Yes, it's very odd. We ran the test twice. Sorry we couldn't help."

"Sure, no problem. You'll send us the remainder of the samples and the report?"

"Yes, well do that as soon as possible."

"Thanks." He hung up the phone, puzzled. In his twenty years of police work he'd never had a blood sample come back as "contaminated" or "unable to determine origin."

Adam sat in the back seat of the battered Ford Escort. Chris veered around a corner too fast, and the car fishtailed and flung him against the door.

"Christ Fuck, man, slow down," Adam said. "I'm trying to roll a joint back here. You want to get us pulled over?"

Karen giggled from the front seat and leaned over to the back. "Almost done? Light it up!"

"Yeah, I would be if your dumbass boyfriend can control himself for a minute."

"Hah, like I'm scared of your old man Andy Taylor and Deputy Barney Fife." Chris laughed and tilted the bottle of cheap vodka up to his lips.

"That's the road, isn't it, sweetie?" Karen pointed toward the barely visible dirt path.

"Yeah, that's it." He swerved the car onto the dirt path which gradually rose upwards into a hill. After about a half mile bumping along the narrow path, it ended at a decrepit wooden house.

"This is it. The gateway to hell," Chris announced. He had explained to Adam earlier about the legend of the house. Some witch had lived here in the 1930s and had murdered a bunch of kids on the property. She had actually succeeded in conjuring up the devil himself, and in the process had opened up the gateway to hell.

Adam grabbed the duffle bag and his flashlight out of the back seat and got out. The bag was heavy. It contained ritual objects that were used to invoke demons; black candles, chalices, a small sword.

They switched on their flashlights and pushed open the door which already stood slightly ajar. Graffiti covered the walls and beer bottles littered the floors and everything was covered with a thick film of dust. Chris led them to a basement door. The stairs groaned and bent as they walked slowly down.

Adam swept his flashlight around the basement. The room was painted in all black except for the dirt floor, and was empty except for a rickety wooden table. There were no windows to let in even a tiny bit of light.

Adam removed objects from the bag and set them on the table. He lit the candles, then picked up the old book he had pilfered from his dad's collection.

"So what do we do?" asked Chris, looking down at the book.

"Well, I read from the book, which is supposed to conjure up a demon."

"What language is that?"

"Latin, I think. Anyway, I read the words, then we have to collect blood and semen in the chalice and drink it."

"Ewe, that's gross!" Karen said, making a gagging sound.

"What? You drink my semen all the time," Chris retorted.

"I meant the blood part, idiot. Anyway, you have to drink it too!"

"Oh, right. That is gross. Do we really have to do that?"

"Well, yeah. That's how you do it."

"How do you know? Can you understand Latin?"

"No, that's what my dad told me. And he would know, he's a demonologist."

"All right, all right. We'll, uh, worry about it later. Let's just get on with it."

They shut off the flashlights and stuffed them in the bag. Adam turned to a page in the book and starting reciting phonetically in Latin. Chris and Karen repeated phrases lamely when he motioned to them.

Adam held out a dagger in one hand, and pointed to each compass point, invoking the demon that resided there, and Chris and Karen repeated.

As he turned to the north, a shuffling sound came out of the corner of the basement, followed by heavy, rasping breathing.

"What's that?" Karen whispered.

The candles blew out before they could answer.

"Shit! I can't see a fucking thing!" Chris whispered.

"Lemme get the flashlight." Adam fumbled around for it in the bag and pushed the switch. The light didn't come on. "Fuck." He grabbed the other as the shuffling sounds got closer, but that one didn't work either.

"Turn the fucking light on!" Chris yelled.

"They don't work."

"Let's just get the fuck out of here." Chris said.

"Yeah, lets go."

They hurried towards the stairs in the pitch dark, bumping against each other, scrambling to get out of there. Behind them they could still hear the rasping breath, growing louder and louder. There was an awful fluttering, as though giant wings moved through thick air, causing a faint movement of air.

They fell through the basement door into the room above. Chris looked around wildly. "Karen?"

Karen wasn't with them.

"Karen!" they both yelled through the basement door. There was absolute silence now.

"Where the fuck is she?" Adam said, looking around the dark kitchen.

"I don't know! Maybe she got out before us?"

"Then where'd she go?"

"Fuck me!" Chris said, growing angry now.

They both called her name from the top of the stairs again.

"We have to go down there and look for her," Adam said.

"Look at what? It's pitch fucking black down there! I can't see a fucking thing! She's not there, she would have answered."

Adam jumped as a shadow passed by the kitchen window. "Someone's outside."

"Maybe it's Karen, trying to be funny. She's probably laughing at us right now."

They went outside, calling her name, but saw nothing.

Chris yelled out, "Very funny Karen. You can stop hiding now."

They walked around the house, peering into the thick of the trees.

"Fuck this. Lets just leave her ass here."

"We can't just leave her here, Chris."

"Then what do you suggest? Besides, maybe she walked home." Chris pulled his cell phone out and flipped it open. "Nothing. Dead zone."

Adam's was the same.

"Come on, let's go. I'll try her once we get out of these sticks."

Adam reluctantly got into the car. "Maybe we should go to the police, have them come out and look?"

"Yeah, maybe. Look, I'll drop you off at your house. No need to get your old man pissed at you about this. I'll try her on the phone, and if I can't get her, I'll go to the police station."

"You sure?"

"Yeah, no problem. Goddammit!" He slammed the wheel with his hand. "All our shit's down there."

Adam held up the book. "Still got this."

"Great."

The ringing noise cut through Cord's sleep. He glanced at the clock, 5:07 am, and picked up the phone. "Yeah?" he slurred.

Johnson's voice was frantic. "Chief, we got a problem. Get out here, right away!"

"Where are you?" Cord sat up, already searching around for his clothes.

"At the town's border. Right by the welcome sign."

"Yeah, okay, I know where that is. I'll be there in a few minutes. What's the problem?"

"I think, I think I'm gonna be sick!"

There was a horrible retching sound, then dead air. Cord snapped the phone shut, got dressed and drove out to the edge of town, muttering to himself, "If this is a dead dog or something, I'm gonna be pissed."

As he got closer, however, his brows drew together. There were two squad cars pulled off the road, cherry tops spinning, in front of the two story high billboard. Two officers, Johnson and Tyler, stood at the side of the road, staring at the top. As he pulled over, he looked up at the billboard. Something was wrong with it. His first thought was some kid had spray painted it red, and he felt his ire rising. *Woke me up at five for this shit?* What was that at the top covering the words "Woodbine?" He stepped out of the car.

"Oh my fucking god. Fuck me." He felt himself shaking, felt the gorge rise in his throat, and struggled to pull himself together.

"Chief!" Johnson yelled and ran towards him. His face was white and his mouth hung open. He stunk of vomit.

"Who is she?"

"We think it's Karen Forman but we're not completely sure. It's hard to tell from here."

Karen Forman, if that's who it was, was hanging upside down from the top of the billboard, naked, her legs spread wide and draped over the edge, held up by something as yet unknown. Her torso had been ripped open from pelvis to neck, and her intestines hung down in long, coiling loops, swaying around her head in the breeze. Her long hair and face were soaked in blood, and a huge smear of blood ran down the wood to the edge, already dried and frozen.

"What's that between her legs?" he said, but he knew what it was as soon as he said it. A cross, as long as his arm, had been shoved into her crotch. He thought he could make out the end of it protruding from her gutted stomach.

"Jesus Christ." The damage done to the girl's body was more horrific than anything he'd ever encountered. The thought briefly crossed his mind that maybe the Manhattan Monster had followed him out here. But this wasn't his MO. In fact, this made the Monster look like a Sunday School teacher.

"How'd she get up there? How we gonna get her down?" Johnson was asking.

"I don't know. We'll have to get a fire truck and a ladder out here I guess. Get Shuly out here with the camera. Call the medical examiner. And cordon off this area.

"Should we call the State?"

"No, I don't think it's necessary. Just get everyone out here." Everyone consisted of a total of four police officers.

Cord conducted the crime scene investigation, assisted by the officers. There was five inches of snow on the ground from the night before, but there were no footprints around the billboard, The only thing on the ground were her ripped, shredded clothes, but there was no blood on them that he could see. He used the fire truck ladder to climb up and photograph and dust for prints, and discovered that the body was being held up with stakes driven through her knees.

When it came time to start thinking about getting the body down, he first tied two ropes around her ankles that hung behind the billboard, pulled out the stakes, then had two officers slowly lower her to the ground. She was about halfway down when Johnson slipped in the snow and lost his grip on the rope, causing Tyler to lose his grip under the sudden full weight, and she fell the rest of the way with a sickening thump, her guts flying out in a fan around her.

"Fucking idiots," Cord murmured, shaking his head.

After the medical examiner took the body to the morgue, he and Johnson drove back to the station with his evidence collection. Tyler would be in charge of notifying the family to come down and identify the body. Cord would afterwards conduct the interview with the family.

He sat at his desk and lit a cigarette, wishing he had a shot of whiskey to go with it. "So what's the story with this girl? You know her?"

"Not that well. I know her parents a little. Boyfriend is Chris Tompkins, he's a pretty bad apple around here, gets in all kinds of trouble. Into that occult devil stuff, you know."

Cord knew who Chris was. Adam's friend. Shit.

After Cord got the call that the parents had identified their daughter, he drove out to their house. They confirmed that Karen had been out with Chris the night before. He called Adam and asked him if he'd been out with Chris and Karen.

"Yeah, I was with them. Why?" he replied defensively.

"I need you to come down to the station. Do you know where Chris is?"

"Yeah, he's right beside me in his car."

"Okay, good. Both of you. I need both of you at the station."

"Why?" he asked again.

"Just get your ass here as soon as possible." He snapped the phone shut then dialed Chris's house. He informed the parents that he would be questioning Chris, and they should be present at the police station.

After questioning Chris and Adam separately, Cord was confident they had no involvement. They were both visibly shaken after hearing of Karen's death. Their stories matched up, and Chris's parents confirmed the time they'd heard Chris come home.

"Why didn't you call the police when you couldn't find her, Chris?"

"I dunno. I was pretty drunk and stoned, I guess. Went home and passed out. Her parents called me this morning asking if I'd heard from her. I was worried, but thought her parents would report it."

"All right. Let's take a trip out to that house, then, before it gets dark."

Cord swung his flashlight around the basement.

"This looks bad for them boys, don't it?" Johnson said in a low voice so Chris and Adam couldn't hear him from the kitchen. "They were with her last night."

"Yeah, it looks bad. But the time of death doesn't match up. She'd only been dead an hour before you found her."

"Well, that's true. But it still looks bad, Chief. People are gonna be real suspicious of them."

"Not if we find the killer."

Johnson let out a burp of laughter. "We ain't gonna find him." He clamped a hand over his mouth as if he hadn't meant to say that.

"What do you mean?"

"Nothing, Chief, just got the jitters."

Cord stood in the basement for a moment and rubbed his eyes. What were the odds? All he'd wanted to do was get away from this kind of shit, and now, here it was again. Murder in Mayberry, Barney Fife is on the case and already declared it unsolvable. He laughed and pulled the bottle of whiskey out of his pocket and took a long, hard swig, and felt a little better.

"So what's the story, Johnson?" Cord sat at his desk drinking coffee and nursing a hangover. He'd spent the early evening before interviewing Karen's friends and acquaintances, then the rest of the evening interviewing a bottle of whiskey at the local bar. He had nothing so far. Chris's car had been impounded for a thorough search, but it was just a formality, he told the family, to rule Chris out. He didn't expect to find anything.

"Huh, what?" Johnson looked up from his paper, perplexed.

"Why'd you say that yesterday, that we're not going to find the killer? You sounded pretty sure of that, like you know something."

Johnson fidgeted for a moment and Cord pressed him, "Johnson, I was a detective for 10 years. I can read people real good. There's something you're not telling me."

"Chief, it's just that, well, we've had a few murders in this town in the past. Never found out who did it."

"When? What kind of murders?"

"The last one was some time ago, 'bout ten years now. We thought it'd stopped, and it had, until now."

"How many murders are we talking about?"

"Oh, I'd say twenty, thirty over the past 60 years. Most was before my time of course. I don't know much about it except what I'd read in the papers and what I learned after getting hired on."

Cord stared at him. "Twenty or thirty? You got to be fucking kidding me. Why didn't anyone tell me this?"

"Chief, like I said, the last one was ten years ago."

"But no one was ever convicted?"

"Nope. It's a real mystery. This town's got a pretty bad past, you see. Kids gone missing too. Never seen again."

Cord said nothing. He could see that Johnson was struggling with something and had more to say.

"That house, out in the woods. That's the old Barclay house. That's where it started, in the 1930s."

"Go on Johnson, tell me about it."

"Elizabeth Barclay lived there. Her and her husband built the house after coming over here from Germany in the early 30s. She was convicted of witch-craft and burned at the stake, and ever since then, we've had these murders and kids disappearin'. People here think it's a curse, that she haunts this town."

"Wait a minute. She was *burned* at the stake? In the 30s? For witchcraft?"

"Yes sir. I know it sounds crazy, but she was. They'd suspected her for a while. Some kids had gone missing, bad things happening to people in the town. Elizabeth's husband had been convicted of raping and murdering a girl and hung some months earlier, and police figured she was bent on revenge. They'd been staking her out up there in the woods with a movie camera, where supposedly she held her rituals. They caught her on film conjurin' up the devil, and eatin' the corpse of a baby."

"Holy christ, Johnson. Are you sure about this?"

"Yeah, yeah. I've seen the boxes of evidence when we moved them from the old storage house a couple of years ago. Never looked at them much, though. I haven't seen the film. But it's all down there. I didn't believe it either, Chief. I hear there's also film of her being burned alive, too, in the town square. She'd just had a baby, too. Her husband's, I suppose, though some people wonder about that."

"What happened to the kid? Is he still around?"

Johnson looked stricken. "No, Chief. He died about five years ago. Lived here his whole life, though."

Cord had a bad feeling in the pit of his stomach. "Name?"

"Randall. Randall Bergen, your grandfather."

Cord searched through the boxes at the evidence storage room, soon finding what he was looking for. His grandfather had become very ill about five years before his death. Ten years ago. Until yesterday, ten years since the last murder, according to Johnson. His grandfather was the son of a witch who'd been burned at the stake. His great-grandmother. Great. Just fucking great.

He carried the box marked "Elizabeth Barclay 1934" to the evidence inspection room and pulled on a pair of latex gloves. Inside were several reels of film in their canisters, a large envelope of photographs, and a stack of documents. The papers were in bad shape, but from what he could make out, two men, a detective and a photographer, had staked out an area behind Elizabeth's house.

Carefully he pulled out the photographs. Mug shots of Elizabeth, staring defiantly into the camera at the police station. She was disheveled, filthy, and wildy beautiful, with long blonde hair and light eyes. It struck him how much Adam resembled her. The old and grainy photos of the crime scene showed a clearing in the woods with a dead bonfire in its center. Closeups of a shallow hole in the ground at the edge. Lying near the fire was what looked like the mangled and chewed up corpse of a very small and very decayed body, and chunks of rotted flesh were scattered around the clearing.

He stared at the reels for a moment and flipped open his phone, dialing a New York number.

"Cord, man how you doing out there in the sticks?" Doug asked cheerfully.

"Nothing a Smith and Wesson couldn't take care of."

"That good, huh?"

"Yeah. Doug, what do you know about old film? I got some here that I need to look at, but don't have a clue what to do with it."

"How old it is?"

"1930s."

"That's pretty old. You'll need to have it transferred to DVD, so you don't ruin the film."

"You know someone that can do that?"

"Yeah I know someone here. What's the film of?"

"A witch burning."

"Cool."

"I can drive it up this weekend. Don't want to take a chance mailing it. How long does it take?"

"Not sure, shouldn't take too long, though, but it depends on how much film you got. I'll give the guy a call and see if he can do it right away."

"Thanks, man. How are things in New York?"

"Oh, just wonderful. The Monster killed *two* women night before last. I think he misses you and is lashing out."

"Yeah, actually I miss him too."

"What's up Cord, got some trouble with kids bashing up mailboxes?"

Cord laughed. "Yeah, that too. I'll talk to you this weekend, okay? I got my own murder to solve."

"Lovely. So we'll hang out and get wasted. You can cry on my shoulder and tell me all about it."

"All right, Doug, see ya."

That night while lying awake in bed, he heard Adam leave the house around 2 a.m. He wondered where he was going so late as he finally drifted off to sleep.

Over the next few days, unable to sleep, Cord had heard Adam leaving the house every night. One night he stayed awake and heard Adam returning around 4:30. After Adam went upstairs, he got up and walked into the kitchen. There was a stench in the hallway, like rotted meat. What the hell was he doing at night? And what was that goddawful smell?

But Cord simply didn't have time to worry about it. He had attended the autopsy of Karen, and the Medical Examiner had determined she died of massive organ damage and blood loss. Her bones were covered with gouges. Though a murder weapon could not be determined, the damage to her tissue indicated she'd been torn open by a sharp object. Nothing to indicate how exactly she'd been hoisted onto the top of the billboard. Someone very big and strong. Or more than one person. No rope marks on her, nothing on the ground at all except for her clothes. No footprints, no ladder marks or tire tracks. The woods around the edge were untouched, not a broken limb to be found. All he had to go on was the cross. Simple, find the owner of the cross, and find the murderer. The cross, along with fingernail scrapings, semen, and other samples, had been sent to the county crime lab. The semen could be Chris's, though. If not, then that would be his biggest break. Chris had voluntarily given a hair sample and turned over his clothing he had worn on the night she was murdered, and was sent to the lab for testing as well.

He also intended to look through the past unsolved cases that Johnson had spoken about, and assigned Tyler to get him a list of all cases of murder and missing persons. There must be old-timers in the town that remembered. All of the police officers had been on the force less than ten years, and the former police chief had died of cancer. Maybe he'd have a talk with old Jasper from the bar, who had to be at least eighty years old. He would surely remember something.

"Don't waste your time, Chief," Jasper rattled, then downed the whiskey shot Cord had bought him.

"What do you mean?"

"You ain't ever gonna find the killer. I can sit here all night and tell you all about it, and I don't mind that, but it ain't gonna do you no good. This is a bad town, it's been that way for a long time, and it'll always be that way. We've pretty much resigned ourselves to it, can't do nothing about it. The town is cursed, so people think. I don't know 'bout that, not much on that superstition stuff, but I know there's somethin' rotten here."

"Did you know my grandparents?"

"Oh yeah, sure, but not too well. They was good, hardworking people. Kept to themselves mostly. Friendly enough, though."

Cord himself knew little about them. Despite the fact they'd lived only two hours apart, his parents hadn't taken him to visit that often when he was a kid. They weren't very close, but he never knew why, and the occasional visits were quiet and a little uneasy. After his parents had died in 1988, he'd had no contact with them at all and they didn't seem interested in contacting him either. He hadn't even attended their funerals. Cord was born and raised in New York; his father had left Woodbine to attend college in New York as a kid and never left.

So what the fuck was he doing here now?

"Did my grandfather know about his mother, Elizabeth?"

"Sure, sure. Wasn't no secret around here. I expect that had a lot to do with him not socializin' too much. You know how people are, suspicious and stuff, especially back then. He moved into the Barclay house after he married Marge when they were pretty young, till they built the new one, the one you're livin' in now."

"So who owns the Barclay house now?"

"Well, I don't think he ever sold it that I know of. It's just an old shack after all. So I expect you do."

"Do you remember Elizabeth Barclay?"

"I don't remember too much about her. I was only about ten at the time. No one ever spoke about what happened, don't expect anyone will now either."

"But you know what they did to her, how she was executed?"

"I've heard the rumors. Don't know anyone who actually saw it, or would admit to it. None of them's alive still of course."

"Of course. What about my grandfather, when he was younger? What was he like?"

"Oh he was quiet then too. But all that had happened to him as a youngster, well it was to be expected, I suppose."

"What happened to him?"

"You don't know?"

"No. I don't know much about him at all."

"Well, he was put into a foster home. Myrtle Snyder took him in. She lived out there in the woods by herself. Twasn't nowhere else for him to go, no one wanted anything to do with him. Everyone believed he was the son of the devil. Myrtle thought that too, but she took him in anyway. She used to beat him real bad. No one did anything about it, or turned the other way. After awhiles he stopped going to school and Myrtle claimed she was home schoolin' him. I guess it got so bad, his mind snapped one day. He was 'bout eight or nine at the time. Anyways, someone went out there to that house, and found him squatted down next to her. She was dead and had been for some time. Her corpse was burnt. He'd been living off her flesh, eating her. He was in bad shape, too, she'd been beatin' him real bad. He was rantin' and ravin', something about the devil being inside him, so I heard."

"Jesus."

"Yeah, well. No one really knows what happened out there. Your grandfather was in a bad state, out of his mind. Wouldn't talk about it afterwards. Wouldn't talk about anything. He was put into the hospital, in the mental ward. He lived there till he was, oh, about eighteen. Till they saw fit to let him out. He met your grandmother right after, and they married and moved into the old Barclay house. That's 'bout all I can tell you about him, Chief."

"What about all of the murders in this town, Jasper? Can you tell me anything about that?"

Jasper downed another shot and gestured at the bartender for another. "Nope. But I expect you'll find out soon enough."

Cord met Doug in New York that weekend and they dropped off the tapes at Doug's contact. The DVDs would be ready in just a few hours, so they grabbed dinner and then went to a bar to drink.

"So what's the story, Cord? What's going on up there in that town?"

"I don't know. All I know is I've walked into something bad, and I'm royally pissed about it. I think that's why they hired me, to clean up their mess." He pulled out the crime scene photos and showed them to Doug.

"This is what's going on. Can you believe it? In that podunk town? Not the first one either. The others were just as bad as this. Bunch of missing kids in the past, too. And these people think the town's cursed or something, by this *witch*, who just happens to be my great-grandmother. I just found out also, my grandfather apparently killed his foster mother when he was a kid, and was put in a mental hospital."

"Nice," Doug murmured, staring at the photos, then asked in a matter-of-fact voice, "Is that a cross in her crotch?"

"Yeah."

"So this is right up your alley then, huh? You think it's occult related, or a ritual sacrifice?"

"Could be, not sure. But that's not the weird part. How the hell did he, or they, get her up on that billboard without leaving any tracks? She was killed there. There was *nothing* on the ground; five inches of snow fresh and untouched."

"Hmm."

Cord could see Doug's mind trying to work that one out, but he'd been over every angle himself.

"Christ, you got me, Cord. That's the most bizarre thing I've ever seen. What about your great-grandmother? You know anything about her?"

Cord tossed back another shot of vodka. "Yeah. She immigrated here from Germany with her husband not too long before she was, uh, executed. Her husband had been hung several months earlier for rape and murder. After that, a couple of kids had disappeared, and they suspected her and staked her out. Couldn't find out that much about her husband, just know his name was Freidrich."

"No wonder you're into the occult stuff. I guess it runs in the family."

"Yeah, and no wonder my grandfather went crazy. Why didn't he just move away from there?"

Doug looked at him over the rim of his glass. "You think your grandfather was involved in anything?"

"The thought crossed my mind. The murders started in 1951, the same time he left the mental hospital. The last one right before he got sick. But if he was, then someone else has taken over now."

"How's Adam taking all this?"

"He seems to be okay, not too happy about living there, though. I didn't tell you the best part. The victim was the girlfriend of Adam's friend. They were the last ones to see her alive."

"Fuck."

"Yeah. Fuck." He hesitated, then continued, "Doug, I don't know what's up with him. He's been leaving the house every night, at the same time, around two, and returning at the same time around four-thirty. Stinking like he's been rolling around with a dead dog."

Cord paused as a thought crossed his mind. Could Adam have left the house again the night Karen was murdered? He'd heard him coming in around one, but had immediately went back to sleep.

"Walking?"

"Huh? No, he takes the car."

"Did you ask him about it?"

"No. Been too wrapped up in this shit. I mean, it's not that unusual for him to stay out late, but to just get up in the middle of the night like that. And that smell. I saw him coming in one night, and he was filthy, and stinking. What the fuck is he doing?"

"Why don't you follow him?"

"Yeah, I thought about it. Not a lot of traffic around there, it'd be hard to stay undercover. Plus if he saw the patrol car, he'd know it was me."

"You need some help? Want me to come out? We could stake him out a couple of days in my car, see what he's up to."

Cord thought about it for a minute. He didn't like the idea of spying on his kid, but with possibly a maniacal killer on the loose, he wanted to know what he was doing, and where he was going.

"Yeah, maybe, Doug. I don't know."

"Just say the word." Doug's cell rang and he flipped it open. "Yo, Bert, what's up? Cool, thanks."

"The DVDs are ready. So let's pick them up, pop some popcorn and watch this baby. I've always wanted to see a witch burning." He let out a loud belch and laughed.

Bert had made two versions of each tape, one was untouched, and the other cleaned up. At Doug's apartment they put in the cleaned up version. The film was surprisingly clear; Bert had done fantastic work cleaning it up.

The footage began with the cameraman following two men through the woods, presumably the detectives. The sun was dipping below the horizon. The silence was eerie as the camera followed the men through the trees. At one point the camera moved away. In the distance, barely visible, was a small wooden house. Cord pointed out to Doug that that was the Barclay house.

The film cuts to a different spot in the woods and it's nearly dark. The camera is still and shows a clearing in the woods about thirty feet away. One of the men is saying something and pointing towards the clearing through the trees.

The film cuts again, now to full darkness. The moon is out, providing some light. About thirty seconds later, a huge bonfire erupts in the clearing, illuminating the area. A hooded and robed figure is standing still in front of the bonfire. The arms raise up slowly and the head lifts up, as if reaching towards something from above. The hood falls back and the robe slides from her body. Elizabeth Barclay, standing naked and very pregnant. She slides her hands across her huge belly, then drops to the ground, crawling, her face covered by her long, waist length hair. She starts digging at the ground, slowly at first, then frantically, clawing at it.

They couldn't see her face, but Cord could imagine what it looked like. Her beautiful, angelic face, contorted and distorted as she dug into the dirt, her full belly nearly touching the ground.

After ten minutes or so, she'd dug a shallow hole and was pulling something out of it.

"What is that?" Doug was leaning forward, as if that would help him see better.

"Can't tell." Then he remembered the crime scene photos. "Shit, it's a body, a baby."

As they watched, she pulled the small body out of the ground. Picking it up with her teeth, she crouch-crawled back towards the bonfire. Cord remembered then about the thing he'd hit on the way into town, the dog-woman with the long hair. It had moved exactly the same way.

She sat up on her haunches, and seemed to be talking, or screaming into the night, She swayed back and forth, her head rolling wildly, hair flying out around her. She lifted the small, stiff body upward—obviously it had been dead awhile —then dropped it down in front of her and crouched over it, digging her face into it. She *chomped* on the body, tearing flesh from the bones, smooshing her face into it, tearing at it with her hands, rubbing and smearing the rotting flesh over her face, breast, and belly, between her legs and her ass, licking and sucking at her fingers all the while.

"Jesus H. Christ," Doug said in a low voice. "This is fucking insane!"

"Look, what's that?"

At the edge of the clearing, something had appeared. Something big. Elizabeth saw it, or heard it, too, and stopped her chomping for a moment, looking back over her shoulder.

The big thing moved jerkily over the ground towards Elizabeth. As it got closer to the light, Doug and Cord yelled out at the same time, "What the fuck is that?"

The *thing* was huge, about eight feet tall, its naked body covered in short fur. The face was hard to see, it was so far above the light, but they could make out horns curling back from the sides of its head, like a ram. Its eyes glowed yellow, and long, muscular arms ended in long, deadly looking talons. It had long, twisted hair that hung down its back. Between legs that were bent like a dog's hind legs, a huge, erect penis protruded up against its furry belly, and testicles the size of a bull's hung down far between the muscular thighs.

"Cord, man. I can't believe what I'm seeing. That's no fucking costume. That thing looks fucking real."

Cord, transfixed to the scene before him, was speechless.

Elizabeth had rolled over onto her back, like a submissive dog. She spread her legs wide as the monster stood over her, and she continued smearing the dead flesh between her legs, rubbing it into herself. The monster thing crouched down between her legs, and ran its talons over her gigantic belly. It leaned over and lapped the dead, rotted flesh from her from her breast, belly, and between her legs, with a tongue that had to be two feet long. It lifted its head for a moment and jerked its hips forward. They couldn't see it but could tell its penis had inserted itself into Elizabeth. Her pelvis rose up, was *lifted* up, by the thing, her feet actually came off the ground, though the man monster wasn't touching her with its hands.

The monster then wrapped its talons around her hips and thrust himself into her, slamming into her pregnant belly. Elizabeth's head fell back in a silent scream, her head rolling wildy back and forth, her hands grabbing and pulling at the penis between her legs, shoving it into herself even further. After several minutes, the monster suddenly withdrew and stood up between her, its penis spraying thick fluid all over her.

Elizabeth continued in her silent scream, her legs drawing back even further. She reached down between her legs, clawing at something, pulling at it. Then, as they watched in horror, her stomach suddenly deflated, and she lifted up the newborn above her, towards the monster, who was still spraying fluid all over her and the baby. The monster ran its talons over the baby.

Cord and Doug held their breaths, as if expecting it to snatch up the baby and gobble it down. But Cord knew he wouldn't. He had just witnessed the birth of his grandfather.

The monster backed away finally, and disappeared into the woods from where it had come. Elizabeth lay still with the screaming baby on her stomach, until the fire died out, the moon slid away, and the film went dark.

"I need a drink, bud." Doug got up and brought back a bottle of Johnny Walker Black and two glasses.

Cord downed the whiskey and poured another. They both lit cigarettes and stared at the blank screen.

"You think it's real, Cord? Or some kind of staged stunt?"

"I don't have the slightest fucking idea. Doesn't look like a stunt. Those were cops for godsakes. I saw the crime scene photos and read the report. That was a real baby she was eating. Where the baby came from, I don't know. Maybe she dug it up from the cemetery."

"What about that, that, bigfoot thing? Some guy dressed up in a costume?"

"I found some hair samples in the evidence box, looks like it may have come from that thing. Couldn't find any analysis on it though."

"You should have it tested."

He thought about the fur he'd sent to the lab. He had a feeling he'd get the same results. Negative.

"God, I hope your grandfather hasn't seen this."

"Me, too. It would explain him being so fucked up, though. Jeez, I don't know. I mean, I really don't have time for this, you know? I gotta try and find out who killed the girl. But I feel like it's all connected somehow. I just don't know how. The people in that town don't like talking about it, either. There was barely a mention of that girl's death."

"Well, look at it this way. You only have about two thousand suspects."

Cord laughed. "So, lets watch the other one."

"Put it in, man. Let's see the bitch burn."

The second DVD began with the camera fixed on Elizabeth sitting inside a jail cell. Her head had been shaved and she was wearing only a cloth tunic. A man in uniform stood next to her, gesturing with his hands, as if speaking to her, but she stared silently ahead.

The film cuts to Elizabeth in the back of a horse drawn wagon being pulled slowly down a dirt road. She is sitting quietly, her staring eyes glazed, with her hands tied behind her back. The film cuts again. Now Elizabeth was being led toward an x-shaped wooden structure surrounded by a large pile of wood. The camera pans around the area, showing a large clearing in the woods. There are about fifteen people standing around and watching. The cops tie her to the stake, her arms and legs spread and bound with rope to the X. Elizabeth doesn't struggle, doesn't say a word. One of the cops reaches up and tears her tunic away, leaving her naked. Her body is bruised and cut all over. Another comes forward with what looks like a gas can and soaks the wood around her, then splashes it on her body and on her face. She winces as the gas is poured onto her cut covered body.

As the cop pulls out a sheet of paper and starts reading, another lights a match, and with little flourish tosses it onto the wood, and steps back as the flames erupt. Elizabeth seems to come alive then. She begins screaming, and her face is twisted with anger and malice. She stares directly at the camera, her lips pulled back, her unknown words spitting venom. The cameraman is obviously shaken, as the camera wavers wildly for a moment, then steadies again. The flames reach closer to her, higher and higher, finally reaching her legs. Elizabeth starts really screaming something then, but her eyes remain on the camera.

It was really unnerving to watch, and both Cord and Doug fidgeted on the couch, as if she were focusing her wrath directly at them, but they were riveted to the screen. Her skin blackens as the flames crawl up her body, finally to her face, her skin literally melting off, then she was finally silent. All that was left was an unidentifiable, crispy fried mess.

The camera, which had moved away from Elizabeth, suddenly jerks and swerves back up again to the charred body. The head is moving, turning slowly, the burnt flesh dripping off, the eyes melted and unseeing. Its mouth opens, and gushes forth a vile looking whitish liquid. The camera starts waving wildly over the liquid on the ground, then steadies. The camera moves in closer. The liquid is moving, writhing and boiling with what looks like thousands of maggots. The camera goes dead.

Cord and Doug stared at each other for a moment, speechless. They were both drunk and not feeling too articulate.

"Cord, man, I was thinking. You could make some money off this shit, you know? A real life witch burning? A witch eating a baby and getting fucked by Satan himself?"

"Who would believe it though?"

"What was that crap she was spewing out? How did that happen? She was a crispy critter by then."

"Christ, how would I know? Maybe the insides of her melted, then just boiled up and exploded."

"Uh huh. Fucking backwoods rednecks."

The following morning, Cord drove directly to the Barclay house on the way home from Doug's apartment in New York. He walked through the woods in the direction he thought the clearing would be where Elizabeth had been filmed. After about 20 minutes, he found it. Actually he smelled it before he found it. The area around the clearing had a putrid, rotted stench that grew stronger as he got closer. Exactly what he'd smelled on those nights when Adam had come home from his nightly wanderings.

In the center of the clearing were the remains of a recent bonfire. He looked closely at the ground, but saw no footprints or other debris. He poked at the ash and wood with a stick, but there was nothing in it otherwise. Is this where Adam was coming at night? Why? And where was that godawful smell coming from? He searched the woods around the clearing, but found nothing.

Back at the station, Tyler handed him a list of previous unsolved or otherwise violent crimes, murders and disappearances.

He stared at the long list. Between 1932 and 1999, there were 6 raped and mutilated girls, 22 missing children, and 18 murders, all unsolved except for the rape and murder Elizabeth's husband had been hung for, which was the earliest one. Except for a few missing cases when Elizabeth was still alive, most had occurred starting in 1951. Christ.

He hated himself for spying on Adam, but he didn't know what else to do. There was a killer on the loose after all, and Cord figured if he asked Adam where he was going at night, he wouldn't tell him.

It was 1:30 a.m. and freezing cold. He had parked the patrol car off the road as far into the trees as he could, and on the far side of the path that led up to the Barclay house so no one could see it on the way in. Using his flashlight, he walked through the woods until he reached the clearing, then hid beyond it in the trees, armed with a Glock. The Glock was for his own and his son's protection, he told himself.

He sat in the cold dark for the next 40 minutes, the whole time thinking this was a bad idea, and he should get up and leave. But just as he stood up, he heard rustling footprints on the other side of the clearing. Someone was coming. He squatted back down and waited.

A figure stepped through trees and into the clearing. It was too dark to see much, but a moment later the fire was lit in the center and illuminated the figure stooping there. It was Adam.

Cord watched, afraid, a sick feeling rising in his stomach. Adam looked dazed and half asleep as he removed his clothes and laid them in a pile at the edge. Then he knelt in front of the fire and closed his eyes. His lips were moving silently, and his head nodding slightly. So much like the film he had just watched, and that scared the shit out of him. Adam's silent words gradually grew louder, his head swayed back and forth and his face appeared ecstatic. He leaned forward on all fours now, trancelike. A movement at the edge brought Adam's words and motion to an abrupt halt. He tilted his head as if listening.

Cord's heart thudded in his chest, expecting to see that huge, monster like creature step out of the dark. He stood up and raised the glock, then stopped. The thing that appeared out of the woods into the light of the fire wasn't the monster, but a woman. Sort of. She was tall and thin and dark skinned. As she got closer to the light, Cord could see it wasn't dark skin at all but short brown fur, covering her from head to toe. Her legs didn't move, she *floated* across the clearing. The hair on her head hung to her buttocks and was matted and filthy. It looked like the thing he'd hit on the way into town.

She carried something in her hand which hung down limply beside her thigh. It was hard to tell but it looked like a very small child, long dead and bloated black. Adam had turned toward her, still on hands and knees, but his eyes remained on the ground. She moved in front of him and dropped the dead baby, and immediately Adam's mouth opened and tore into the rotted flesh of the stomach with his teeth like a ravaged dog. Adam grew increasingly frantic, and he suddenly sat back on his haunches and lifted the corpse onto his lap. Cord could see Adam's erection disappear into the stinking mushy flesh. His head flung back, and his mouth opened in loud gasping howls as he shoved the corpse onto himself, its flesh tearing off in chunks between Adams fingers.

The furry woman stood before Adam, looking down at him, watching him. After a few minutes, the woman reached down and pulled the corpse from Adam's lap. Adam looked up at her, gasping with a pleading look, as if he weren't finished.

The woman floated away the way she'd come, still carrying the remains of the corpse and disappeared into the trees.

Adam picked himself up and dressed, as if nothing unusual had happened, spread dirt on the fire to quell it, and walked away into the woods.

Cord stayed still and waited, his mind racing. After several minutes, convinced that Adam wasn't coming back, he stood and turned on his flashlight and walked to the clearing. There were bits of flesh still on the ground. He hadn't brought any evidence vials with him, but didn't think it mattered. The child had been dead for a while, thank god for that. Adam hadn't killed anybody, right? He was filled with disgust and apprehension. What the hell was that and what did it want with Adam?

He left and drove home. He couldn't bear to face Adam now, what would he say to him? *Son, I know what you're doing and I'd rather you not eat and fuck dead corpses anymore?*

And what about that woman? Was that for real? It certainly looked so. How is it that they were doing almost exactly the same thing as he'd seen in the film from seventy years ago?

His grandfather was involved, or had been, he knew that. And his father may have known, perhaps that's why he left the barrens.

He remembered the boxes of his grandparent's belongings he'd put in the basement when he first came out after his grandmother's death. Among the boxes was a small, locked filing cabinet. Was there something there? He intended to find out.

He pried open the filing cabinet with a crowbar, and after a few moments of rummaging through the papers, found a letter dated February 4th, 1999, from his grandfather to his grandmother.

Dear Marge,

Please forgive me for what I am about to do, but I cannot continue living this way. You believed in me, helped me get straightened up after being released from the hospital so long ago, and I was always grateful to you for that. And I really tried, I tried to forget everything, but I couldn't, and I can't go on pretending everything is okay, because it's not. You will be better off without me. I've done some terrible things, but I did them because of her, and she'll never leave me alone. She's always been there, seeking me out, she would come to me in the night, making me do terrible things. When I got sick, I guess I should have been relieved, but I wasn't. She'll never let me go. I know this is the only way to relieve myself of this nightmare I've lived my whole life. You must contact my grandson. You will have no choice and she will not have it any other way. She's waiting for me, and I have to go now. I love you. And I'm so sorry.

Love always,
Randall

Great, Cord thought. His grandfather had offed himself and had not died of his illness. And so he was brought here to carry out Elizabeth's curse? His grandmother had left everything to him in her final will, so apparently she had agreed to her husband's wish. But why? Why would she want to continue this? But as Randall had put it, perhaps she really had no choice. Maybe Elizabeth had made sure of that.

But Cord did have a choice. It would end here. The next morning he rented a trailer, packed up everything, and said goodbye to that godforsaken town. Adam seemed nonplussed, not caring one way or another. Elizabeth would not have him or his son to carry out her revenge. If the bitch wanted Adam, she'd have to come get him. Fuck them. Fuck the town and the rubes who lived there, who seemed to be resigned and unwilling to put a stop to the mayhem.

As they drove up the Jersey turnpike, the skyline of Manhattan suddenly came into view. He thought of his old nemesis, the Manhattan Monster. Cord smiled. At least the Monster was human. It was good to be home.

Two weeks later, Cord lay awake at 4:30 am in his New York apartment bedroom. He heard the front door softly open and close. A moment later, the stench of decay and death seeped into his room.

Rat King

Jeffrey Thomas

I APPRECIATE THE DRINK, my friend, but please don't take pity on me; those boys meant me no real harm. My face frightens them and bullying me gives them control over their fears. It is easier to be cruel to the maimed, the weak, the cowed. We don't respect these things, they fill us with disgust . . . because we don't want to become them.

And please, don't feel sorry for me on account of my disfigurement. After all, I did this to myself. Literally, of course. But also, I earned this face. My face changed to become what I had become. It was a miracle that I could fire a bullet from a .455 through the roof of my mouth and live. It is nothing but that; a true miracle. God did not want me dead, my friend. Death would be too quick and merciful. God spared my life through divine intervention so that I could grow old as I have . . . and suffer the contempt of boys. And suffer my memories of that pit . . .

When I was a boy myself I once went out on the broken ice of a pond to save a friend's dog from the water. I might have died, rescuing that animal. How, then, did I become the man I was in 1945? What changes in my heart, in my soul, shaped me . . . led me . . . fated me to become an SS guard at the camp of Bergen-Belsen?

Thinking of that dog reminds me of an experience my cousin had while he himself was an Oberschaarfuhrer at Auschwitz. His name would be unknown today, but you Americans glorify some mass murderer who has killed only five, maybe a dozen people. My cousin personally gassed many *thousands,* with his fellows. He murdered enough people to fill towns.

He had a wolfhound, a great beautiful animal he told me, and one day the dog had run into a fence while playfully bounding about. The fence carried 6,000 volts and the dog was instantly electrocuted. This dog died just outside one of the crematoriums, where my cousin's victims were incinerated. While he told me this story his eyes grew moist, I noticed. He blamed himself for killing his beloved pet, as he had been throwing a stick for it to fetch. He felt guilty for the animal's death . . . outside that crematorium.

But let me tell you about myself, as I started to. Myself, and Belsen . . .

I understand that after a time the prisoners would no longer smell the stink of death and excrement that reached for miles, reached into the peaceful and lovely town of Belsen like a great tentacled monster which was invisible because the people of the town chose not to see it. We became accustomed to the stench also, though not fully immune, as we did not dwell in those horrid shacks. It was useful that we could still smell the stench. It filled us with repulsion for our charges, and repulsion made it easier to abuse them. It was useful that, starved and sick as they were, the prisoners came to look unearthly; animate skeletons barely sheathed in skin, no longer truly male or female . . . not so much less than human as other than human. Hideous, ghastly. Their ugliness made it easier for us to treat them as *things*. Things not human, things worthy of contempt. The way those boys see me now.

We manufactured these things, at our factory death camps. We were manufacturing obliteration. We unmade people. We meant to unmake cultures, races. It was an ambitious project, one might say.

This was hell, as Dante saw it. The prisoners were the damned. And that made me one of the demons. I know that now . . .

The British came, on April 15, 1945, and captured Belsen before we could even hope to do away with all the human evidence. The British saw no grand vision at work here. They were appalled. Great pits were dug. Then, we ourselves were forced to bury the dead. We SS were now the wretched enslaved.

The British could not expect us to bury the dead with dignity; they had to be buried as quickly as possible, there were so many of them, all decaying, and all having lost their individuality in any case. They were all one same tortured soul, in effect, and they all went into one great grave in a jumble, in heaps, in mountains, until at last that vast grave was full of thousands and covered and we went on to the next.

For days we slung the pathetic figures into these pits. Their numbers seemed never to exhaust themselves; our labors, Dante-like, would seem to be eternal. You read of the numbers killed and find it hard to conceive of those numbers as lives. I carried these bodies, I *saw* how many there were, but I myself could not grasp that reality. As in life, we treated those dead as things. Sacks to be slung up onto truck beds. Slack mannequins to be dragged on their faces to the pit and slung over the edge to flop and sprawl atop the piles. They were horrible things; with slit eyes and twisted snarls, long-limbed and rubbery. Yes, rigor mortis is only a temporary condition. I could tell you more about the characteristics of a corpse than could a dozen morticians.

On the first day of this forced labor I had stumbled back from the lip of the first pit, my uniform soiled with sweat and befouled with human waste and smeared with decay. My shoulders ached, as I had slung bodies over them at times because it was faster than dragging. I mopped my face with a handkerchief, and saw that a British officer was moving toward me. I was weary but a defensive fury was rising in me. He was going to order me back to work and I was going to tell him to go to hell, even if he whipped me with his pistol for it.

But instead of withdrawing his revolver, the officer produced a tin of cigarettes and extended it to me. I nodded with a grunt meant to sound polite, and accepted one, which he also lit for me. Then the man dropped his gaze into the pit as he inhaled on his own cigarette. His eyes were squinted in revulsion, as if they half wanted to close and shut the scene out.

He said to me in English, "How could you people do this?"

"We didn't murder these people," I told him.

He looked to me suddenly; at first I thought he was surprised that I spoke English, but then I realized he was shocked at the words I had spoken.

"What do you mean, you didn't kill them?"

"They starved. And most of them were very sick. This camp was intended originally to house privileged Jews with Allied nationality. American, British nationality." I nodded at him. "Conditions here were very good. But this winter they began transporting great numbers of prisoners here from . . . elsewhere . . ." Elsewhere meant the camps of Sachsenhausen, Natzweiler, Mittelbau and others. Like Auschwitz. "We became hopelessly over-crowded. Conditions necessarily worsened. And they made us a center to receive sick prisoners, mostly. So it was these conditions that killed these people you see. We did not exterminate them."

"How can you look me in the face and say that, man? If . . . if you were to abandon a newborn infant in the forest, you'd be murdering it through neglect. Murder is murder. You're only insulting my intelligence and your own."

I shrugged, drew on my cigarette. The taste of smoke helped mask the stench of death that had even coated the inside of my mouth. "You will be murdering us by exposing us like this so closely to these rotting diseased bodies."

"A fate well deserved, my friend, I'm sure. And some of you we will murder quite consciously, I assure you. On the gallows."

"Yes, of course you will. So don't look down on me, 'my friend.' You murder for your purposes, we murder for ours; as you say, murder is murder."

Again my words made the British officer gape at me. "Ten thousand unburied dead, we estimate here. Three hundred dropping dead every day, I'm told. No, SS man, don't think to compare your motivations to ours."

"You have your notions of justice, and we have ours. It's what makes the world so colorful." And I grinned broadly.

"Colorful. Yes. Blood red."

I had expected the man to strike me then, but he was still too much a gentleman, too British. He simply strode away. And I turned back to my labors.

I was going to flick the end of my cigarette into the pit but my eyes locked with the foggy but weirdly direct gaze of a young man down there, and oddly, I dropped it to my feet and stamped it out instead.

The next day I was actually down in the pit, spreading the dead out more evenly, as they tended to clump up where those above pitched them down. At last I was relieved, picked my way not too delicately through the carpet of bodies and climbed up and out. Waiting there was my friend from the previous afternoon, the British officer. My earlier words did not dissuade him from offering me another cigarette.

I had no doubt he had sought me out specifically, and now I understood why. It amused me somewhat but I was careful not to show this. The man was a homosexual, as we liked to claim all British men were, in addition to their all being alcoholics. I knew this because I was very handsome then, my friend . . . yes, it is ironic now indeed. I had been told all my life how beautiful I was. Heroic, god-like, my admirers had gushed; but for my dark hair I was the Aryan ideal. Many times I had seen women act in this man's manner . . . seeking me out after an initial meeting, trying to make it look accidental, casual, trying to seem aloof but churning inside with desire so that I felt the vibration of their lust in the air between us. Even now in this horrid air I felt it.

And maybe that was part of it. You know? Death has a strange glamour, even in its most hideous forms. Your beloved serial-killers, as I say. I think it was subconscious, with this individual. I'm certain that outwardly he truly was appalled at our crimes, and agonized at the loss of lives. I am not saying he condoned our actions. But I think he was drawn to the darkness he perceived in me. The allure of the dangerous hidden under the beautiful. No, don't be naive, don't protest. It goes beyond mere morbid fascination; it's the seductiveness of evil. Look at the new Nazis you Americans have. Your Klan. Your obsession with us real Nazis in films for decades! You find us as beautiful, our uniforms as beautiful, as did the most devout of us! We love villains, criminals. Gangsters. Monsters. We all have that inside us, after all. Maybe it's our way of accepting that side of us.

He appeared properly contemptuous, anyway, standing there in his neat, unstained uniform. "Now you need a shower, SS man. Now you stink. Now you have lice, no doubt."

"And maybe typhus."

"Good. How do you think the people in some of those barracks have felt? I went into one that I could only stand in for less than a minute, on account of its stench. The living people lay amongst the dead people and I couldn't tell them apart from each other. They were too weak to move, most of them. Many were in a coma. Just covering the floor. How do you think they have felt lying there?"

"I don't think those individuals really feel much of anything anymore. But they came here sick, most of them. Already sick, as I've told you."

"Oh, how innocent you are. How could even one human being let this happen? Do you know that if we all had true empathy for one another, could do something so simple as put ourselves in each other's shoes, there would be no murder, no war, and no inhumanity?" He gestured with his cigarette into the vast grave. "Look there, my friend. You see that woman? She could be your wife. She could be your sister."

I smiled. "I have neither."

"Don't be so bloody smug, you bastard. You know what I'm saying. She could be your mother, your daughter, she could be *you*."

"But she isn't. She's a Jew. She's a woman. She's down there and I'm up here."

"Your positions will some day be reversed."

"On Judgment Day, eh?" I chuckled mockingly. I knew I shouldn't provoke his anger, repulse him. Perhaps I could use his attraction to my advantage. My pride aside, I would rather have become his secret lover than hang. But I didn't think he would ever chance an outright relationship with me. Still, I knew I should try to benefit myself from the situation, to flirt with him, beguile him, in the same way I had skillfully mesmerized women. After all, I had consciously enthralled ugly women, women I wouldn't have slept with. In my vanity, I simply enjoyed the attention. The power. Looking back now, I wonder if my flirtation with the officer was motivated less by my attempt to better my situation than it was by this feeling of power. Maybe it made me feel superior to the man, less a prisoner. I was still a Nazi then, of course. I still believed in mastering others.

In any case, when the officer proffered another cigarette and lit it for me, I lightly cupped my hands around his. I felt a light tremor flinch through him at this contact but he didn't jerk his hands away. He was indeed smitten, and he was indeed afraid of me, which I think made him more smitten.

Both of us said nothing for several minutes as we watched others drop one emaciated being after another over the side, like mummies being reinterred, but without the finery. I flicked a louse off my arm; the officer had been right. Parasites. We had called the Jews parasites. Vermin to be exterminated with no more compassion than we would feel spraying insects, or killing rats.

These conversations, philosophical as they were, put me in mind of our motivations as Nazis, brought to mind the analogy of vermin. And seeing the interlaced arms and legs, the entwined skeletal bodies below, made my thoughts take another leap. But a very strange one, unsettling. I shuddered unaccountably; it was the first time staring into the pit, staring at the heaped corpses, actually brought out goose flesh on my arms.

"Have you ever heard," I asked my new found friend, "of Rat Kings?"

We looked at each other; he said, "No."

"My grandmother told me about them. Of course, it's always grandmothers who tell you such things. In any case, she told me that when rats were more plentiful amongst us than they are today, sometimes in a nest of rats a Rat King would be found. This was a group of say a dozen rats or more, whose tails had all tangled together so that they couldn't pull apart, with their heads all facing outwards. Because they were stuck together like this they couldn't move very far, and were often found pitifully starving or already dead. They seemed like many-headed monsters to those who found them, and that was why they were thought of as Rat Kings. Did you know there is a Rat King in *The Nutcracker?* But they call it a Mouse King."

"Yes . . . that's right. But all this about rats with their tails knotted up sounds like wives' tales and nonsense."

"Perhaps it is, though my grandmother swore to me that such things were truly discovered. As a child she herself had a neighbor who supposedly found one in their barn consisting of two dozen rats, which was why she told me about all this. It could be that huddling together in the winter, it was their own frozen urine that was linking their tails together. In any case, only the attic rat, as we Germans call them, have been found as Rat Kings. These are the black rats. They're smaller and more rare than the brown rat . . . mostly because the bigger and stronger brown rats have preyed on them and diminished their numbers greatly. Nearly wiped them out. The brown rats are the more successful and superior species."

"An interesting science lesson. But why would only the weaker black rats get bound up into these Rat Kings, then?"

I shrugged, smiled enigmatically. "One of the many mysteries of life, friend."

The officer drew up closer to me, and thus nearer to the edge of the pit. He gazed down into it on today's cairn of corpses, one hand cupped over his lower face as a filter. "Here's a mystery of life for you. I just can not *accept* this. Look at these bodies. So wasted. Many of these men were once muscular and strong. Tanned. Many of these women were lovely, shapely, fussed over their hair. Now they all look the same. Horrid. Are you really *looking* at them? Look at that young girl. See. Look at her posture."

I looked. Her arms flung, her legs spread. Her patch of pubic hair seemed too large for her skeletal frame. It was so bluntly exposed. Probably swarming with lice. Pubic hair and sunken eyes sockets were the black areas that showed up most against all the masses of white torsos and limbs. There was something very disturbing, even I had to admit at that moment, in seeing so many naked figures so shamelessly exposing private parts that in life they would have shyly hidden. Had these same women been alive and healthy, seeing them naked and sprawled on a bed would have aroused me greatly. This motionless orgy of plaited cadavers, however, made me wonder how I would feel the next time a woman spread herself for me. Would memories of these images get in the way of my view? Would I fear that black nest of hair? Fear its smell of rot, and the lice hiding there in wait for me?

I grew irritated with myself. What effect was this delicate British fop having on me? Was I actually letting him stir feelings of guilt in me, with his admonishments?

My contempt for him at this moment gave me the perverse desire to exploit his interest in me further, to manipulate him as he was seeking to manipulate me. I reached out and picked a piece of lint from his jacket's breast. He stepped back from me, a look of potential alarm in his eyes, but I showed him the lint before I blew it out of my fingers. I then lightly patted the place on his breast where I had plucked the lint, as if dislodging some dust that actually wasn't there.

"A handsome uniform, my friend," I told him.

"Thank you."

"It makes me embarrassed for you to see me this way. Filthy, sweaty. I take pride in my appearance. I wish I could talk to you clean and smelling properly, like a human being."

"I'm sure I prefer you this way. I have no interest in seeing you in your SS uniform."

"As I say, we both wear uniforms. We both do our jobs. But if we were both naked right now, we would be the same, wouldn't we? Not German, not English. Not demon and angel. Just two men. Together. Talking." And I spread a slow smile for him, like the bearded smile between a woman's legs.

I saw his adam's apple bob once. It gave me a weird satisfaction. I felt more in control again, after my stumble of guilt.

"I know you despise me, my friend," I told him, "but I, in fact, enjoy your company. I respect you and enjoy talking with you. Perhaps this evening after I have bathed and changed I could join you for a cigarette and some more stimulating conversation? Then I would feel less ashamed of my condition."

"It sounds to me as though you mean to trick me, SS man, and take me off guard. Grab for my pistol. Hold me as hostage and try to escape."

"Oh, come now. Are you afraid of me? We can meet in full view of others. The guards, your men. But if you'd rather not, then so be it . . ."

"I'll come and get you. I find you unpleasantly . . . educational. But if you try anything foolish I promise you I will put a bullet through your head."

"Thank you. I look forward to conversing with you more as a gentleman."

"You can bathe and change, sir, but you will still not be a gentleman, and you will still have every right to be ashamed of your condition."

Yes, I thought, but you'll still keep that date, won't you? And your heart will be beating heavier as you come to search me out . . .

I had no intention of attempting escape. Of inflicting harm on him. As I told you, I just wanted to see if I could use him to my benefit. And I liked to see his adam's apple bob.

My officer fetched me after dinner, after the sun had set. Lights washed the camp, leaving few dark corners, and he must have felt safe enough to stroll with me. Straight off he had given me one of his cigarettes, and while he lit it for me a soldier patted me down for hidden weapons. As we walked off I asked him, "Did your superiors ask why you were permitting me this pleasant liberty?"

"I told them you were talkative. They asked me to write down what you tell me in my report."

I laughed. "Will you write about Rat Kings?"

"I may have to, but I was hoping you would tell me more in depth what your people did here and at the other camps. The death camps."

"I have never been to one of these alleged death camps, sir."

"Listen, I can take you back and let you be hanged with all your knowledge intact. Or maybe you can be cooperative and make things easier for yourself."

Ah, so this was how he had justified our date to himself. He was going to question me as part of an investigation. He was going to probe the criminal mind. I remember how amused I was at his desperate attempt to rationalize or excuse his interest in me. As earnestly as I could sound, thus amused, I told him, "Sir, I am only a simple soldier. I acted on orders. The vision I followed was that of men far removed from me. But I can tell you what my responsibilities were, as that soldier. I can cooperate to that extent. But if I am to hang . . . well . . . what would be the point in helping you?"

"Your superiors will no doubt hang. I hardly think we will hang every last guard and soldier; we are not barbarians like you fiends are. I was only trying to frighten you."

"Well, I am relieved. I will help you. But you have to promise to protect me. Please." I stopped to face him, and he faced me. We were still within view of posted British soldiers, but were too far for anyone to hear our words. "Please protect me . . ."

"Write down a full report of your activities here. Everything you learned about operations, your superiors, anything you think would be valuable to us. You've seen the film crew. We need to make the world believe this horror really happened. Maybe in some small way you can exonerate yourself."

"And you will take care of me?"

"I told you, I'll do all I can."

I took his hand and clasped it in both of mine. Squeezed it. He stood silhouetted against a flood lamp; had his adam's apple shifted? "What is your name, my friend?" I asked softly, still holding his hand.

In a hesitant, uncertain voice, he told me. But I will not tell you what he said. He was a fine officer. A good man. I would not want to sully his reputation, even if he should be dead now. I was trying to corrupt him, confuse him. I was finding vulnerable places in him. It is my reputation that should be sullied. I am the one who should feel embarrassed.

We strolled on, smoked another cigarette. He walked, I noticed, so that his holstered revolver was on the far side of him. His nervousness, his tension, was electric in the air but I don't think he was really nervous that I would assault him.

Why did we walk at last to the pit? Remember, I had become immune to much of the stink of Belsen, but my companion surely hadn't. I think now that we ended up there because it was as deserted a place as the camp had to offer. It left us in intimacy. And thus far, the pits had been the place of our rendezvouses. Like a garden where lovers meet.

This particular pit had not been filled to capacity, that evening, so it had not yet been plowed over by the bulldozers. It gaped as a huge crater, and was black except for the far wall, where one flood beam slanted into it. There were thousands of people down at our feet, and yet we felt alone.

"Here we are, drawn back to the nightmare," I had to remark. "It fascinates you."

"It horrifies me! I can't comprehend it!"

"Yes. But it fascinates you. Just as you find me interesting. Perhaps fascinating."

"I find you disgusting."

"But you met me tonight," I said in a near whisper, stepping so close to the man I'm sure he felt the breath of my words on his cheek.

I heard him swallow. It amused me, but I think my game of seduction had started to consume me, really. By projecting those energies toward him, I think I had actually started to become aroused by the game. His reactions to my manipulation were giving me a very odd gratification. My attempt to dominate him was resembling those times I had coaxed some young girl out of her virginity. The desire in her, but the fear. Then the succumbing . . .

I am not a homosexual. And yet, at that moment, a hungry warmth spread through my lower body and it was almost dizzying. So I reacted to it, without thinking. If I thought anything at all, I suppose I justified my actions to myself as an attempt to seduce him utterly, so that he would let no harm come to me. That's what I told myself then. But I know now it was the warmth in my belly.

What I did, you see, was step even closer to him, and press my lips onto his lips. I reached one hand down to lightly cup his testicles. My tongue began to slide into his mouth, where the taste of our cigarettes mingled.

But it was only an instant, and then the blow under my jaw sent my head back with a snap. I had bitten my tongue badly. Light filled my vision as if a spotlight had fallen on my face. In his fury, the officer had struck me with incredible force.

Thus dazed, I stumbled back from him. And in stumbling back, I toppled into the pit.

I rolled down the dirt incline. Then I sprawled on my belly across the floor of the pit. And the floor of the pit was an ocean of bodies. An ocean of stench. Totally dark. It was more the bottom of an ocean, and the stench was drowning me, filling my lungs. One of my boots had wedged between several bent limbs, and in thrusting out my hand it slipped off a set of ribs and slid into a space between bodies so that my arm became buried to the shoulder. I grunted, spat blood, fought to extricate my arm and roll over, tangled as I was.

A hand brushed my cheek.

It was light, a caress, then gone. But I hadn't imagined it. In my fall I had caused the heaped bodies to shift, I thought . . . for a body then rolled onto the backs of my legs. It must have tumbled from a bit higher up the slope.

I couldn't hear the officer up there. Had he stormed off in disgust, embarrassed, enraged? Had he thought I deserved nothing more than to be left down here, where a monster like me belonged? I had not been able to roll over yet to look. As I struggled to do so, another body rolled onto my back and the back of my head, pressing my face down against flesh. Pressing my lips against flesh. I made a convulsive effort, at that point, to jerk my buried arm free.

I jerked, but it resisted. Something down below me in the heap had snagged the cuff of my sleeve.

Fingers, it must be . . . bent into claws in death, I thought. The idea horrified me; hooked claws or not, I should be able to rip my arm free. But I couldn't, when I tried again. And now a terrifying idea came to me. A vision born of my growing desperation as it approached panic. I imagined that it wasn't fingers that had caught hold of my sleeve . . . but teeth.

A hand slid across the left side of my face, one finger trailing teasingly into my ear as it went, and I screamed.

I rolled onto my back with a surge of strength, a burst of adrenaline, and in so doing it seemed I upset an entire hill of corpses looming just beside me, for the hill then toppled over me, and what I saw of the night sky for a moment was eclipsed when I was suddenly and utterly buried beneath a languid, rubbery avalanche of the dead.

I had watched that mass of bodies descend, as in slow motion. It was a heavy and crushing blob of darkness woven from light scarecrow figures. It had descended on me like one many-armed creature, but this mass was only a part of the creature, I realized . . . and I was screaming again, at the realization. Clawing, squirming, desperate for breath as I realized that the bodies beneath me were also a part of this creature. The bodies all around me. Linked, locked, braided and meshed. They were all weak as individuals, but as this one unified mass they had become amazingly strong, and they had trapped me. And their intent, of course, was to absorb me into the mass. To make me one of them, and thus a part of *it*.

I blubbered crazily for help. The weight seemed only to press me down deeper. Were more of them from either side moving in waves to pile further atop me? Were dead bodies not yet dragged from the barracks now slithering across the camp on their bellies and toppling themselves into the pit?

A girl's long hair had fallen across my throat, her face nuzzled into my shoulder. A bush of pubic hair ground against my forehead in a terrible moist kiss. Fingers had hooked in the back of my shirt collar, the nails lightly scraping my skin. I shrieked and began to sob outright, hopelessly, like a woman, lifted my neck as best I could away from those nails . . . but my cheek pressed against the sharp ridge of a spine barely painted in skin.

It was as though the sharp bones above and below me were fangs that meant to impale me, fanged jaws that meant to rend me, devour me.

They're not all dead, I reasoned in an effort to remain sane. That was it! The officer had pointed it out himself. In the barracks, the dead lay thick upon the floors mixed in with the living so that you could not tell one from the other. Living people must have been thrown into the pit with the dead in our haste to finish all the burying. That was why the hands seemed so purposely to be reaching to me, taking hold of me. That was why the cadavers seemed to have purposely rolled atop me, covered me . . .

That some of the bodies were alive is not very possible, but it may be. True or not, it didn't comfort me much. Was it that the living mixed in with the dead sought to have revenge upon me . . . or that the pale starved spirits of all those dead had somehow merged into one powerful entity? Both possibilities were equally hideous—rational or supernatural. Because either way, I was helpless. Either way, they would have their revenge.

Because I was never getting out. I was going to suffocate, or my chest would be crushed, or my heart would burst, or that hand at the back of my neck and others were going to curl around my throat at any moment . . .

Nails raked down my face. I squeezed my eyes shut as the nails raked my eyelid. I wanted to die at that moment, my friend. Right then. Before the other nails came. And the strangling hands. And the teeth. I wanted it over with because the officer had had his revenge on me, too—he had abandoned me—and I would never escape this pit.

The bodies were churning atop me, moving more actively, and a hand took hold of my arm in an unmistakable grip.

Then the pressure eased from my chest and I looked up to see a face hovering above me, the eyes glittering, the teeth grimacing. A flashlight beam fell upon my face. More bodies were lifted off me, and I realized this was the reason for the feeling of activity above me. More hands took hold of me. I was passed up to other men, all British. I pawed crazily at the dirt slope of the grave, probably hindering their efforts to rescue me in my frenzy.

"What happened?" I heard one man ask. "Did he attack you?"

"No," I heard my officer say. "He just . . . fell."

Those were the last words I heard from him, as the man never spoke to me again.

I was out now, standing on the edge of the pit. I had been rescued from hell. I turned to look back down, and in the new lights I could see the creature. It had many eyes, some catching the light. I saw many mouths, smiling in that odd little expression of faint amusement so often seen on the dead.

What I did then was inexplicable. Like kissing my British officer. But I had been driven mad. It didn't matter that I had been rescued. The monster was smiling at me, staring at me, it knew it had shattered my mind and my soul and its will was strong, it commanded me to give myself to it. It would have me yet. It was the only way to exonerate myself, to repent, to pay for my sins. The British would not execute me. I must execute myself . . .

And I had to die, I felt, as I reached out to my officer and snatched the revolver from his holster. Dying was the only way I was ever going to escape those eyes.

And dying was the only way to empathize with it in the way the monster demanded of me.

The soldiers clawed at my arms to stop me. Maybe that was why the bullet went wrong, up through my nose and into my eye socket rather than into my brain. Or, as I have suggested, it may have been the will of God that I should not have escaped my punishment so neatly.

I never much believed in God or in punishment, until after I had met that officer. Until after I had met that monster.

They are a monster in your country, aren't they? Strong and unified, rich and powerful. Can I blame them? They are a monster in Israel, smaller but tougher and with very sharp teeth. I have a deathly fear of both countries. Of their retribution. Monsters always turn on their makers.

You think I'm still insane, the way I'm talking. That after that night I never regained my sanity. But I did, my friend. I am sane now. In fact, I didn't really go mad when I fell in the pit. It was up until that point—before I fell—that I was insane.

And maybe I was saved when they pulled me out of that hell. Maybe my eternal soul has been burned clean and saved. But maybe not.

So that is my story. I see you don't believe certain mysteries I've suggested. Just as the British officer didn't believe me about the Rat Kings. And now that you know my past, you find me repellent, as he did. Repulsive, now that you know the truth about me. You can call me a demon, a monster. Something other than human. Just like we called the Jews and the rest. Anything, so long as you can say that I'm not a man like you.

Yes, you found my story a trifle unpleasant, eh? But like my officer . . . you wanted to listen.

The Caterpillar

C. Dennis Moore

IT WASN'T MY FIRST CHOICE, and I was pissed at my parents and my sister for saying no, but whatever. So when I came back to town I wound up staying with my cousin Judy and her husband Jeff in their basement. I don't think they wanted me there, more likely they were just too polite to turn me away. I showed up on a Tuesday and hauled what I could in through the garage to the basement, then parked the moving truck in front of the house so Jeff could have the driveway and went inside to thank Judy, again, for letting me stay.

I heard a door close down the hall and then Judy appeared, emerging from the dark with a towel in one hand and an empty bowl in the other. I'd forgotten about their daughter. Jessica was ten and we'd never met. But I knew about her.

She was a second-generation Thalidomide baby. According to the FDA, only 17 American children were born with Thalidomide-related deformities. Jeff's mother had been one of them. While another article, published in DRUG SAFETY, assured the drug did not cause further defects, and yes Jeff had been born normal, Jessica suffered from Amelia, which meant she'd been born with no limbs.

I followed Judy into the kitchen, thanking her, as she put the empty bowl in the sink and laid the towel on the counter.

"No," she said, "it's okay. You get settled. It's good to have you home."

I wondered how sincerely she meant that. I'd been in Florida for ten years, involved in a number of businesses, all of which had failed. I had a moving company, owned a miniature golf course, a bar, a skateboard shop, just to name a few. I had good ideas, just bad luck. And maybe bad business sense. So after a decade of failure, I decided it was time to come home and just live a life again where I wasn't dodging creditors all the time or watching my possessions being sold at auction to pay my debts. Not to mention the cost of living is a lot cheaper in the Midwest.

I returned every few years to attend reunions or show off my success for a weekend, but I always left before my cash ran out or the bill collectors tracked me down. I never stayed in town long enough for the cracks to show. And I rarely kept in contact with any of the family. So it came as no surprise when I detected reluctance in Judy's tone. Not to mention I'm sure she and Jeff had enough problems with Jessica without worrying about me in there, too.

Just a couple weeks, I reminded myself.

Judy said to make myself at home, asked if I was hungry. I was, but I said no. I commented on how they had a nice house. She said thank you. Then I returned to the basement to start unpacking.

Jeff came home a few hours later and we moved the rest of my things into the basement, then dropped off the truck at the U-haul, while Judy got dinner ready. We all finished at the same time, then met in the kitchen.

It was just the three of us at the table and I asked, "Does Jessica not eat out here?"

They exchanged glances, then Judy said, "Usually. But not tonight. She's coming down with something, so it's just soup and juice in bed."

I nodded, twirling spaghetti onto my fork. "I've been here all day and haven't even said hello. I can't believe she's ten and I've never met her."

"You will," Judy said.

I tried to think back, but couldn't remember one family reunion where Judy had brought her daughter. Understandable, I guess. It's one thing to live with it and get used to it every day, but to then be surrounded by two dozen people who didn't know anything about it or didn't deal with it daily, that was something else.

"How's your mother?" I asked Judy.

"Fine, fine," she said.

We ate mostly in silence. I doubted that was normal for them, but I was a stranger in their house, despite the fact I'd spent my younger summers at Judy's house in the country. That was decades ago and now I was an intruder.

Dinner was delicious and filling and I said so, then went back down to my lair to continue unpacking. Their basement was spacious, one long open room with the laundry and a full bath off to the side. The carpet looked new. They already had a couch and chair down there. There were spiders fucking everywhere, though. Afterward, I took a shower and stretched out on the couch.

I dozed off, and woke only once or twice during the night to more thumping overhead, one of them on the way to the bathroom or the kitchen, I couldn't tell.

The next morning began my job search. I'd thought about taking a couple days to acclimate, but the vibe at dinner had put that out of my head real quick; it was obvious I didn't belong there. So for everyone's sake, I'd determined to be out as soon as I could.

Home had changed in those ten years, but the bones remained the same. Before I started the job hunt, I stopped at the houses of a few friends, discovered two of them had moved, but the last, Jerry, was home. Jerry worked construction but was between jobs, so we sat around and caught up for a while, drank a few beers. He said things were good, but the state of his living room said differently, thrift store furniture he'd had since before I left for Florida, and the years showed in them. A few hours and several more beers into the afternoon, he said he'd been thinking of starting his own construction company. He had the business plan all mapped out and just needed backing.

"That sounds like a plan," I told him. My mouth felt numb and too thick for my face. "How much you need to get started?"

He told me and old habits returned; I calculated how much I'd have to borrow from how many people in order to get in on Jerry's deal. He was a good worker and knew his stuff, so if I contributed a hefty sum of the start-up money, he'd be working for me and I could sit pretty and not worry about a job just yet.

I had a lot of old friends in town, buddies I used to run with. Plus there was family. I could sell half the stuff in Judy's basement. I could get the money. I left Jerry's house late that afternoon full of a warm buzz, partly from the beer, but mostly, I thought, from how good the future looked and suddenly I was glad I'd moved back.

I didn't bother looking for a job that day. Jerry's plan was solid and I still had some savings, surely enough to live on until he got things moving. I wasn't paying rent at Judy's, so it was money to eat and put gas in my car and having dinner at the house, I knew I could stretch that money quite a bit.

Even so, to keep them from worrying, I'd tell them I had a job anyway, then tomorrow morning I'd just come back to Jerry's.

So I went to the park and left my car doors open with the stereo cranked and sat in the grass. Summer was a month from over and the sun felt good. Midwest sun is a much subtler thing than Florida sun. I sat and watched the cars drive by and worked through my buzz. Birds sang and bugs flew. A butterfly landed on the grass by my foot, but took off again when I shifted my legs.

I stayed there, soaking up the sun and watching women stop by with their kids. I think it was close to six before I got up and climbed back into my car. The buzz was long gone and I figured dinner would be ready soon, so I headed back. Parked in the driveway and used the garage door opener Judy'd given me to enter through the basement. Took a piss and splashed water in my face, then went upstairs to tell them the good news.

"That was fast," Jeff said. "You start tomorrow? Already?"

"Yeah," I said, piling meat onto a tortilla shell at the stove. "My buddy, Jerry, says I showed up just in time, this parking lot job could take a while and he was short one guy, so I guess everything works out."

"I guess it does," Jeff said. Judy sat at the table picking at the lettuce and cheese from the pile on her shell, which wouldn't stay folded.

After dinner, I returned to the basement and sat on the couch, drinking another beer from a cooler I'd stored in the garage yesterday. I listened to them move about upstairs, talking. I heard muffled voices, but couldn't make out the details. They sounded a little worked up, too fast, urgent, and forced.

I knew they were arguing about me, but what was I supposed to do? It was two more beers and another hour of their voices before I fell asleep on the couch. In the morning, I got out almost as soon as I woke up.

Jerry was home again and as I'd hoped he had restocked his beer from the day before. We got buzzed up again and spent the day laughing over old times. I hinted I might have some money coming pretty soon if he was serious about starting his own company. He said hell yeah he was serious and we drank to that. The time got away and pretty soon I'd missed dinner at the house, so Jerry and I had cold pizza from his fridge, then I went home, in through the garage again, and passed out on the couch. It was late morning the next day when I woke up, sloppy and disoriented. My head was paying the price for last night. It had been a while since I'd drank like that.

I'd woken up to some noise coming from upstairs. I couldn't tell what it was, but it droned on and on. I stumbled into the bathroom and showered. I tried to lean against the shower wall and close my eyes, but every time I did, it felt like I was falling through the world, so I fought to keep my eyes open and work through the hangover.

I got out, toweled off, and that alarm or whatever it was hadn't stopped. Maybe Judy was running the vacuum.

I went upstairs to say good morning. The living room was empty and I called for Judy or Jeff but no one answered. That noise was louder and less muffled. It wasn't the vacuum, it was crying, but this wasn't any crying I'd heard before. It was weak and raspy.

I called out again and the crying stopped.

"Judy?" No answer as I wandered the house looking for someone. The crying came from Jessica's bedroom. I knocked on the door and asked, "Hello?"

I cracked the door and peeked in. Judy wasn't here, but Jessica was lying in her bed, staring at the crack in the door like all the angels in Heaven might issue forth bearing gifts and ice cream. I'd never seen her before.

For a horrible, shameful moment, I thought "Caterpillar".

She was a normal-looking girl, there was just less of her. She was beautiful, actually, took after her mother but had Jeff's eyes. I don't know what I'd been expecting, but I realized then that no limbs didn't mean horribly disfigured.

"Um, you okay?" I asked. "Hang on, I'm gonna try to find your mother."

I started to back out, but she called to me before I could retreat.

"They're not here," she said, getting herself under control. The sobbing had stopped, but there were still hitches and gasps. "I think they're gone."

"They should be back soon, though. You need something?"

"They're not coming back," she said. "They left me here because there's finally someone else to take care of me. They don't love me anymore."

"No," I said, easing back into the room, "they wouldn't do that. I think maybe you just woke up from a bad dream. They'll be back."

I was talking down to her and she knew it and called me on it.

"I'm not dumb," she said. "I'm ten. They packed last night and left really late. They think I don't hear anything in here, but I knew what they were doing."

And then I knew what was wrong. I'd detected, but had been too wrapped up in the crying and the shock of seeing Jessica for the first time, I hadn't given it much thought. But now the smell hit me like a shovel.

"I couldn't help it," she said, "there was no one here to help me."

"Um . . . Okay, hang on," I told her. "I'll go get something."

All I could think of were baby wipes and diapers, but this wasn't a baby, surely her parents didn't keep her in diapers. I went into the bathroom and came back with a wet wash cloth. A voice in the back of my head asked me what the hell I was doing, but come on, she couldn't do it herself, could she?

I leaned down to lift her up and clear away the sheets. I wrapped one hand under her to pick her up—she couldn't weigh anything, surely—and my hand slid under her back, my fingers scraped against some bony nubs, I didn't know what but it freaked me out and I yanked my hand out and backed away, looking down at her.

"It's okay," she said. She'd stopped crying finally, but her face was still smeared with tears and snot. Her eyes were swollen.

"No, I'm sorry," I said. I knew this was a delicate situation, but looking at her now, I realized it was delicate for Jessica, too. Obviously she had enough problems without some drunken washout cringing over her.

"That's Joon," she said.

"What's June?"

"Joon," she repeated. "I'll tell you about her, just please help me?"

Shit. Let's see if I can get this all straight the way she told it. The Thalidomide syndrome wasn't enough. Jessica had been one of two conjoined twins. As she told it, sometimes one twin is too strong and it absorbs the other one. This is what happens when you hear of someone who goes to the doctor with stomach pains only to find out the growth in their stomach is their unborn conjoined twin, a fully formed fetus in their gut. Or, as in Jessica's case, extra limbs where the twin used to be but hadn't been fully absorbed back into the dominant one. Jessica told me about a case of a woman with the small, fully-formed body of her twin growing from her own torso. The head had been absorbed back into her in the womb, but only the head.

In Jessica's case, she'd reabsorbed all of Joon except her limbs, tiny, barely formed, maybe three inches long, growing from her back. She also had an eye and a tiny, crooked mouth with three nubby teeth at the base of her neck.

Denied limbs of her own, she had to live knowing her unborn twin had them, if nothing else.

It was the most grotesque thing I'd ever seen. Part of me suddenly understood the stress they had to have been under and why they'd never brought Jessica to meet anyone.

I tried to hide the shaking of my hands as I cleaned her and put her into clean clothes, then set her in her wheelchair and changed her sheets. Her chair sported a breath-controlled remote and Jessica was independent, at least in regards to moving about. Having put her dirty sheets in the wash and come back upstairs, I found her in the living room, watching Nickelodeon and asking, "Can I have a Pop Tart?"

I gave her two, chocolate, and laid them on a tray across her chair where she could eat them on her own. Having lived like this her entire life, Jessica didn't give her actions a second thought, but it was all a huge shock to me.

"You gonna be okay for a bit?" I asked. She nodded, chocolate smeared in the corner of her mouth and I'd wipe that off later. I returned her nod and grabbed the phone, then went into Judy and Jeff's bedroom.

Most of their possessions were still here, but you could tell stuff was missing. There were gaps in the closet where they'd taken what clothes they wanted to keep. I dialed Judy's cell number, but learned the number I'd dialed was no longer in service.

I called Judy's mother, but she hadn't heard from her daughter in weeks, she said. She was surprised to hear I was back in town and staying with Judy.

"I think she and Jeff might have vanished," I said.

"What do you mean?"

"I mean Jessica's here and they aren't. She says they left late last night and she's afraid they just up and left her."

"I don't believe they'd do that," she said. "I mean, I can't say I'd blame them if they wanted to, but I don't think they would."

Can't blame them? What the fuck?

"Just tell her to call if you hear from her, okay?" And I hung up before I had to hear any more.

I went back out to the living room and asked, "Do you know any of your parents' friends? Where they live?"

She shook her head. "They never took me anywhere like that. Can we go swing in a little bit?"

The world swirled around me and I knew I'd had to have lost my mind. I was dreaming all this, brought on by the booze at Jerry's house, that had to be it. I glanced out the kitchen window and saw Jessica's swing set, the swing one of those rubber harness designs they make for babies.

She seemed incredibly calm given the situation. I wondered if maybe that was because she'd always had her parents to handle any crisis. She understood what had happened, but I was left to deal with the consequences. Then she said, "I'm sorry they left me for you to take care of."

No, this wasn't happening. They'd taken off for a couple days just to get away and be with each other, that was it. They'd be back. There was a note somewhere around here, I just hadn't found it yet. Or they'd forgotten to write it. But that was the answer. It was a few days' getaway, but they'd be back.

I woke up later that night and heard something thump overhead. I jumped off the couch and stumbled up the steps, knowing they'd come back, ready to yell at them for not warning me. I burst through the basement door, into the kitchen, the house quiet and dark. They weren't back. I'd dreamed the sound. Or Judy had raccoons. Whatever, it wasn't them. I listened for Jessica, but her room was silent. I went back down and tried to sleep, tossed and turned for a while.

In the morning, I helped Jessica in the bathroom, then gave her toast. She could eat anything, although sometimes it would need cut or broken up, but she never seemed to mind. I think it was that day I began to admire her. I had a good thirty years' experience over her, all my limbs, and I was barely holding together at the thought her parents might be gone for good.

I spent that morning going through everything, looking for an address book or anything that would lead me to someone who might know where they'd gone. Not a trace, not a scrap of paper. Wherever they'd gone, it was a well-kept secret. I didn't even find any old credit card statements, nothing I could trace at all. By late afternoon that day, I collapsed on the couch and Jessica asked, "Shouldn't you be at work?"

I looked up. She had toast crumbs in the corners of her mouth. I grabbed a hand towel from the kitchen and wiped her face, then answered, "Not today."

By this point, I had no idea what to do. I couldn't track them. The few people I got hold of, no one had heard from them. I wondered if they'd been planning this and had shut themselves off from everyone they knew. Then I looked at Jessica and thought of all the care she had to require, not to mention Joon—and that still made me shudder—it would be understandable if the reason I couldn't find their friends was they didn't have any.

My last resort was the police. But if they really were gone, what would happen to Jessica? Would they send her to Judy's mother? Or leave her with me since I was a relative living in the house? Or foster care? Who knew? If that happened, she'd no longer be my problem, and let me tell you, this was one problem I did not need. At the same time, none of this was her fault. I didn't want to punish her any more than she already had been just because her parents couldn't deal anymore.

After a week, the doubts I'd been having about their return were stronger than my hope. By the end of the second week, I knew they weren't coming back. It was slim pickings in the kitchen and my savings were about gone. I had to get a job. For real this time.

I saw a commercial on television for school bus drivers and one of the selling points was how it allowed one driver to be home with her daughter. That was the job for me. It only kept me out of the house for a couple hours each day, in the morning and later in the afternoon, and the rest of the time I was home with Jessica.

I bought a monitor and put it in her room. I still slept in the basement; I couldn't bring myself to take over Judy and Jeff's bedroom, it felt lifeless in there and cold. But if Jessica needed me in the night, the monitor solved that problem. She refused to come with me on the bus, insisting she could manage those couple hours on her own, as long as the tv remote lay on her tray and she'd gone to the bathroom before I left.

Caring for Jessica felt strange. I'd dated girls with kids before, but didn't have any of my own. The less attention they needed, the better, as far as I was concerned. But she would always need this kind of care, wouldn't she?

I just wanted to go down to Jerry's, get wasted and talk about good times.

My dreams of contributing to his business plan were still in the back of my

186 C. DENNIS MOORE

mind and I thought if the business picked up and we started making some real money, I could hire a nurse to take care of her. I didn't mind making her breakfast and parking her in front of the television, but baths were a problem, and Joon still scared the piss out of me.

I lay downstairs, stretched out on the couch, listening to the white noise from the monitor, drifting off. I heard bedsprings screech, and then a thump. I knew what it was, but exhaustion said if Jessica was hurt, she'd cry out.

I did hear something, a moan or a groan, but still I was too beat to react to anything other than "Help!" What I heard didn't sound like pain, she was probably dreaming.

Then I heard the skittering.

Something moved across the floor above me, very fast, and I sat up, thinking something had gotten in, a raccoon or squirrel. I leapt off the couch and tried to cross the room in the dark. A strand of spider web brushed my face and I jerked, stubbed my toe, got the web out of my eye, and ran up the stairs. I flipped on the kitchen light and looked around, listening for whatever was in the house.

My heartbeat pounded and my breath in my ears made it hard to hear, so I stood a second, trying to calm myself down. I scanned the living room and the hallway, but my eyes felt so heavy, I couldn't make out anything. Then I heard it again, a scritch in the dark by the television. I looked and waited, but nothing moved, so I went across the living room and flipped on the lamp.

Jessica lay on the floor there, her blank face staring up at nothing through closed lids. My first thought was how did she get out here, but then she moved. Her body scooted forward, like she was floating, moving toward the hall. As she got closer, I saw what had been lying under her by the television: a candy bar wrapper. I'd bought it earlier at a gas station, then forgot it, had tossed it on the table by the door with my keys. The candy bar was gone, but the wrapper lay torn open. Then Jessica scurried around the corner and down the hall, on her back, and I knew that wasn't possible, so what the fuck?

I followed her, silently, and watched her enter her room again, then climb up the cover to the mattress and lay down again. I didn't turn her over, but I saw as she sat up to get back into bed, Joon's short, half-formed arms reaching out and pulling herself up. I thought if I went in there and looked, Jessica's face would be clean and sleeping, but if I turned her over, I might see a smear of chocolate on Joon's tiny, misshapen mouth. For a moment I couldn't breathe.

I wondered if that was the real reason her parents had taken off and, I hate to admit it, I didn't blame them at all.

* * * *

It shouldn't even be an issue to mention I stayed awake the rest of the night. The questions stormed my brain, pounding around inside my skull like steel-toed boots. In the morning, I climbed the stairs and went into Jessica's room to help her get up. All I could think of was Joon climbing back into bed. I wanted to ask her about it, but couldn't think of the words. I didn't even know if Jessica knew about it. She'd been sleeping, that was plain to see at the time, but this couldn't have been the first time, obviously.

I sat at the kitchen table and watched her dip her face toward a bowl of dry Fruit Loops, take a mouthful, then drink milk from the straw in the glass next to her bowl.

Her unborn twin's stubby limbs bulged at the back of her T-shirt, a white cotton one with Hannah Montana across the front. She wasn't a monster. She wasn't someone I should be cringing from. She was just a little girl, one who'd had her life fucked up before she was even born.

I sighed and stood up then; time to go to work. I asked once about her own school, but Jessica said her parents had home schooled her because it was easier than dealing with parents, teachers, other students who wouldn't understand why she was born the way she was. That made sense. But with her parents gone, there was no one to teach her. I barely graduated high school.

"Do you have to go to the bathroom before I leave?" She shook her head and smiled and said, "See you soon."

I nodded, grabbed my keys, didn't look at the torn open candy bar wrapper I hadn't been able to make myself pick up yet, then left.

I came home for the afternoon, then back out again on the return run, then home to make dinner and put Jessica to bed. We adopted this routine for the next couple of weeks.

Our interaction was limited. I knew nothing about kids, and after what I saw the night before, like it or not, she freaked me out.

Another two weeks passed and still no word from Jeff and Judy. I started to hate them and I sometimes regretted moving back now. I'm not going to go into a big riff on how I'd been alone all my life and Jessica showed me what it was to live, she wasn't the missing piece to my life and she didn't fill my heart with joy. She was a helpless kid. As much as I hate the responsibility, if I didn't take care of her, who would? And I still wasn't letting her go to strangers; I've heard plenty of stories of how those kids are treated and she's defenseless enough without adding that kind of pressure. But still, every day there, knowing what I knew now about Joon, it got harder and harder to keep going.

That tiny body scurrying around on those stumpy limbs like a giant spider, and Jessica's sleeping half dead to the world, her face calm and empty while her body is hijacked by a fluke of nature.

Even after two weeks, I shivered every time I thought of it. And eventually I found out Jessica knew.

We sat at the table one night. I'd ordered pizza, then cut up Jessica's into smaller bite-sized pieces and I was staring out the kitchen window when she said, "You don't have to be afraid of her."

"What?" because I hadn't been paying attention in the first place.

"Joon," she said. "She can't hurt you. She just gets hungry sometimes, but she didn't mean to freak you out so bad."

"What are you talking about?"

"I know why you've been acting so different, because you saw her that night, and now you're scared."

"I'm not scared," I said. But maybe I was. And maybe part of me felt ashamed that she knew it.

"You didn't tell me about that," I said, trying not to sound accusatory, but feeling it a bit anyway. "I thought she was just a deformity."

"I didn't want you to get scared and go away like they did." She teared up. "Nobody likes me," she said and started bawling.

Christ.

I got up and went over to her and sat in the next chair. I wanted to hug her, but, honestly, the thought of touching Joon's arms . . . I can't tell you how careful I was when I had to move Jessica to keep from touching any part of Joon. Instead I put my hand on her side and said, "That's not true and you know it."

"Oh yeah?" she yelled back at me. Her lips were wet and spittle flew off them to land on the table. "Who else is there? I only know three people and two of them left. Now you hate me, too!"

"Jess, come on," I tried calming her down. "I don't hate you. And I'm not going anywhere, I promise you."

"You don't even want to be here!" she cried.

"You can't say that. I didn't ask for this situation, I'll be honest, but I'm not about to up and leave."

"Why didn't they love me enough?" she asked me, and at that I was speechless.

I shrugged and hugged her anyway. I brushed one stubby arm and moved my hand to the middle of her back, but I held her and ssshhhhhhh'd in her ear until she stopped crying. I kissed her cheek and went to get something to wipe her nose.

"You wanna watch Nickelodeon or something?" I asked. She nodded, looking up at me with big wet eyes. I moved her into the living room and put her pizza on the tray in front of her. She ate and watched SUITE LIFE for a while. Later I put her to bed, turned on the monitor, and went downstairs to shower. Afterward I stretched out on the couch, thinking about how much I hated my cousin and her piece of shit husband right then.

The weekend came and I realized part of what made Jessica so miserable may be that her parents kept her cooped up in the house most of the time. So I put her in the car and we drove. The sun shone and I bought her a pair of green plastic sunglasses because green was her favorite color, and we drove around the streets, through the parks, around the boulevards and avenues with the radio blasting Carrie Underwood, another of her favorites, and not thinking about anything. I asked if she wanted to get out at the park and swing, but she only looked down at where her lap wasn't and said, "No, thanks. Maybe when we get home."

My instinct was to tell her nonsense and take her anyway, but if she wasn't comfortable with it, I wouldn't force her. In time, I figured.

We drove home then, going through McDonald's first because they were giving away brain teasers in their Happy Meals and Jessica loved being able to solve those. She got Chicken McNuggets, which she ate whole from the box, taking them in her mouth, dipping them in honey mustard, and chewing the entire thing with her cheeks bulging and trying not to laugh.

It felt good to see her being a kid and enjoying some time in the sun.

I put her to bed not long after; she said she'd never been so worn out which I thought strange considering pretty much all she did was sit there, but what do I know? She slept on her side and now that I knew about Joon, I knew why. I kissed her goodnight on the cheek, then went out to the living room. I wasn't tired just yet and I turned on the television, but kept the volume down.

Nothing much on TV, so I watched some countdown on VH1, flipping between that and some investigation thing on one of those crime channels. I'd spent about an hour at this when I heard Jessica coughing.

I muted the tv and sat quiet, listening for her to call for me. She never did, though, but I left the sound off a little longer just in case. After about five minutes, she coughed again and this time I went in to ask if she was okay, did she need a drink?

Jessica was asleep. But the coughing continued and I realized it was Joon.

I leaned over to check her. Her tiny crooked mouth worked, opening and coughing. Something in her throat. If she had a throat. Her little eye crinkled shut and the mouth opened wider and another cough shot out, along with something else.

I figured it to be a piece of food. I found it on the edge of the mattress. It was crawling back toward Joon. Without thinking, I swatted it away, off the bed and into the dark. She coughed again, hard, hacking something up, and another one shot out, this time hitting my arm before falling back to the mattress. I looked down at it, trying to see in the dark with what little light came in from the hall. It was a spider. Tiny, but definitely a spider. And it was alive and crawling toward Joon.

I swatted this one away as well, but she coughed up another, then another, and a fifth. I stared down at her and watched two more spiders crawl from her mouth, up over her face, vanishing into the tangle of hair that fell over Joon's face. Jessica moaned in her sleep and moved her head around as if trying to scratch it against the pillow.

The spiders kept crawling, up Jessica's head, down to the pillow, and over the side of the bed, disappearing to wherever spiders go. The coughing stopped and nothing else came from Joon's mouth. They were both fast asleep again.

I felt my heart about to plummet into my stomach and my knees almost refused to hold me upright. I returned to the living room wondering what in the holy fuck I had gotten myself into.

I somehow managed to doze off back on the couch and awakened again late into the night—I think the clock read 2:00 AM—to Jessica's voice. I jumped up and ran halfway down the hall when I realized she wasn't calling for me. She was screaming at Joon.

"Stop it, I won't let you!" and "I don't care, I'm still bigger than you!" There were other noises coming from the bedroom, things being knocked over, thumping. I got in and flipped on the light and found Jessica on the floor—or rather, Joon on the floor, Jessica was a helpless passenger. Or maybe not so helpless anymore because as Joon tried to move around, Jessica, who had most of the control of her torso, threw her center of gravity around, knocking Joon off balance, causing her to stumble. But she still tried to crawl around, despite Jessica's best attempts.

"What?"

It was all I could get out. The rest of the question was pointless.

They didn't seem to notice me anyway.

"Joon, stop it!" Jessica yelled. "I don't care, no! We're going to be fine, you have to listen to me!"

She threw her head to the right and that knocked Joon over, then Jessica hurried to scramble onto her stomach so Joon's stubby limbs would have no purchase.

"Get downstairs," Jessica yelled up at me. "She'll get tired soon, just go."

That stumped me even more than watching them fight. Why was she warning me?

"What the hell's going on?" I asked, then stooped to pick her up.

"Don't touch me!" Jessica shrieked. "Stay away from us!"

I jumped back and stared at her, asked again, "Jessica, what's going on?"

"She thinks you're going to leave," she said. One of Joon's misshapen arms came up and grabbed a chunk of Jessica's hair, pulling until she screamed. Acting on instinct, Jessica bucked against the tugging, and that helped Joon gain some momentum and flip herself back over. She let go of Jessica's hair and scurried toward me across the floor.

I backed away and, without thinking, yanked the bedroom door shut before she could reach me. I heard her head thump when she hit it.

Through the door I called, "Jessica, what is she doing?"

"She thinks you're gonna leave because of her."

"Why does she think that?"

"Joon, stop it!" she screamed again. "Stop it right now!"

I heard a grunt and another thump, then a moment of quiet. Jessica panted as she spoke. "Before they left us, our parents started being nicer to us. They bought us stuff, cds and cartoon dvds. Then they left. Joon thinks you're going to leave because you were so nice today."

"That's not the same," I told her, told both of them. "I'm not your parents."

"I know that," she said. Then the struggles picked up again. They knocked over what sounded like the small white wicker table beside the bed. Then another question occurred to me.

"Jessica, how did she plan to keep me here?"

She didn't answer. And she didn't have to. I saw them when I looked up.

The spiders. I'd only seen her cough up seven, but who knew what she'd done before, or after that. I didn't even try to count the spiders on the ceiling in the hall. Nor did I need to; their work spoke for itself. They moved about as if it had been choreographed, covering the walls and ceiling in the hall with an intricate web of thick strands, then across, from wall to wall, and if I'd been distracted long enough, the web would have blocked my path. I don't think it would have held me, but maybe that wasn't the point. I don't know everything there is to know about Joon, but what I'd seen already told me not to underestimate her. The web only had to slow me down. Whatever she was going to do to me, she would do herself.

I slunk back away from the hall and the spiders, and stayed close to Jessica's bedroom door. It wasn't like they could reach the handle and open it. Then again, Joon coughed up spiders. Anything felt possible at that moment.

I heard another crash from the bedroom, and Jessica kept screaming at her twin.

The spiders continued working their trap while the battle went on inside the bedroom, and I stood outside in the dark, helpless and in shock. It sounded like they'd knocked over the dresser and I wondered what the fuck they could be doing in there. They weren't big girls.

I heard the spiders clacking back and forth over the walls and ceiling, watched them drop on the webs, spinning and weaving. I had nowhere to go. I almost burst back into the room, and I'm ashamed to admit I didn't because Joon scared me more than ever.

I yelled through the door, "Joon, I'm not going anywhere, I'm right here, I'm not leaving you. Do you hear me?" It was the first time I'd addressed her.

Something shattered in the bedroom and I knew it was serious, threw open the door and ran in despite what I may find. Jessica lay on the floor at the foot of her bed, bleeding, and I rushed over.

"Don't," she said before I could touch her.

I looked her over and saw a couple shards of mirror from her closet door— shattered closet door, now—one lodged in Joon's right arm, another up into her mouth. Tears leaked from her one deformed eye. They were thick, like pus, and slightly yellow.

"Are you alright?" I asked.

Jessica said, "I'm okay." But she was crying. "Don't touch me yet, okay?"

I didn't know what was going on, so I had to trust she knew what she was talking about and I knelt there beside her and waited.

Joon looked up at me, her eye rolling lazily in its slitted socket. There was hatred in that glare, and I couldn't figure out why. All I could imagine was putting myself in her place and realizing just how badly you'd been fucked over by life even before you were born. What kind of hate must that fill a person with? Before tonight I would have questioned whether she was even aware enough to feel something like hatred, but I didn't doubt it for a second now. Joon knew exactly what was going on, she knew what she was, and she knew how unfair it was.

I stayed there, watching, waiting. I watched Jessica cry and waited for Joon to reach out and scamper up my chest and latch onto my face before filling my mouth and eyes with webs shot from her mouth. Or something like that. But that didn't happen. She died slowly, bleeding and moving her pathetic limbs, trying to do something, anything, to show she still existed.

I pulled the glass from her and bandaged the wounds as best I could. Joon never twitched. Jessica said she was dead and I believed her.

Jessica spent a week in mourning, not eating much, not even wanting to watch television. I took those first few days off my bus route to stay with her, but went back before I lost my job. And a week later, to the day, she stopped. From there it was only a matter of time, no more than a month, and Joon was gone for real. The deformed limbs dried up, shriveled, finally scabbed over and kind of just . . . fell off. Jessica and I were both disgusted by it, but we kept quiet and I scooped them up as they fell away and threw them in the garbage. Joon's eye closed and grew over, as did her mouth. Soon Jessica was just Jessica. She turned eleven and we began the weekend tradition of driving around and enjoying time alone together out of the house. She was a smart girl, beautiful and funny.

Soon we stopped wondering about her parents and took it as a matter of course that they were just gone, and neither of us, I don't think, ever truly missed them after that.

I tried to talk her into going into regular school. I showed her a school for special needs kids in the next town over. She shot that down.

"It'd do you good," I told her, "to make some friends, get a real education. There's more to life than your dirty old cousin."

But she wasn't having it. Eventually, I learned why she was so adamant.

On Jessica's twelfth birthday I came into her room with cupcakes for breakfast, bite-sized chocolate ones, and a present. A book of Mensa puzzles. But she wasn't there.

I thought she'd maybe tossed and turned to the foot of the bed, but she was just gone. Maybe she'd fallen out, hurt herself, and was underneath it. But she wasn't there, either.

I tore that bedroom apart looking for her, and it was almost fifteen minutes before I found her, and even then I didn't realize it at first. In her closet, stuck up into one corner, Jessica, asleep, hidden inside a giant, translucent cocoon. I could just make out her peaceful face through the silk. I don't know how long she'll be in there, nor what she'll be when she gets out, but I can't stop thinking about Joon, and my first reaction to Jessica, and I'm not ashamed to admit, I'm terrified at the sounds I hear coming out of that thing.

"Poor Brother Ed"
or
The Man Who Visited
Ralph Greco, Jr.

As IF A SLIGHTLY DRUNK ballerina had entered the shed, The Wizard's two-inch heel boots kicked up dust off the wood floor as he stepped from one shaft of light to the next. Here the taste of the Pacific mixed with the smells of thick musty curtains and creosote from the boardwalk only a block away. The ancient carnie lived and loved the fantasies and submerged disappointments in the boxes of this room; stuffed canvas bags of memories spilling over the bowing shelves above his head; casks and bottles of various perverted potions leaning up against the crinkly sepia stained walls. In this grimy rollaway shed were the reminders, remainders and reenactments of all the years that The Wizard had lived among the ruins of 'the show'.

But when the man shook his hands free of his pockets the crane of his eighty-years lifted off him as if he was shaking arthritic crumbs from his limbs. He stood fully then, all five feet seven of him and decades flittered up and away through the muted sunlight spilling through the pair of crusty windows over his head. Like delicate birds alighting from a tree around him, The Wizard poked the air with his still nimble digits, reaching for the formidable casket standing upright at the eastern corner of the shed. His usually quiet penis engorged to erection, his high brow burned with a quick sweat, his tiny blue eyes opened wide, the old man opened the lid of the coffin to himself.

"Brother Ed," the Wizard said to the 105 year-old petrified corpse, a mummy really, he revealed.

The Wizard reached in and rolled out his star attraction, very much like— and with the requisite same sound—unraveling wrapping-paper from a soft cardboard tube.

"Full moon once again," The Wizard said as he lean the reed thin, paper-mache' like body of the man once known as Joshua McKinney out and to the side of his coffin.

In life, Joshua 'Ed' McKinney had been a drunkard, semi-outlaw who had lived his final days on a cattle ranch in southern Oklahoma at the end of the nineteenth century. With Joshua's pappy not near in attendance any of the boy's formative years; his mother a drunk, blind in-one-eye and spit-evil with the other; a sister who had begun taking money for her ample worn favors at the age of thirteen and a sadistic spinster aunt who visited her brother's brood every year or so, only to engage and investigate her young nephew's rumored unusually-sized appendage, there wasn't much else for poor Joshua to do except get out as far and as fast as he could and make the best of this days . . . short though they would be.

Joshua learned to rustle some, cheat at cards and to use his obvious street wit and his cold blue eyes (and that rumored ample body part) on as many and as young a woman as he could entice. That last year of his life though, while he was actually working a *real* job on a kind cattle-rancher's farm, the thirty year-old man began to 'court' the only daughter of a half gypsy woman named Mama Lee.

'Dating' Mama Lee's daughter would prove to be Joshua McKinney's undo-ing.

Mama's only daughter Beb, only fourteen at the time, began seeing Joshua as often as she could sneak. The man was as unwelcome around the young girl as Mama Lee could sternly warn, but the older woman realized there would be no stopping such a willful beauty as Beb. Knowing he was dancing in a fire pit, Joshua still took his opportunities with the dark-haired woman/child as often as he could; in backyards, farmyards and in sheds, the girl was continually rent in vagina, anus and mouth by the crude, yet filling 'love-making' of the man she fantasized would one day be her husband. Of course all Joshua (or *Ed,* as his aunt had nick-named *that* part of him) wanted was to continue his prodding and poking of such nubile willing beauties. When Beb began making overtones of a more lasting arrangement, the man 'pulled out' . . . literally and figuratively.

Glad for the halting of their romance but hurt by her daughter's rejection, Mama Bell decided to get back at Joshua, 'Ed' the only way she knew how. Relying on her Creole lineage and the magic supposedly still surging through her veins, Mama Bell met up with the unlucky Mr. McKinney one fine spring day, confronting him on the town's main street, of all places!

"Know for the rest of your days . . ." the stout woman shouted down the dusty busy street as Joshua faced her wide-eyed, smirking . . . and drunk ". . .

whether dead or alive, Joshua McKinney, you will always a'wander for the touch of feminine flesh."

The town people who reported witnessing the incident that day told of Mama Bell turning on her ample heels while Joshua called after her—a choice few phrases no church-going woman could repeat—then stumbled back to the local tavern. This drinking soon killed Joshua though, for not a full year later the man died from an imploded liver. His age notwithstanding, the pure rot gut potato whiskey the man could only ever afford, his less then nutritious eating habits and the constant barrage of hard labor (when he did labor) killed young Joshua but quick.

Buried in a potters' field a week later, it was then that the true infamy of 'Brother Ed' began.

To the horror of a pair of gravediggers, Joshua McKinney actually split open the top of his coffin as it was being lowered! Puking the most horrific cry ever heard by the two shocked men, the suffering corpse sauntered off flaying into the night, following well the old Creole curse coursing through him. As most of the townsfolk remembered well that fateful day Mama Bell had confronted Joshua, it was simply assumed the dead man was up and walking to quench his never-to-be-satiated, cursed lust.

It was decided that Joshua McKinney should be found and his body burned to avoid any further wandering by the unfortunate dead man.

A posse was assembled but there was an enterprising duo, Hap Seasons and his only son Brady who lit out a day before the search party. Hap and his son were about done with their time in this not-good-for-even-one-horse town and were looking for an opportunity to light out for pastures west. The older man had seen his time in circuses when he was younger and now his wife dead, the motherless boy and widowed dad were aching to put dad's old carnie know-how to work; what could an honest-to-goodness zombie fetch on the tent-show circuit, Hap wondered?! Hap had a cousin who could probably help set-up the show and . . .

But first the men had to find the suffering cursed corpse of Joshua Ed McKinney and do so in a day's time.

Although The Wizard was the age he was he still managed to shimmy Ed's brittle light body to the door of the shed. Just beyond, in the carnie's home trailer, the permanent one he kept here in California, not the one he used to drag behind his truck when his carnival was traveling the byways of America, a bright-eyed seventeen year-old girl squirmed on The Wizard's immaculate bedspread. As The Wizard opened the single thin metal door of the shed he didn't smell it, but he knew Brother Ed certainly could; the pheromone rush from that squirming scared girl wafting clear across the backyard lot to them.

"First one's on me ol' friend," The Wizard said holding both the single door wide and Brother Ed's left stretched bicep. If not for the red flannel shirt it might have been impossible for the old carnie to hold to, let alone find any muscle in the desiccated, leathery covering that was Brother Ed's skin.

"Go 'head," the man said and smiled across to the grimacing sunken face of the dead man in his arms.

"Go 'head," he repeated releasing his hold on his ancient charge.

For a fleeting few seconds The Wizard feared his old friend was going to teeter back into him, but then the slightest shimmer passed through that rail thin reed-of-a-corpse and Brother Ed was standing on his own, all in for the game.

The Seasons men made *Willard's Eve* that very night. Although there were two towns on a direct path from the potter's field, Willard's had the distinction of being the only one to house a whorehouse. In fact, father Seasons had recently brought his son Brady to the red brick building only two doors down from the bank, to deflower the sixteen year-old boy. It *was* possible that Joshua had simply fallen out, and was rotting someplace in the hilly and dry country between Willard's and that lonely potters field, or he could be laying down with a sow, not being able to distinguish species only gender, but the Seasons men, like the posse behind them, believed Mama Lee's old curse was working well. If Joshua Ed McKinney was destined to seek female company he would have to be led right to the "Purple Parrot" and the fine ladies within.

As Brady would explain years after they had made their fortunes and sold 'Brother Ed': "My daddy said the man was being led by his johnson, more then most. Those ugly old whores had him if anybody did!"

No sooner had the men arrived in town then they heard the screams from the house of ill repute. Luckily the local sheriff was none too hurried to visit the local eye-sore and the minutes it took for him to finally get his large self into his shirt sleeves and suspenders, Brady and his dad barged in, bid helloes to the Madame they had only just visited a month before and walked right down the hallway to room number four.

"Damndest thing I'd ever seen . . ." Brady continued his account. ". . . there was Blue-Eyed Molly, nice and big boned as she was, half dressed with Joshua pawing at her. She didn't seem as frightened—those ladies of the P.P. had seen their share—as she was simply humored! She screamed that the 'man' had snuck in through a window to simply lie down beside her as she was resting for what

Molly assumed would be a busy Saturday night. Damn, she was busy a'right with that dead man rolling and huffin' next to her, the dirt from his grave staining her sheets more then what big Molly was used to them being stained with!"

The Seasons' men managed to spirit the zombie to their wagon, tying him tight in the back. It was a hell-ride Brady would later recall with unabashed horror mixed with glee; Joshua moaning and flapping as they drove west the entire night. Neither son nor father spoke about their prize until they were well over the state line and hiding out waiting for Hap's cousin to find them.

"She's the prettiest little thing," The Wizard was saying as he and Brother Ed executed the slow walk to the trailer.

The Wizard knew that as a man ages he needs more then just the sight and smell of a woman, he needs to consider her, pine for her a bit, anticipate her being there in a myriad of possible poses. Now no man was as old as old' Brother Ed so he needed this attention more then most, The Wizard reasoned. True, his old boss Preeson and those men who had kept Ed before him had probably not taken the time like this, but The Wizard had been Brother Ed's keeper longer then any of those men and he had made a quiet fortune with the man: he owed him pure and simple, let the man have this walk now. The Wizard didn't even especially mind disposing of the bodies as he had all these long years. Like giving Ed his 'walk', The Wizard had come to see his part in all of this and was proud of what he provided.

"I think she's Mexican, if I'm not mistaken," the old carnie whispered. "You know how much fire they have."

It was at times like these, heat finally waning under the full midnight moon of a July night, that The Wizard felt, sensed even, telepathy from the 'man' plodding next to him. He had never, nor would he ever expect a reply, that was simply too much to ask—Brother Ed *was* dead after all—but the old carnie knew his words were getting through, knew he was understood and somehow *felt* silent acknowledgment. Let's face it, there were very few folks left in 'the show' anymore and certainly none as old as The Wizard or as odd as Brother Ed!

If these two men couldn't have a kinship, and unspoken communication, who could, The Wizard wondered?

'The Wizard' was Arny Ullman when he first saw 'Brother Ed' enter the carnival he was working the summer of 1922. Ed had just come under the care of Arny's boss, an enterprising amateur magician and professional con artist named Robert Preeson. While not exactly sure what Ed was, the lanky Preeson did know a potential money making opportunity when he saw one, 'buying' Ed from Hap and his cousin when their battered and broke tent-show carnival passed through the orange groves of a pre-Hollywood L.A. Robert had seen plenty gimmicks in his time—quite a few he perpetrated himself in his rusty stage act—so the weathered body was an oddity but not so much to dissuade the budding entrepreneur. But when he was told there was indeed no gimmick, that Ed was an honest-to-goodness animated dead man, Robert couldn't have been happier with his purchase! Further more, much to Robert's amaze and amusement, Ed's pria-prismic pride still seemed intact as he rolled, moaned, and walked to every pretty woman who passed by him to the horror of onlookers and delight to the man who owned him!

Dead men do not make the best of lovers but they can grope, slobber and shuck themselves at legions of paying ladies and their titillated mates. Brother Ed would spend his days quiet, dead as he was, until nighttime when his coffin was opened to the full view of a tent-show audience who had paid well to view him. With the whiff of perfume on the air, or the sound of light tittering laughter, Ed would begin to stutter and shake in his coffin and in no time would be lunging forward to the lip of the stage for the women in the audience he had been cursed to hunger for.

Robert had learned from the Seasons' men and his own time with him that all Ed really needed was to take a little 'taste' from time to time. If the poor man's lusts were satiated Brother Ed could be counted on to never venture far even on his nights off. All that was ever needed, as Hap and his son had told an entranced Mr. Preeson, was for a willing lady to be procured from time to time. Nothing as perverse as copulation had to be even attempted, ol' Ed was content to just lie down next to a lady for a few minutes, maybe have a friction if possible.

It was a simple thing to ask, really.

Robert Preeson, as had the Season men before him, began to scour the local whorehouses wherever his carnival happened to stop, buying Ed local prostitutes or any woman really who could be convinced for a few pieces of silver to spend time with the man in the box. It was a creepy request to be sure, but as the Season men had, Preeson merely convinced the women that this was *his* particular fetish (which in a way it was); he had a dummy for his show that he liked to see bedded down with a real live lady. Most women agreed, especially for the handsome Preeson, but found they had allowed more then they could have ever bargained for when the *dummy* they lay next to began to rub himself against them! One lady even stayed long enough to have Brother Ed reveal his now withered, yet still considerable cock to the side of her leg and begin humping her thigh like a Border collie!

The light from the trailer shone down on the ancient friends. To the uninitiated, out here in the wash of high moonlight, it would seem as though two very old men were standing admiring the abundance of stars in the southern California night. It would take a closer inspection to realize the condition of the thinner man, the pallor of his face and his leathery sunken looks, the cobalt dead-fly stare of his open eyes.

Brother Ed had never really gone to rot. Sure he was an 105 year old corpse, his flagging skin had peeled pretty much to leather and what hair remained on the man's head, though unusually thick and shiny given the state he was in (dead) grew to the consistency of straw. But his body was so well preserved one would believe the man was just recently deceased. True, Ed had been embalmed but still a body would never keep as well as Ed had if not for some other element in the mix . . . mainly the mojo of Mama Bell's spell those many years ago. The old half-gypsy woman truly was determined to have Joshua McKinney wander the backwoods and alleyways searching, so his body had stayed pretty much intact.

"Give a look," The Wizard said standing then with Brother Ed at his bathroom window.

Through it they could see the bathroom door, left ajar by The Wizard only a half hour before. Beyond the doorway, lying on the bed, tied and gagged, lay a brown-skinned girl, naked save for the red bandana The Wizard had bade her wear after he paid her the requisite hundred dollars for what the waitress assumed would be this old man's quick fun.

Jeanne was not a working girl, far from it, but she'd let an ancient harmless man have his way if he bought her dinner (which he had), drove her around all night to bars and friend's houses (which he had) and begged her enough, for one hundred dollars, to "just strip and let an old man feast his eyes on what he used to be able to put his hands on." Sure, she'd tie the bandana around her neck; fuck, Jimmy had never been this polite or sweet and he had taken a lot more off her, that's for sure! Maybe this was even a way she could make some extra cash, the guy seemed to have enough of it and truth be told she had always fancied herself pretty enough to be a model . . . Christ she had the tits for it and hers were at least real!

What the seventeen year-old girl did not count on though was the old man's agility and his damn quick way with ropes!

* * * *

In the second decade of the new century a carnival such as Preeson's never stayed in one place too long. The stories about the odd man in the box and the ladies who met him retreated like so much locomotive steam as the popular carnival jumped from town to town. Business was good, as good as could be expected with movies an all-too-new and all-too-present-booming entertainment.

Counting ragged receipts was one thing for the prematurely graying magician, but it wasn't long until he tired of procuring lovelies for Ed. Of all things the carnie owner was jealous, jealous that his once ashen, slightly mysterious looks had gone to seed with the tensions of running his enterprise and jealous of how quick women took his money for his odd 'request'. These ladies, some not even prostitutes, would barely ever even bat an eye *his* way unless more silver was forthcoming.

In his roiling rage, soon Preeson allowed the unthinkable! The very thing the family Seasons warned could never pass; Preeson began to let Brother Ed out on his own!

While no lady was actually hurt during Ed's midnight wanderings and he'd usually be content to trawl only once or twice a week, Preeson still turned a mighty blind eye to the idea of a sex-cursed zombie walking into the latest town to steal some time with an underage lass or a budding bride-to-be! Rumors abounded, stories followed, there was even once a reporter who managed to catch up with them in Oregon, but Preeson managed to dissuade actual fact into innuendo so he could spend the few days with his carnival, bilk the marks for as much as possible then be on his way as the story of 'the man who visited' became part of the folklore, a 'maybe it was, maybe it wasn't' fright time story one would tell their children as they walked the midway or made their way back home.

Preeson sold the carnival and all its possessions to Arny 'The Little Wizard' as his last bequeathed request to his best worker, in that dusty hellhole season of '48. Arny took to Brother Ed as he did the acquisition of the rest of his old boss's carnival, dropped the 'Little' from his name and Brother Ed soon had a new owner and friend. The Wizard came to understand and subsequently sympathize with his new, most famous charge more then the men who had owned Brother Ed ever could. The Seasons' men had brought prostitutes and joked as Brother Ed took his need, Preeson grew resentful, too horny for his own good and let the zombie loose on his own, but The Wizard felt a kinship to Ed. He knew he owed it to this 'man', his alter ego, to provide the best he could on the special nights when the moon was full and The Wizard could take his time to find a lady.

And while prostitutes would suffice, 'real' women, not those 'in the show' were what The Wizard wanted for his best friend.

Of course there was simply no way a woman who had been tied down, forced to copulate with a zombie, wouldn't tell her tale. But with his skill with ropes, his still flexible sinewy muscles and carnie wit, The Wizard found he could procure women about as easily as he could dispose of them. Even with those who managed out of the bonds from time to time (usually after Brother Ed had had his way) The Wizard was there to dispose of a flaying, running girl before she got past his trailer door.

With Brother Ed satiated—at least for that month—Arny could sleep contented knowing he had provided his cursed partner with the very best he could afford and allow. Sure he would have loved to have done more for Brother Ed but it seemed that as the years slowed The Wizard down they had also slowed the curse in Joshua McKinney; one woman a month seemed enough for him now.

They came to the front door of the trailer, these two old men, one dead, one close enough he smelled of it. The Wizard opened the door for the zombie shuttering next to him, the single stone step challenging most of Brother Ed's brittle resolve. But for what lie within scared and unknowing on The Wizard's bed, the zombie would muster the strength. He had done so all these decades on the nights of the first full moon as he would continue to do until no one came for him anymore, to open his box. The Wizard practically beamed as he stood in the doorway, watching the achingly slow progression of his friend, executing tight paper steps down the hallway to the woman-child who lay beyond.

This was truly the very best part of the anticipation The Wizard knew, as he stood there in the hall, unzipped his fly and released his now raging member. As old as he was, The Wizard would still sport quite the erection as these scenes unfolded: the girl began to thrash as she saw the bedroom door open even wider and assumed the 'game' was now afoot; then there was that quick squeaky sensation of the bed moving, then muffled squeals, the bed rutting against the wood floor once again and the sensation of utter horror seeping through the walls as the girl tied to that bed saw Brother Ed and realized she would not be indulging The Wizard's need this night . . . but something quite a bit more sinister!

What the Wizard would love to know, but would go to his grave not knowing, was whether these women knew they were going to die? Did they think Brother Ed was The Wizard playing dead-man dress-up? Did they even conceive what it was that was actually bending down there to roll next to them? Could they even imagine what the next few minutes would be like?

Did they even ever see the flash of The Wizard's blade after the zombie got off them?

The Wizard imagined Brother Ed's movements as he heard his old bed groan with the added weight of the dead man. The living man grabbed his purple stump-of-a-cock and began pumping his fist wildly to what he imagined was happening in that room beyond. But The Wizard wasn't on himself for more then a minute when he felt a clutch across his chest. His eyes tearing, his left arm thumped his side as he heard a soft intake of female breath from his bedroom . . . then the old carnie fell dead from a massive heart attack.

"And this is where . . ." Benny said to the wind as Teresa Riner turned to him. ". . . nah forget it. Just one of those urban legends."

"Where what?" she said.

With blue eyes that lustrous Benny was hard pressed to ignore any request this woman made and truth be told he had purposely taken this moment, here in the buzz and scrape of the bulldozers below to entice the lady architect with some horrific folklore.

"Benny, we go back a long way," Teresa said. "You got some good gossip, you just got to spill it."

Truth be told, although Teresa's architectural firm had hired Benny's builders (that was actually the name of his contracting company, "Benny's Builders") for this very expensive and expansive condo site, the red haired lady had yet to be out here at the site. Now that she was, Teresa felt a strange chill she was damn sure did not emanate from the breeze blowing off the near ocean. She pulled her arms tight to herself, silently reveling in the fact that her covered, yet ample cleavage pushed up at the handsome foreman facing her.

"The way I heard it," Benny said, leaning in so close the heat between the pair was palatable. For simply too many years Benny and Teresa's firm had worked together and an attraction had always bubbled unrequited.

"There was an old trailer here, shed too I think, that the locals burned after *that* night."

"That night? What night?"

"The night that girl came runnin' out, the night they found the two old guys raping her," Benny said.

Involuntarily leaning even closer, the couple spied the progress of the machines and men down the hill from them. Mixed with Teresa's undetectable pheromone secretion was the sweet "Oliva Bath Perfume" she had added to her bath the night before. But that odd chill, just what was it exactly that was gnawing at the deepest pinpoint of her belly?

This combination of the woman's scents and reactions worked its unique spectrum of brightness though the stale smelling development on this California shore and down to the hidden grave not three feet from the man and woman. Below, eight feet down just to be sure, now covered in concrete and mesh and a new condo water pipe system, lay a man who could smell the welcoming scent, even though he was in the box that had been provided by a shocked yet sympathetic populace.

That sad and cursed ancient man smiled to the possibility of a visit sometime in the future.

About the Authors

JOHN BRUNI—John Bruni's work has appeared (or will appear) in *Shroud, Cthulhu Sex, The Monsters Next Door, All Hallows, Trail of Indiscretion, Detective Mystery Stories, The Nocturnal Lyric*, Niteblade's *Lost Innocence* anthology, and a number of other publications. He was the editor of *Tabard Inn*, and you can visit him at www.talesofquestionabletaste.com. He lives in Elmhurst, IL, and he much prefers whiskey to mescal.

GARRY BUSHELL—Garry Bushell cut his teeth on the Socialist Worker before writing for the UK rock weekly Sounds. He compiled the first four *Oi!* albums, fronts veteran punk band The Gonads and has interviewed everyone from Joe Strummer and Jerry Dammers to Debbie Harry and Ozzy Osbourne. His books include pulp fiction crime novels *The Face* and *Two-Faced, Cockney Reject* (the authorized story of Jeff Turner), *Dance Craze—the 2-Tone Story* and *Running Free* (the authorized story of Iron Maiden).

RAMSEY CAMPBELL—The *Oxford Companion to English Literature* describes Ramsey Campbell as "Britain's most respected living horror writer". He has been given more awards than any other writer in the field, including the Grand Master Award of the World Horror Convention, the Lifetime Achievement Award of the Horror Writers Association and the Living Legend Award of the International Horror Guild. Among his novels are *The Face That Must Die, Incarnate, Midnight Sun, The Count of Eleven, Silent Children, The Darkest Part of the Woods, The Overnight, Secret Story, The Grin of the Dark* and *Thieving Fear*. Forthcoming are *Creatures of the Pool* and *The Seven Days of Cain*. His collections include *Waking Nightmares, Alone with the Horrors, Ghosts and Grisly Things, Told by the Dead* and *Just Behind You*, and his non-fiction is collected as *Ramsey Campbell, Probably*. His novels *The Nameless* and *Pact of the Fathers* have been filmed in Spain. His regular columns appear in *All Hallows, Prism, Dead Reckonings* and *Video Watchdog*. He is the President of the British Fantasy Society and of the Society of Fantastic Films.

Ramsey Campbell lives on Merseyside with his wife Jenny. His pleasures include classical music, good food and wine, and whatever's in that pipe. His web site is at www.ramseycampbell.com.

RANDY CHANDLER—Randy Chandler is the author of *Bad Juju, Hellz Bellz*, and co-author of *Duet for the Devil* (with t. Winter-Damon). He's the author of numerous short stories which have appeared in such books as *Shivers IV, Damned Nation, Exit Laughing*, and *Darkside: Horror For The Next Millennium.*

Randy's very first horror tale was published under the title of "Fungoid" in 1986 in *Doppelganger*, a small-press zine with a tiny readership, but it was a completely different story. He says the first "Fungoid" is probably best forgotten and that he resurrected the title when he had a story funky enough to do it justice.

TIM CURRAN—Tim Curran lives in Michigan and is the author of the novels *Hive* and *Dead Sea* from Elder Signs Press, and *Skin Medicine* from Hellbound Books. Elder Signs Press will also be publishing the next three volumes of the *Hive* series. Upcoming projects include *The Corpse King*, a novella from Cemetery Dance, and *Four Rode Out*, a collection of four weird-western novellas by Curran, Tim Lebbon, Brian Keene, and Steve Vernon, also from Cemetery Dance. His short stories have appeared in such magazines as *City Slab, Flesh & Blood, Book of Dark Wisdom*, and *Inhuman,* as well as anthologies such as *Horrors Beyond, Flesh Feast, Shivers IV,* and *Hardboiled Cthulhu.*

RALPH GRECO, JR.—Ralph Greco, Jr. is an internationally published author of short stories, plays, essays, button slogans, 800# phone sex scripts, children's songs and SEO copy. Ralph is also an ASCAP licensed songwriter/performer and Internet radio D.J. He lives in the wilds of suburban New Jersey, where he attempts to keep his ever-expanding ego in check.

C.J. HENDERSON—CJ Henderson is the creator of the Teddy London supernatural detective series, and the author of such varied titles as *The Encyclopedia of Science Fiction Movies, Black Sabbath: The Ozzy Osbourne Years*, and *Baby's First Mythos.* The first book in his new series, *Brooklyn Knight*, will be coming from Tor/Forge in early 2010. He is also the author of hundreds of short stories and comics and thousands of non-fiction articles. For free short stories, a chance to tell him what you thought of his story in this anthology, or just a chance to waste more time on-line, feel free to visit him at www.cjhenderson.com.

Z.F. KILGORE—Z.F. Kilgore is a retired police detective. He is currently writing and compiling a collection of short stories centered around the character

Cord Bergen, paranormal investigator. "The Devil Lives in Jersey" is the first of the series. Z.F. lives in the pine barrens of New Jersey with Brock, a one-eyed German Shepherd and retired police dog, who now spends his days chasing rabbits instead of crooks. They have both actually seen the Jersey Devil.

SEAN LOGAN—Sean Logan's stories have appeared in more than a dozen publications, including *Black Ink Horror, New Traditions in Terror* and *The Vault of Punk Horror*. He lives in northern California with his lovely wife and a shockingly handsome rottweiler. Aside from writing unpleasant stories, he enjoys skateboarding, going to sleazy punk rock shows, and anything else that is A) likely to end in an injury and B) totally inappropriate for someone who's nearly 40 year's old.

GRAHAM MASTERTON—Graham Masterton is the author of more than 100 novels, including thrillers, historical sagas, disaster novels and horror novels. His first horror novel *The Manitou* was filmed with Tony Curtis playing the lead role. He has also published more than 100 short stories, several of which were televised by Tony Scott for his "Hunger" series. He was the first Western horror novelist to be published in Poland after the collapse of communism and has a plaque in the foyer of the prestigious Bristol Hotel in Warsaw. A former editor of Penthouse magazine, Graham has also published a series of best-selling "how-to" books on sex. He was awarded a Special Edgar by Mystery Writers of America for *Charnel House*, and shortlisted by the MWA for best original paperback for *Trauma*. Numerous other awards include the Prix Julia Verlanger, the Tombstone Award and the International Horror Guild award. He has constantly pushed the boundaries of horror fiction: his story "Eric the Pie" was banned by British booksellers. "Sepsis" was written to push the edge even further. Graham Masterton currently lives in England with his wife and agent Wiescka. His official website is www.grahammasterton.co.uk

ANGEL LEIGH MCCOY—Angel Leigh McCoy lives in Seattle, where the long, dark winters feed her penchant for horror and dark fantasy. Her short fiction has appeared in several anthologies. Over the years, she has designed RPG material for companies such as White Wolf, Wizards of the Coast, FASA, and Pinnacle Entertainment Group. She worked for Microsoft Game Studios, writing articles as Xbox.com correspondent Wireless Angel. Currently, she is a game designer at ArenaNet, where she is part of a vast team effort to make the coolest MMORPG ever: Guild Wars 2. In her spare time, she serves as head editor at WilyWriters.com.

C. DENNIS MOORE—C. Dennis Moore has been called 'an author worth keeping an eye on' and 'one of the suspense genre's best kept secrets.' His fiction has appeared in over 50 publications and this glamorous lifestyle has allowed him to indulge in his true passion, which is inventory control, for at least 40 hours a week. To further your CDM experience, please go to www.cdennismoore.com.

STEFAN PEARSON—Stefan Pearson is a founding member of Edinburgh-based spoken word performance group, Writers' Bloc. His fiction has appeared in *Nova Scotia* (the Scottish speculative fiction anthology), *Read by Dawn Vol 1*, and *Ruins Terra*. Further fiction and journalism has appeared in the Scottish arts magazine, *One Magazine.*

BRIAN ROSENBERGER—Brian Rosenberger lives in a cellar in Marietta, GA and writes by the light of captured fireflies. He is a member of People for the Ethical Treatment of Werewolves and a staunch supporter for equal rights for the Undead. News about upcoming and recent publications can be found at http://home.earthlink.net/~brosenberger.

JEFFREY THOMAS—Jeffrey Thomas is the author of such novels as *Blue War, Deadstock, Health Agent, Monstrocity, Letters From Hades,* and *A Nightmare on Elm Street: The Dream Dealers,* and such collections as *Punktown, Voices From Punktown, Voices From Hades, Unholy Dimensions, Doomsdays* and *Thirteen Specimens.* His stories have appeared in anthologies like *The Year's Best Horror Stories XXII, The Year's Best Fantasy and Horror #14, The Solaris Book of New Science Fiction #1* and *The Thackery T. Lambshead Pocket Guide to Eccentric and Discredited Diseases.* Thomas lives in Massachusetts, and has a blog and message board at his web site www.jeffreyethomas.com.

SCARS

THE MAGAZINE THAT LEAVE MARKS

WWW.SCARSMAGAZINE.COM

ALSO AVAILABLE FROM COMET PRESS

DEADLINES AN ANTHOLOGY OF HORROR AND DARK FICTION

In this deadly trip down the darkside of human nature from 20 authors of modern terror you will encounter:

MURDEROUS ANATOMICALLY CORRECT DOLLS
ZOMBIE SKINHEADS
SICK SERIAL KILLERS PLUS PLENTY OF MAYHEM!

AVAILABLE AT OUR WEBSITE AND AMAZON.COM

WWW.COMETPRESS.US

www.myspace.com/cometpress   www.twitter.com/cometpress

MORPHEUS TALES

MAGAZINE OF HORROR, SCIENCE FICTION AND FANTASY

"Featuring...
JOE R. LANSDALE,
MICHAEL LAIMO,
RAY GARTON,
JOSEPH MCGEE
and many more!"

MORPHEUS TALES IS A QUARTERLY MAGAZINE
FEATURING THE HIGHEST QUALITY FICTION, ARTWORK
AND REVIEWS OF THE LATEST BOOKS AND FILMS.

www.morpheustales.com
(on myspace at)
www.myspace.com/morpheustales

HORROR IN CULTURE & ENTERTAINMENT

RUE MORGUE

VISIT OUR NEW ONLINE PRESENCE AT

RUE-MORGUE.COM

CINEMACABRE MOVIE NIGHTS

NEW, RARE, CLASSIC & CULT HORROR MOVIES!

THIRD THURSDAY OF EVERY MONTH EXCLUSIVELY AT THE LEGENDARY

BLOOR CINEMA

CHECK LISTINGS AT WWW.RUE-MORGUE.COM

RUE MORGUE RADIO

Hosted by

TOMB DRAGOMIR

Featuring

INTERVIEWS BY STUART FEEDBACK ANDREWS
THE BLOOD SPATTERED GUIDE
THE CAUSTIC CRITICS

WWW.RUEMORGUERADIO.COM

ALL NEW SHOPPE OF HORROR!

SHOP ONLINE FOR OFFICIAL
MERCHANDISE FROM RUE MORGUE.

OPEN LATE!

Lightning Source UK Ltd.
Milton Keynes UK

176656UK00002B/59/P